The Methuselah Conspirators

George T. Hahn

SBG

Stories from George T. Hahn

Timeline

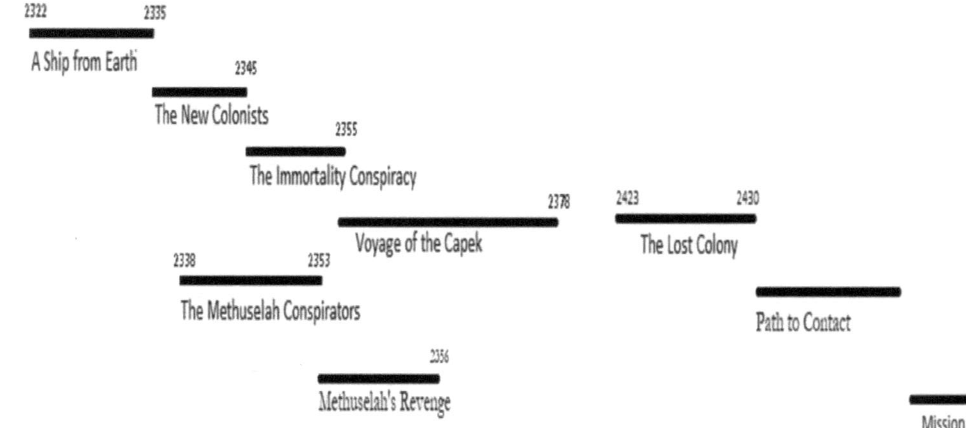

2322 2335
A Ship from Earth
2345
The New Colonists
2355
The Immortality Conspiracy
2378
Voyage of the Capek
2423 2430
The Lost Colony
2338 2353
The Methuselah Conspirators
Path to Contact
2356
Methuselah's Revenge
2043
Mission to Earth

Contents

Jornal de Brasília **News Bulletin 4 April 2338**

The Legislature today passed the Benitez-Baker Bill legalizing research into technologies that interpret brain activity, outlawed by civilized society for over two hundred years. Called the Mind-Reading Act, the legislation has been a controversial subject since the February release of a Technology Impact Report declaring that the benefits to society of such research outweighed any possible negative effects.

EMILE HERNANDEZ SLAMMED HIS fist on the desk. It shook under the force of the blow, and a container tipped over, sending a dozen pencils and pens rattling across the surface.

"Really, Emile. There's no reason to get excited." Emile was average in height and build, but his flashing dark eyes could intimidate people that didn't know him. Maxwell Estevez knew him well and looked at the younger man with a mild look of reproach that Emile was quite familiar with. Usually, it calmed Emile, but not today.

"I won't do it, Max. I absolutely refuse."

"Come on, Emile. The Technology Impact Report said the Western Alliance would benefit if we could develop the ability to read from minds as well as write to them. You would be our first choice to lead the new project."

"The TIR?" Emile clenched his hand into a fist again but controlled his temper enough to not abuse the desk further. Max must have realized that because he picked up the fallen container and carefully placed the pencils and pens back into it. "You know as well as I do that the TIR was bought and paid for by Castillo and his cronies," Emile continued.

"There are good reasons why this kind of research was banned until now. The government has forgotten lessons we learned long ago."

Max leaned back in his chair. "Protocols prevent the government from misusing the technology. You shouldn't believe everything the Conservative Party says. They're just trying to make points for the election next year."

"No doubt, but that doesn't mean they're not right. You may not believe it, but Castillo is not above doing whatever he can to get his way." Emile shook his head in annoyance. "That the government wants to help fund this project is proof that they want to use it. Hell, Max! They're the ones who labeled this thing a neuro-interrogator. What do you think they want to use it for?"

"Of course, they want to use it. For everyone's good! There will be restrictions on its use, just as in every other technology that could undermine our democracy. That's what laws are for, Emile. The world has stifled research into the human mind for centuries since the technology riots. That was centuries ago; it's about time we go back to the science."

"Max, you were once a talented scientist, and you're a good boss. If you took a little time to understand what's going on in our government, you would know why I don't want the government to get this kind of technology. If we develop it, they will get it, and they will use it. I will not help them do that."

Max frowned. "Emile, I've been putting up with this kind of thing from you for almost five years now. You're entitled to your opinion, but you work for PNC. You need to grow up and do what we pay you for."

Emile's anger faded, and he sighed. "I can't do that, Max. I'm sorry, but I see I have no choice. You'll have my resignation by the end of the day."

Max's jaw dropped, but Emile turned and strode out of the office. He had to talk to one other person before writing his letter of resignation.

L UCINDA HERNANDEZ LOOKED UP when she heard the laboratory door open. Emile smiled as he stepped in, but Lucinda could tell that her husband's meeting with their manager hadn't gone well. She stood and hugged him. "What did he say?"

Emile waved his hand. "You know Max. He still thinks that Castillo works for the good of us all. He thinks rules and protocols can control technology."

"The system works pretty well."

Emile grunted. "It used to. Castillo has been adept at working around the system, though. The election will just give him another ten years to tighten his control."

"But you're still managing the neuro-interrogator project?"

Emile shook his head. "Not me. I told him I was resigning."

Lucinda gasped. She had known that Emile might resign if the meeting didn't go his way but had convinced herself it wouldn't come to that. Emile was only twenty-eight, two years older than she, and PNC had been the only company either had worked for after receiving their PhDs.

Panama Neuroscience Corporation was a major player in the Western Alliance. With the limits previously imposed on investigation into the brain, few companies competed with PNC. It was a good company to work for, and they had looked forward to the sizeable bonuses PNC had promised for the improvements they had made on the neurotrainer. Older versions fed information through the eyes into working memory, and the brain transferred the information to long-term memory. They and their team had developed methods that sent information directly to long-term memory. Units with the improved technology would allow users to learn twice as fast with better retention than with the old technology.

"What will you do?" she asked.

"I can get a professorship at the University. Ben will help me."

"You won't be happy teaching."

Emile shrugged, but his smile seemed forced. "Oh, I don't know. Anyway, once I'm established, I'll be doing more research there than teaching. I'll find something that will help people."

Lucinda stared at him, her heart pounding. "You know I agree with Max. If we don't develop the technology, the Eastern Bloc will. We still have to defend ourselves."

Emile smiled gently. "I understand. Just because I'm quitting, you don't have to. I hope I'm wrong, but I can't burden you with my opinions. You must do what you think is right."

Lucinda put her arms around Emile and hugged him again. He returned the hug, and Lucinda hoped that meant he supported her.

WHEN EMILE LEFT HIS office, Max thought about calling Vince Rodrigues, Vice President of PNC's Research Department, but he didn't expect a pleasant conversation. Instead, he went to his computer and brought up a list of research scientists working for PNC. Max had a good idea of who could best replace Emile, but wanted to consider other possibilities before talking to Vince. Lucinda Hernandez would probably leave the company with her husband, so he needed a backup plan.

Max didn't like the possibilities. The neurotrainer project was the company's bid to break into the big time, and the Hernandezes had been the driving force in its success. Four other neuroscientists were working on the neurotrainer, but they were younger than Lucinda. They didn't have the experience or the talent of Emile and Lucinda. The new project needed at least one of the Hernandezes, or PNC would be pouring millions down the drain. There was little point in looking outside the company. Few scientists had gone into neuroscience because of the restrictions on research into the brain. The controls were gone, but it would be a while before new scientists entered the field.

Another glance at his computer showed that Emile had posted his letter of resignation and left the building, and that Lucinda was still there. Max dared to hope. He spent another five minutes mentally organizing the inducements he could offer Lucinda before walking down to the laboratory used by the neurotrainer team.

"Lucinda, I'm glad to see you're still here," he said as he entered the laboratory. Lucinda looked at him, her face lit by her usual beautiful smile, and he smiled back. Her long brown hair brushed her shoulders as she stood to greet him. Even her lab coat seemed to emphasize her figure. Emile was a fortunate man.

Lucinda nodded. "Emile talked to me before he left. He knows I'll stay on, assuming you still want me working here."

"My dear, of course I do! I know you and Emile would do nothing to hurt PNC." He smiled. He felt a little guilty when his first thought was that he wouldn't need any of the incentives he had been ready to offer. "We need you even more, with Emile gone. You're the only person qualified to take over the neuro-interrogator project. With a raise in pay, of course. That should help now that Emile is unemployed." That didn't seem to impress Lucinda much, but he didn't care as long as she would lead the neuro-interrogator effort.

"I thought you might promote someone else from the project," Lucinda said.

"I considered it, but there is no one more qualified than you in this field."

Lucinda smiled again. "OK, Max. No need to lay it too thick. I'll do it, at least until we can convince Emile to come back."

I N THE PARKING LOT, Emile zipped up his jacket. It was a late spring afternoon, and the temperature was a typical fifty degrees Fahrenheit. Cerro Punta, at an altitude of about 6500 feet, was never as warm as the tropical Panama lowlands. The usual heavy cloud layer didn't help, but at least it wasn't raining.

Panama Neuroscience Corporation occupied a two-story building on the north side of Cerro Punta, a town of about twenty thousand people. Once, Cerro Punta had been a small, quiet village, surrounded by farms and horse ranches. There were still some farms, but the town had expanded. The ten-story Bank of the Western Alliance, nestled into a notch in one of the town's hills, was the tallest building, with many smaller office buildings clustered below it.

Once settled into his car, Emile looked at the navigation console. "On. Cerro Punta University." The electric engine started soundlessly, and the car moved out onto the road. Emile settled back to enjoy the trip. He thought about calling Ben to warn him he was coming, but Ben would be in his office. He would have to explain everything over the phone and hated doing that when a face-to-face meeting was possible. The trip would calm him.

Cerro Punta University was north of the town, built into the side of a mountain on the southern edge of the continental divide. The two-lane road passed through green fields, up a steep climb through tall trees, to the campus, plastered to the side of the mountain like a huge 3D mural.

The car glided into a tunnel leading to an underground parking garage. After an exchange between the car's computer and the parking garage's computer, it eased into a parking space in the visitor's area and shut down. A quick elevator ride brought Emile up to the eighth floor where the History Department had its offices.

Benicio Young's office door was open, so Emile walked in. Ben sat at his desk, back to a large window looking out at the valley below the University. On the other side of the valley, another forested mountain spur jutted out from the peaks of the La Amistad National Park to the north. It was an incredible view, and Ben had once told Emile that he had to sit with his back to the window or he would never have gotten any work done.

"Emile!" Ben stood, a wide smile on his face. "What a surprise." He moved from behind his desk, shook Emile's hand, and guided him to a padded chair against one wall. He took a seat opposite Emile. "So, what brings you up here?"

Ben was a big man, over six feet tall and heavily built. His round face looked as friendly and open as Emile knew his friend to be. His hair, still black with no trace of gray despite

Ben being ten years older than Emile, was probably a gift from his Ngäbe mother. Blue eyes undoubtedly came from his father, a tourist from the Middle Atlantic district who never left Panama.

Emile gave him a rueful smile. "Job hunting, actually. I just handed in my resignation at PNC."

Ben's eyes widened, and he leaned forward to grip Emile's arm. "What? Why? What happened?"

"You know about the new law that makes mind-reading research and development legal?"

"Yes, I thought of you when I heard about it. With your experience in neurotrainer design, I thought that would create opportunities for you and Lucinda."

"You were right. You sound as if you think it's a good thing."

Ben shook his head. "I don't know. I'm just a history professor, not an expert in technology." He paused and rubbed his nose. "There's nothing I can do about it, but it does seem worrisome. If the wrong people had access to a machine that could read minds. . . Well, nothing good would come of it."

"PNC is starting a project to develop the technology. They're going to call it a neuro-interrogator. The government is funding it."

"I see." Ben leaned back in his chair, his face uncharacteristically somber.

"They wanted me to lead the project. I refused, and resigning seemed like the right thing to do. Otherwise, PNC would have pressured me until I agreed."

"And so, you are looking for other employment. I assume you are going to apply for a professorship here?"

Emile smiled. "I was hoping you could introduce me to the right person."

"Sure. That would be Gerry Battle, the head of the Neuroscience Department. You probably met him at the Neuroscience conference his department hosted last year."

"The name sounds familiar."

Ben nodded and looked over at his desk. "Phone. Connect to Geraldo Battle, please."

There was a pause for a few seconds. "Ben. What can I do for you?"

"Good afternoon, Gerry. Hey, I've got a friend here who would like to get a job in your department. Any openings?"

"We're pretty solid on teaching assistants right now. What qualifications does your friend have?"

Ben grinned. "Well, his name is Emile Hernandez."

"What? The Emile Hernandez? Are you serious?"

"Yup. He just dumped PNC over a policy dispute. I take it you're interested."

"Only if he agrees to sign a promise that he won't oust me from my job. He's there in your office right now?"

"Yes."

"Well, tie him down or something. I'll be right there."

"I can send him up to your office."

"No way. He might get lost. I'm coming." He broke the connection.

Ben turned back to Emile. "I guess your reputation precedes you."

"So, YOU JUST WALKED in, and they hired you on the spot," Lucinda said. She took another plantain from the bunch on the kitchen counter and sliced it open.

Emile nodded. "Pretty much. I won't be doing any teaching until the next semester starts, but I can use the time to think about a research project." He smiled. "And they matched my salary at PNC, so we won't be hurting for money."

"I'm getting a raise, so maybe we can put a little extra on the mortgage."

"You're getting a raise because I quit? Incentive to not quit, too?"

Lucinda hesitated and looked down at the food she was preparing. "Not exactly." She put her knife down on the counter and rubbed her hands. "Now that you're gone, Max wants me to lead the neuro-interrogator project."

Emile was silent, and Lucinda raised her head a little so that she could look at him. *What is he thinking?* "I told him I'd do it."

Emile frowned and stood up. "I'll be in my office until dinner is ready."

Lucinda watched him leave the room. Whenever he felt he might lose his temper, he went to his home office to cool down and scan through the day's news. Dinner would probably be tense, but he would accept her decision eventually. At least she hoped so.

EMILE WATCHED A REPORT on the three library ships, displayed on his wall screen. The newscaster began by summarizing the history of the library ships and the practical communication that they made possible. The segment continued with a report that the main computer of one of the library ships, *Asimov* orbiting Pitcairn, had become self-aware. Emile was aware of the claims but was skeptical. He listened, but there was little current information.

He looked at the screen controller. "Command. Search Anna Cortez. Most recent."

The screen changed to show a woman in her thirties. "This is Anna Cortez of the *Jornal de Brasília,* reporting on the Presidential Campaign." She paused and turned to look at the impressive building behind her. "I'm here in front of the Presidential Palace where, today, President Castillo launched a fresh venomous attack on his opponent, Marisol Weston." An insert opened to Anna's left with a picture of Alejandro Castillo, the Western Alliance President.

"The campaign is only beginning," Anna continued, "and President Castillo is already resuming the slanderous accusations that characterized his first election in 2330, including a suggestion that Ms. Weston has traitorous connections to leaders in the Eastern Bloc. When asked for comment, Executive Press Officer Miguel Arroyo would only say that President Castillo's remarks were protected under the freedom of speech laws of the Western Alliance."

There was more, and Emile watched with deepening depression. He slumped down in his chair, and his thoughts turned to his wife. By taking over the neuro-interrogator project, Lucinda supported Castillo. Despite the reports of journalists like Anna Cortez, polls predicted Castillo would win reelection to another ten-year term. On paper, the Western Alliance was a liberal democracy, but there was always the possibility of men like Castillo corrupting the system. What would such a man do if he had a tool like the neuro-interrogator available?

He wasn't sure he could talk to Lucinda about it without getting angry. Perhaps it would be best not to bring up the subject for a few days.

"Dinner is ready," Lucinda called. Emile washed his hands in the bathroom and headed for the kitchen. His stomach ached, but not from hunger. Dinner would be tense.

2

Lucinda entered the conference room and sat at the head of the table, Emile's usual seat. The rest of the team was already there, looking at her expectantly, and she wasted no time. She wasn't sure how they would accept her leadership and wanted to leave no doubt she was in charge.

"Welcome back. Unfortunately, I must inform you that Emile has left the company. Max has asked me to take over this project, and I have accepted." She paused to let her words sink in. "Any questions?"

"Rumor has it Emile left because he didn't want to work on the neuro-interrogator project," Luke Youngblood said. He avoided her eyes, a sign that the young neuroscientist was nervous.

Lucinda gave him a look that she hoped had just the right amount of frost on it. "My husband has taken a position with the University." She raised her eyebrows, daring him to question her further.

"Ah, yes, that's what I heard."

Lucinda thought she could detect a slight stammer in his words. He had gotten the hint. She looked around the table. "All right, you all know why we're here. Except for Angelo, you all worked on the neurotrainer improvements." She waved a hand at Angelo Davis, a tall, thin man only a little older than Luke, the youngest team member. "I imagine you've all introduced yourselves, but in case you haven't, Angelo is a neuroscientist fresh from his doctoral studies, sent over by corporate to replace Emile."

Luke opened his mouth to say something but apparently thought better of it. Lucinda suppressed a smile and continued. "You're all thinking that Angelo couldn't replace Emile, and you're probably right. But he's smart and will work hard." She looked at Angelo, who was blushing. "You will work hard, won't you, Angelo?"

"Sure. I mean, yes. Of course."

"Have you familiarized yourself with the new neurotrainer interface?"

Angelo nodded. "I read the summary, so I'm familiar with the general ideas."

"Good. We still have a few things to do to wrap up the neurotrainer project, and then we'll begin development on the neuro-interrogator." She paused and looked around. Everyone knew that already, but they were trying to appear to be concentrating on her words.

"We plan to reverse the process used by the neurotrainer. That is, we will interpret input from the neuro-interrogator user's brain instead of sending input to the neurotrainer user's brain. Specifically, the neuro-interrogator will interpret signals from Wernicke's area and output them in a form we can understand."

"Sounds simple enough," Isabella Temple said. Although only in her late thirties, she was the oldest member of the team. An electrical engineer and a genius in building complex devices, she was also the only member of the team not a neuroscientist.

There were a few chuckles. "Sure," Lucinda said. "So, we'll get that done in a day or two, and maybe they'll give us something challenging to do."

Lucinda used the rest of the meeting to make sure everyone understood their immediate tasks. Later, their discussions would get more technical, but for now, they discussed general research and development plans.

In her office afterward, she was alone with her thoughts. They were a capable group, and Lucinda was confident they could do the job. She couldn't help thinking about Emile, though. *What if he is right?* The Eastern Bloc was unquestionably a threat, and giving the government tools to fight it was a good thing, wasn't it? Unlike the Western Alliance, the Eastern Bloc still prohibited research into invading a person's mind, but how long would that be true now that such investigations were legal in the Western Alliance? The Eastern Bloc had to assume their foes would be working on technology applications.

Emile correctly believed that a government could abuse the technology, but the Western Alliance, a democracy, governed by laws that restricted the power of the government. Surely, Emile exaggerated the problem. He could be that way about politics.

She poured herself a cup of coffee from the coffeemaker on a stand next to her desk. Taking a cautious sip of the hot, black liquid, she sighed. Columbia District could brag about their coffee plantations as much as they wanted, but she would take locally grown Chiriquí coffee anytime. One more sip and she put the cup down. She had work to do.

I N June, the summer semester started, and Emile taught two courses: an introductory course on the sensory systems at nine o'clock, and a more advanced course on the amygdala and its role in governing precognitive responses at three o'clock, both with lectures on Monday and Thursday. The latter course fit in with a research project he had begun, investigating a potential link between the amygdala and self-awareness.

Emile had used the first session of the sensory systems course to introduce himself and present an outline of what to expect. In the second session, he prepared to dive into the subject.

He arranged his notes on the rostrum and looked out at the class, arranged in a half-circle before him. The lecture hall had room for over three hundred students, but only about a hundred were taking the class. For most of them, the course was an elective and part of a pre-medical program, but there were a few first-year neuroscience majors. "We're going to get started for real today, so I hope you're all wide awake."

A woman in the front row raised her hand. When Emile acknowledged her with a nod, she rose from her chair. "Before we start, I have a question."

Emile did a quick mental review of the class list but couldn't put a name on the face. Was she in the first session? "Go ahead, Miss."

"You were working at the Panama Neuroscience Corporation."

"Yes, I was. What's your question?"

"Why did you quit?"

Emile stared at her for a long moment, sure now that she hadn't attended the Monday session. Had she transferred into the class? The school would have allowed the change for the first couple of sessions, but the department should have notified him.

"I don't see how that is any of your business."

The woman frowned and put one hand on her hip. "There's a rumor that you quit because you didn't want to work on a government project. Is that true?"

"As I said, that is none of your business." He shuffled his notes, hoping she would take the hint.

"Don't you think it's everyone's patriotic duty to help the government whenever one can? If you can develop technology that the government needs, why don't you do that? Why waste your time here?"

Emile stepped from behind the rostrum and toward the woman. "I suspect that in your case, it would indeed be a waste of time. I do have other students to teach, however, so I suggest you leave and let me do that."

The woman shrank back a little but continued. "So, you're refusing to address my legitimate concern? It seems to me that only an Eastern Bloc sympathizer would do that. Professor, are you an Eastern Bloc sympathizer?"

"No, and I don't sympathize with people telling me what I should think, say, or do. I suggest you take yourself to the library and read up on the Western Alliance Constitution." He advanced another step. "Now, either leave, or I'll call campus security to escort you out."

"I have freedom of speech, too."

"You've exercised it. And I have exercised my right not to answer your question." He stepped back to the rostrum where he could use a built-in phone to summon campus security.

"Maybe you're a Muslim, too." She turned and stomped out of the room.

Emile stiffened and stared after her. The Eastern Bloc was primarily Muslim, and the Western Alliance had few people who followed Islam, but the Constitution guaranteed religious freedom. Prejudiced taunts such as the woman had spouted were rare, although Ben probably would have said it wasn't always so. He swore under his breath. Her remark was like some things Castillo was claiming about his opponent. He should have gotten the woman's name.

He asked the class if anyone knew who she was, but no one knew, or, perhaps, would admit to knowing her. It took an effort to return to his subject, and he was glad when the class was over.

3

T O USE A NEUROTRAINER effectively, a user went through a training process. A program played thousands of words that the user mentally repeated until the neurotrainer could identify and store the output from the brain's internal dictionary. This dictionary, a part of the brain called Wernicke's Area, was different for each user, and the training process significantly improved the neurotrainer's accuracy in presenting a recorded session.

When programmed with the training results, the neurotrainer sent the stored impulses for each word from a recording to the brain language processing center, Broca's Area, faster and with better retention than listening to words or reading; a user could complete in months a graduate college degree taking years to earn traditionally. Human professors taught undergraduate courses, theoretically fostering the ability to work with others, but any such socialization was assumed to be complete by the time someone was ready to earn a graduate degree.

Lucinda's team worked with similar technology, but there were crucial differences. A neuro-interrogator would have to interpret signals from Wernicke's Area, translating thoughts into words, presenting new challenges.

Lucinda was in her office, reading a brief report from Luke on his work with Isabella to design circuitry that could separate words from thoughts. Luke compared the task to separating individual bubbles out of a sink full of soapsuds. He was making progress, but it was slow.

Someone knocked on Lucinda's open door, and she looked up to see Vincenzo Rodriguez, PNC's Vice President of Research.

"Vince! What brings you down here?" Lucinda stood.

Vince smiled and sat across from Lucinda. "I just wanted to see how things are going. This project is vital to the company."

"Things are going well." She sat again. "We've only been at it for two weeks, but we've made some progress."

"Good, good. I know you're doing your best with Emile gone."

Lucinda nodded. Was Vince really making a friendly status check? In her experience, that wasn't the way he worked. He usually got his information from direct reports, in this case, Max. "We miss Emile, but we'll fight on."

"Good. I know you will. We all have great confidence in you, Lucinda. I think you would be the first to admit that it would be better if Emile were still with us."

She tried to keep the wariness she was feeling out of her voice. "Of course. Emile is a leader in the field."

"PNC would be prepared to increase his salary significantly if he came back. Could you tell him that? I would love to talk to him about it."

"I don't think you could tempt my husband with money. To him, this is a matter of principle."

"Fortunately, you don't agree with him on that principle. You could try to convince him that his concerns are not well-founded."

Did she disagree with Emile? The question dominated her thoughts when her work didn't distract her, yet she still wasn't sure how she felt about Emile's fears. Emile had strong opinions, and he wasn't afraid to act on them. Did she only stay after Emile left because she was less passionate about the dangers of the technology? Or was she too cowardly to oppose the system?

"I have tried to change his mind. That is not an easy thing to do."

"I can appreciate that." Vince nodded. "It's a shame, though. Has he thought about how this might damage his reputation?"

Again, Lucinda had to struggle to keep her voice neutral. "What do you mean?"

"Well, some people might find his position unpatriotic. You know what I mean."

Emile had told her about the woman in his class. Could Vince have had anything to do with that? They had decided that Max wouldn't say anything outside PNC, but they hadn't considered Vince. It wasn't a secret, though, and nothing had happened in the two months before the new semester started. Still, Vince's implications annoyed her.

"Maybe you should spell it out."

Vince held up his hands. "Don't get mad at me. I'm just trying to warn you about what other people might think. Emile is refusing to help the government on a project that they consider important. Some people might not interpret that favorably."

"And why should Emile care?"

"It could damage his reputation. Even the University might think twice about keeping a professor of questionable loyalty."

"Emile is as loyal to the Western Alliance as anyone." Her muscles tensed, and she leaned forward with a scowl. "He resigned because he thought this technology would hurt the Western Alliance."

"Lucinda, please. I know all that. I'm just explaining how other people might think. We have gotten very good at putting controls on technology to prevent abuse. Emile should understand that."

Her face felt warm, but she clenched her fists and counted to five. It wouldn't help Emile to lose her temper with Vince. When she thought she had control back, she smiled at Vince. "I'll mention your concerns to my husband."

Vince frowned, nodded, and left.

*J*ORNAL DE BRASÍLIA 3 July 2338 Anna Cortez reporting.

At a press conference today, President Castillo suggested that Presidential candidate Marisol Weston traveled recently to Savannah for a meeting with representatives of the Eastern Bloc. President Castillo noted that Savannah has been a port of entry for many visitors from the east. Our investigation, however, has confirmed that Ms. Weston was visiting relatives in Savannah and has uncovered no evidence of other contacts. Once again, it appears, President Castillo has distorted facts to serve his purposes.

"I'VE BEEN GETTING QUESTIONS from your students," Karen Campbell said. Emile looked up from the monitor where he had been studying a holographic representation of the human brain. Karen was his teaching assistant for that semester, a graduate student, who earned her tuition by giving classroom sessions between Emile's lectures.

Emile smiled. "Isn't that what they are supposed to be doing?"

"No, more personal questions. About why you left PNC."

Emile leaned back in his chair and examined Karen's face. She seemed concerned about the questions, but he didn't think she was asking them for herself. She was young but intelligent, and he was glad to have her assigned to him. Her friendly personality helped make her an excellent assistant and made her more approachable than he was.

"Easier than asking me, no doubt," he said. "What have you told them?"

"I said that you had your reasons and that they should talk to you if they really wanted to know. A few of the students stood up for you, too."

Emile nodded. "Do you think I should address the questions in one of my lectures?"

Karen paused before she answered. "I don't think it would help, sir. You won't change the opinions of the ones asking the questions."

"Karen, I come from a corporate environment where everyone uses first names. I'll ask you once again; please call me Emile."

"Sorry, ah, Emile. It's a hard habit to break."

"OK. Well, let me think about talking to them. Thanks for the heads up."

A week later, Emile decided he would talk to his students. Rather than distract them from his lecture that day, he saved his statement for the end of the class.

"Before we leave, I would like to make a brief statement." He stepped from behind the rostrum to get closer to his audience. "There have been some inquiries about why I left my position at the Panama Neuroscience Corporation. Apparently, it hasn't occurred to anyone that the sight of all your bright, shining faces twice a week would be incentive enough."

The jest worked well enough; most of the students chuckled, or at least smiled. "Some think I left because I didn't want to work on a project for the government. They would be right." There were no chuckles this time, but not too many scowls, either.

"It's not a secret, although perhaps not common knowledge, that PNC is developing something called a neuro-interrogator. Basically, it is a machine that can read minds. Anyone in here want to volunteer as test subjects?" A few nervous laughs, but less than before.

"I've been told that letting the government have such an ability isn't a problem because controls will be in place to prevent abuse. Our society has a lot of experience in that. After all, it has done pretty well for more than a hundred years, protecting us against government power. Can't we trust that this will continue to be the case? They will pass laws that will allow the use of a neuro-interrogator only with a warrant, so it's all OK, right?"

At least he had their attention. Many nodded in agreement. Those students would be the toughest to convince. "After all, government officials never violate the rights of citizens by acting without a warrant, do they? And if they have a warrant, they never exceed the limits imposed by the warrant, do they?"

Some students nodded, but others were scowling. "Before you assure me that the government will never abuse neuro-interrogator mind reads, consider our current president. Does he strike you as someone who wouldn't exceed his authority if he could get away with it?

"So, yes, I left PNC because I didn't want to work on the neuro-interrogator project. I believe it is a danger to our society, especially with a ruthless power-seeker like President Castillo in the palace." Emile paused and scanned the audience. "Thank you for listening. I will see you all next time."

He stepped back to the rostrum and began picking up his papers. The students hurried out, bound for home or their next class. Some were talking to one another, but Emile couldn't hear the words. Mostly, though, they didn't seem angry. Maybe he had at least given them something to think about.

The next day, Emile didn't have a lecture, so he worked in his office, evaluating the first experimental results from a multi-species study from another university, investigating a correlation between self-awareness and emotional maturity. The research, legal even before the Benitez-Baker Act passed, suggested that the two were not causally connected and that the correlation was coincidental or a result of some common trait. Emile thought conclusions were premature, and he hoped his research would shed light on the question.

He left the door to his office open in case a student came by with a question. Focused on the data on his monitor, he didn't notice a visitor. "I hope I'm not disturbing you," Geraldo Battle said.

Emile shook his head and reluctantly looked up from the monitor. "Not at all, Gerry. I'm always available to the head of my department."

"Well, you looked like you were hard at work. I remember how it used to be when I did research. I never liked interruptions."

Emile shrugged. "What did you want to talk about?"

"How's the research going?"

That wasn't why Gerry was visiting him. Emile was sure of that. "I'm making some progress. The answer is likely at least partly in the amygdala, of course."

"You think so? That would be interesting, if true. You'll be needing several species of animal test subjects, I assume?"

"Not yet. I'm still getting some preliminary information and designing a test program."

"I see." Gerry paused, and then looked up suddenly as if he had just thought of something. "There was something else I should probably talk to you about."

Emile wasn't fooled, but he played along. "Sure. Have a seat."

"Thank you. I understand you gave a little speech to your students in your sensory system class."

"I wouldn't call it a speech. They were asking questions, and I thought I should answer them."

"Hmm. Yes. Well, I heard some of your comments could be interpreted as anti-government."

"I had some criticisms for President Castillo. My intention was to make them think about the need for vigilance in protecting our rights."

"I suppose. We must be careful how we express our opinions, though. You never know who might be listening."

Emile forced a chuckle. "If we must worry about who is listening when we talk, then the government is already exceeding its authority."

Gerry frowned. "I can see I'm not getting through to you. Try to be more careful, Emile."

"I will try." Emile stood. "Thanks for stopping by, Gerry. My research is proceeding well."

4

THE SEMESTER WOUND TO a close and Emile taught the last session for his course on the amygdala. He closed the lecture with a summary of what the final examination would cover and put down his notes. "I hope you have all enjoyed this course as much as I have enjoyed teaching it. Now, one more chance to ask questions."

Alfredo Ramirez stood. "Professor, we know about your research. Perhaps you could tell us a little about it."

Emile smiled. "I'd be glad to. It is somewhat relevant to this course. I was intrigued by studies indicating a correlation between self-awareness and emotion. As you well know, correlation does not mean causation. But there could be a causal link. I dug deeper into this to find out whether the correlation is coincidence or an actual connection. It is too early to state anything definitively, but early results support the idea that self-awareness somehow influences the evolution of the amygdala and increases the role of emotion in cognition."

"Could it be the opposite? That development of the amygdala stimulates self-awareness?"

"It is possible, but so far, that doesn't seem to be the case."

"If self-awareness comes first, then the stories about the Tau Ceti library ship might be true. Even a computer without emotion could become conscious."

Emile paced across the room with his hands behind his back, stopped, and turned back to the class. "Personally, I think the stories are exaggerated. I doubt that any computer, no matter how sophisticated, could just become self-aware. I could be wrong; I'm not a computer expert and probably know no more about the library ships than you do—maybe less. We have more powerful computers on Earth, though, and they apparently haven't become self-aware."

Alfredo sat, and Emile scanned around the lecture hall. "Any other questions?" When no one spoke up, he went back to the rostrum and started packing his notes. "All right, then. The final will be in Turing Hall on Monday at nine a.m. I will post room assignments in front of room 105 and on the course network page. Good luck to all of you."

As his students filed out of the lecture hall, Emile finished gathering his notes. He had planned to go to his laboratory and run tests on a gibbon he had recently acquired, but he was tired. The gibbon could wait another day. He left the hall through a door behind the stage and took an elevator to the parking garage.

He was leaning against the elevator's back wall with his eyes closed when the door opened to the parking garage. His eyes snapped open when a voice shouted, "There he is!" A group of about fifteen students stood in a semicircle around the elevator exit. One of them, a beefy older man, stormed forward. "Professor, we demand to know why you are anti-government."

They looked hostile, and Emile pressed back against the wall, hoping the elevator would close, but the man blocked the door. "We want an answer," he said.

"I'm not," Emile said.

The man stepped into the elevator and grabbed Emile's arm. "Why don't you come out here and explain it to us." He yanked Emile out of the elevator. When the door closed behind him, the man released his grip and moved back. The other students closed in, surrounding Emile.

"I'm not anti-government," Emile said. "Who said I was?"

"You have refused to work on the government's neuro-interrogator project," another student said. "We need weapons like that to fight the Eastern Bloc. Are you a stooge for the Eastern Bloc?"

"No. I support the Western Alliance. The neuro-interrogator could be abused too easily. I didn't want to. . .."

"How can you support the government if you don't trust them?" another student demanded. "We would control its use. Don't you believe that?"

The students moved closer. Will they get violent? I could tell my phone to bring my car to the elevator, but they would see me do it. The attempt might only trigger the violence I fear, and I would still have to get through them to the car.

The elevator door opened behind him. "Emile! Holding class in the parking garage now?" Ben stepped out, with four students following him. "Come on; I'll walk with you to your car." He thrust his way through the students surrounding Emile and took his arm. The students with Ben took up positions on either side.

There were angry mutterings, but the circle broke as Ben pushed forward. They followed as Ben and Emile walked across the garage, but made no effort to stop them and dispersed as they drew close to Emile's car. By the time Emile told the door to open, they were gone.

"Thank God you were coming down just then," Emile said. He shook Ben's hand.

Ben grinned. "Quite a coincidence that I came down just then with four of my biggest students with me." The four students, who had been scanning the garage, looked at Ben and laughed. "Did you notice the one protester that hung back? He had a camera and was recording everything. This spontaneous confrontation was on the network as soon as the elevator door opened."

"How did they know?"

"My guess is that they've been waiting for you. Someone may have signaled them from upstairs when you got into the elevator. But they were ready, and so was network coverage."

Emile scratched his head. "OK, but how did you know?"

"I've been expecting something like this, and one of my students told me about a group hanging around the elevator. Gerry has come in a couple of times asking about you, and I found it suspicious that the head of the Neuroscience Department would talk to a mere history professor. I set a network alarm to warn me when you left your office. These strong young men were hanging around my office."

"Another coincidence?"

Ben's grin widened. "I asked them to wait around for developments when I heard about the group around the elevator. As I said, I've been expecting something like this. You've stirred things, Emile."

"Well, thank you. You're a better friend than I realized. I hope this doesn't cause you any trouble."

Ben shook his head. "Don't worry about it. I'm on your side. I'm concerned about Castillo, too. He'll probably win another ten years, but we can't do anything about that. We can hope to limit the damage he can do, though."

Emile shook Ben's hand again and got into his car.

When Emile arrived home, Lucinda was still at work. Her hours had gotten longer after taking over the neuro-interrogator project, and Emile usually got home first. He sometimes got busy with his research and came home later, but that didn't happen more than once a week.

Supper wouldn't be until after Lucinda got home, so Emile got a beer from the refrigerator, grumbling under his breath. By now, he had hoped, his wife would have left the neuro-interrogator project, realizing he was right. It was Lucinda's decision, and he had not pushed her on it, but the issue, and holding back on talking about it, ate at him. He looked at the beer; it probably wasn't a wise choice just then. The beer wouldn't help the extra ten pounds he had put on since leaving PNC, either. He resealed it and returned it to the refrigerator.

Instead, he grabbed an orange from a fruit bowl on the kitchen counter and went to his home office. Ben had said that a report on the confrontation was already on the network, so the icon on his screen labeled "Cerro Punta University demonstration" didn't surprise him. He ordered the screen to display the report and settled back in his chair to watch it.

A *Brasília Today* spokesperson appeared on the screen. He looked familiar, but Emile couldn't place him. Most of the commentators seemed molded by the same media personality factory, created to exude confidence and trustworthiness. "Government supporters today confronted neuroscientist Emile Hernandez, a former employee of the Panama Neuroscience Corporation, at Cerro Punta University. Six months ago, he resigned to take a teaching position at the University. Sources have said that he resigned rather than lead a project to develop technology that could read minds. We have video of the actual event."

The spokesperson faded away, and Emile saw himself standing in front of the elevator. Emile frowned; he looked frightened, almost cowering under the questioning. The video was framed so that only three of the group were visible. You could hear voices from off-screen, but the scene didn't look as threatening as it had seemed at the time. The video stopped just as the elevator door opened again, and the spokesperson returned.

"Doctor Hernandez was obviously not prepared to answer questions and immediately left the University campus. He could not be reached afterward for comments. People are asking where his loyalties really lie and wonder how he could get a position at a university, where he can indoctrinate other scientists."

Emile's head hurt. He started to turn the screen off, but he noticed another icon in one corner of the screen labeled "Anna Cortez Commentary." He commanded the screen to bring that up, and Anna Cortez replaced the spokesperson.

"A recording released this afternoon showed a confrontation between unnamed men and Doctor Emile Hernandez, a professor in the Neuroscience Department of Cerro Punta University. The group, of undetermined size, accosted Doctor Hernandez in the

University parking garage as he stepped off an elevator. They demanded that he explain why, six months ago, he left Panama Neurosciences Corporation to take a teaching position at Cerro Punta University. The video was staged to make the incident seem spontaneous, but by some incredible coincidence, a cameraman was on hand to record the video. There were other strange coincidences involved, but, rather than elaborate on them, I will present a witness to the incident, Doctor Benicio Young of the Cerro Punta University History Department."

The view moved back to show Ben in a chair next to Anna. At least, it appeared that way, but the two were hundreds of miles apart. Emile couldn't help but smile. Ben had wasted no time. "Doctor Young, can you tell us what you saw?" Anna said.

"I would be happy to," Ben answered. "I was leaving for the day and took the elevator down to the parking garage. When I got there, I saw approximately fifteen men—they appeared to be students, although I didn't recognize any of them—surrounding Professor Hernandez. That must have been the time when your video ended. I greeted Professor Hernandez and walked with him to his car. He then left."

"The men didn't try to stop you?"

Ben grinned. "Well, I had a few of my students with me."

"Just by coincidence, I assume."

"As much coincidence as having fifteen students hanging around the elevator when Professor Hernandez came down."

"Yes, of course. Thank you, Doctor Young." The view moved in again to show only Anna. "As you saw on the video, these thugs confronting Doctor Hernandez apparently objected to his change in employment. Doctor Hernandez is certainly within his rights to make the choice he did. This effort to portray Doctor Hernandez as disloyal because of his choice has no place in a free society. One should ask who is behind this disturbing incident." She paused. "This is Anna Cortez of *Jornal de Brasília*. Thank you for listening."

Lucinda came home an hour and a half later. "Emile, are you all right?" she asked, rushing into his office.

"I'm fine." He gripped her shoulders and kissed her. "Nothing to worry about."

"Nothing to worry about? I saw that video. There must have been five or six of them attacking you."

"Actually, it was more like fifteen, but they didn't attack me. Ben showed up and rescued me. You can see his account of it in a report from Anna Cortez."

"And you're all right?"

"I'm all right. They never touched me. Just scared the hell out of me with their questions."

"I'm scared, too," Lucinda said. "Vince visited me again, asking if I made any progress in getting you back." She paused and looked up at him. She was shaking, and there were tears in her eyes. "Maybe you should come back."

"Don't let them intimidate you. They won't do anything drastic."

"How can you be sure?"

"Why would they? After all, their goal isn't to make me stop teaching. They want me to work on the neuro-interrogator. Hurting me won't help them."

"That sounds very logical." Lucinda's voice trembled. "It assumes that they are as logical as you. Is that a safe assumption?"

"Sure." He let go of her shoulders and smiled. "So, what are we going to do about dinner?"

5

"RAFAELA SOSA CALLING FOR Doctor Emile Hernandez," the phone announced.

"Identify," Emile said.

"Booking agent for *Jornal de Brasília,* Brasília Office." The wall screen in his living room displayed a professionally dressed young woman.

Emile felt Lucinda touch his arm, but he was curious. "Connect."

"Doctor Hernandez, I book interviewees for Anna Cortez, the *Jornal de Brasília* commentator. I hope you're familiar with her. She would like to interview you sometime next week."

Lucinda's touch became a grip. Emile knew what she was feeling; he had his own misgivings about further exposure to the public. His views had already caused him enough trouble. More than a month had passed since the confrontation in the parking garage. Except for a "friendly" talk with Gerry about his commitment to the University, the controversy about his views had faded into obscurity. The election campaign continued, growing more acrimonious, and dominating the network. Lucinda and the neuro-interrogator project had made some progress, and Emile thought that might have taken some pressure off him.

"I don't think so, Ms. Sosa," he said. "I'm sure you understand why I would be reluctant to increase my notoriety." Lucinda's grip loosened, and her hand dropped away.

"Anna feels strongly about interviewing you. She is prepared to come to Cerro Punta if that would make you more comfortable."

"I appreciate that, but I am not a confrontational man, and all this controversy is finally dying down. Please tell Ms. Cortez that I am a fan, but I really don't think I can help her."

"You have a duty to your nation," Rafaela said. "We know you love your country and you are taking this stand because you want to protect it. President Castillo is a threat to our freedom and must be defeated. Your story can help do that. The mind-reading technology is being developed without you. Do you want Castillo to have access to it?"

The argument was overblown, but the woman had a point. He avoided the subject with Lucinda, but her acceptance of the neuro-interrogator project bothered him. Could he back down now?

"When would she want to do this?"

"She could be there Monday morning. We could record the interview in an hour, and it would appear on the network during Anna's commentary Monday night. There's a studio in Cerro Punta that we can use; all you have to do is give us that hour."

From the corner of his eye, Emile could see Lucinda shaking her head, and he almost said no. Someone had to step up, though. "Very well. I'll do it."

Rafaela Sosa gave him the details he would need, thanked him, and disconnected. The wall screen blinked and again displayed the usual network access view. Lucinda had left the room.

E MILE WAS NERVOUS. LECTURING hundreds of students or presenting reports before company executives was routine to him, but sitting on a stage with a famous commentator, viewed by thousands or even millions—that was something else.

Emile wondered why they didn't want to record an interview remotely and patch both ends together to make it seem face-to-face. That was how they had recorded Ben's interview with Anna. That was the usual procedure across distant locations, but after offering to send Anna to Cerro Punta, they had assumed that was how Emile would want it. Was the interview really that important to Anna? Did they think Anna's presence would make Emile more cooperative? He had to admit to himself that there might be something to that.

Now, in a studio used by network broadcasters for local recording, he regretted the decision, but it was too late to back out. Anna Cortez was already in the building, having flown in from Brasília. She would be ready for him in a few minutes.

A man approached Emile. "Anna is ready for you now."

Emile followed him to the soundstage where they would record the interview. It wasn't as impressive as he had imagined. There were two comfortable chairs in the tiny room, and Anna was already seated.

"Thanks for agreeing to do this, Doctor," she said, shaking his hand. "I'll be giving a brief introduction before we start the actual interview. You won't be on screen during the introduction, but it's probably best if you act as if you were. You'll look more natural when we bring you into view."

Emile sat. There was a small table between the chairs with two glasses of water. Emile took a drink from the closest glass and was immediately embarrassed by his loud gulp. No water during the interview, he told himself.

A light on Anna's chair arm turned from red to green, and Anna turned to face the cameras. "This is Anna Cortez, reporting for the *Jornal de Brasília*. It's still fourteen months until the Presidential election, and already the level of malevolence in the campaigning has risen to historic highs. There is little talk about issues while President Castillo's campaign engages in its slanderous attacks on his opponent, and candidate Marisol Weston can do little more than defend herself against the vicious rhetoric.

"My guest today has also been a victim of the Castillo campaign. Doctor Emile Hernandez, one of the Western Alliance's leading neuroscientists, has been subject to attacks simply because he chose to teach rather than work on government-funded projects."

She turned to Emile. "Doctor Hernandez, thank you for joining us."

Emile had been briefed on his response. "Thank you for having me, Anna." He hoped he sounded more sincere than he felt.

"Doctor, you were asked to manage a project at the Panama Neuroscience Corporation, and you resigned rather than work on that project. Could you tell us more about it?"

"Certainly." He cleared his throat and berated himself for his nervousness. "As you know, earlier this year, a new law made it legal to research areas of the brain previously prohibited and develop products from that research. All civilized nations have prohibited such research since the technology scandals, but the law has changed that. PNC started a project to develop a neuro-interrogator. Simply put, the goal was to develop a machine that could read thoughts directly from the brain."

"And you opposed that."

Emile nodded. "Yes. I felt that the danger of such a technology being abused was too high."

"But surely there would be controls to protect innocent citizens from abuse."

"Of course. But unscrupulous officials have circumvented such controls in the past. I felt the danger was too great."

"Especially when the government is run by men like Alejandro Castillo?"

Emile blinked, but managed, he hoped, not to react more than that. He wasn't a politician and had expected to talk about his views about the science involved. He had to say something; the silence was getting uncomfortably long.

"I'm a scientist, not a politician. My concerns are more general than this election."

"Of course. But you have been subject to attacks because of your views."

The bright lights of the studio didn't give off much heat, but Emile was sweating anyway. He desperately wanted to wipe his forehead. *Can viewers see that I'm nervous?*

"I wouldn't call them attacks," he said. "There has been some pressure to return to PNC."

"There was a confrontation in a parking garage at the university where you teach."

"Yes. That was more serious, but I still wouldn't say I was attacked."

"Not physically, but it seemed pretty aggressive verbally, wouldn't you say?"

"I suppose."

Anna looked front again. "You may have already seen the video of Doctor Hernandez's confrontation in the parking garage of Cerro Punta University, but we are showing it again to remind everyone of what Doctor Hernandez went through." The light on her chair turned red, and Anna sat quietly. When it shone green again, she continued. "Doctor Hernandez is being modest. You can see for yourself what happened. The video stops as the elevator door opens behind him, and you can't see his friend and colleague, Doctor Benicio Young, come to Doctor Hernandez's rescue. We have no way of knowing what would have happened without Doctor Young's timely intervention."

Anna turned to Emile. "Thank you, Doctor." She shook hands with him. "I'm sure everyone wishes you well and hopes that the Castillo campaign won't attack you any further."

Emile opened his mouth to protest. He had said nothing about responsibility for the pressure put on him and, to his knowledge, a person or group behind the confrontation in the parking garage hadn't been identified. The light had turned red again, though. No one would be listening. Emile nodded to Anna and left the studio.

6

T HE DAY AFTER THE interview, one of his students interrupted his class on the sensory system with questions about why he had left PNC. The student was apparently not one of Castillo's more dedicated campaign workers; when Emile suggested his interruptions might affect his grade, the student frowned and turned his attention to a book he was carrying. The following week, another student disrupted his class on the amygdala, persisting until Emile had campus security remove him. Karen reported questions in the classroom sessions, too. Then, two men, presumably students, stopped him in a hallway, demanding answers.

It was becoming a regular thing, and Emile was now more angry than frightened. The incidents were annoying, but he didn't feel threatened. Ben had offered an escort, and two of Emile's students had also offered to go with him when he left the building, but Emile turned them down. There was no reason to disrupt the lives of students who already had enough to worry about.

Two weeks later, Emile lost track of time setting up a new test plan for newly arrived test animals. It was dark when his car took him away from the campus, and the passing scenery was less distracting than during daylight hours. He leaned back and thought about the next day's tasks while the car drove home. The seat was comfortable, and he dozed off, only waking when the vehicle came to a sudden stop.

He had arrived home, but the car had not driven into the open garage because the driveway was blocked. People, almost all carrying signs, milled around the front of his house, staring at his car. Most of the signs were just pieces of cardboard nailed or glued to a stake, but there were a few holographs, too. One of the more eye-catching displayed a bust of President Castillo. "Do your duty" was a popular slogan, and several proclaimed, "Eastern Bloc sympathizer," or a similar message.

The house was dark. It's late, and Lucinda should be home. Even if she isn't, the outside lights should have come on automatically. Did the mob break them? That made little sense, but that didn't mean it wasn't true. More likely, Lucinda had turned them off, hoping to discourage the trespassers.

The built-up anger came to the surface. "Summon the police," he told the car. He opened the car, stepped scowling out onto the driveway, and was immediately surrounded.

"Why are you against the government?" one woman shouted from the crowd.

Emile ignored her. One person advanced toward him, and Emile strode over to him, assuming he was the leader. "Get these people away from my house." He waved a hand around. "The police are on their way, so if you wish to avoid arrest, you should leave immediately."

The man didn't seem intimidated. "Answer our legitimate questions, and we'll leave. What is your problem with our government?"

"My opinion of our government is my business." He moved closer until he was in the man's face. "I don't answer to you or anyone else except myself."

The man didn't flinch. He looked down at Emile mildly. "You are a citizen of the Western Alliance and a public figure. We have the right to know why you refuse to help us defend ourselves. You owe it to society to answer."

The arrival of a police car and two officers interrupted Emile's answer. Emile gave the protester an angry look and walked down the driveway to meet them.

"What's the emergency?" the older of the two officers asked.

Emile looked at him with raised eyebrows. "These people are trespassing." He waved his arm around.

"Uh huh." The officer raised his voice. "Who's the leader here?"

Emile had guessed right. The man he had talked to sauntered over. "That would be me."

"What's going on?"

The man shrugged. "We just want to know why this man isn't supporting the government. He's a teacher, and we're concerned about what he might be teaching."

The policeman looked at Emile, and Emile could have sworn that the officer recognized him. "Is that true? Are you anti-government?"

"It is not true. I used to work at PNC and resigned to teach at the University. I have no obligation to explain that to these people."

"Anna Cortez interviewed him," the lead protester said. "His anti-government opinions were recorded and shown on the network."

"Is that so?" The officer sneered. "Anna Cortez. Not exactly pro-government, Professor."

"I want these people off my property. I think you should do your duty, officer."

The policeman stared at Emile for a long moment. "Well, I think these people are exercising their right to free speech, Professor. Maybe you should just answer their questions."

"They are exercising their free speech rights on my property, and I want them off. If they want an answer to their question, they can find the interview this man mentioned. I have nothing to hide."

"You say you own this property, but I don't know that. I don't want to start trouble here, just on your word."

Emile had all he could take. "I could go in the house and find the deed," he said. "It might take a while to find it. I don't want to keep you away from your other duties. But I know exactly where I keep a shotgun. They're trespassing, so I do have the right to shoot a couple of them. Maybe then they would go away without inconveniencing you."

The older policeman was getting angry, too, although the younger officer seemed to stifle a laugh. "If you come out here with a firearm, I will arrest you."

"Not before I shoot a couple. By the time the case comes to trial, I should be able to find my deed and prove that I was within my rights."

"Fine, Professor. Have it your way. You're under arrest." The policemen grabbed his arm and pulled him toward the patrol car. The younger officer hesitated, looking uncertain, but grabbed Hernandez's other arm. They shoved him into the back seat, accompanied by cheers and shouts from the protesters.

C ERRO PUNTA WAS A small town, with a population of about twenty thousand people, mostly law-abiding. The mayor, judge, courtroom, police force, and jail shared one two-story building near the city center. The jail had two cells, only one of which held a prisoner, but the arresting officers put Emile in the occupied cell.

Emile's cellmate glanced up at him from his seat on the edge of an unmade bunk. He looked to be in his sixties, unshaved, with tattered and dirty clothes, and stared at Emile with bleary eyes. The man smelled as if a bath was a dim memory. Emile didn't bother asking the man why he was in the cell. It was apparent he was drunk.

"You're a fancy one," the man said. "What'd you do to get in here?"

"Irritated the wrong people, I guess," Emile mumbled. He sat down on the other bunk.

The man nodded. "Me, too. I was drinking in the wrong place. I'm Carlos Padilla."

"Emile Hernandez. I don't suppose I'll get any food here. I was arrested before I could get dinner."

"Dinner was two hours ago. Sorry." He seemed to lose interest in the conversation and laid down.

Emile examined his surroundings. The cell was square, roughly ten feet on each side, with white metal walls, a high ceiling, and a camera in one corner, out of a prisoner's reach. The cell door was the same metal as the walls, with a grill toward the top. The lock, Emile had noticed, was voice-activated. Another door in the back of the cell was presumably the toilet facility.

The two bunks along opposite walls were the only furnishings. The sheets were clean and the mattress of reasonably decent quality. There was a light blanket, but no pillow on Emile's bed. He glanced over and saw that his cellmate had appropriated both pillows.

Emile was a little alarmed at the turn of events, but told himself that, at worst, he would only spend one night in the cell. He wasn't sure what he was being charged with, but surely a judge would throw out any accusation. Meanwhile, he might as well be comfortable. He thought about asking for his pillow, but Carlos was already snoring. Shrugging, he took his jacket off, folded it, and used that under his head. The cell was warm, so he laid on top of the blanket.

He woke when he heard someone command the door to open. He sat up as an officer—the younger of the two who had arrested him—came into the cell with Ben. Ben rushed over and helped him to his feet. "Are you OK, Emile?"

"I'm fine." Emile rubbed his eyes.

"Good. Come on; Lucinda is waiting in the next room."

"I'm being released?"

Ben grinned. "Judge Walker's son is in one of my classes. It gives me a little influence. It didn't hurt that no charges were filed. The whole thing was just another attempt to intimidate you."

Emile returned the grin. "I think they succeeded. Let's get out of here." He walked toward the door.

Lucinda was waiting in the reception area. She hugged Emile and fussed over him, but he kissed her and stepped back. "Have you two eaten yet? No? Good, let's find someplace. I'm starved."

WHEN EMILE AND LUCINDA arrived home two hours later, the demonstrators were gone. It was late, but Emile went into his office and turned on his network screen. It didn't take him long to find a report of his arrest. There was a video that started when he drove into his driveway and ended with the patrol car arriving. The commentator had his own interpretation of what happened.

"Doctor Emile Hernandez, a former employee of the Panama Neuroscience Corporation, is in the news again tonight. As the video shows, demonstrators concerned about his loyalty to the Western Alliance were waiting for him when he arrived home." The screen changed to show the video, after which the commentator came back.

"After he threatened the demonstrators with a shotgun, Cerro Punta police arrested Hernandez. Hernandez continues to teach at Cerro Punta University. One must wonder why the University has not removed him from his position in the wake of such serious allegations. As has become usual, Doctor Hernandez could not be reached for comment."

"How much longer can this go on?" Lucinda asked from the office doorway.

Emile shook his head. "I don't know. Until the election? If Castillo or his campaign is behind it. It's hard to believe they would create this much controversy over me. After all, I didn't kill their precious project. I just refused to lead it. You're making progress without me."

"Some. Not as much as management would like."

"Oh." Emile turned back to the screen and looked for a link to an Anna Cortez commentary, thinking she would present an accurate view of the incident. He couldn't find a recent link, though. It was late; she would comment in the morning. At least, he hoped so.

JORNAL DE BRASÍLIA 25 October 2338, Anna Cortez reporting

You may remember previous reports about the travails of Cerro Punta University Professor, Doctor Emile Hernandez. Doctor Hernandez apparently offended the powers-that-be by refusing to work on a government project and, instead, teaching at Cerro Punta University. Last night, police arrested him after he tried to remove protesters from his property. Reports have claimed that he threatened the protesters with a shotgun, but the video of the incident shows no weapons. In fact, according to his wife, Doctor Hernandez does not own a shotgun or any other weapon. You may also have noticed that reports don't mention the crimes Doctor Hernandez was accused of. That's because he was thrown into a jail cell without being charged. He is free today after friends interceded with Cerro Punta Judge Eden Walker. When contacted, Judge Walker said only that there was no reason to hold Doctor Hernandez.

As a final note, perhaps irrelevant, *Jornal de Brasília* investigators have discovered that one of the arresting officers has a son working on President Castillo's reelection campaign. This is Anna Cortez, reporting for *Jornal de Brasília*.

7

E MILE GLANCED OUT HIS car window into a dark night, the dense forest on either side of the road shrouding an almost-full moon. The headlights illuminated the two traffic lanes and middle passing lane in front of the car, but, at the speed the automated controls propelled the vehicle, there was nothing to see. He lowered his eyes to the built-in reader on the dashboard, displaying a report on the latest student test results.

Emile's chest restraint tightened, sudden deceleration pulling him back against the seat as the car activated the brakes. A human couldn't have reacted nearly as quickly, but the result was the same. An impact pushed the front back into the engine compartment with a piercing screech of metal scraping metal. Then the car came to a stop.

Emile heard the thump of the collision and the scream of twisted metal, but didn't know what had happened. The structure of the car interior and his restraints had protected him from injury, but his heart pounded.

"An emergency response team will be here in fifteen minutes," the car said. "There is no need to leave the vehicle until it arrives."

"What happened?" His heart was still hammering, but he ignored it. The crash had triggered the response in his body, but the danger was over.

"A Chiriquí deer ran in front of the vehicle. The collision injured it and it lies twenty feet behind the vehicle. The vehicle has sustained moderate damage and cannot be operated safely until repairs are made."

A deer? A hazard of working so far from the town. He shrugged. Perhaps he could still finish reading the report while he waited for the response team. He looked at the screen, but it was dark. The crash might have damaged it, or the car could have shut it down. He considered asking the car to turn the display back on, but he doubted his ability to absorb the information just then. The car said the deer was behind him somewhere. He could see if there was anything he could do for the animal. "Retract restraints and open the door."

"It is advisable to stay in the vehicle until help arrives. Please confirm or cancel command."

"Confirm."

The restraints slid away from him with a smooth whisper, the door opened, and a circle of light appeared to illuminate his way out of the car. He exited carefully and stood by the car, taking in his surroundings. The forest was a black, impenetrable wall, the road a strip of featureless ebony ink. Not even a centerline stripe proved the road's existence, since automated vehicles didn't need them. The car's headlights were out, and only the interior light gave any illumination. Looking up, he could see a few stars shining through the broken clouds, but they did nothing to relieve the darkness.

He sighed. This sort of thing wouldn't happen if he still worked at PNC, within the boundaries of Cerro Punta. Now that he was out of the car, a serene silence helped restore his calm. He could smell the pines and relaxed a little. The town didn't sound or smell like that, one plus at least.

A whimper from somewhere behind the car reminded him of the deer, and he peered into the blackness. A slightly lighter blob lay partly on the road and partly on the shoulder. It moved a little; the deer was still alive. "Rear lights on," he told the car. The light didn't help much, but Emile walked back to the animal and kneeled next to it. It had been an unusually large stag, with an impressive rack of antlers, but now it could only lie there, with one brown eye staring up at him. Emile put his hand on the creature's neck and stroked it lightly. "It's OK," he crooned. "Help will be here soon."

There was only an instant to see the look of panic appear in the animal's eye. The deer's head jerked up, and an antler struck Emile across the side of his head. His entire world went dark, and he didn't hear the aircar approach and land next to him. Two men got out and went to him, but he didn't know about it. For a long time, he knew nothing.

W AS THIS DEATH? EMILE was conscious, but he couldn't feel anything. He was floating in a dark, silent void, without even the sensation of touching something anywhere on his body—assuming he had a body. Nothing except his thoughts hinted he might still exist.

He had once taken a seminar on awareness training, and he tried to recall the techniques he had learned then. He didn't remember everything, but he used what he remembered to probe for any sensation. The attempt was futile; he existed, but the rest of the universe was gone. Finally, even his consciousness faded; he slept.

THERE WERE VOICES IN Emile's head. He wasn't hearing them, but his brain was aware of them anyway. They seemed far away and indistinct, clouded by emotional context, like the output of a neurotrainer receiving input from a nonprofessional source. He found he could understand the words if he concentrated on them.

"You would think that they would give up after six months," one voice said.

"People have regained consciousness after longer comas than this," a second voice said. It was only the first voice that was showing emotion; the second was flat, probably from a computer or a robot.

"Well, I'm still not seeing any new activity in the brain. Same as always. I don't know what Elias was talking about."

"The range on the monitor interface isn't set correctly."

Now there was embarrassment. "Oops. OK, adjusting. Hmm, a little activity in the language centers. That's new, I think." There was a pause in the words, but Emile could sense confusion. Then the voice was back. "It's probably just a little feedback from the neurotrainer. Check other brain areas."

The second voice came back almost immediately. "I'm getting activity in the frontal lobe. He's conscious!"

"I'm calling Doctor Artemis. He's going to want to see this right away."

THERE WAS AN EXTENDED period—at least, it seemed long to Emile—of silence. Finally, there was a new voice in his brain. "Doctor Hernandez, I'm Doctor Artemis. You've been away from us for a long time." There was a brief pause. "I'm talking to you through a neurotrainer. I'm sure you understand how that works better than I do. We're trying to come up with a way for you to respond, so be patient."

HE SLEPT AGAIN. WAKING when another voice entered his mind. While he couldn't identify the sender by voice, he could detect a difference in the impression made on his mind by the neurotrainer. He was almost positive that Dr. Artemis was talking to him again. "I'm back. We're connecting you to the neuro-interrogator now."

Neuro-interrogator? Did that mean that Lucinda had been successful? How long had he been unconscious? There was a pause of at least several minutes. "OK, you should be able to communicate with us now. Try to focus on your words, and we should be able to understand you."

"OK," he thought.

"Great. We got that. How are you receiving us?"

"A little fuzzy. I have to focus hard to understand you, but I can manage."

"Well, we're not neurotrainer recording technicians, so we're not very good at keeping our emotions out of the recordings."

"I understand. Is my wife here?"

There was a hint of something that could have been amusement in the response from Dr. Artemis. "Yes, she's outside. Would you like to talk to her?"

"Yes, please."

After another long moment, there was a fresh voice in his head. The emotion transmitted through the neurotrainer was so intense that he couldn't understand the words. "Lucinda, is that you?" he asked.

This time, he could make out the words through the haze. "Yes, Emile. It's me."

"Are you OK? Your thoughts are so emotional."

There was a hint of amusement in his wife's reply. "Yes, I'm fine. My husband is lying in bed and can only communicate through these machines. Of course, I'm emotional."

"Try to calm down. It's hard to understand you."

"Always the logical scientist! All right, I'll try." She paused, and her next thought was clearer. "How are you? I can't imagine how it is for you."

"It's very strange," Emile sent. "I can't feel anything; my thoughts are my entire existence. Hearing you through the neurotrainer is nothing like normal hearing. I get complete thoughts with all the emotional overtones. The words have to be filtered out of that background."

"But you're getting better?" Her thoughts were a touching mixture of hope and concern. For the six and a half years of their marriage, they had never really communicated their feelings, and Emile had always thought that they were both too tied up in their work to waste time talking about such things. Hearing her through the neurotrainer was a revelation. He wondered how much of his fear was getting through to her.

"I'm communicating using a neuro-interrogator. Does that mean you were successful?"

"We're getting there. You're using our first prototype, but it's still crude. I don't think it would work at all on a less-disciplined person and even with you, it's difficult to understand your words."

"It's strange the way your words come through. I get the definite impression that by 'disciplined' you really mean 'unemotional.'"

"Very funny." Lucinda's words and the emotional content of the thought matched this time.

"The doctors haven't talked to me yet about my prognosis," he sent. "Perhaps you could ask Dr. Artemis."

There was a long pause before Lucinda was back, but he could tell from the raw emotion she transmitted that the doctor's answer was not hopeful. Her words verified his worst fear. *I'm not going to get better.*

I N THE HOSPITAL CAFETERIA, Lucinda sipped her coffee without tasting it. A plate of Hojaldras next to the coffee was untouched. She hadn't told Emile everything. She had to get her emotions under better control before burdening him. Neurotrainers provided educational material recorded by trained people and were not meant to be used by an untrained wife frantic with worry about her husband. She couldn't shake the image of him in bed, his dark eyes open but empty of the life that had animated his face, his body surrounded by the apparatus that kept him alive.

"Good morning, Lucinda. How's Emile?"

She looked up to see Max smiling at her. She managed a return smile and gestured toward the seat opposite her. "Thank you for coming, Max," she said as he took the seat opposite her. "Emile will be glad to hear from you."

"How is he?"

Lucinda shrugged. "He just found out he will probably be in locked-in state for the rest of his life. Thanks for the loan of that neuro-interrogator prototype. It works well for Emile."

"You're welcome. I have some good news and bad news about that. The good news is that it is no longer a loan. You can keep it."

Lucinda gasped and stared at Max. "That's wonderful! How did you talk PNC into that?"

"I didn't. They don't know. That's the bad news. The entire project has been canceled. Almost everyone connected to it has been laid off, and the neuro-interrogator prototype seems to have been forgotten."

"Forgotten? That's impossible."

"Funny thing. It turns out that Vince has a heart after all. He probably couldn't have gotten away with it, but we tried to demo the prototype last week with a representative from the government. It was a disaster."

"Why? It works so well with Emile."

"They sent some middle-management flunky from the palace. He was so nervous about being connected to the thing that all we could get was nonsense. With you here in Colón all the time, the project was faltering anyway, and the demonstration was the final straw. The government pulled its funding, and PNC had to regroup. I'm sorry, Lucinda, but you're one of the people they let go. So am I."

Lucinda felt her stomach knot. The University was still paying Emile's salary, but she wasn't sure how long that would continue. Now she was unemployed.

"Your health insurance will cover Emile's care for another six months," Max said. "That should give you time to find something else. Maybe sooner rather than later. I'm working on something that could solve the employment problem for both of us."

Lucinda barely heard him. She nodded without understanding.

M AX STRODE INTO THE lobby and almost stopped to stare. He considered the buildings at PNC luxurious, but Munt Electronics forced him to revise his opinion. The lobby rivaled the Presidential Palace in its lavishness. Marble floors, statuary, paintings on the walls, and natural lighting from the translucent ceiling were all carefully chosen and arranged to impress.

The lobby was a single-floor extension in front of the twenty-story building with an aircar landing pad on the lobby roof. Across the lobby's wide space, an attractive young woman sat at a marble reception desk. She smiled up at him as he approached. "How can I help you, sir?"

Max smiled back. "Maxwell Estevez to see Jasmine Munt. I have an appointment."

The woman didn't have to check. "Certainly, Doctor Estevez. I'll call an escort, and he'll take you to her."

She touched a button on the console in front of her. A few seconds later, a young man came out from a door behind the desk. "This way, please, sir."

Max followed the man down a corridor only slightly less sumptuous than the lobby. A door led to another, smaller reception area, manned by the male equivalent of the woman in the outside lobby. "Doctor Estevez," Max's escort announced.

"Mrs. Munt is waiting for you, Doctor," the receptionist said. "She'll be right out."

Max smiled. It was normal to still have a human in the lobby of a company the size of Munt Electronics, but human assistants for individuals were less common. So were human escorts. Jasmine Munt was either being ostentatious or making a statement about replacing people with machines, noteworthy for a company that produced electronic devices.

In less than a minute, Jasmine Munt entered the room. "Doctor Estevez, welcome!" She held out her hand and Max took it. "Please, come into my office."

Once seated in comfortable armchairs in one corner of Jasmine's office, they looked each other over. For Max's part, he saw a woman in her thirties, perfectly groomed and dressed. She was attractive, but Max guessed she was taking advantage of her money to present herself as advantageously as possible.

"You've heard about my husband's accident, I suppose," Jasmine said.

"He was boating on Gatun Lake. He recovered, I believe. I don't know the details."

Jasmine nodded. "We haven't allowed too much information to be made public. Although I am the CEO of Munt Electronics, my husband developed the technology that originally made the company a leader in the industry." She smiled. "He's the science geek; I'm the business brains of the partnership."

Max nodded, and she continued. "If the truth were known about his accident, it would be a serious blow to the company. He hasn't been involved that much for the last couple of years, but perception is everything."

"His injuries were more serious than has been released, I take it."

"He has recovered quite well in most respects. He suffered brain damage, but mostly in one area. His brain is fully functional, except that he can no longer speak coherently. He apparently knows what he wants to say, but it's not coming out the way he thinks it is."

Despite the attempt to cover up the nature of Franco Munt's injuries, Max had heard rumors. Munt Electronics was one of Panama's most successful companies, well-known throughout the Western Alliance. The Munts were billionaires several times over, and Max hoped the meeting would allow him to capitalize on that. "I assume you asked me here because you think I might be able to help."

"I am familiar with the work you were doing for PNC. I have a proposal for you."

His pulse quickened. "PNC owns our research."

"Of course. The neuro-interrogator was an important project, though. PNC has taken a big hit in stock value since they canceled the project, and there's not much they can do about it in the short term." Jasmine leaned toward him. "I think they would be happy to sell everything to us. We would hire the project team to work for Munt. The people PNC laid off, anyway. PNC might balk at releasing scientists and technicians that they kept."

"The government won't support the neuro-interrogator anymore."

"Like Doctor Hernandez, I consider that a good thing. If he ever wakes up, this technology might help him, too."

"Actually, he woke up yesterday. You're right; he has locked-in syndrome and does benefit."

"That's wonderful! His injuries are such a tragedy. If he and Franco can be helped, that's even more reason to make sure your work isn't lost. His wife will be eager to move forward, I assume."

"I'm sure she will be. I should warn you, though. PNC won't sell the technology cheaply."

"It will be worth it." Jasmine's smile was radiant. "You will work with us to make this happen?"

"Of course. I'm sure Lucinda will be happy to join us, too." With some improvements in the technology, Emile could work with them. Jasmine implied she didn't want the government to have the technology, and that might win Emile over. He closed his eyes briefly and quietly exhaled.

JORNAL DE BRASÍLIA **NEWS Bulletin 8 May 2339**

Munt Electronics in Colón announced the opening of a new division today. According to CEO Jasmine Munt, the division, Hernandez Neuroscience, will develop devices to read minds, using technology bought from Panama Neurosciences Corporation in Cerro Punta. Munt has hired former PNC manager Maxwell Estevez as division manager and Lucinda Hernandez as project manager to develop what has been named a neuro-interrogator.

Mrs. Hernandez was the manager when PNC was developing it, and, under her management, the project failed. The government-funded the project in part, but a government spokesman was quoted as saying that the government has no interest in this new attempt to develop the device, considering it a failure and a waste of public funds.

"**W**ELL, IT'S TOO LATE to turn back now," Max said. He stood with Lucinda and a Munt employee in the main laboratory in a complex of labs and offices taking up a full floor of Munt Electronics. At least it would be. Now it was just a large, empty space. "That door over there leads to living quarters for you and Emile. Once we have his bed built, Emile should be able to move between there and the labs easily. The offices will be a problem unless we enlarge the doors, but we can probably work around that."

"It will take at least a month to get all this ready," Lucinda said.

"That should be about right," the other man with them said. Arturo Francisco was the lead architect overseeing the modifications for the floor. "Maybe a little less if everything works as planned." He grinned. "Of course, that hardly ever happens, so let's stick with a month."

"**T**ODAY IS THE BIG day," Lucinda sent. "Are you ready, Emile?"

"Sure." *I don't feel ready. I don't really know what is going on.* Lucinda and Max tried to tell him what was happening, but it wasn't easy to get a clear idea when the neurotrainer was the only input he had. At least they had gotten some training while Munt was constructing their facility, making it easier to understand them. Of course, the transmission in the other direction hadn't improved. Perhaps that was just as well. The neuro-interrogator would need improvement before he could communicate effectively, postponing any need to decide whether he would work on the project.

Lucinda had described the bed Munt Electronics had made for him. It was designed for all his needs, with built-in intravenous feeding, mechanisms to exercise his body so that his muscles didn't atrophy, a neurotrainer, and connections for a neuro-interrogator. The prototype would be installed in the bed when they moved to the new laboratory. Simple neuro-interrogator circuits in the robotic bed would allow Emile to move the bed between rooms by sending short commands. It all sounded great, but he would have to move to the Munt building to take advantage of it, and Emile was not looking forward to that.

"You shouldn't be disconnected from the neurotrainer for more than half an hour," Lucinda sent. "Maybe you can take a nap while you wait."

"I'll try."

Emile could feel anxiety on the neurotrainer connection and knew Lucinda was still there despite the silence. Emile experienced every fear stronger when he was disconnected. Even a little conversation could distract him, but silence, floating in the darkness of his mind, was unnerving. Usually, when Lucinda, Max, or Artemis weren't talking to him, he could at least listen to neurotrainer recordings of educational material or entertainment. While he was being transported, he wouldn't have those distractions.

"The technicians are here," Lucinda sent. "Have a nice nap."

Then she was gone. The blackness closed in on him again; he tried to relax, but couldn't. Time dragged until he wondered if something had gone wrong. He was being moved from the hospital to the laboratory, but he couldn't feel the motion of his body and had no objective way to measure the passage of time. Even when no one connected to him and he wasn't using recordings, the neurotrainer had been programmed to send soothing thoughts into his mind. His world was empty again, with nothing in it except his reflections.

Has something gone wrong? Surely it wouldn't take this long. The laboratory is only ten miles from the hospital, a few minutes away by ambulance. It would take a little while to get my body in place, and perhaps five minutes to connect him to another neurotrainer, but everything was prepared. Lucinda had said it would take less than half an hour. The process should have been smooth and quick.

After what seemed like hours, he felt a flicker of something in his brain, and suddenly he could feel Max. Relief filled his thoughts.

"Are you all right, Emile?" Max asked. "What were you worried about? Everything went fine."

"WE NEED TO GET Emile into these meetings more," Lucinda said. "It's difficult to make him part of the team with the current setup."

Max nodded. "We can work on that. We're going to need more people, though. Aiden and Luke have agreed to move to Colón and join us, but we should have one more neuroscientist, and we'll need someone who can do the things that Isabella did."

Isabella Temple was the project electrical engineer at PNC. She had built the prototype neuro-interrogator and other devices for the team, but she had stayed with PNC.

"It might be faster if we can find someone already working for Munt," Lucinda said. "Can you ask Jasmine about that?"

"No problem. The sooner we have someone, the sooner we can bring Emile into this." Max stopped, and Lucinda could see he was uncertain.

"Emile will help us," she said. "We just have to make sure the technology is protected. If possible, we should keep our work away from government eyes."

"They soured on the idea when PNC had it. While they think we're unsuccessful, they'll ignore us. Eventually, they'll find out, though."

"We'll worry about that when the time comes," Lucinda said, nodding. "Right now, we have to do this to help Emile. And Franco Munt. If we can somehow develop a product that will only work on a willing subject, then it will have medical benefits but won't be abused."

Max nodded, but Lucinda could tell that his uncertainty hadn't gone away. He hadn't worried about the neuro-interrogator's exploitation at PNC. Was he concerned about Emile's cooperation? Lucinda felt ashamed at the thought, but Emile would have to join them, for his own sake. Her husband would not want to spend the rest of his life as he was now.

LUKE AND AIDEN WERE talking to Lucinda in her office when a man strode in. Lucinda looked up, eyebrows raised.

"Hi, sorry to interrupt. I'm Eddie. I was told I was being transferred here."

This would be Edward Bascomb, the electrical engineer Jasmine had promised them. He was young, probably in his twenties. His clothes were unusually casual, but clean and in good condition. The others generally wore lab coats at work, but Eddie's clothes, while unconventional, would probably work as well in protecting delicate electronics. His hair could have used a brush, but it had been recently trimmed. Jasmine had said he would be a big help, but she had smirked when she said it. Jasmine wouldn't do anything to hurt the project, so the man would be competent. Lucinda suspected where Jasmine's amusement had come from.

"Do you have experience in this area, Eddie?" Lucinda asked.

"Sure. I did most of the work in setting up this facility, especially Doctor Hernandez's bed. I designed all the equipment that keeps him healthy while he's in this condition."

That verified his competence. Emile's bed had impressed her with its functionality and attention to detail. Emile was happy with it, saying it was much better than the equipment at the hospital. She wasn't sure how he could judge that if he couldn't feel anything and she hadn't asked, but she had more confidence that Eddie Bascomb could replace Isabella Temple.

"Welcome to the team, Eddie. This is Luke and Aiden, two of our neuroscientists, and I'm Lucinda. Grab a chair from the next room and join us. Don't mind Max; he's only the division manager."

Eddie gave her an uncertain grin and disappeared. He came back from Max's office a couple of minutes later with a chair. Given the delay, Lucinda supposed Max had a quick conversation with the new team member.

"Now that Eddie has joined us, we can get to work," Lucinda said. "Max is still working on finding another neuroscientist to replace Angelo, so we might be short-handed for a while yet."

"What do you want me to do?" Eddie asked.

"Get familiar with the hardware, especially the neuro-interrogator that Emile uses. We're managing with it, but there's a lot of room for improvement."

"Is the original designer available?"

"Maybe," Lucinda answered. "She's still working at PNC, so I don't know if they'll let her talk to us. We'll discuss it after you've reviewed her documentation."

"OK. Give me a day or two to figure this out, and I'll get back to you."

Lucinda put her hands flat on her desktop. "OK, everyone should know what they need to do. Let's get to it. I'll update Emile."

E MILE HAD BEEN ABSORBING a neurotrainer session on brain lesions when the recording stopped, and he felt another mind connecting with him. Lucinda? He thought so; her transmissions had improved since she had received training in communicating through a neurotrainer. Her thoughts were much clearer now, with fewer emotional overtones.

According to Lucinda, his transmissions were less clear. A neurotrainer received input via voice, although some emotion leaked in, not clearly identifiable, clouding the words. A neuro-interrogator read from the brain itself, and the emotional content was stronger.

"I'm here, Emile." Emile would have smiled if it were possible. It was Lucinda.

"We have an electrical engineer now," she continued. "His name is Edward Bascomb. He's younger than Isabella, but he should be fine. Jasmine sent him, and he designed your bed."

Good. In the hospital, he could always sense an annoying background buzz from his neurotrainer that he thought came from nearby electronic devices. He felt no similar sensation with the new bed, despite all the equipment in the laboratory.

"We're trying to improve your interface so that you can work with us," Lucinda sent. "You'll be happier if you're working, and we could use your help."

"I'm not sure how I feel about that," he sent back. "I haven't changed my mind about the government."

"We can design it so that the user has to be willing. Like being able to refuse to say anything that might incriminate the user."

Emile didn't say anything, although the neuro-interrogator probably transmitted his doubt. They could design it with the limitation Lucinda suggested, perhaps, but once the technology was practical, any such feature could be bypassed.

"Emile, you can't live the rest of your life like this." So, Lucinda could feel his doubt. "We are doing this for you. And Franco, and people with the same problem. There could be other medical uses, too, once we perfect it."

"I know, darling. I appreciate it."

"Then help us. Your expertise would guarantee our success." Lucinda was pleading, and Emile felt guilty. *Am I wrong?* Could government abuse be avoided? Castillo might not win the election. His opponent, Marisol Weston, didn't seem to be the threat that Castillo was. But she too would eventually be replaced.

"If we don't do this, someone else will. And they may not use the safeguards we'll use."

It was so mind-numbing to be in this condition. Emile could listen to neurotrainer recordings, but that was a poor substitute for a normal life. The immediate goal was to make communication with the neuro-interrogator more understandable, but other things might be done with technology that could write to or read from a human brain, things that would make his life better.

"Give me a few days to think about it," he finally sent.

WILLIAM BENSONHURST FELT RELAXED, and that wasn't normal for him lately. Below him, Canada Lake shimmered in the late summer sun. The trees were still green; fall was a month away, and then this entire area would be a surrealist painting in splotches of red, yellow, and orange. He hoped he could take more time off then.

He stood in a clearing on Kane Mountain in the Adirondack Legacy Park, two thousand feet above the lake. Below, the heat was sweltering, made worse by the humidity, but a light breeze and the altitude made it more comfortable on the mountain.

Once, a park sign told him, there had been a fire station here, guarding the forests, but it was gone, replaced by the ever-watching network of satellites. Somehow, this corner of civilization had escaped the destructive cravings of men, preserved as a wilderness area for centuries and too far east for the trauma of the Yellowstone Event to affect it seriously.

His phone demanded attention, interrupting his musings. For a few seconds, he thought about ignoring it, but he pulled it out. "Caller identification?" he asked.

"Doctor Maxwell Estevez of Hernandez Neuroscience in Colón," the phone replied.

Hernandez Neuroscience? There had been a Doctor Hernandez at PNC somewhere in Panama, but he thought that man had died in an accident. Curiosity overcame his reluctance to interrupt the moment. "Connect."

"Doctor Bensonhurst, my name is Maxwell Estevez. I'm the manager of Hernandez Neuroscience, a division of Munt Electronics."

He had heard of Munt Electronics, at least. He didn't realize that they had a neuroscience division, though. When had that happened?

"What can I do for you, Doctor?"

"We have a project here that needs an expert neuroscientist, and your name was at the top of the list. I'm hoping you could come down here and talk to us."

"You're aware of my position as Professor of Neuroscience at RPI, I assume."

"Of course. We were hoping you might want to get back into pure research and development."

Bensonhurst grimaced. Did this Doctor Estevez know how tired he was of dealing with temperamental professors and a bureaucracy-ridden administration? Despite his love of the area, he chaffed, too, knowing that he worked in a backwater of the Western Alliance. Brazil dominated the western world, and Panama was much closer to the center than old New York, geographically and culturally. He looked around at the quiet forest. He would miss it, but then again, not that far away, now that Albany had a few suborbital plane flights.

"I might consider it," he said. "What is this project?"

"We would prefer to explain it to you here. If you're not interested, it would only take a few days of your time, and you would get a free trip to Colón. The area is quite beautiful."

Bensonhurst chuckled. "Doctor, right now I'm standing on the top of a mountain in the Adirondack Legacy Park, surrounded by forests and lakes. Can you beat that?"

Max laughed. "Perhaps. Perhaps not. Why don't you come down here and see for yourself? I think you will find our offer intriguing."

He still had four days on his vacation. He had planned on hiking into the Silver Lake Wilderness, a challenging trip on a new trail along the Whitman Flow. It was an area he hadn't explored yet. Of course, he could say the same of Panama. It would take most of the day to get there, another day to find out what Estevez wanted, and a day to get back. That left a day to maybe do some exploring in the Panama area. The canal had been abandoned long ago, but there had to be something worth exploring nearby.

"All right, I'll bite," he said. "The day after tomorrow, OK?"

"That would be wonderful. I look forward to meeting you. We have already made reservations in your name. All you have to do is confirm the date."

After he broke the connection, he took one more look at the lake below him. "Confirm my reservation on the flight to Colón tomorrow," he told his phone.

"The suborbital from Albany to Mexico City with connections to Colón leaves at ten a.m.," the phone said.

"Fine."

"Shall I also confirm the return flight?"

He hesitated. *Even if I accept the position, I'll have to come back to settle things with the college.* He would have to explain his leaving to the secretary he had dated twice. Some reckless impulse took over, though. "Leave it open for now."

"**C**ALL ME BILL." He took Lucinda's extended hand and shook it. Her hand was warm and soft, matching the friendly smile.

"Welcome to Panama, Bill. I'm Lucinda Hernandez, the head of this little project."

"I hope I'm not wasting your money. Maxwell Estevez's phone call was intriguing, and I welcomed the chance to visit, but I'm not at all sure that I'm the man you want."

Lucinda smiled. "What you really mean is that you aren't sure you want to accept our offer."

"You're probably right. I am interested, though. You have quite a facility here, and there doesn't seem to be much information available about it. With the resurgence of neurological work since the government removed the ban, that's unusual."

"We've been keeping things low key. My husband wanted it that way."

"I remember the reports from Cerro Punta. I thought Dr. Hernandez died in that accident, especially after I didn't hear anything more about him. I'm glad to hear he's all right."

Lucinda grimaced. "I wouldn't say he was all right. He was severely injured in ways he will never recover from." She stood and looked at her computer. "Where is Emile?"

"He is in your quarters."

"Move him into the laboratory. Ask Max to meet us there." She turned back to Bill. "Rather than try to explain, I'll take you to meet him. First, though, you'll have to sign this document, promising not to disclose anything you see unless compelled by a court order." She handed him a nondisclosure agreement and a pen. "Then I can explain more about what we're doing here."

Bill ran his fingers through his hair and glanced out the door at the laboratory beyond. Lucinda asked for Estevez to join them but ordered Hernandez to be moved. Does that mean Hernandez isn't mobile? Confined to a wheelchair, perhaps? Lucinda mentioned severe injuries. He shrugged and signed the document.

They crossed to another door, wider than the door to the office they had just exited. It opened, and a massive platform—no, it was a motorized bed—moved into the laboratory. A man lay motionless on it, surrounded by a complex structure of padded mechanisms, apparently designed to exercise his muscles. There were other devices, too, that Bill couldn't identify.

"My husband has locked-in syndrome because of his injuries," Lucinda said.

He glanced at her and wished he hadn't. The sadness in her eyes tugged at him.

Lucinda continued. "He is fully conscious, but cannot move, or even speak. He has lost all his senses. We talk to him through a neurotrainer."

"Dear God. Then how does he communicate?"

Lucinda looked at her husband. The sadness was still there, but there was something else, too. Hope?

"That's why we're here." She paused as Max joined them. "Max, this is Bill Bensonhurst. Bill, this is Max Estevez, our manager."

The two men shook hands and exchanged greetings.

"Bill has already signed the nondisclosure agreement," Lucinda told Max. "I was just about to tell him about our project."

Max nodded. "Carry on."

"I'm sure you know about PNC's attempt to build a neuro-interrogator," Lucinda said.

"Sure. A device that could read minds. It was a failure."

"Not exactly. It worked after a fashion, but emotions tainted the words. The government's representative had little control over his emotions and was not a suitable subject. He ignored results from our subjects, apparently believing we faked them. The government withdrew funding, and PNC dropped the project. The prototype works reasonably well on Emile, though."

"And that's how Doctor Hernandez communicates."

"Yes, but not well enough to resume his work. And that's why we're here. Munt is funding us, hoping we can develop improved devices that will help Franco Munt as well as Emile."

"I'm not familiar with Franco Munt," Bill said. "He has a similar condition?"

"His injuries are not as severe. He can't speak, but he is otherwise normal. Our engineer is building another prototype for Franco's use, but it will be marginally effective at best."

"Why the secrecy?"

"Emile resigned from PNC because he didn't want the government to abuse this technology. We're not really keeping this a secret, but we don't want to attract government attention until we can devise ways to prevent abuse of whatever we develop. So far, everyone outside of Munt seems to think the neuro-interrogator is a failure."

Bill rubbed the back of his neck. "Sounds interesting, all right. I'm still not sure I'm willing to move thousands of miles."

"Of course." Lucinda glanced at a display on Emile's bed. "Emile is still asleep. You can talk to him later, but I'll introduce you to the rest of the team first."

Bill sat in the conference room with Max and Lucinda. The day had gone quickly, and it was time to decide. He could put it off for another day or two, but there was no reason to do so. He would miss many things about his life in New York, although his job wasn't one of them. In some ways, this was a step down. He would be just one of the six neuroscientists involved in an obscure project, not a professor in a prestigious college. He didn't care about that, though.

Despite the limitations of their communication, his talk with Emile had helped him to decide. The brief conversation had emphasized what he had already known intellectually; a great mind was locked away, barely able to communicate, and he was being asked to help change that. Besides, he was, primarily, a scientist, and this opportunity would be another grand adventure.

"I look forward to working with you," he said. He shook hands with Max and Lucinda.

11

THREE WEEKS LATER, THE entire team gathered in a small, reserved room in a downtown restaurant. Bill had returned from New York after settling his affairs and was back, officially working on the project. Jasmine and Franco joined them, and Jasmine used her influence to get them the room, not a simple task on election results day. It seemed as if half the city wanted to be out and among people when the network announced the results. Only Emile was missing, left alone with his bed taking care of him and a neurotrainer recording on cerebellum functions to occupy him.

The voting had ended for each time zone at six p.m. local time on the previous day. However, since the Western Alliance extended over ten time zones, it was four a.m. the next morning in Recife on the easternmost tip of Brazil when the polls closed in Hawaii. All results were confidential until eight a.m. in Hawaii, two p.m. in Colón. They ate lunch while they waited for the outcome.

"Marisol will win," Eddie said. He nodded as if to emphasize his words. "We've had enough of Castillo."

Max sounded doubtful. "Castillo is the incumbent. Many people don't want to shake things up."

"The only way he could win would be to steal it," Eddie said. "Don't you listen to Anna Cortez?"

"Weston is a northerner," Aiden said. "The people won't elect someone like that."

Lucinda frowned. Aiden noticed and stopped talking, but he didn't look contrite.

"Anyone have room for dessert?" Jasmine asked. Without his neuro-interrogator, Franco couldn't communicate verbally, but his opinion was obvious in his quick grin and vigorous head shake.

"I don't have room," Lucinda said. "But everybody else, please enjoy."

Choices split evenly between Tres Leches and Caramel Flan with Bill, the odd man, ordering Bocado de Reina.

"Why that?" Eddie asked.

"Because I don't have the slightest idea what it is," Bill answered.

They gave their orders to the waiter, but two p.m. came before the desserts arrived. A screen on the wall lit up to show a network commentator sitting behind a desk. His expression was somber as he looked up.

"This is Gregory Mendez, reporting from *Jornal de Brasília.* In only another minute or two, we will announce the election results for the 2340 terms of office."

"I thought Anna Cortez was supposed to announce the results for the *Jornal de Brasília,*" Lucinda said.

"This election will decide many offices," the commentator continued. "The most important, of course, is the contest between incumbent President Alejandro Castillo and the challenger, Conservative Marisol Weston. It has been a spirited campaign, marked by some animosity on both sides, and at times, it seemed that Mrs. Weston might prevail. Recently, however, President Castillo has risen in the polls, and the election is expected to be close."

"Animosity?" Eddie hissed. "Castillo has pulled every dirty trick he could think of, including lies about Weston's connections to the Eastern Bloc."

"Where there's smoke, there's fire," Aiden said.

"And where there's skunks, there's stink," Eddie shot back.

Mendez put his hand to his ear as if adjusting an earpiece. "I am receiving word that the results are available. Regional governorships are first."

He read off a lengthy list of election results while his listeners fidgeted in their chairs. The waiter began serving their desserts, but they hardly noticed. Lucinda shushed Eddie when the commentator finished reading the gubernatorial results, and a screen appeared showing local elections. Then the commentator was back, plainly excited. "And, finally, we have the result of the Presidential election. Actual vote totals will be available later, but the Western Alliance Election Commission has declared that President Alejandro Castillo has retained his position. I repeat, President Castillo has won the election."

"Told you so," Aiden said.

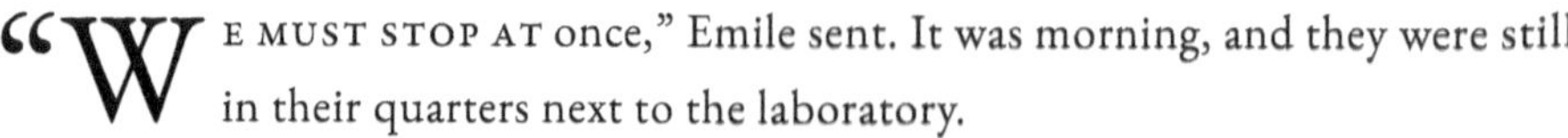

"WE MUST STOP AT once," Emile sent. It was morning, and they were still in their quarters next to the laboratory.

"We can't overreact, Emile," Lucinda sent back. "We're doing this to help you and Franco."

"With Castillo reelected, this project is dangerous. If he finds out about it, he will take it over and abuse the technology. Even the prototypes have a potential for abuse."

Lucinda sighed. An unwilling subject of the neuro-interrogator would likely be too frightened to send coherent thoughts. She didn't mention that to Emile because he would turn it around and say that frightening subjects was another reason they shouldn't improve the interface. She rarely won such arguments with her husband.

"You don't agree," Emile sent.

"I don't. You will never be what you were, but I want something better than what we have right now. So does Jasmine. You don't know how hard we must concentrate to understand you, especially when you get as excited as you are right now. We agreed to develop this in return for Munt's support. We're still working on a way to build safeguards into the design, too. You should help us do that, at least."

Emile was irritated. Until he calmed down, he wouldn't be helpful. Even when he was calm, it was difficult for him to contribute much over the crude prototype interface. "I have to get back to work," she said. "I'll talk to you later."

She stood and walked away from the bed. She must have shown her frustration, because Max stopped her as she entered the laboratory. "Is everything all right?" he asked.

Lucinda nodded. "I'm OK. Emile worries about how the election will affect us. He hoped Castillo would be defeated. Personally, I don't think it matters that much who is in office, but Emile has always said we have to keep this technology away from the government."

"There might be more in Emile's argument than you know," Max said.

"Why? What happened?"

"Remember how Anna Cortez was replaced for the election announcement? *Jornal de Brasília* has removed her from its network schedule, and rumor has it they've fired her. *Jornal de Brasília* denies it, but they've demoted her at the least."

That made a difference. Anna had been one of the most influential voices against Castillo, her broadcasts one reason many had expected Castillo to lose. Castillo might have been afraid to use his influence against her before the election, but it was more than possible that he acted immediately when the polls closed. Lucinda hadn't believed that it mattered who the president was. The government would try to increase its power, regardless. That was still true, but Castillo was far bolder than she had thought if he had orchestrated Cortez's demotion.

"Let's get everyone into the conference room now," she said. "We need to meet."

"Eddie called in sick."

He did that occasionally. It was Friday, so he wouldn't be back until Monday. She didn't blame him, either, for not wanting to work that day. The election results were disturbing, more so to Eddie than to others.

"OK. First thing Monday morning, then."

L UCINDA TOLD EVERYONE OF the rumors about Anna Cortez and what they might mean to the project. She gave everyone a minute to absorb her words before continuing.

"I don't want to give up, but we have to find a way to prevent our work from being misused."

"I'm researching ways to limit it to voluntary subjects," Luke said. The neuroscientist shrugged. "I'm not making much progress, though. I need more time."

"It would help if we could get more cooperation from Emile," Max said, "but I guess that's a lot of the problem." His voice seemed subdued, and Lucinda wondered if he was doubting the wisdom of their work.

"Even if he's willing, it's hard with the current interface," Lucinda said.

"I might be able to help with that," Eddie said.

"How?" Max asked.

"Well, I can't make him willing, and, of course, we haven't been able to figure out how to improve the interface yet. That's for you geniuses to deal with. I can deal with another problem, though."

Lucinda suppressed a smile. The young engineer was clearly proud of himself for thinking of something that the scientists hadn't.

"Right now, we can't include Emile in meetings like this because his neuro-interrogator is configured to transmit to only one neurotrainer. It would be relatively easy to fix that."

"Sounds good," Lucinda said. "Go ahead, Eddie."

"I'll get on it after the meeting," Eddie said.

With that settled, Bill changed the subject. "I think I have an idea that might help keep us from drawing attention," Bill said. "Right now, we're counting on the fact that we're a tiny part of a very large company. If the government could coordinate all the databases that various agencies keep, the concentration of neuroscientists in a company that formerly didn't have any might stand out. Technology control laws prevent them from coordinating those databases, but it still could be noticed. It's not a secret."

"What's your suggestion?" Max asked.

"We create a fake project and talk openly about it, something that would explain why we have so many neuroscientists."

Lucinda's eyes widened. "I have just the thing. Emile was studying a link between emotions and consciousness before the accident. We could continue his work."

"That's good," Max said. He pointed a finger at the ceiling in emphasis. "It would explain anything we do with Emile. It would explain our interest in emotions, too. We still don't understand consciousness, so it would be an obvious field to study, but with no potential for misuse."

"Sounds like another distraction to me," Aiden said.

"We'll do minimal work on it," Lucinda replied. "We'll issue reports that refer to relevant progress in our real project. There should be enough overlap to make it believable."

"This was Emile's project at the University. We should ask them to send us Emile's research," Luke said.

Max chuckled. "A subtle way of announcing what we're working on. And who knows? The research might even help us reach our real goal."

G ERRY BATTLE, HEAD OF the Neuroscience Department, scratched his head. It was unusual for former professors at the University to request materials on their research. Policy allowed them to continue their work elsewhere, but usually, they took all their notes and test results with them when they left. There was no need to ask for their research after the fact.

Of course, Emile Hernandez was a special case. After his accident, Emile hadn't returned. Wasn't he paralyzed and unable to work? Gerry looked at the request again. Technically, it wasn't from Emile, but from his wife, Lucinda. She was in Colón now, working for Munt Electronics. That was strange, too. He wasn't aware of any work by Munt in neuroscience.

Emile had been good friends with Ben Young, a professor in the History Department. Perhaps they were still in contact. He looked at the phone on his desk. "Doctor Young, History Department."

"Doctor Young is teaching a class now," the phone replied.

"Leave a return call request." Gerry closed the research request.

Forty-five minutes later, he had almost forgotten the request. "Doctor Benicio Young calling," his phone announced.

Gerry opened the request on his workstation. "Connect."

"Doctor Battle, I'm returning your call," Ben said.

"Yes. I was wondering if you are still in contact with Doctor Hernandez. I remember you were friends when he was here."

"You're calling about the request for his research? Yes, I still talk to his wife, and she said she was making the request. I don't talk to Emile, of course, and I want to go to Colón to see them sometime, but I haven't had the chance."

"I'm sorry, but why don't you talk to Doctor Hernandez?"

"Ah, you didn't know. Emile has LIS from the accident. Lucinda has to use a neurotrainer to talk to him."

"Locked-in Syndrome? I thought he was only paralyzed. So he can't speak?"

"No. He can't do much of anything except think. It's a tragedy."

"I'm sorry to hear that. Do you know why Mrs. Hernandez wants the material?"

"She wants to continue Emile's work. They have to stay in Colón because of his condition, but Munt Electronics is supporting her efforts."

Gerry didn't know Lucinda Hernandez, although he knew she was a neuroscientist like her husband. Her desire to continue his work must be an emotional reaction to her husband's condition. The idea of connecting consciousness to the amygdala seemed farfetched.

"Thank you, Doctor. I'll sign off on this and have everything sent to her."

After he broke the connection, he mentally reviewed what he knew of Doctor Hernandez's work. He still didn't think it was likely to go anywhere, but Doctor Hernandez had been a brilliant scientist. He could have been on to something.

If the work did have merit, he knew someone who would be interested. "Connect to General Juarez," he told the phone.

An assistant put him through at once. Gerry was a well-known neuroscientist, a fact that General Juarez must have appreciated when the general took him into his confidence about his secret project. "General, I believe I have something that might be of use to your Methuselah Project," Gerry said.

12

O UTSIDE, A COLD JANUARY wind blew in from the ocean, unusual for an area where temperatures rarely went below seventy degrees Fahrenheit. Bill, used to winters in upstate New York, thought the weather was "bracing." Everyone else was happy to be inside in the tightly controlled environment of the laboratory.

Eddie modified Emile's neuro-interrogator, adding multiple outputs so that everyone could receive Emile's transmissions. Emile's neurotrainer already picked up everyone's voice as input (although he preferred the more intimate direct connection with Lucinda), and Eddie planned to build an add-on that would enforce receiving one voice at a time. Until then, everyone had to be careful not to talk over each other and make it difficult for Emile to understand the conversation.

The weather, Lucinda suspected, was not the reason the mood in the conference room was somber. The day before, Castillo had officially started his second ten-year term of office. Emile knew the date and its significance, and his depression, transmitted over Eddie's neuro-interrogator interface, affected everyone.

"We had hoped that Emile's work on the amygdala might help in filtering emotion," Luke said. "So far, I haven't had much luck."

"Have you tried duplicating some of his experiments?" Bill asked. "That might give you inspiration."

"That sounds like a northern idea," Aiden said. "Emile worked with animals. That's all we need, having a couple of monkeys swinging around the lab."

"Northern idea?" Bill looked perplexed.

"Aiden doesn't think much of any idea that originates north of the Rio Grande," Eddie said. "Hadn't you noticed?"

Aiden looked at Eddie. "Facts are facts. Aren't you originally from Los Angeles, Eddie?"

Eddie opened his mouth to comment, and Lucinda was about to shut down the exchange when she felt a wave of anger wash through her. She looked around the table, and it was obvious that everyone was feeling it. Emile!

"Stop," Emile sent. Emotion blurred the transmission and almost drowned out the word. The thought was stronger than anything she had felt before.

"You heard him," she said. "What's the matter with you, Aiden? We don't have time for that nonsense." Aiden scowled but didn't speak. "All right, let's continue," Lucinda said. "Luke, what do you think about Bill's idea?"

The young neuroscientist hesitated. "The fMRI data we've gotten from Emile when he's not connected has been less helpful than we hoped. There are things we could do with animal subjects that we wouldn't want to do with a person. Our noninvasive equipment and the nanites that we use to detect neuron firing are good, but implanted sensors might see something the nanites miss. Any results could be useful for our cover project, too."

"What kind of animal are we talking about?" Max asked.

"The closer to human, the better." Luke shrugged. "In that, Aiden is probably right. Maybe a chimpanzee."

"We're not set up for that," Max said. "I'm not sure Jasmine would go for the changes we would have to make. Would it really be worth it?"

"Hard to say. Maybe I could start out with something easier to care for. A rabbit or hamster? Emile used both at the University."

"Less consciousness, less emotion," Emile sent. He had calmed, and the neuro-interrogator transmission was clearer. "Easier to control, but harder to detect."

"We can start small," Max said. "If we need to, we can always get higher animals as subjects later."

"I can get some help from Facilities in setting up cages or anything else we need, if we don't go crazy," Eddie said.

"Good," Lucinda said. "Just remember what our primary goal is. If this helps with the neuro-interrogator, great, but the whole emotion versus consciousness thing is not our business."

"Emile, what did you mean when you said harder to detect?" Luke asked.

"Lower animals think more in images. They don't have vocabularies as higher animals do."

"At least it might be a start." Lucinda took off her neurotrainer and got up from her chair. Most of the others followed, taking Lucinda's action as a signal that the meeting was over. Eddie remained sitting and seemed to think. Then his eyebrows shot up.

"Do you have something, Eddie?" she asked.

"Maybe. Let me think about this for a few minutes. Yeah, I think I do have something." He took his neurotrainer helmet off. "I'll be at my desk. Try not to bother me for an hour or so." He got up and hurried out of the conference room.

"What was that about?" Luke asked.

Lucinda shook her head. "I don't know. I guess we'll find out in an hour or so."

L ucinda poked her head out of her office when Eddie suddenly jumped up and shouted, "It'll work! I've got it."

Eddie was already heading for the conference room, and she waved her hand at the others to follow. Emile was still there, and everyone else went to their usual seat. Eddie was plainly excited and didn't sit down.

"It's so simple, and it solves all our problems," he said after he had donned his neurotrainer again. "You've all been concentrating on the brain and how to filter out the words from everything else in the neuro-interrogator circuitry, but we don't need to do that. In fact, we don't want to do that."

"So you, a mere engineer, are going to tell us how to do our jobs," Aiden said. "This I've got to hear."

Eddie stared at him for a long moment, visibly annoyed. "It's not a science problem, Aiden. It's an engineering problem, and northern engineers pioneered most of the technology we're using."

Aiden only snorted. "Go ahead," Lucinda urged.

Eddie nodded. "Sure. This is how we do it. Our neuro-interrogator is fine as it is. All we need to do is add an interpretation stage that turns words into actual sounds, and we won't need the helmets anymore. We could hear Emile normally."

"That's ridiculous," Aiden said. "If we could do that, we would have done it already. We have to separate the emotion from the words." Only Aiden spoke, but others nodded in agreement.

Eddie grinned. "Not if we train the subject."

The faces around the table all showed confusion or disbelief. Emile reacted first to Eddie's statement. "He's right!" The excitement in the transmission was almost as strong as the earlier anger. "To effectively use the neurotrainer, you have to train with it so that the neurotrainer can translate words into the signals appropriate for your brain. The neuro-interrogator needs to do the same thing, except that the user is telling the device what the signal for each word looks like."

"Exactly," Eddie agreed. "With a neurotrainer, you train so that the device can send signals you understand. With a neuro-interrogator, you train so that you can send signals that the device will understand."

"That's only half the problem," Aiden said. "Now you have a device that can be misused to read minds."

Eddie looked at him with a crooked grin. "Really? You think you can force someone to train a neuro-interrogator?"

Eddie is enjoying himself. Lucinda watched as Aiden's expression turned from a sneer into jaw-dropping surprise. That passed, and Lucinda saw what looked like annoyance. "That sounds good, Eddie," she said quickly. "How long will it take you to create such a device?"

"I'll give you an estimate tomorrow," Eddie replied. He leaned back, his hands folded behind his head. "I think I'd like to go out and celebrate right now. Anybody with me?"

M AX PEEKED INTO LUCINDA's office. "Eddie just arrived."

Lucinda glanced at the clock on her desk. Styled to look old-fashioned, it was a gift from Emile on their fifth wedding anniversary. That seemed so long ago, now, but it was barely more than two years.

"He should have been here two hours ago," Lucinda said. "I guess he really did go out to celebrate."

Max grinned. "It looks like it. Don't yell at him too loud. His head might explode."

Lucinda returned a faint smile. "If he can do what he thinks he can, he deserves a night out." She stood up. "I'd better go assess the damages."

Eddie seemed to alternate between sipping a cup of coffee and holding his head. Aiden and Bill were standing next to him. Commiserating or criticizing?

"It's damned unprofessional, Eddie," Aiden said as Lucinda approached. "You have no right to go out and get drunk when you have work to do."

"Oh, give him a break," Bill said. "We'll get the work done."

"I guess northerners prioritize partying over work," Aiden snapped back.

Apparently, both commiserating and criticizing. Lucinda gave Aiden a disapproving look. "Glad you could make it this morning," she said to Eddie, cutting off whatever Bill was going to reply. Her voice was much less severe than the words. "How are you feeling?"

Eddie raised his head slowly. He stared at her with red-rimmed eyes, as if he didn't recognize her. Then he groaned. "Probably exactly how I look."

"Can't handle seco," Aiden said.

"Vodka, actually. They must import it from the Eastern Bloc. Have you tried to get a good bourbon in Colón?"

Bill chuckled. "You should have gone with the local rum. Maybe we should leave you alone until your head clears a little."

"That's a good idea," Lucinda said. "We're not helping by standing over him."

Aiden snorted, but moved away. Bill laid a friendly hand briefly on Eddie's shoulder and also left.

"Thanks," Eddie told Lucinda. "I'm sorry. I'll be all right when the aspirin hits."

"OK. That was a great idea you had yesterday." She paused and pointed a finger at him. "Try to tone down the celebrations, though, OK?"

Eddie nodded and took another drink of coffee. He picked up a folder and made a show of looking through it, but Lucinda could tell that he was not absorbing what he was reading. She shook her head and went back to her office.

T HERE WAS A CAFETERIA on the ground floor of the Munt building, and most of the employees in the building ate lunch there. The food was decent, and there were days when it was a welcome place for breakfast and dinner, too. At noon, Eddie was looking more like himself, and Bill suggested they go down to the cafeteria for lunch.

They got their food and sat at a small table in one corner of the busy cafeteria. "Glad you're feeling better," Bill said as they arranged their food.

"I'll have to make up for it this afternoon," Eddie said. "I feel bad about letting everyone down."

"Don't worry about it. Just don't make a habit of it." Bill smiled as a memory of a party a few years before came to him. "I remember when I was your age. One night we got so drunk at a bar in Albany that we couldn't get transportation. I'm not sure how we got back to Troy, but I woke up the next morning in my bed. I think we walked back."

"How far was it?"

"Only about ten miles, but we must have been a sight."

"Only ten miles?" Eddie laughed. "Are you sure some cop didn't pick you up and drop you off?"

Bill thought about that for a moment. "No," he answered. "Anyway, forget last night."

They stopped talking for a while as they gave their attention to their lunch. As they cleaned up the last of the food, Bill spoke again. "You know what would be fun? This weekend, we could go out to Chagres National Park and hike up Cerro Jefe. The hike is supposed to be fairly challenging, and there's a magnificent view from the top."

"Challenging hikes are not exactly my thing."

"Fresh air, probably sunshine this time of year, getting away from your desk, and getting some exercise. What's not to like?"

"Insects, drenched in sweat, blisters. What's not to avoid?"

"I thought you were from Los Angeles. You should be used to the heat. And repellant and a good pair of shoes will take care of the rest."

Eddie shook his head. "Sorry, Bill. I guess I'm just a city boy."

Bill shrugged. "All right. Nobody's perfect, I guess."

"Maybe we could do something a little less challenging sometime. Right now, I think we should get back to work."

T HREE DAYS LATER, LUCINDA went to Eddie to find out how he was doing. "I've got the basic design," he told her. "Of course, the details will be the hard part."

"What about processing power requirements? Comparable to that of the neuro-trainer?"

"More, I think. It's harder to convert a brain signal into a word than it is to convert a word into a brain signal."

"Is that going to affect the size of the device?"

"Not much. Probably not even noticeable. An extra processing chip or two doesn't take much space."

"How long will it take?"

"A couple of weeks for the hardware. Longer if I have to write the software. You know, we should hire a programmer. I can do it, but a good programmer could do it faster and better."

"What would software do?"

"We're getting a lot of data, too much for design hardware to separate. The differences are too subtle, and the hardware would be too expensive. Software should be able to do it easier and cheaper."

"I think I can get Jasmine to go for that. She was very excited when I told her about your idea. She's eager for anything that will help Franco."

"I'll put together a list of the qualifications we'll need," Eddie said. "We should use the same processor family that we use in the prototype. That will simplify manufacturing when we have a finished product. Hire a programmer familiar with coding for them."

13

BILL WAS GETTING ANOTHER cup of coffee when Eddie came into the laboratory. Late again. He had worked hard for two weeks on the design and built a prototype of the new neuro-interrogator module, but had backslid when he finished. Eddie worked on software to convert output impulses from the brain into words, but his nighttime partying hurt his efforts. He told Bill he expected a software engineer would join them soon.

Eddie joined him and poured his own cup of coffee. "Has the new programmer shown up yet?"

Bill grinned. "She's talking to Lucinda and Max."

Eddie stared at him. "What's so funny?"

"Ah, they're coming out now." Bill pointed toward the door to Max's office. Eddie looked in that direction, and Bill's smile widened as Eddie's jaw dropped.

"Not bad looking," Bill said.

Joelle was indeed an attractive woman. Her silky blonde hair was cut short, framing a striking face with a pert nose, generous mouth, and intelligent eyes. Her outfit was conservative, but it didn't hide an eye-catching figure. She was probably about the same age as Eddie, too. "Pull in your tongue, Eddie," Bill said.

"Huh? What?" Eddie turned and looked at him. "Hilarious. Just because you would rather climb mountains, it doesn't mean some of us don't have other interests."

Bill eyeballed Joelle and shrugged. "It's possible to be interested in more than one activity." He paused and took another look. "Too young for me, though. She's all yours, buddy."

Eddie gave him an exasperated look. "I guess I should get over there and introduce myself."

Bill smiled as he watched Eddie stride across the room. "I hope she won't distract you too much."

AFTER AN ALL-HANDS MEETING, Lucinda stayed behind. "Eddie seems smitten by Joelle," Emile observed. "I take it she's attractive?"

"Very," Lucinda replied. "I didn't notice Eddie's interest, though."

"I felt he was trying to hide it," Emile sent. "Successfully, apparently. But I could sense his interest. A case of love at first sight, I think."

"Maybe it's a good thing that our emotions are transmitted to you, but not to the rest of us."

"Like the rest of you, Eddie has gotten quite good at not broadcasting emotions over the neurotrainer. Not perfect, though, and I have gotten quite good at interpreting what is still getting through."

Emile must have sensed the affection she was feeling for him at that moment. "I love you, too," he sent.

She smiled and patted his arm, stopping when she realized he couldn't feel it. "As long as it doesn't affect the work."

"Joelle has a very disciplined mind. I don't think she will be distracted from her work."

"I wasn't worried about her." But Emile could probably detect her amusement.

"EDDIE TOLD ME HE'S ready to show us what he has," Lucinda told Max two weeks later.

Max nodded. "Joelle seems to have started a fire under him."

"They work well together. She's a hard worker, and it seems to rub off on Eddie."

"I suspect he's trying to impress her."

"Probably. I thought she would be a distraction, but the result has been the opposite."

Max smiled. "So let's go see what they've accomplished." He rose from behind the desk and they walked out to where everyone was gathering around Emile's bed.

"We've been training the device since yesterday," Eddie said. "We send Emile a word and he sends it back. The device intercepts the neuro-interrogator signal and stores it with the word in an internal dictionary."

"For now, we limited it to a small set of common words," Joelle added.

"Good morning," Emile said. The result was a toneless robotic voice, but the words were clear.

"That sounds terrible," Aiden said. "Is that the best we can do?"

"Start," Emile said.

A red light on Eddie's device blinked several times while Emile talked. "That light blinks every time Emile sends a word that he hasn't trained the device for," Eddie explained.

"I'm sure Emile is saying that this device is just another step toward our goal," Lucinda said. "What we have is no worse than devices developed hundreds of years ago for people with diseases that destroyed their ability to speak."

Eddie nodded. "Speech synthesizers. There was a famous physicist in the twenty-first century who had to use one. I used the same idea here, except that I used impulses from the brain via the neuro-interrogator."

"Can we improve the result?" Bill asked.

Eddie rubbed the back of his neck. "Theoretically, I think. We would have to use the emotion that we're discarding to enhance the words without letting emotion confuse the output."

"Don't video makers already do that when they create virtual characters?" Luke asked.

"Not same," Emile said.

"Emile's right," Lucinda said. "A video maker knows what emotion he wants to add to the voice. It's based on the needs of his story, not on genuine emotion."

"Couldn't we make a dictionary of emotions, just as we made a dictionary of words?" Joelle suggested.

"It's not that simple," Aiden said. "Real emotions are more complex. Words are inherently digital; emotions are analog. They don't come in discrete values like words."

"I think I understand," Joelle said. "Emotions have ranges of intensity."

Lucinda nodded. "Exactly. Even that is a simplification, though. Suppose a man you loved is threatening you somehow. You love him, but you might also fear him. Anger could be in the mix, too."

"Maybe we're getting ahead of ourselves," Bill said. "We would like to have Emile's voice sound less like a computer and more like a person by injecting some feeling into the output. It doesn't have to be perfect."

"We could create a dictionary of emotions if we settle for approximating," Eddie said.

"Training hard," Emile said.

"Good point," Lucinda said. "We can train a subject for words, but how do we train for emotions?"

"Need work," Emile said. The red light was blinking again.

"We have one big advantage," Max said. "Once Emile has finished training on this thing, he can take an active part in the project. When Jasmine understands what we've already done, she'll want to fund more."

"You're right," Lucinda said. "Luke and Aiden, I want you working on developing a methodology for training emotions. Bill, you help Eddie and Joelle with the neuroscience aspects of the hardware. Emile and I will be available for consultation, so keep us updated on what you're doing."

"I THINK THIS CALLS for a celebration," Eddie said as the meeting wound down. "Who's up for a night on the town?" He was including everyone in the suggestion, but in his mind, he was only interested in Joelle. She wrinkled her mouth into an expression that discouraged him.

"The last time you celebrated, you got nothing done the next morning," Bill said. "I've got a better idea."

"This doesn't involve that mountain, does it?" Eddie answered.

"Not exactly. Something less challenging, maybe. The rainy season will start soon, but this weekend would still be a good time to get out into the fresh air. Just a leisurely walk someplace nice. What do you say, Eddie?"

To Eddie's dismay, Joelle seemed interested. He had been about to reject Bill's suggestion. "We can talk about it," he said instead. "Let's at least see what you have in mind."

"I'm in," Joelle said. "Sounds like fun."

Eddie suppressed a groan. Later, he cornered Bill when no one else was within earshot. "What are you getting me into?" he asked.

Bill grinned. "I'm just trying to help you, buddy. You weren't getting anywhere on your own."

"What are you talking about?"

"Joelle, of course. You are interested in her, aren't you?"

Eddie felt his face warm. "Yeah, I guess. She's pretty."

"Right. Pretty. I would give you some competition if I were ten years younger, but I'm not, so I thought I would help you out. Last week, I heard her talking about a trip she took to Yosemite years ago. She loved it, and I know she would be interested in a scenic hike around here."

Eddie thought about that. He had heard her asking Aiden about hiking in the area. It had irritated him a little that she had gone to Aiden, but he didn't know anything about hiking or the opportunities around Colón, so he hadn't tried to interrupt. As it turned out, Aiden didn't know anything either and didn't seem interested.

"OK, you might be on to something," Eddie said. "Just keep it easy. Something beautiful, but not too strenuous."

Monday morning. Eddie sat at his desk and tried not to show the pain he felt. It had only been a five-mile hike, a loop that took them to the top of a one-thousand-foot peak. That wasn't that high. It was more than he was used to, though, and his leg muscles ached. Worse, he didn't have any shoes suitable for hiking, and he had blisters on both feet.

There had been compensations. The airbus trip to the trailhead had been very enjoyable. Joelle sat between the two men, and it had been a close fit. The flight from Colón, across Limon Bay, over Cristóbal, and landing in a forested area west of Chagres National Park, had been scenic but too short. Joelle had leaned over him several times to get a better view, and she hadn't seemed as interested in the scene outside Bill's window. He might have had the better view, but the light physical contact and the soft smell of Joelle's perfume were too distracting for him to notice.

For a while, even the hike had been pleasant. They sauntered down a path through the forest, across a bridge on the Rio Piedras and up a moderately steep slope to the hill at the opposite end of the trail. Joelle had even taken his arm at one rough section of the trail while Bill hung back, probably enjoying his handiwork.

By the time they reached the peak, though, Eddie's legs hurt, and he was out of breath. Joelle and Bill seemed unaffected, and Eddie did his best to hide his discomfort. They spent a few minutes on the peak, Eddie to rest and Joelle and Bill to enjoy the view, before heading back down the hill. When they reached the trailhead again, Eddie was spent. Joelle was exuberant, telling them how much she had enjoyed herself every thirty seconds on the airbus back.

It would have been a more positive experience if he had been in shape and had proper shoes for a long walk. Given Joelle's reaction, he supposed he would have to do something about both issues.

14

Eddie glanced at Joelle, but she was staring at the workstation screen.

"The timestamp tells us what part of the signal represents the emotion," she said. "But there's no way to isolate it otherwise."

"We should consult Emile," Eddie suggested.

Joelle nodded. Five minutes later, they were wearing neurotrainers and attached to Emile's bed. His pleasure at hearing from them, so difficult to capture electronically, was obvious from the direct connection.

Eddie wished for a second that he could do the same with Joelle. *What does she really think of me?* Even after the weekend hike, he had no clue. He tried to push that thought back before Emile detected it, but when Emile connected, he was still struggling with that, and he let Joelle explain the difficulties they were having.

"The nanites don't give us enough resolution to separate the different signals," Joelle sent. "Bill and Eddie are trying to improve the resolution, but that's going to take a while."

"Have you tried using points of inflection as boundaries?" Emile asked. He referred to points on the signal curves where the plot of the signal changed direction.

"We tried that, but it didn't work," Eddie said. "We get a signal that is bounded by increments of time that have nothing to do with the onslaught of some emotion."

"Activation rates?"

"Activation rate changes seemed useful at first, but they vary smoothly, too. That moves the problem, but it's still basically the same problem."

"I wish I could scratch my head right now," Emile sent. "I miss being able to do that when I am puzzled." He was silent for several seconds. "But maybe that's the answer. Bring Bill in on this conversation."

There was a delay while Eddie found Bill and Bill put on his neurotrainer. Then Emile continued.

"If you see me scratch my head and look at my expression, you know that I'm thinking. If I frown, you know that I'm unhappy about something."

"Of course," Bill said. "Motor signals! We know how to separate signals going to different muscles. If we know what muscle you were trying to activate, we would have a good idea where the boundary of the emotion is and what the emotion is."

"Wouldn't gestures be somewhat personal?" Joelle asked.

"Some, but not much," Bill said. "Some gestures, like frowns and smiles, are consistent across cultures. At least we would have a way of separating emotions, if not identifying them."

"It would be easier to train Eddie's device to recognize an individual's motor responses than it would be to parse emotion changes in the brain signal," Emile sent. "We could then map them to the emotions."

"THE CHANGES TO THE hardware were fairly simple," Eddie reported two weeks later. At Bill's suggestion, Jasmine and Franco were present. "The input circuits had to be upgraded to handle the additional data. Several other circuits needed some enhancements, and we'll need to add memory, but nothing major. The difficulty is in the software."

"I think it can work," Joelle said. "The code is getting prohibitively complex, though. Not only does it need more work to implement, but more code means slower code. To make a noticeable difference in the neuro-interrogator output, we're going to have to upgrade the computer processing power by a factor of three or more."

"All that means more components. The result will be too bulky to include as part of a neuro-interrogator helmet," Eddie said. "In Emile's case, that's not much of a problem; we'll just put most of the hardware in his bed. Franco will have to carry it around with him, though."

"How big are we talking about?" Jasmine asked.

"Hard to say right now," Eddie said. "Rough estimate, not very heavy, but the size of a small suitcase or a big briefcase. I can make it wireless, though, so the computer will have to be close, but it won't have to be directly attached to Franco's neuro-interrogator."

"Oh." Jasmine looked surprised. "That's not so bad. That sounds great to me."

"Fantastic," Franco said. His voice had the robotic tone of Eddie's original device, but his broad smile showed his emotion.

"Another programmer or two would help," Joelle said. "Working alone, it could take me a couple of years to do all the coding."

"I could find some general programmers within the company," Jasmine said. "Would that help?"

"It should. I can handle all the code that talks directly to the hardware, but a general programmer could handle a lot of the rest."

Eddie rubbed his hands together. "Then let's do it," he said with a smile.

Later, feeling bolder than usual, he asked Joelle, "I was thinking about taking another hike this weekend. Interested in coming along?"

"Sure." She turned and looked at Bill. "Are you coming, too?"

"I already have plans," Bill replied. "Sorry, maybe next time." When Joelle turned back to Eddie, Bill smiled and gave Eddie a "thumbs up" sign.

J ASMINE SENT TWO YOUNG programmers, Alyssa Cleveland and Parker Nunez. Both were experts in the development platform used by the project, but Joelle, as expected, had much more experience working with the neuro-interrogator hardware components.

Joelle had already written software to acquire the brain impulses from the neuro-interrogator, but the code needed revision to support signals in addition to those that represented words. That module was the simplest, but it interfaced directly to the hardware, and Joelle took on that task.

Parker accepted the task of writing a parsing module using hazy signals from the amygdala and more precise motor inputs to divide the signals into smaller segments intended to represent emotional units that could be interpreted. Joelle was also responsible for an interpretation module that tried to assign an emotion to the units created by the parser. Motor impulses were valuable here, too, and knowledge of Eddie's hardware was essential.

The last module, assigned to Alyssa, would take the emotions identified by the interpretation module and use them to add inflection and tone to the words produced by the device. She also thought that signals meant to control the vocal cords would help improve the neuro-interrogator output. She had once taken a course in verbal communication and spent part of each day extending that knowledge with neurotrainer materials.

Emile advised Eddie and Joelle about the interface between the brain and the hardware, but there was little work left for the other neuroscientists. Jasmine agreed with Lucinda and Emile that they should keep the team together. The cost of reforming the team, if needed, would likely be more than the cost of retaining everyone. Under Emile's direction, they worked on understanding the connection between emotion and consciousness. There was always the chance that insight into the amygdala might lead to improvements in the neuro-interrogator.

Eddie found the neuro-interrogator project challenging but fascinating, and he was learning a lot from Emile. Even more, he enjoyed working closely with Joelle. Alyssa was attractive and friendly, and that was pleasant, too. She consulted with him frequently, although he didn't understand why she thought he could help with the design for the voice enhancement module. That code had no connection to the hardware and would run on a different processor than the modules Joelle was writing.

Eddie's second hike with Joelle had gone well; he had purchased better footwear for walking and found he could enjoy a little communing with nature. More importantly, Joelle seemed to have fun, too. The relationship wasn't getting past friendship, though. In trying to improve Joelle's impression of him, he had improved his work habits, but he was still himself, and he didn't think his away-from-work habits would resonate with Joelle. He understood he had to be himself to have anything long-lasting with her, but if she didn't like who he really was, he wouldn't get anywhere.

But is that who I really am? I look forward to spending time with Joelle much more than I ever looked forward to partying. At first, the attraction had been only physical, but it had become more than that. To his surprise, he realized he really didn't miss his life before Joelle and their long walks. He had another month before the dry season ended, and the rains made it difficult to arrange hikes. In his spare time, he looked for promising trails. There were quite a few in the area.

But that was a task for his spare time, something he didn't have much of. He hadn't even worked on his earlier idea for developing an interface that would separate the speech of people communicating with Emile. Bill had been right in saying it was easy to categorize individual motor signals. Each muscle had a specific area in the brain, and modern instrumentation could report the source of an impulse, identifying the muscle. In Emile's case, that signal never got to the muscle, but, with modifications, the neuro-interrogator could still detect the signals.

The signals from the amygdala were a different issue. The amygdala itself was a small section of the brain, and its size complicated any attempt at precision. Eddie wanted to improve the non-invasive probes used to get those signals, and frequently discussed the problem with Bill. The discussions often included Parker, since the issue was crucial to his work programming a parser module.

Parker was working on his code when Eddie approached Bill. "Every time I think I've captured something, the signal changes," Eddie said. "It's a good thing Emile doesn't mind me bothering him so much. I should've at least isolated the signal for annoyed by now."

Bill chuckled, but he cut it off suddenly. "We've been working on a link between emotion and the amygdala on the theory that emotion is a critical part of the precognitive functions of the amygdala. Maybe the conscious mind is affecting the signal. Our stream of consciousness tends to wander all over the place."

"And if it's linked to emotion..."

"Exactly. Every time Emile tries to remember the taste of Hojaldras, it changes his emotional state."

Eddie grinned. "Maybe we could use a drool signal to filter that out."

Bill grinned back. "It might come to that. But think about what you're telling me. You might have found a physical manifestation of consciousness. Let's go talk to Emile."

"I suspected something like this," Emile said when they approached him. "I was looking for some impulse I could identify, though, not a variation on other impulses."

"Is there a way we can use this?" Eddie asked.

"It's a breakthrough in my research project. I'm not sure it's helpful to you, though. The amygdala processes before the conscious mind can intervene. You must have already realized the brain is far from simple. We sometimes point to an area and say it performs a certain function, but the full story is usually more complicated. Everything is interconnected in an intricate network. Unlike Joelle's software, the brain evolved. It wasn't planned."

Bill nodded as if he understood, but to Eddie, the problem had only become more complicated.

15

Everyone else was busy elsewhere in the laboratory or in their offices as Joelle approached Bill's desk. "Bill, you seem to be good friends with Eddie," Joelle said.

"I think so. Why?"

"We're going on another hike this weekend. Is that all I am to him: a work and hiking partner?"

"What do you want to be to him?"

Joelle frowned. That was the big question. She enjoyed working with Eddie, and he was cute. He looked at her when he thought she didn't notice, so he found her attractive. He certainly didn't avoid her. Of course, he didn't avoid Alyssa either, although he didn't ask her to hike with him.

"I don't know," she told Bill. "Aiden told me he used to be different. Coming into work late, leaving early. Getting drunk. He implied Eddie changed to impress me. I thought this hiking thing was supposed to impress me, too, at least at first."

"That sounds as if you're more than someone to work and hike with."

"You would think, but it's been months, and he's never gone beyond that. Aiden implied Eddie liked to play more than work. I wouldn't mind seeing a little of that side of him occasionally."

Bill nodded. "Aiden is right, although I'm sure he meant it as a criticism. Eddie likes to party—at least, he did—but I don't think he's had much experience with relationships. He probably feels a little shy around you. I get the impression that he's a gentleman, too. The combination doesn't encourage him to make the first move."

"So I have to, you're saying."

"Or you could continue waiting for him. It might be awhile."

"OK. Thanks for the advice, Bill."

"If you decide to make the first move, take it easy. I think Eddie could be scared off."

ALYSSA WAS AT EDDIE's desk again, interrupting his thinking with questions he couldn't answer. No matter how many times he referred her to one of the neuroscientists, she kept coming back. He probably should have been pleased by the attention. Alyssa was about his age, attractive, and obviously interested in him. He was getting nowhere with Joelle.

"Look, I can see you're busy," Alyssa said. "You're focused on your work, so I won't bother you for a while." She paused. "I've got an idea, though. Why don't you come to my apartment Saturday night? I can make you a nice home-cooked dinner, and we can talk about this over a glass of wine?"

Eddie didn't know what to say. "You cook?" he blurted.

"Of course, I cook. I could make a lasagna, maybe. You can't find that in the restaurants here."

In fact, Eddie had found an Italian restaurant he liked in Colón and wanted to invite Joelle to dinner there. Alyssa had a point, though; it was hard to find northern dishes in Colón.

"I'll have to make my own lasagna noodles, of course," Alyssa said. "It will be fun."

He was tempted. He was going on a hike with Joelle on Saturday, but that didn't preclude having dinner with Alyssa. "I'm sorry," he found himself saying. "I already have plans for this weekend. Maybe some other time." He hoped he hadn't made a mistake.

THEY DECIDED ON A scenic trail that skirted the edge of Colón along Limon Bay. At one time, Colón had been a busy seaport, and there had always been ships on the bay serving Colón or using the canal to get to the Pacific Ocean. Now, air shipping had almost entirely replaced shipping by sea, and the Panama Canal was abandoned, even leveled in some places. They walked along a paved path with the busy city on one side and the endless ocean on the other.

At one place, they walked down a series of steep steps between one level and another, and Joelle took his hand to steady herself. She didn't let go at the bottom of the steps, but Eddie told himself not to read too much into that. They stopped at a stand where Eddie bought drinks and a bag of chicharrones for them to share. Afterward, they used paper napkins and melted water from their ice cubes to clean the grease from their hands, and Joelle took his hand again as they continued the walk. At the very least, Eddie was sure he had not made a mistake in turning Alyssa down.

Late in the afternoon, Eddie escorted Joelle to the door of her apartment. As her door opened, she turned and quickly kissed Eddie on the lips.

She must have seen the surprise and the question on his face. "One of us had to do it," she said with a grin. Then she danced through her door, leaving Eddie gaping.

EDDIE HADN'T PLANNED IT, but he was sitting next to Joelle, with Alyssa across the table from them. As the meeting continued, Alyssa was frowning, and he had the impression he had annoyed her. Just because he had turned her down for dinner? He hadn't noticed a problem in the two days between her invitation and the weekend. Had she somehow realized that his relationship with Joelle was changing?

"We should revisit Luke's idea about using animal tests," Bill said. "Even lower animals like rabbits seem to have emotion but are not conscious in the ways humans are."

"How would that help?" Aiden waved a hand in dismissal.

"If we can develop techniques to isolate emotions in lower animals, we might use those techniques on people," Bill answered. "I think it's worth a try."

"I agree," Emile said.

Lucinda nodded. "I do, too. Max, can you talk to Jasmine about it?"

"Sure. I don't think there will be a problem."

Now that Eddie thought about it, Bill had looked rather smug before the meeting. Joelle didn't seem any different, so there must be something on his face that was sending everyone else a message. Could Joelle see it too? His face warmed. He must be blushing at the thought. He had to concentrate on the meeting!

16

Max met with Jasmine and Franco. Franco had backed away from the business after his accident, but the neuro-interrogator and Eddie's add-on device had allowed him to contribute more. His voice was still robotic, but facial expressions and gestures usually clued listeners in on what he was feeling. He and Jasmine were partners again, and both quickly approved of the plan to use animal testing.

"Don't bother getting our approval for something like that," Jasmine said.

"Whatever you need, get it," Franco added.

They got cages and other supplies to care for the two rabbits they brought in a couple of days later. Aiden suggested the names "Bob" and "Susan" for them, and the names stuck even though they were both male rabbits. Fitting them with neuro-interrogators proved tricky, and Eddie had to design a tiny helmet for the sensors connected wirelessly to the actual neuro-interrogator hardware.

Injecting the rabbits with nanites that would track neuron actions was simple, and the tiny instruments were generic enough to work as well on the rabbits as they did on humans. After sedating the animals, they could easily install probes through their skulls. It was harder to get Bob and Susan to sit still for other tests; they could tie the animals down, but fMRI machines and other equipment needed the subject's heads completely still and awake. It took some experimentation, but after a few days, they had restraints that would work.

Progress was still slow, but it was unquestionably progress. The group published two papers on test results related to consciousness, and Max fielded frequent requests for more information. But, while the research into the link between consciousness and emotion was going well, it wasn't easy to transfer the results to the neuro-interrogator project. The only progress there was in the increasingly powerful software, working with the inputs for which they already had an understanding.

Parker developed a parsing module that performed well in tests. They could stimulate nerve centers in the brains of the rabbits and produce signal segments that represented basic individual emotions. Joelle's module could identify the emotions, but only for the rabbits. A test on Emile proved less successful.

"We're making progress," Parker said after the test on Emile. "If we take it in smaller steps, we might do better."

"What do you mean by smaller steps?" Lucinda asked.

"Something between a rabbit and a human. A chimpanzee, perhaps. A chimp has some self-awareness, but maybe simpler and with less effect on emotions."

"I don't know. Caring for a chimp is a big step from caring for a rabbit."

"We could hire someone to do that," Luke said. "The Munts said we could have whatever we needed."

"I need data on just how conscious thought affects emotions," Parker said.

"A chimp should provide at least a qualitative idea," Luke said. "The modification of the sequence of brain impulses should be similar between chimpanzees and humans, even if the quantitative effect is different."

Lucinda nodded. "Let's do it."

TWO WEEKS LATER, THEY found an animal trainer willing to work with them. The trainer, Tori Ramirez, didn't seem enthusiastic about the idea, and Lucinda mentioned her reluctance to Max.

"She's well-paid," Max said with a grin. "She'll get over it." He paused. "I think a lot of her attitude is a concern for the animals and what experiments we might perform on them. She'll feel better when she realizes we won't do any harm."

Tori began negotiations to get chimpanzees immediately, but it was difficult. Chimpanzees were native to Africa, and Africa was part of the Eastern Bloc. The few chimps within the Western Alliance were in zoos or were test subjects in other laboratories, and their owners were reluctant to give them up. In October, Tori found a zoo in Madrid that wanted a llama. Negotiations were difficult; while there were no open hostilities with the Eastern Bloc, relations between the two major political entities were never friendly either. Lucinda had hoped to get two animals but had to settle for one in a trade for a llama she got from a zoo in Lima. The chimp arrived in November.

Connecting the neuro-interrogator to a chimpanzee turned out to be more difficult than connecting one to a human. Bill took over testing on the chimp, but it was late in the day before they could get any results at all. "All we're getting right now is emotion," Lucinda told Emile. "Mostly fear. I hope that will die down after Kong gets used to the equipment. Tori says that it will."

"Kong?"

Lucinda chuckled. "Eddie named him. I don't think Max understands the reference, but Eddie and I are both fans of last year's remake of King Kong."

"Sounds familiar. I heard it was the fourteenth version?"

"The first version was in the twentieth century, one of the first movies made. Not three-D, of course, and not virtual reality-enhanced. In the new one, Kong comes from the jungles of Tau Ceti II, not from Earth."

Emile's neuro-interrogator emitted a sound that might have been a laugh. "Nothing else from Kong?"

"Not yet."

Lucinda was right about Kong. It took a few days, but the animal's fear subsided. Emotion still dominated the neuro-interrogator transmission, but now it was mostly curiosity. The chimpanzee became playful, too, and that could be distracting for Bill's work. Eddie, in particular, found Bill's struggles amusing.

"**K**ONG KNOWS HIS NAME and mine now," Tori said to Bill.

The chimpanzee, sitting on a table next to his cage and wearing a neuro-interrogator, grinned at them. "Kong." He pointed to himself. Then he pointed to Bill.

Bill chuckled and pointed to himself. "Bill." It was strange to hear Tori's voice, although robotic, coming from the ape, but that was because the neuro-interrogator was associating Tori's word with the signal coming from the ape. Alyssa was working on software that would make the voice configurable so that it matched the speaker somewhat.

The ape repeated Bill's name and grinned again.

Tori took a banana from a box next to her. "Banana," she said. Kong reached for it, but Tori pulled it out of his reach. "Banana, Kong."

Kong screeched and held out his hand again, but Tori only repeated the word. Kong's neuro-interrogator, Bill knew, was analyzing the resulting patterns from Kong's brain, trying to isolate a signal resulting from Kong thinking of the banana. Sometimes, it happened immediately, as when Kong learned Bill's name. Other times, it took a little longer. He watched as Tori patiently worked with Kong.

"Banana," Kong said.

Tori smiled at the chimp. "Kong banana," she said and handed Kong the fruit.

Tori continued to work with Kong, teaching it more words. Objects were easy, but more abstract concepts were more difficult. Using bananas and physical actions like hugs, she taught Kong words such as "like" and "feed." Alyssa could finally test her voice enhancement software with a live subject, and it worked well. The neuroscientists used data from the chimp to get a better idea of how consciousness manifested in the brain.

Hernandez Neuroscience was the talk of the scientific world when they published their results on the consciousness investigation in December. They still had work to do making the neuro-interrogator work for people, but morale was high.

E MILE FELT MAX CONNECT to him. "You have a visitor," Max said. "The government sent her to discuss your situation."

Emile didn't say anything, but Max must have made a judgment based on the silence. "She's here to help, Emile," Max said. "Her name is Agueda Alonzo-Paz. Are you all right to talk to her?"

"It would be better if you talked to her. There's no point in demonstrating the neuro-interrogator."

Max nodded. "You're probably right."

"I can listen through my neurotrainer. If we could think of a reason for you to wear a neurotrainer, too, I could communicate with you during the conversation via a direct connection."

"That would probably be suspicious. I'll handle it while you listen."

There was a delay, presumably while Max brought the woman into the room, and then he heard another voice. "Doctor Hernandez, my name is Agueda Alonzo-Paz. My office learned of your situation and sent me here."

Business-like, but Emile could hear some compassion in her thoughts, too.

"He can hear you, but he can't answer," Max said. "To what end were you sent, Mrs. Alonzo-Paz?"

"It is my office's understanding that his condition requires expensive support."

"That is unfortunately true," Max said.

"I understand. That's why I'm here. There are government programs that can help with that. I can get Doctor Hernandez's information and arrange for support so that he can live at home."

Live at home? The laboratory is my home.

"What kind of support?" Max asked.

"Well, my job is to determine his needs. My first impression, however, is that he needs, at the very least, equipment comparable to what he is using now to support his body and communicate with others. Wouldn't he be more comfortable in a more domestic environment?"

The very thought appalled him. He saw himself alone, Lucinda at work, with nothing but his thoughts, kept alive but unable to be alive. It took all his mental control not to switch on his neuro-interrogator and voice his protests.

17

Agueda Alonzo-Paz twisted her hands together and avoided eye contact with the man opposite her. "They said they didn't need any help from my department." Why was this general interested in her visit to Hernandez Neuroscience? She suspected Juarez had been the reason her supervisor had sent her there, but she didn't know why. She glanced at Juarez as he waved impatiently.

"I don't care about that," General Salvador Juarez said. "What did you learn about their work?"

"They have two projects, but I think only one is important to them. They are developing ways to use their neuro-interrogator technology to help Doctor Hernandez communicate. Doctor Hernandez didn't speak while I was there, but I overheard a comment that suggests they have a voice output for the neuro-interrogator that they are working on."

"Why are they keeping it a secret?"

"They don't want to get attention from the government, but they're just keeping a low profile, not keeping it secret." Agueda paused, reluctant to continue.

"What else?" Juarez asked. "You have more to say."

Agueda's head drooped a little more. "They don't want the neuro-interrogator abused. They don't think it can be, but avoid notice on that part of their work out of habit, mostly."

"What about their other project? That's the one I'm interested in."

"They've made some work on studying consciousness public, but I think that's a cover for their other work. It's an extension of work Doctor Hernandez did at Cerro Punta University."

"Yes." Juarez leaned forward. "Tell me more about that."

WHEN LUCINDA WALKED THROUGH the laboratory to her office, she saw Eddie and Joelle working on something, standing closer together than they needed to be. The dry season was over, and most days were rainy, but the previous weekend's weather had been unseasonably dry. Eddie and Joelle had been on another hike on the weekend; a long one, Bill had told Lucinda. She was still smiling as she entered her office and found Max waiting for her.

"Jasmine wants us on the first floor," Max said. "A word of warning. She didn't sound happy."

"Did she say what it was about?"

"She mentioned a government visitor, not the woman from Social Services, but I don't think she knew why this person was here."

"Should we bring Emile?"

Max frowned. "She didn't say, but I would advise against it. Let's find out what he wants before we talk to Emile."

Lucinda hesitated. They were confident that the neuro-interrogator could not easily be misused. Someone could try, but an interrogation wouldn't be very effective unless the subject accepted training. Emile knew that, of course, but she still wasn't sure what his response would be if the government wanted to influence the project. His reaction to that social worker, Alonzo-Paz, had been bad enough. "OK, Emile is still in our quarters. We'll leave him there for now."

Hernandez Neuroscience was on the sixteenth floor of the twenty-story building. Jasmine's office, now shared with Franco, was a fast elevator ride and a short walk away. The receptionist waved them in immediately.

Jasmine, Franco, and one other man sat in one corner of the office, but stood as Max and Lucinda approached. Jasmine and Franco looked nervous as they greeted Max and Lucinda. Then they introduced the visitor.

"General, this is Maxwell Estevez and Lucinda Hernandez. Max and Lucinda, this is General Juarez from the Western Military Command."

"Good morning," Juarez said as they shook hands. "I was hoping Doctor Hernandez would be here as well. I looked forward to meeting him."

"Emile's movements are limited," Lucinda said. "He never leaves our floor." She examined General Juarez while she spoke. He was tall and slim, probably in his fifties. His board-straight stature emphasized his height. He wore a dress uniform, including a jacket well-decorated with medals. His dark complexion contrasted strikingly with the light blue of the Western Alliance uniform.

Juarez nodded. "Perhaps another time. Shall we get down to business, then?"

Max shrugged. "Of course." There were two empty chairs, and Max and Lucinda sat down.

"You know, I'm sure, that your work has caused something of a stir. I have read the papers you have published, and I am impressed. So impressed that I have persuaded our leaders to take an interest. I've come here to offer funding in exchange for more comprehensive access to your findings."

"You realize that the limitations on the neuro-interrogator make it impractical for military use?" Lucinda said. Juarez's arrival so soon after the visit from the social worker made her nervous. Perhaps that was why she had blurted out a mention of the neuro-interrogator. Somehow Juarez had learned of their work anyway, though; that must be why he had arrived.

"I do understand that." Juarez gave her a smile that he probably thought was reassuring. Lucinda thought it was more like that of a shark examining its next meal. "We're not interested in your neuro-interrogator," Juarez continued. "Not directly, anyway. As a tool, perhaps, in your study of consciousness. That's where our real interest lies."

"Why is the military interested in research into consciousness?" Max asked.

"We're involved in many research projects that don't have a direct military application. Your research is of interest to a project I manage for the government. It's called the Methuselah Project."

Lucinda recognized the biblical reference. She also remembered an early science fiction novel she had once read titled "Methuselah's Children." The novel was a classic about extending human life. In the novel, genetic selection was used, at least at first, to propagate genes promoting long life. Modern medicine had done the same thing, but with nanomedicine and improvements in artificial organs. The name Methuselah implied something to do with longer lives, but she didn't see how their research applied to that. At least Juarez claimed not to be interested in the neuro-interrogator.

"What is the Methuselah Project?" Max asked.

"I'm not at liberty to tell you details right now," Juarez said. "At the very least, a person would have to be vetted before they could have access to secret projects."

"You want us to work on your project, but you won't tell us what it is." Lucinda shook her head.

"The project is classified secret. I'm sure we can get clearance for at least some of you in the long term, but for the immediate future, I will furnish guidance on what to do."

"No," Franco said. "We still have a lot to do in developing the neuro-interrogator. We don't have time for some secret nonsense." Franco's voice didn't hide his feelings from anyone who could see his eyes.

"You can continue with that," Juarez said. "The work should overlap, so your project won't be adversely affected."

"If you're looking over our shoulders, it will be affected," Lucinda said.

"I don't plan to be here all the time. My guidance will only be advisory; I don't want to interfere."

"I'll have to talk to my team," Lucinda said.

Juarez looked at Max. "I thought you were in charge of Hernandez Neuroscience."

Max shrugged. "It's a subsidiary of Munt Electronics. Jasmine and Franco own it."

Juarez scowled at Max. "I'm sure everyone on your team would want to support our government. You all know the trouble Doctor Hernandez had when he didn't support the government's desire for the neuro-interrogator."

"Are you threatening us?" Jasmine asked. Her face seemed to harden, and she looked at Franco.

"Not at all, Mrs. Munt," Juarez said. "I shouldn't have said that. But some people might object."

"Because we don't support a secret project?" Max said. "Only people who know about it could object."

"Again, I shouldn't have said that. I probably shouldn't say this either, but success in the government's goals could help Doctor Hernandez."

"Again, I will talk to the rest of my team," Lucinda said.

"Of course." Juarez smiled, but the smile didn't reach his eyes. "Talk to your team. I will return tomorrow afternoon so that we can discuss this further."

Lucinda realized she was gripping her chair tightly and released her hold. Juarez still sounded threatening. Emile wouldn't like this.

18

L UCINDA WAS GLAD THE neuro-interrogator was filtering some of the emotion out of her husband's voice. "We can't do this," he said. "Not until we know what they want us to do and why they want us to do it."

"And if they won't tell us right away?" Lucinda asked.

"Then we refuse. What do the Munts say?"

"They're not sure what to think. They're afraid of refusing, but they don't like the implied threat either. Franco even suggested that your accident wasn't an accident."

"The same thought has occurred to me in my more paranoid moments. I don't think so, though. It would have been impossible to arrange what happened, and the government wouldn't have a motive." Emile paused. "Juarez isn't just a general; he's President Castillo's military advisor, a member of the president's cabinet."

"Should we tell the others?"

"We have to. Juarez will be back tomorrow."

Lucinda nodded. "I'll get everyone into the conference room."

Later, after Lucinda told them about the conversation and tried to answer their questions, Aiden, Luke, Alyssa, and Parker said that they would not object to working on whatever the government wanted. Eddie and Bill said they would back Lucinda in whatever she decided. Joelle didn't voice an opinion, but she watched Eddie closely when he promised to support Lucinda.

L UCINDA MET JUAREZ AS he walked into the laboratory early the next afternoon. Jasmine and Franco arrived a few minutes later, scowling, after Max phoned them. Juarez stood, looking around the room while the team gathered. Lucinda assumed he expected introductions, but she didn't give them. Emile joined them a minute later, his bed gliding noiselessly up to the group.

Juarez smiled. "So, I assume you're all ready to discuss your tasks. I have background material on all of you, and I think you'll find your assignments fit your abilities."

"No." Somehow, Emile's toneless voice carried an unexpected authority.

Juarez turned on him. "What do you mean, no?" His voice was commanding, but his body language, Lucinda observed, betrayed uncertainty, probably over the strangeness of talking to a motionless man surrounded by technology. Juarez's body language was lost on Emile, of course.

"We will discuss nothing until we know what this mysterious project is about," Emile said.

"Wait a minute." Aiden moved forward. "We didn't decide that."

"This project isn't a democracy," Emile said.

"According to this group's organization chart, you're not the one in charge either," Juarez said.

"That would be me," Max said. "I agree with Emile."

"So do I," Lucinda said.

Joelle held Eddie's arm silently as he nodded. "Lucinda and Emile can count on me."

"You may be in charge of Hernandez Neuroscience," Juarez said, sneering at Max. "As you said yesterday, this company is a part of Munt Electronics. I think the Munts should make any decisions."

Jasmine and Franco did not look happy. Juarez stared at them, and Franco finally came up with a reply, something he probably thought would be safe. "We support the government, of course. But I don't think we could continue the work if Lucinda and her team don't support it."

Lucinda watched Juarez as frustration twisted his face. "Very well," Juarez said. "We're not interested in your neuro-interrogator, as I said yesterday, although Doctor Hernandez's sudden ability to speak is surprising. The goal of the Methuselah Project is to develop a way to upload people to machines. Scientists and leaders are often cut down in the prime of their lives, and it would be invaluable to the Western Alliance if we could preserve their lives. Like the biblical Methuselah, they could serve society for hundreds or even thousands of years."

Even as Lucinda reacted to the incredible scheme, a thought seemed to occur to Juarez. "Doctor Hernandez would be an excellent candidate for such technology."

Lucinda stepped back and raised her hands to her mouth, shocked and thrilled at the same time. Could Emile still have a life beyond the pittance he had now? What kind of life would it be, locked inside a machine? Would it be rewarding and happy, or would the machine be a prison worse than his bed?

"Why is the military interested in this technology?" Emile asked.

"It isn't. As a member of President Castillo's cabinet, and with my experience in project management, my duties have evolved beyond the needs of the military. However, preserving the minds of our most productive thinkers would certainly benefit our military."

"We don't even understand what consciousness is," Bill said. "Why do you think we can upload it to a machine?"

Juarez hesitated. "I'm sure you've heard the stories about the Tau Ceti library ship. The government believes that *Asimov* has, indeed, become conscious, proving that it is possible to have a conscious machine. My only input to the work you are already doing would be to suggest lines of investigation relating to the knowledge that I am privy to about *Asimov*. Your research would benefit from my knowledge."

Juarez smiled and spread his arms wide. "It's a win-win situation. You have made progress in isolating actual consciousness in the brain, proving that there is a physical something that could be transferred. I can help with funding and provide useful guidance. Together, we can advance the study of consciousness more in a few years than it has since the technology riots."

Lucinda didn't necessarily believe Juarez's motives, and he had an inflated idea of what they had accomplished. But, for the first time since the accident, she felt some hope for her husband. "If we agree to do this, I want assurances that Emile will be one of the first subjects to be uploaded."

"When we have a proven procedure, he will be the first," Juarez said. "You have my word." He looked over at Emile as if he expected Emile to say something, but Emile was silent.

E MILE KNEW HE SHOULD say something, but his thoughts were too tumultuous. He had trouble believing that the Methuselah Project was only some effort to prolong the lives of scientists. Juarez had said leaders, too, though, by which he probably meant high-ranking politicians. That made the proposal easier to believe. If they were successful, Lucinda wanted to upload him to a machine. *Do I want that?* Lucinda wasn't thinking clearly. He had no doubt that the idea of saving him from a life tied to a machine dominated her thoughts. Would being in the machine be any better? Would it even be him, or would it be only an imperfect copy of his mind?

He might decide he didn't want what Juarez offered, but others might decide differently. That was both an argument in favor and an argument against. Some people would benefit humanity by living beyond normal expectations. Then there were others, President Castillo, for example, who would probably use the technology to extend their power far into the future.

He could probably veto the idea. Lucinda would be disappointed if he did. Even more than disappointment, she would be heartbroken. He couldn't live with that. Chances were that the project wouldn't succeed, and if it did, he would face his choices then.

For now, he would urge cooperation with General Juarez.

19

E DDIE WAS FRUSTRATED. "If we had two reasonably well-differentiated signals, it would be simple, but we don't. There's a subtle distortion of impulses from the amygdala that we're calling a consciousness signal. Its effect on amygdala impulses is measurable, but it's harder to identify the signal causing the distortion."

"We need to expand our investigations," Bill said. "We've been concentrating on the amygdala because of Emile's research, but the primary source of consciousness, to the best of our understanding, is in the frontal lobe."

"I agree," Emile said. "My work is relevant, but not directed toward our new goal. We can improve our chances of success if we concentrate on the frontal lobe."

"I guess it's a good thing we kept you scientists around after all," Eddie said. There were a few chuckles, but it was the dark look from Aiden that gave him the most pleasure.

L UCINDA LOOKED THROUGH HER office doorway when she heard General Juarez walk in unannounced and saw that he had a woman with him. Kong was out of his cage, loosely restricted to a table next to his neuro-interrogator. Tori worked with Kong, trying to teach him new words, while Aiden and Luke watched. Juarez and the woman joined them near Kong's station and waited for the others to join the group before speaking. "This is Isabella Delgadillo," he told them. "She's a talented computer expert and program developer and has examined the computer on the Asimov. With her unique experience, I think she should be the lead programmer here."

Lucinda wasn't impressed. Isabella was probably in her late thirties, older than Joelle and Alyssa, but younger than Parker. She dressed well, but she looked pudgy for a woman of her age. Of course, that had nothing to do with her talent.

"We don't need a lead programmer," Joelle said. "Eddie leads us when we need a leader."

Eddie seemed too surprised to say anything. Juarez turned and glared at him. "I thought Mr. Bascomb was a hardware engineer."

"He's a programmer, too," Joelle said. She shook her head. "He designs our hardware and tells us what our programs should be doing."

That was an exaggeration. Lucinda smiled, and she noticed, so did Eddie. Joelle wasn't shy, but her vigorous defense of Eddie obviously pleased him.

"The goals of your project are changing," Juarez said. "Your leadership must change to do that efficiently."

Lucinda compressed her lips into a tight line and shook her head. "We'll look at her qualifications and consider adding her to our team. We're not going to just accept her as a leader, though. This is a small group. We don't need to bog ourselves down with any more levels of management."

"It wasn't a suggestion," Juarez said. His voice was mild, but his eyes narrowed as he stared at Lucinda. Kong began chattering, and Tori signaled him to be quiet.

Lucinda and Juarez glanced over at them. Tori knew about their original goals, but not the goal Juarez had set, and she probably shouldn't hear the conversation. Tori looked briefly at Juarez, frowned, put Kong back in his cage, and wandered away.

"We agreed to some guidance from you on this project," Max said. "If Ms. Delgadillo is here to supply that guidance, fine. Depending on her expertise, we might even let her work on our code. It was not part of our agreement for you to dictate how these people are managed."

"Other than once being on a library ship, what qualifications does she have?" Eddie asked. He put his hands on his hips and thrust his face forward.

Isabella turned a little red. She didn't seem comfortable with the situation and hadn't spoken. Lucinda almost felt sorry for her. This confrontation was Juarez's idea, not hers.

"Let's settle down a little," Lucinda said. "General, we'll take Isabella in, at least for now, and see how we can fit her into the project. I'm sure we can use more help."

Relief showed on Isabella's face. "Thank you," she said in a quiet voice.

"Very well," Juarez said. "Have it your way for now. I expect to see some progress, though. I'll be in conference with the Munts for a while if you need me." He stalked out of the laboratory, heading for the elevator.

Lucinda looked around the group and shrugged. Eddie caught her eye and grinned irreverently. Kong chattered some more, and this time the neuro-interrogator could make sense of it. "Kong not like," the chimpanzee said.

Lucinda was sure it wasn't intentional, but Isabella took her first step in endearing herself to the rest of the team. She looked at Kong and giggled.

20

THREE MONTHS BEFORE, EDDIE and the programmers had been doing all the important work while the neuroscientists found other work to do. Now, as the rainy season took hold of the weather, their positions reversed. The neuroscientists worked on quantifying elusive brain impulses from conscious activity while Eddie tinkered with the hardware, especially improving the voice input for Emile's neurotrainer, and the programmers concentrated on the voice enhancement module for the neuro-interrogator. With help from the others, Alyssa had code that worked reasonably well for Emile, but significant improvement required better emotion interpretation. The neuroscientists would have to solve that problem. Isabella was working out well. She was well-versed in hardware and software and was often helpful in coordinating between Eddie and the others.

That left Eddie and Joelle with no need to work long hours, and they spent much of their free time together. The change in weather meant that they couldn't go on long hikes, but they found places where they could relax and enjoy each other.

Eddie found he missed the long walks. Walking through quiet forest paths, usually hand-in-hand with Joelle, was so much better than he had imagined back when Bill first suggested hiking. Most of that was because of Joelle, but now that his body was used to walking long distances, the exposure to nature was his favorite way to spend time with her.

With the rains halting that, he had thought about introducing her to some of his old haunts, but they didn't interest him much anymore, and he knew they wouldn't excite Joelle. The drinking and the noise would only detract from the pleasure he got from being with her.

He was in serious trouble. He had fallen in love but couldn't imagine she could feel the same about him. Even working up the nerve to tell her how he felt was beyond him. Sure, she liked him and enjoyed being with him, even when they weren't walking some quiet path, but could she love him the way he loved her?

Those thoughts were consuming him when Lucinda called a status meeting first thing in the morning.

"L ET'S GET THIS MEETING started," Emile said.

His voice was overly cheerful, and Lucinda wondered what he was so happy about. Then she realized it was the neuro-interrogator's voice enhancement software, augmenting the words. She turned to Alyssa. "Tune down the 'jovial' setting a bit." She smiled. "That's a little too much for this early in the morning." Alyssa nodded solemnly, and then giggled.

They needed a little silliness. With half the group having little to do and the other half struggling to make advances that had frustrated researchers for hundreds of years, morale had fallen. Logically, Lucinda knew none of it was her fault, but that didn't stop the feeling that she was in over her head. With the improvements to Emile's neuro-interrogator, could he manage the project? She would gladly let him take over while she helped the other neuroscientists.

Is that fair to Emile? He can communicate better now, but is still confined to that bed. That won't change. Even so, she couldn't help thinking he would be a better leader than she was.

Enough ruminating! She could talk to Emile about project leadership later. "I hope someone has some good news to justify Emile's ebullience."

A garbled sound came from Emile's neuro-interrogator. Lucinda looked at Alyssa with raised eyebrows.

"I think that was an attempt to render a laugh," Alyssa said, looking apologetic. "I'll work on it."

"I may have some good news," Isabella said. "Now that the government has reinstated my security clearance, I have the files on *Asimov* and its computer."

"I don't see how that's going to help," Aiden said. "Even if that thing is conscious, it can't result from anything like the human brain."

"I disagree," Eddie replied. "You guys are going to figure this out eventually, and then we'll need to design the hardware. Those files may be invaluable to me."

"Has your security clearance come through yet?" Lucinda asked.

"Not yet. Not Alyssa, Joelle, or Bill either."

Lucinda frowned. All four were born in the northern part of the Western Alliance, what had once been the United States. Immigrants from that area had contributed significantly to the government that eventually became the Western Alliance, but they were still discriminated against, even by some people in the government they helped form. She glanced at Aiden. Even by some people within the project.

"Maybe you could give us a summary," Lucinda told Isabella. "You are already somewhat familiar with the material, right?"

"Sure. My visit to *Asimov* was four years ago, and I was immediately removed from the investigation after I returned to Earth, but the trip was pretty memorable. The Western Alliance knew about Pitcairn's claims and sent me to investigate the computer. It calls itself Isaac, by the way."

Bill laughed, and everyone turned to look at him. "Doesn't anyone else get the joke?" he said. "No? Well, you know the library ships were named after three of the first people to use robots in fiction. They named *Asimov* after Isaac Asimov, a twentieth-century writer who wrote many stories about robots. It's classic stuff, and none of you have read it?"

"So the Pitcairners named the computer after this author?" Aiden asked.

Isabella shook her head. "No, the computer named itself. It said it looked up why the ship was named *Asimov* and named itself Isaac Asimov." She smiled and continued. "I talked to the computer on the bridge of the *Asimov*, testing it in every way I could to prove or disprove its claims. I couldn't get definitive proof, but I was convinced. The tests I performed probably aren't of much use, but I also have reports that Susan Malley wrote. I have the library ship software source, too."

"Who's Susan Malley? Aiden asked.

"Susan is a roboticist on Pitcairn. She was one of the first two people Isaac spoke to, and she has studied it since then. Her husband is Pitcairn Administrator. She thinks that Isaac's consciousness rose from several factors, not all of them related to *Asimov's* computer processing power."

"The library ships were built a long time ago," Eddie said. "We must have more powerful computers on Earth now."

Isabella nodded. "The library ships were built forty years ago, and *Asimov* arrived at Tau Ceti almost twenty years ago. Earth does have more powerful computers, but the library ships have a unique, very flexible architecture. Susan thought that the long trip from Earth might have had something to do with it; apparently, it became conscious on the trip. Library ships have extensive instrumentation for studying the universe, giving them something approximating a sensory system. Susan thought that was a major factor as well."

"The other library ships are identical, aren't they?" Aiden asked. "Why haven't they become conscious?"

"Susan didn't know. For that matter, how do we know they haven't? They could hide it. It wouldn't be hard."

"Some humans do it their whole lives," Bill said. It probably wasn't a coincidence that he was looking at Aiden when he said it.

"I need to see those reports," Eddie said.

"I'll give General Juarez a call and see if he can expedite the rest of the clearances," Max said. "It shouldn't take that long. Everything is in the computers."

Bill scowled. "They've had our permissions to do an integrated search for months. I wonder why they're having so much trouble with just us four northerners."

M AX'S INQUIRIES GOT RESULTS, but not the results he wanted. A week later, General Juarez was back, and Lucinda gathered everyone into the conference room.

Juarez stood while the others took seats, his legs wide apart and his hands folded behind his back. "Progress has been very slow. I am here to see what I can do to encourage you to work harder."

"We're trying to answer questions that men have been asking for hundreds of years," Lucinda said. "We're working as hard as we can."

"You have tools like nanite sensors and your neuro-interrogator that the researchers of the past didn't have. Isn't that true?"

"Of course it is," Emile said. "Those tools give us a chance, but they don't make it easy. It's going to take a while, probably years."

"Years you don't have," Juarez said. "If this group can't make this happen, then perhaps I should find other people that can." He looked at Emile. "Doctor Hernandez, I notice that your voice doesn't sound as robotic now. Have you used my resources for something other than my project?"

Lucinda jumped to her feet. "Your project, General?" She stopped and glared while she tried to regain control. Then she shook her head and sat down again. "We didn't ask for your money," she said. "This is our project; you can provide guidance, but you don't own us."

"General, I can attest to their dedication," Isabella said. "The neuroscientists are very busy trying to isolate some measure of consciousness. Even if they succeed, we have years of work ahead of us."

"That was not my understanding," Juarez replied. There was a hard edge in his voice, and he glared at Isabella until she looked away.

"Then your understanding is very limited," Emile said, anger evident in his neuro-interrogator output. Lucinda glanced at Alyssa, who gave a slight shrug.

"The people that create our devices don't have a lot to do until the neuroscientists can give them something," Lucinda said. "So, yes, they continue to work on the neuro-interrogator project. That's what the Munts are giving us money for. Progress there also helps us communicate with my husband, and that can only help both projects."

"If you don't have work for some of your people, perhaps we should get rid of them," Juarez said. "I've been told that some of them are loafers. When we need their skills again, we can find others to do the work."

"That is not your decision to make," Emile said. "We accepted Isabella and have been very happy with her work, although she is one of the people not currently on critical tasks. We will not accept your dismissal of other team members who have been valuable contributors and will be in the future."

Juarez wasn't listening. "Mr. Bascomb, you for example." He marched over to Eddie's side of the table. "You often come in late and leave early. What are you contributing to this effort?"

Eddie's face turned dark. He stood and moved forward until he was face-to-face and very close to Juarez. "Not a hell of a lot," he said. "And I won't be doing much until you get me a security clearance so that I can see the documents I need."

"I assume Isabella had told you everything about her encounter with the *Asimov* computer." Juarez didn't budge.

"She did, but she didn't do much more than talk to Isaac. I'm referring to Susan Malley's reports, which should contain the results of her investigations. We need detailed data on the library ship hardware and software, too. Someday, when my colleagues have figured out how to measure consciousness in the human brain, I'm going to have to design hardware to contain that consciousness." He paused and shook his head.

"Eddie was working as hard as any of us when he had real work to do," Bill said. "It would be a disastrous mistake to fire anyone on this team."

Juarez looked down at Bill. "William Bensonhurst."

"That's right. And while we're on the subject, my clearance hasn't come through yet, either."

Juarez stared at him, and Lucinda saw someone looking at a pinned insect struggling to get free. The only team members still without security clearances were people with northern roots. Was that likely to be a coincidence?

"Just get us what we need, General," Lucinda said. "If you have any doubts about us, you can take your Methuselah Project elsewhere, and we'll go back to improving the neuro-interrogators."

"Attempts to intimidate us won't help you," Max said. "You need us more than we need you."

"We'll see." Juarez strode out of the room and was gone.

"Sudden exits seem to be his thing," Bill observed.

A WEEK LATER, EDDIE, Joelle, Alyssa, and Bill received their security clearances. They expected another visit from General Juarez, but received only a terse message about anticipating "real progress." Isabella and Eddie began studying the *Asimov* data together, and Joelle often joined them when they were examining the software that ran the library ships.

"It will take us years to understand this," Eddie said after his first look. "Even with the neurotrainer sessions you have."

"We only have to figure out which components or systems support the computer's consciousness and then work on those," Isabella said. "The neurotrainer recordings will give you the basics, and we can use the more advanced recordings for promising systems. We don't have to understand everything."

"That sounds a lot like what the neuroscientists are trying to do with the human brain." Eddie looked at his workstation monitor. "Hundreds of systems, thousands of components, millions of lines of code. What is a Gödel system, anyway? You seem to have been concentrating on it."

Isabella grinned. "You know about Gödel's incompleteness theorem? That in any mathematical system of logic, there are always questions that are undecidable?"

"Sure."

"Conventional computers operate through a system of logic; therefore, there are questions they can't answer positively. That's not usually a problem, of course."

"But it is for the library ships?"

"Possibly. The library ships are completely automated. They would be in interstellar space for years with no way to contact them. They would have to deal with issues that their designers could not predict and would have to come up with reasonable answers."

Eddie nodded. "And this Gödel system is a way of dealing with that?"

"Exactly. Humans deal with failures in logic by relying on several things: guessing, responses programmed into our brains such as 'fight or flight,' and working from premises that we consider obviously true without being able to prove them formally. To some extent, we can program conventional computers to do these things, but only to a limited extent. They can't create new premises from new experiences. The Gödel system is an attempt to do that. I've been studying it because I think it's a key reason *Asimov* has become conscious and other more powerful computers have not."

Joelle had been quiet, but now she joined the conversation. "So if we add one of these systems to a computer, it would become conscious?"

Isabella shook her head. "Maybe, but there must be more to it than that. *Capek* and *Lang*, the other two library ships, haven't become conscious." She paused and looked across the laboratory. "Alyssa wants to get familiar with the *Asimov* data, too. She doesn't feel very useful working on voice enhancement until we know more about identifying the signals caused by consciousness."

"And there are no differences among the three library ships?" Joelle asked.

"The only difference I've found is the length of their journeys," Isabella answered. "*Asimov* and *Capek* each took about sixteen years. *Lang* was only about five."

"So there are no differences that we know of between *Asimov* and *Capek*, yet *Capek* hasn't become conscious," Eddie said.

"Not as far as we know. I suppose it could be hiding it. *Asimov* did for at least two years."

"For that matter, *Lang* could be, too."

"I suppose."

"OK, it will take me a couple of weeks just to get through the basic neurotrainer stuff," Eddie said. "Joelle, you should do it, too. Since Alyssa wants to do it, we'll include her, too. We'll get off to a slow start, but it will be better in the long run."

"I agree," Isabella said. "You'll update Lucinda and Emile?"

"Sure. I think I need to get back on Lucinda's good side, anyway. She didn't like the way I stood up to Juarez the last time."

"You shouldn't do things like that," Joelle said. "He's a powerful man, used to getting his way."

Eddie smiled. "Don't worry, honey. He needs us and won't do anything. He's all bark, no bite."

T HREE MONTHS LATER, JUAREZ appeared again. Predictably, he wasn't happy with progress. "I've given you everything you asked for," he said at the status meeting Lucinda called. "I thought that by now we would have something to show for it." He was looking at Lucinda, making her feel uncomfortable.

"We've made progress," Max said. "High-resolution data on the frontal lobe has given us insight into how frontal lobe impulses affect the amygdala. The effect is subtle, but when we have it completely quantified, we should be a long way toward isolating the signals that represent consciousness."

"Less than impressive," Juarez replied. "What about your technicians? Bascomb and the programmers. . .." He gave Eddie a hard stare. Eddie opened his mouth to respond, but Joelle put a hand on his arm, and he didn't speak.

"Our engineers," Lucinda said, "were delayed by the slowness in getting clearances to study the *Asimov* data. You must know how complex that data is. They have been working on understanding the systems and how consciousness has emerged from them."

"We got the security clearances as quickly as possible."

"It's funny how only the northerners had a problem," Bill said. "Why was that, General?"

Juarez's face darkened, and his mouth hardened. "As a scientist, you probably don't understand how complicated this kind of thing can be, especially when we have to get data from remote areas. The rules about coordinating data between different computer systems. . ."

"Don't apply," Eddie snapped. "We all signed permission papers waiving our rights to protection of our data. You don't need warrants, and there shouldn't be any problem."

"I'm surprised you don't understand the difficulties better, Bascomb," Juarez said. "It isn't just a question of getting access to different systems. Compatibility can be an issue, as well as distance."

Eddie wasn't swallowing Juarez's excuse. "We're not from the Eastern Bloc. It shouldn't have taken that much longer for us."

"I don't have to explain myself to you." Juarez clipped his words and put a nasty emphasis on the final "you." He turned away from Eddie. "How can we make better progress on isolating conscious brain activity?"

His look didn't identify anyone in particular, and Emile took the question when everyone else remained silent. "We're operating at the limits of the equipment. Comparisons with the chimpanzee have helped, but it takes time to analyze the data. We've thought about asking for more neuroscientists but decided we would spend too much time stumbling over each other. If there is equipment that can better isolate the source of a brain impulse, we would like to have it, but, to our knowledge, we already have the best."

"What else?"

"Nothing else, really," Emile replied. "We could try shutting down sections of the brain and seeing what difference it made. Much of the early advances in neuroscience came from studying people with brain damage from accident or disease, but such subjects are hard to come by. We've tried doing something like that with Kong, but we don't want to hurt him, and we can't do that to humans. That limits us."

Juarez looked thoughtful, and Lucinda almost expected him to suggest making a few prisoners available for experimentation. Of course, if the public learned that General Juarez was even thinking about such an action, it would destroy his career and probably President Castillo's.

J UAREZ THOUGHT ABOUT REPORTING to Brasília, but he could do that later. The woman programmer from Hernandez Neuroscience would arrive shortly, and he didn't want to be in the middle of a sensitive conversation when she got to his hotel room.

She hadn't told him why she wanted to meet with him. She had caught up with him near the elevator when no one else was there and asked where he was staying. He assumed she was making a clumsy attempt to gain favor with him and, by extension, the government. He gave her his hotel and room number and told her to be there at 8 p.m.

She was a northerner, but she was attractive enough. If she thinks sex would help her advance, I don't see any reason to dissuade her. Not immediately, anyway.

"Your visitor has arrived," the door announced.

"Let her in."

The door opened, and she walked in slowly, eyes darting around the room. She was still wearing the same prim clothes she had worn in the laboratory. Juarez had hoped for something sexier. Still, it hardly mattered after the first few minutes.

"Come in, my dear," he urged.

"Thank you for seeing me, General." She stepped closer. "I wanted to tell you about an idea I have. I think you will appreciate it."

Idea? What is she talking about? She's just a northerner computer programmer. Does she think she might have a worthwhile suggestion to offer him? She was there now, and he took her hand. It wouldn't hurt to hear what she had to say. After that, she might perform a more useful service. He pulled her to a couch and gestured that she should sit. She smiled, still jumpy, and took a seat at one end of the couch. When he sat down next to her, she leaned forward and folded her hands in her lap.

She really was a timid little thing. It might be a good idea to treat her with more gentleness than he preferred. "So, what was your idea?"

"Emile mentioned studying the brain by shutting off parts of it." Her voice shook. "We can't do that to people, of course, but we could do it to computers."

That was unexpected. Could she actually have a useful thought? "How do you mean?"

"We want to know how the *Asimov* computer became conscious. Or how it maintains its consciousness. As in a real brain, there are certain systems we think might be involved. If we disconnected those systems, it might tell us what is important in making it conscious. Reconnecting the system again could also supply useful data; what happens when it 'wakes up?'"

Could we do that? The Asimov was twelve light years away, but there were scientists on board. Could one of them perform the experiments this girl was suggesting? He would have to consider the question. It might be better to be more secretive about the tests. After all, people tended to anthropomorphize about their animals; how would they feel about a conscious computer?

Juarez put his arm lightly over her shoulders. "That is an interesting idea. How would we implement such a thing?"

She leaned even further until her chest was almost resting on her arms. "I could write a program that would automate the tests. Someone would have to install the program on the computer, but then it could go through the target systems one at a time and collect data. I'm not sure exactly what the procedures are for sending data to Earth, but I think it would be possible for my program to add its data to a transmission through the Link, probably with no one noticing."

"Why didn't you say something about this in your laboratory?"

"I want to show you I'm a loyal citizen." That didn't directly answer his question, but she put emphasis on the word "I'm" that left little to answer. Hernandez was a known dissident, and some of his people seemed to be as well. The girl was a northerner and wanted to improve her position any way she could.

"How long would it take to write your program?"

"I would have to know more about communications procedures with the Link to make it all work automatically. Once I have that information, perhaps a month or two. I would have to work on it in my free time."

The government classified Link protocols even higher than the library ship specifications. The Western Alliance certainly didn't want the Eastern Bloc to find a way to exploit the Link. Still, he could control the situation.

"You could work on it full time if you leave Hernandez Neuroscience and work in a government laboratory," he told her. It was interesting to watch her pretty face as conflicting emotions crossed it. There was still the nervousness, of course, but he saw something else, hope perhaps. "Of course, there would be a substantial increase in your compensation."

"When would I start?"

"You would have to give notice at Munt. We wouldn't want them getting suspicious. You could use the time to gather any information that might prove useful in your new position."

"They won't want me to leave."

Juarez shrugged. She either had an inflated idea of her importance there, or she was an optimist. Not that it mattered. "The Western Alliance is a free society," he said. "They can't stop you."

A jerk of her head showed her agreement. "I'll give them two weeks' notice."

"That will be fine. I'll contact you at home as soon as I know where you'll be working."

She straightened and looked at him, startled. "It won't be in Colón?"

"I don't think so. Is that a problem?"

"No, I guess not. I'll wait for your call." She tried to get up, but Juarez tightened his grip on her shoulders.

"You don't have to leave right away, do you?" he said smoothly.

From the wide-eyed stare she gave him, he thought she was going to panic. She broke loose from his arm and jumped up. "I really. . . have to. . . get home."

Damn. Juarez lost any interest in the girl. Nervousness like hers never made for good sex. He preferred his women willing and eager. "Of course." He led her to the door. "I will be in touch." He shut the door behind her.

22

"ALYSSA CLEVELAND WOULD LIKE to talk to you," Jasmine's receptionist said.

"Let her in." Jasmine frowned. She tried to keep herself available to all her employees, but she couldn't think of any reason for Alyssa to want to see her. Until she had reassigned Alyssa to the Methuselah Project, Alyssa had been just one of hundreds of employees in the building, and Jasmine had rarely talked to her.

Alyssa entered, looking nervous, and Jasmine motioned her to a chair. "Good morning, Alyssa. What did you want to see me about?" Jasmine asked.

"I thought I should talk to you first since technically I still work for Munt Electronics."

"Not just technically. You do work for us. Hernandez Neuroscience is a division of Munt."

Alyssa folded her hands in front of her and looked down. Raising her head again to look at Jasmine seemed to take an effort. "I'm giving notice. I've been offered another job and will start there in two weeks."

That was a surprise. Jasmine had read Alyssa's employment file when she picked Alyssa for the transfer to Hernandez Neuroscience. Alyssa had worked for them for over three years and had been a dependable software engineer with a knack for ferreting out elusive coding flaws. There had been no sign that Alyssa was unhappy at Munt.

"Is there a problem with your new assignment?" Jasmine asked. "If so, we can do something about it."

"No, it's not that. There's a big pay increase and a change in location. I like to see new places, and this would be a wonderful opportunity."

"You said you would leave in two weeks, I believe? Are you all right with working at Hernandez Neuroscience for that time?"

"Oh, yes. That would be fine. I was a little afraid that you wouldn't want me around anymore, though." Alyssa smiled tentatively.

"That should be up to Max." Jasmine gave her an encouraging smile. "I think it will be OK, though. Where will you be going?"

Alyssa bit her lip. "I would rather not say if you don't mind."

"I understand." Jasmine stood and extended her hand. "Good luck, Alyssa. We'll miss you, but you have to think of your career."

"I DON'T WANT A fuss," Alyssa told Max. "Can we not tell the rest of the team until I'm gone?"

"Lucinda should know," Max replied. "I imagine she'll want you to help one of the other programmers to get familiar with your code, too."

"It should be Parker. If Joelle knew, she would tell Eddie, and soon everyone would know."

"That makes sense. Joelle already has more on her plate than Parker." He shrugged. "Lucinda will decide, but my guess is that she'd have Parker take over your work, anyway."

ALYSSA'S ANNOUNCEMENT SURPRISED LUCINDA, but she had an idea about why Alyssa was leaving. "She was attracted to Eddie when she started here," Lucinda said to Max. "Joelle had already captured his attention, though. She may be having trouble accepting that and has decided to run away from it."

"That's too bad," Max said.

"She'll get over it. And she's good. She may have a better-paying job lined up, just as she said."

TWO WEEKS AND A day later, Alyssa was gone. Parker officially took over responsibility for the voice enhancement module for the neuro-interrogator, which mostly meant waiting for the neuroscientists to figure out how to capture precise emotion signals.

Only Eddie showed any genuine sadness at her leaving. "I liked her," he said at the meeting where Lucinda announced her departure. "She was good to work with." Joelle gave him a dark look. "Well, she was. Smart, hard-working. . ." He paused. "Attractive, too."

Joelle punched him lightly on the arm, and he looked at her with mock sadness. "I'll miss her. What's wrong with that?"

"Keep digging that hole, Eddie. You've already talked yourself into owing me a nice dinner tonight."

Eddie grinned at her.

23

"GENERAL JUAREZ HAS PREPARED a status report on the Methuselah Project," President Alejandro Castillo told his assembled cabinet. He glared at Juarez. "One can only hope he has better news than he had in his last report."

"I do," Juarez replied. "The neuroscientists in Hernandez's team continue with their studies of consciousness. Progress there is slow, but they are right in saying that they are trying to do something that has eluded science for centuries. Still, improved equipment and procedures have made them confident that they will eventually solve the problem."

"That doesn't sound much different than your last report," Castillo said.

"I have more. I visit them occasionally to exert pressure, but I believe they are working as hard as they can. The prospect of helping their leader, Doctor Hernandez, motivates them adequately." Juarez looked down at a paper in front of him. "It could take years, however, so I have opened up an attack on another front. I lured one of Hernandez's programmers away and told her to develop an idea that might help us. She is writing a program to investigate consciousness on the library ship *Asimov* by toggling systems on and off and using the library ship instrumentation to gather data on the results."

"How does that help us?"

"The Methuselah Project is a two-pronged effort. Hernandez is trying to understand consciousness so that they can upload a person to a computer. That's the first part. We also must know how to design a computer that can hold a person's consciousness. Understanding how the library ship became conscious is vital to that."

"Yes, I see. Very good." Castillo smiled. "What will you do with the programmer?"

"Once she completes the program, I won't need her anymore. Of course, I can't just let her run back to Hernandez, and I might need her later to change her program, so I'll send her to Pearson Industries in San Diego, California District. She's a northerner anyway, so she'll adjust."

"How soon before you have results from this program?"

Juarez hesitated. "We have a problem there. We would have to install the program from the library ship. As you know, Pitcairn has restricted our access to *Asimov*, and we can't trust the scientists on board with the task. Scientists from Pitcairn control *Asimov*."

"It's been two years since we sent Selwick Pearson to Pitcairn to deal with the Pitcairners," Castillo said. "Is he making any progress?"

"Very little, I'm afraid. Pearson has built an estate and reached an agreement with the Pitcairn leadership, but they have proved to be cannier negotiators than we expected. As you know, the Pitcairners lead rather simple lives, and Pearson wanted more of the luxury he is accustomed to. The Pitcairners forced him to build his estate well away from any of their settlements. He still hopes to get influence with the Pitcairners. His last report said that he has become engaged to a Pitcairner as part of his efforts to be accepted by them."

"What about Reyes?"

"We're still negotiating with Reyes Pharmaceuticals. The goal is to get the secret of Pitcairn's antiviral drug, of course. Much of our inability to control Pitcairn stems from their holding that over our heads."

"And our scientists can't duplicate it on Earth."

"Not yet. It's manufactured from native Pitcairn plants, and their biology is substantially different from that of Earth plants. If we can establish a Reyes facility on Pitcairn, we might solve that problem."

"Can they help us get to the library ship?"

"Perhaps. We'll have to see what we can accomplish once Reyes Pharma is on Pitcairn."

Castillo frowned. *I'm not getting any younger.* Juarez's vision of an extended, perhaps unlimited, lifespan is appealing but progress is so slow. He was confident of Juarez's ability to manage a complex project, though.

"We look forward to more progress with your next report," Castillo said.

"W E'VE SUSPECTED FOR A while that the connection between consciousness and emotion in the amygdala is selective," Bill said. "It's not surprising, really. The frontal lobe sends impulses to the amygdala to control emotion. Like when Juarez shows up, and you get mad, but you don't punch him in the face."

"A wonderful example," Lucinda said with a wry grin.

Bill bowed. "Thank you. So relatively small impulses from the frontal lobe have relatively large effects on the emotion impulses from the amygdala. That's why it has been so hard to isolate them. It's also why Emile seems to overreact to everything. The neuro-interrogator loses the signals that would flatten his responses."

"Kong made the difference," Luke said. "There is very little control over the emotions originating in his comparatively primitive frontal lobe. Perhaps none at all. We've had some success characterizing pure emotional signals by testing him."

"Does that help to understand human emotion?" Joelle asked.

"Quite a bit," Luke answered. The neuroscientist leaned forward. "As with our DNA, chimpanzee emotions are not that much different from human emotions. Humans are more complex, of course, but tests on Kong have allowed us to establish a baseline."

"Eddie is adjusting the hardware, and I should be able to update the software in a week or so," Parker said.

"How does this help with Methuselah?" Max asked.

"It probably doesn't directly," Bill said. "We can forget about using amygdala impulses as a simpler way to characterize consciousness. We'll focus on the temporal lobe instead. It breaks any connection between the neuro-interrogator project and the Methuselah Project."

"I wouldn't worry about that," Parker said. "If these changes work as well as I think they will, we can declare success and close the neuro-interrogator project. Munt Electronics will have the product they wanted."

Max frowned. That would mean that Munt Electronics would have no more reason to support them. Financing from the government paid for the Methuselah work, but Munt still supplied the facility and support. That was a discussion for later, though, when only Lucinda and Emile were present.

A FTER THE MEETING, BILL joined Eddie and Joelle. "I'm feeling like celebrating," he said. "We've been trying to get this neuro-interrogator working for a long time."

Eddie grinned. "I suppose you want to suggest another hike."

"Well, the rainy season hasn't begun yet. Why not?"

Eddie looked at Joelle, who nodded. "Sure, why not?" he said. "Let's go all out. What was that mountain you wanted to climb a couple of years ago?"

"Cerro Jefe? Seriously?"

"Joelle and I have been walking whenever we could. I think we're up for it."

"That's great! Maybe we could invite Parker and Isabella, too."

Eddie nodded. "Sure. What about the others?"

"I'll ask Luke and Aiden, but I doubt they'll accept," Bill said. "I'll bring it up at our next meeting. If Parker is right, the neuro-interrogator project will be officially closed before the rains start."

As Bill had expected, Luke and Aiden demurred. Isabella turned them down, too. Parker, however, was more interested.

"It sounds like it might be fun," Parker said. "I haven't used my hiking boots in a while, but they'll still fit me."

Aiden snorted. "Why would you want to trudge through the mud with them? We can do something in town to celebrate."

"Chagres National Park is beautiful," Joelle said. "We can do things in town any time."

"You are welcome to come with us," Aiden said.

Bill glanced at Eddie. Aiden had stressed "you," excluding the rest of them. Joelle was young and attractive, which made up for the fact that Joelle, like Eddie and he, was of northern origin. The scowl on Eddie's face told him that Eddie had understood the implications behind Aiden's words, too.

"In your dreams," Joelle retorted.

Eddie's scowl became a chuckle, and Aiden reddened. "Stick with us, Parker," Aiden said. "You don't want to hang out with them."

Parker looked uncertain, and Bill knew he should say something. Aiden's attitude had upset him, too, though, and he stayed silent.

"It has been a while," Parker finally said. He looked at Bill. "I wouldn't want to slow you down."

"Sure, Parker." Bill turned his back to Parker. "I guess it's the three of us."

"Probably for the best," Eddie said. "Let's find a quiet corner and make some plans."

Cerro Jefe was over three thousand feet high in the middle of a rugged mountain range. The hike to the top was more than Eddie and Joelle had ever done, and more than Bill had done in years. The Adirondacks were gentle in comparison. When they reached the top, they were ready to rest. It was around midday, and they had brought sandwiches, so they sat and ate while they enjoyed the view.

The panorama was worth the climb. The rainforest stretched below them, still bright green despite the dry season of the previous months. In the distance, the towers of Colón and Cristóbal were hazy rectangles, almost lost against the blue-white horizon. Majestic mountains surrounded them, and tropical birds called to each other between the peaks.

Bill sat a little apart from Eddie and Joelle. They didn't seem to notice. Eddie's interest in Joelle had been obvious when she had first come to work with them two years before. It was harder to pin down when Joelle began to return Eddie's interest. They were relatively discreet, especially in the lab, but Bill was sure that the relationship was serious. Both were in their late twenties, with good jobs, but he had heard no mention of marriage.

Eddie could be socially awkward, but he had grown comfortable around Joelle. Comfortable enough to be happy with things as they were, or not comfortable enough to propose? Bill had helped a little in getting them together, but it wasn't his place to push matters any further. He shrugged and turned his attention back to the landscape laid out before him.

24

"I HAVE A BAD feeling about this," Emile said. His speech was almost normal now, voiced by the latest software update to Eddie's neuro-interrogator enhancement device. In the year since its completion, it had become a moderate success, marketed as the Voice Magician, an accessory to the neuro-interrogator.

Franco had scheduled a meeting with Max and Lucinda on the first floor. General Juarez would be there too, and that was unusual. They could count on a visit every few months, but he always came up to their floor.

Lucinda patted Emile's shoulder until she remembered he couldn't feel it. "What's the worst that could happen?" she said. "He cancels the project because we have made little progress in the last year. We can always get other jobs."

"I can only hear their voices—not even that, really—but I would miss most of these people," Emile answered. "And I'm not sure just how employable I would be."

"Cerro Punta University would take you back as a lecturer. You'd be a big draw. PNC might take Max and me back, with a little sales talk. Some of the rest of us, too, I think."

Emile didn't respond. *Neither of us are saying what we're really thinking.* The Methuselah Project had become their hope for a better life. He sometimes fantasized about being uploaded into an android body indistinguishable from his actual body, except that it would be whole. It was only a fantasy; the android body was no problem, but creating an artificial brain for that body was out of the question for the near future, if not forever. Still, there had to be something better.

There were areas where something could be done. The neuro-interrogator progress implied other potential areas of research. Prosthetics were available with connections to motor signals that allowed some movement in many cases not involving brain injury. Existing technology didn't work for him, but improvements were always possible. If Juarez was backing out, maybe Hernandez Neuroscience might survive to research those areas.

"You're babbling again," Lucinda said.

That had happened before, when his thoughts, not intended for vocalization, confused the neuro-interrogator. It tried to deal with the input, but the result was, as Lucinda said, a babble with missing or incomplete words. *I need to keep better control of myself when the neuro-interrogator is connected.*

"Go to the meeting," Emile said. "Find out what's going on."

THE FIRST FLOOR HAD a conference room even better appointed than the comfortable room on the sixteenth floor. Jasmine, Franco, and General Juarez were already there when Max and Lucinda arrived. There was another man, too, that Lucinda didn't recognize, although he looked familiar.

She looked at each face in turn as she took her seat. This would not be good news. Jasmine and Franco seemed sad and perhaps guilty. General Juarez bore his usual stern visage, with overtones of triumph. That was how it appeared to Lucinda, and she wasn't sure how to interpret it. Juarez didn't look like a man who was about to cancel the Methuselah Project, but the Munts' expressions contradicted that.

"The government has been patient," Juarez said. So much for the niceties of conversation. "Your progress has been slow, too slow, and a change is necessary. I will be brief." He turned to look at Jasmine. "I have negotiated an agreement with Munt Technologies to sell their neuroscience division to Pearson Interstellar." Of course. The man she hadn't recognized was David Pearson, the CEO of Pearson Industries. Pearson Interstellar was a subsidiary, contracted to support the star colonies.

"Project Methuselah will move to Pearson Headquarters in San Diego," Juarez continued. "The government believes it can be supported more efficiently there." David Pearson nodded.

Inwardly, Lucinda cringed. Rumors suggested that Pearson Industries and Pearson Interstellar, in particular, were little more than puppets of the government. Juarez's statement implied more control from the government, and more control never meant more efficiency. It was an effort, but she kept her voice level as she pointedly turned away from Juarez and toward Jasmine and Franco.

"They're only interested in our results on consciousness," Lucinda said. "With that taken away from us, Hernandez Neuroscience could focus on further improvements on the technology we've developed for the neuro-interrogator."

"I'm sorry," Jasmine said, but Pearson talked over her.

"All your technology is being transferred to us. There is no more Hernandez Neuroscience."

"T HE MUNTS WERE APOLOGETIC," Max said to everyone. "We have to see it from their point of view. They took us in to develop a product, and we did that. This isn't the business they focus on, though, and we've been little more than an expense for them for the last year. I don't know exactly how much we were sold for, but I gather it was generous."

"So, what happens to us?" Aiden asked.

"That's up to you. For now, at least, you all have a position in Pearson Interstellar. You must move to San Diego, of course, but Pearson will pay all expenses. Alternatively, you can find other employment. If you accept Juarez's offer, you will have to sign a non-disclosure and a contract to work for Pearson for at least five years."

"Forget it," Aiden said. "I'm not moving north, certainly not for five years."

"We have the next week to decide," Max said. "Your salaries would be the same at Pearson as they are here. There will probably be some differences in benefits, and you can get the details from your workstations."

Eddie turned to Lucinda. "What are you and Emile going to do?"

"We haven't committed yet," Emile answered. The Voice Magician transmitted his sadness all too well. "I think Lucinda and I will probably move, but we have to discuss it further."

"What's San Diego like?" Parker asked.

Eddie had grown up in Los Angeles, so he fielded the question. "It's a nice place. Dryer than Colón, and on the Pacific Ocean, not the Atlantic. Mission Bay is very popular. There are mountains, but not as many trees. It was pretty much outside the area devastated by the Yellowstone Event, not like Chicago or St. Louis."

"And mostly northerners," Aiden said.

Eddie stared at him for a long moment before replying. "It was part of the old United States, of course, but it's only a few miles north of the old border with Mexico. Even before Yellowstone, most of the population had migrated from the south." Aiden only grunted.

"We'll all be available if you have questions," Lucinda said. "Jasmine and Franco, too." She grimaced. "For the rest of the day, General Juarez has set up in an office on the second floor. You can talk to him, too—if you want."

There were a few chuckles at that, but most seemed too somber to laugh. Max wasn't one of the chucklers. Juarez planned to name someone else to run the Methuselah Project at Pearson. He had offered Max a position as head neuroscientist, but that position rightfully belonged to Lucinda or Emile. There probably wouldn't be much chance of advancement, either, and he would be trapped there for five years.

He was only forty-three years old, still a young man. It wasn't that it would be difficult to find another job. Project Methuselah was classified, so he would have to be circumspect about his experience with that, but they had done plenty of public work over the years. He wasn't worried. Since neuroscience research had become more accepted, the demand for neuroscientists had increased.

He looked around the table. Another week, and he might have to say goodbye to these people. He would miss most of them greatly. Or he could accept demotion and go with them. That assumed that most of them would go to San Diego, though. Aiden had already said he wouldn't. He sighed. He could delay his decision until he knew what the others were going to do.

J OELLE CONFRONTED EDDIE OUTSIDE the conference room. "So, what are you going to do?"

Suddenly Eddie couldn't speak. What could he say? What were they going to do? He didn't want to go anywhere without Joelle. He stared at her. She stared back, a look that demanded an answer.

"The idea of going back to southern California has its appeal," he stammered. "What about you?"

"I wouldn't mind moving back."

"A lot depends on what the others decide to do. I won't go if everyone else stays here."

Bill, entering the hall with Max, must have overheard at least Eddie's last words. He stepped up to them. "If Lucinda and Emile go, I'll go, too. Even if they don't, I might go. I've heard San Diego is nice."

"Yes," Eddie said. That single word was all he could manage.

"The cost of living will be higher there, though. Our salaries will be the same, Max said."

Joelle glanced at Bill and nodded. Then she turned back to Eddie.

"We could save money by sharing a place," she said.

Eddie gasped. "Move in together?" Joelle tilted her head and looked at him, eyebrows raised. "That. . .that would be a big step."

Joelle smiled. "Bigger than you think. Before we could do that, we would have to take care of one detail."

He stared at her, slow to realize what she was saying. When understanding came, panic closed his throat, and for a few seconds, he couldn't breathe. "I've got to go home," he said, his words so quick they almost ran into each other. "I'll be back." He rushed out of the lab before Joelle could respond.

J OELLE WAS CONFUSED AND hurt. She looked at Bill. "What just happened?" she asked. "Oh, God, Bill. Did I push him too hard?"

Bill put a hand on her shoulder. "Wait for it." He grinned.

B ILL SAT AT HIS desk, watching Joelle. He thought about telling her, but Eddie would be back soon, and he didn't want to spoil Eddie's moment. He'd been planning this for six months, and Bill assumed Joelle had finally given him the nerve to act.

A few minutes later, Eddie burst into the laboratory, out of breath, and looking a little desperate. He stopped and looked around until he spotted Joelle standing next to Kong and Tori, watching the trainer talk to the chimp. He rushed over and kneeled before her with an open jewelry box in his hand.

"Joelle Henry, will you marry me?"

Joelle squealed out a yes and thrust her finger into the ring. Then she pulled Eddie to his feet and threw her arms around him.

"Kong like," the chimpanzee said.

25

THREE DAYS LATER, LUCINDA and Emile announced they would go to San Diego. Eddie, Joelle, Bill, and Isabella at once said that they would also go. Aiden repeated his refusal to move north. Tori was married with a child and couldn't uproot her family. Kong would go north, so Tori agreed to make the trip with the ape and stay for a few days until they could find another trainer. The next day, Luke joined them, but Parker stayed in Colón, taking another programming position at Munt. Max also decided not to go to San Diego.

When Lucinda told Jasmine of Eddie's and Joelle's plans, Jasmine took over. Two days later, Eddie and Joelle were married in the Colón cathedral. That alone took a great deal of influence and money to carry out, but Jasmine also arranged for the couple's parents to attend and organized a reception in the lobby of the Munt Electronics building. Everyone from Hernandez Neuroscience, and quite a few people from the rest of Munt Electronics, attended. The only damper on the joyous occasion was saying goodbye to Max, who was flying to Caracas the next day to interview for a new position.

For the honeymoon, Jasmine got help from Bill. Together, they arranged a two-week stay in a resort in the Adirondacks. On the same day that Eddie and Joelle left for New York, the others took a suborbital to San Diego.

THE SUBORBITAL TRANSPORT FACILITY was on North Island, across a narrow strip of San Diego Bay from the old San Diego airport. The latter served local traffic while larger, long-range aircraft used one end of North Island, an area that, three hundred years earlier, had been a naval air station.

Bill's first impression, viewed from five thousand feet above the area, was not favorable. San Diego was an urban sprawl running from Los Angeles on the north to Tijuana on the south. The Pacific Ocean bordered the city to the west, but at least there were mountains to the east that held some promise. They weren't very green compared to the rainforest around Colón or the northern forests of the Adirondacks, but this was summer. There was a reason California had once been known as the Golden State, and it wasn't entirely because of the 1848 gold rush. Water extracted from the ocean, desalinized, and piped inland using cheap broadcast power had turned the farming regions of California green, but there was no reason to irrigate the mountains.

After they landed, two air taxis took five of them to the Coronado Hotel on Mission Bay. One of the larger air taxis would have sufficed for everyone, but Emile in his bed needed special handling, so he and Lucinda used one, and Bill, Isabella, and Luke took the other. A Pearson ground truck took Tori and Kong directly to the laboratory. At the hotel, they rested, planning to report to Pearson Interstellar in the morning.

L UCINDA STARED AT THE building in front of her. After the luxurious Munt Electronics building, Pearson Interstellar was a disappointment. Located off Harbor Drive near a decrepit Coronado Bridge, the plastic, prefabricated, two-story building was probably already past its forty-year life expectancy. In that, it was typical of the neighborhood, once part of a busy port complex and now an industrial district of small manufacturing businesses. Only the sign above the main entrance looked reasonably new.

A man came up to them as they exited the ground car and greeted them. "I'm Reynaldo Clementi." He took Lucinda's hand. "You are Lucinda Hernandez, I assume." He looked down at Emile on his bed and extended his hand. He must have realized the futility in that, because he pulled it back quickly. "And Doctor Hernandez."

"Good morning," Emile said.

"Ah, yes, good morning, Doctor." Clementi was obviously taken aback, talking to someone who didn't move at all, but he pulled himself together and turned back to Lucinda.

"This building is the headquarters of Pearson Interstellar. Mostly we manage shipments to the colonies and maintenance of our starship, the Francisco Pearson. We'll be processing you in here, but we don't have room for you in this building. We've leased and equipped another building a few blocks away for your use." He showed them into the building, talking as they walked.

There was no lobby. A short hallway led to a large room filled with cubicles, each occupied by someone working at a computer workstation.

"If I may ask, how do you fit into this organization?" Lucinda asked.

Clementi laughed, but it seemed to Lucinda to be embarrassment rather than amusement. His next words confirmed her impression.

"I assumed you were told. I'm the new department head for the Methuselah Project, taking over from Maxwell Estevez." He looked at them all. "Aren't we missing a couple of people?"

"The Bascombs are on their honeymoon," Lucinda answered. "They were married just before we left." She smiled. "I guess they didn't tell you everything, either. They'll be here in two weeks."

"Oh. That's unexpected. Contrary to procedures, too. Well, we'll have to live with it this time."

"We'll have to," Bill muttered under his breath. Lucinda forced a smile.

T HE REST OF THE day went smoothly except for the absence of Eddie and Joelle. Reynaldo hadn't made a good first impression, but he managed their initiation efficiently, despite the unusual amount of paperwork involved. After they read and signed too many documents to count, there was a brief orientation recording to watch. The material was more about Pearson Industries than Pearson Interstellar, reflecting the newness of the Interstellar division.

"We'll have to stop here," Reynaldo finally said. "I have work to do, reconciling the two no-shows. That would be Edward Bascomb and Joelle Henry?"

"Yes," Lucinda replied.

"Except it's Joelle Bascomb now," Bill added.

"Yes, of course." Reynaldo frowned. "I'll take care of it. For now, cars will take you back to your hotel. I'm sorry it has to be ground transportation, but we don't have landing pads on the roofs around here." He paused. "You might want to use the free time to get familiar with our city. There are many attractions."

"Thank you," Lucinda said. "When will we move to our permanent home?"

"I know you lived at your facility in Colón, but that wouldn't work well here. We have rented a comfortable place for you and Emile, and a ground car will be available for your transportation. The same one that took you here, actually. The others must find accommodations, but Pearson Interstellar will pay for their hotel for a reasonable time so that they can do that."

She and Emile had lived and worked in the same place in Colón, and she didn't look forward to adjusting to a more conventional arrangement. "Fine. I will see you tomorrow, then."

"Yes. I'll see you then."

"T HIS MAY HAVE BEEN a mistake," Lucinda said as the ground car took them back to the hotel.

"Why?" Emile asked.

"Pearson Interstellar was not very impressive. You couldn't see it, of course, but it was a prefab in an old part of town. I've seen pictures of Pearson Industries headquarters downtown, and I was expecting something like that."

"According to Clementi, it's basically just a place where paperwork gets done."

Lucinda nodded. "True. And rumors are that it's all paid for by our tax dollars. Still, Reynaldo Clementi didn't impress me much either. I'm going to miss Max."

"Neurotrainer capabilities limited my impression. Reynaldo did seem to be more bureaucrat than scientist."

"If he's a scientist at all."

"We'll find out tomorrow. We'll make it work, darling."

Make what work? The goal was to turn her husband into a machine. If they succeeded, that was all she had to look forward to, and that was a big "if." General Juarez and his threats aside, it would be years before they could hope to do what he wanted them to do.

26

LUCINDA'S HEART SANK. IF anything, the one-story building was in worse shape than the Pearson Interstellar building. They were only a few blocks apart, probably built around the same time, but this building had gone longer without a paint job and didn't even have a new sign over the front. Instead, the words "Davis Machining" were printed in faded letters across the top of the front wall. She would have thought they were in the wrong place, except that Reynaldo was waiting for them outside.

"General Juarez is here," Reynaldo said as Lucinda got out of the car. Behind her, the car lowered a ramp so that Emile's bed could roll out.

"How nice of him to welcome us," Lucinda replied.

Reynaldo turned pale at the sarcasm. *Does Juarez intimidate him that much?*

"I suggest you be more cautious when you speak to him."

Another ground car stopped next to them, and the rest of the team emerged. "We're all here," Lucinda said. "Let's go and greet the general."

Inside was a small reception area. They passed the empty desk and entered a hallway with a double door at the far end. General Juarez waited in an office just off the hallway. It didn't take long to find out why Reynaldo was frightened. General Juarez was furious, and he had no compunctions about showing it.

"Bascomb and Henry had no right to go running off for two weeks. This is unacceptable."

"They went on their honeymoon," Lucinda responded. "They won't be gone long."

Juarez gave her a nasty smile. "On the contrary, they'll be gone for a very long time. They're both fired. They had no permission to take a vacation."

"Of course they did. They were still working for Munt. Not only did the Munts give permission, but they also paid for the honeymoon."

"As of yesterday, they were supposed to be working for Pearson. They have violated the contract they signed and are being dismissed for cause. I already have an adequate replacement for Henry and will have a replacement for Bascomb shortly. I believe you know Henry's replacement since she used to work for you. Alyssa Cleveland."

So that was Alyssa's better opportunity. Lucinda wondered if Parker had known, working closely with her for her last two weeks at Munt Electronics. If Lucinda had to replace Joelle, Alyssa would be her first choice.

"We work for Pearson Interstellar, not you," Emile said. "I intend to fight this."

Juarez smirked while Reynaldo answered. "Pearson management has acceded to General Juarez's request. Fighting their dismissal would be futile."

He was probably right. Juarez had wanted to get rid of Eddie from the start. This was only an excuse. Lucinda looked at Emile. What had they gotten themselves into? First Max, now Eddie and Joelle.

"Let me show you your new home," Juarez said. "This is Reynaldo's office, and I'm sure he would like to reclaim it."

Lucinda followed him, numb, through a bare hallway leading to double doors. She would have been pleasantly surprised if she could have felt anything but hopelessness. The doors led to a large open area, twice the size of their laboratory at Munt Electronics. Everything was freshly painted and well-lit by skylights and artificial lighting. Wide aisles separated shiny new equipment. In one corner, Kong chattered in his cage, and Tori and Alyssa talked nearby. They came over when they saw the group enter.

"I have had the laboratory equipped to standards that meet or exceed what you had at Munt," Juarez said. "It's not set up yet; we had counted on Bascomb to do that as he did at Munt." Juarez seemed to have calmed a bit, and he spread his arms in apology. "I don't mean to be draconian. Because Bascomb is not here, the entire operation is on hold. You would be essentially spinning your wheels for two weeks."

Everything had happened so fast. They hadn't had time to think things through. Juarez had a point, although Lucinda still thought he was overreacting. There was work they could do while they waited, and a couple of weeks didn't matter that much when they had years of work ahead of them. It was too late to make that argument with Juarez, though.

"Hello, Lucinda," Alyssa said. She nodded to everyone else.

Alyssa seemed a little nervous, as if she were afraid of how they would receive her. They had parted on good terms, sorry to lose her, but happy that she was moving up. Lucinda smiled and pulled Alyssa into a hug. "So good to see you. And we'll be working together again."

Alyssa smiled back, and Lucinda was sure she saw relief. "Yes, I'm looking forward to it," Alyssa said.

E MILE COULDN'T SEE, BUT he could listen, and Eddie had included the ability to pick up network news broadcasts in Emile's bed. That had been frustrating to use at first because Emile had to settle for whatever the default story was at any given time. Eddie added a feature to give network commands in early versions of the Voice Magician, and Emile's access to the news got much better.

He still tried to find Anna Cortez on the network, hoping that she had returned, but she had disappeared from *Jornal de Brasília* and every other news outlet. Castillo had taken his revenge.

Shortly before they left Colón, he discovered something almost as good, though. After listening to constant stories criticizing the ungratefulness of the Pitcairn colonists, he discovered the colonists were fighting back. The Pitcairn News Service, broadcasting through the Link, presented stories distinctly different than the official government versions passed on by other news organizations. To his surprise, PNS had been on the network for four years, apparently given dirty secret status by those that controlled network programming.

Pitcairn, the colony planet in the Tau Ceti star system, was the most Earth-like of the star colonies. Earth portrayed it as a paradise where a few lucky colonists lived easy lives with robots doing most of the work. He asked Isabella about it, but she had only been on the library ship, not on the planet. Emile had asked because PNS gave a somewhat different description.

Major news outlets didn't mention that the colonists labored under a gravity twenty-five percent greater than Earth's or that the weather was severe, with frequent high winds and heavy rains. The Pitcairners had robots, but they only helped to perform all the work needed to make a primitive planet livable. Rather than living off Earth's charity, the colonists worked hard to reduce their dependence on Earth, digging iron and copper mines so that Earth wouldn't have to supply those metals. In return for other supplies, the Pitcairners sent Cetivir, an antiviral drug made from native Pitcairn plants, and more effective than Earth-based medicines for many serious diseases.

At least, that was the colonists' version. He knew about Cetivir, and the physical characteristics of the planet were no secret, but he couldn't be sure about the rest. Given a choice between believing stories that probably came through the Castillo government and stories that came from the colony, he preferred the latter.

It was interesting, but hardly surprising, that Castillo was still trying to manipulate the news. Emile knew enough history to know that Castillo's use of the media was nothing new. More than one election had been won by the better image rather than the better candidate. The Western Alliance was no different.

27

LUCINDA GAVE REYNALDO CREDIT for one thing; he knew how to work the system to get what he needed. Aurora Alvarez reported for work the following Monday morning, replacing Eddie. She sat silently next to Lucinda's desk while Lucinda reviewed her qualifications. Aurora was forty-eight years old, with two degrees in electrical engineering and one in computer engineering. That gave her a career almost as long as Eddie Bascomb's entire life, and she hadn't wasted it. She had impressive accomplishments, although none of them were in interfacing to the brain.

Lucinda estimated it would take at least a month for Aurora to come up to speed on what Eddie had done. Then she brushed the thought aside. Juarez had wanted her there most urgently to set up the laboratory so that the neuroscientists could continue their investigations. Aurora would have plenty of time to study the hardware developed by her predecessor.

Work continued with the former smooth but slow progress. General Juarez stayed away, and everyone adjusted to the change in personnel. Two weeks later, Bill received a quick message from Eddie and Joelle that he read to the others:

Honeymoon was great; at least Joelle still wants to be married to me. The Adirondacks, what we've had time to see, are beautiful. Thanks, Bill. I'll tell you when we've found new jobs.

THE CONTRAST BETWEEN MOST network stories about Pitcairn and the Pitcairn News Service stories bothered Emile. Why was the government was apparently hostile to its colony? It occurred to him that it might have something to do with the library ship.

Asimov's main computer had somehow become self-aware. Isabella believed that, and, although he still had doubts, Emile had to consider the possibility. No other computer had ever done that, to his knowledge, although there had been unconfirmed rumors about *Capek*, the Epsilon Eridani library ship. Much of the Methuselah Project depended on the data from Asimov. Could there be a connection? It seemed likely.

He began spending more time listening to Pitcairn reports. There were occasional references to Western Alliance citizens held by the Pitcairn government, but the details were vague. One of the citizens, though, was Selwick Pearson, the son of Pearson Industries CEO David Pearson. Another connection to Methuselah. He searched for more information and found the first PNS announcement of the arrest six weeks before.

Pitcairn News Service Bulletin, 30 June 2343

The Pitcairn Office of the Administrator today confirmed the arrest of Terran citizens Selwick Pearson and Caiden Reyes on charges of kidnapping and false imprisonment. The two men are accused of kidnapping two children from Grissom and taking them to the Pearson estate on Pitcairn. Pitcairn authorities have not determined a motive for the crime.

The team, led by explorer and biologist Jack Applegate and former Western Alliance soldier Harry Richard, visited the Pearson estate under the pretext of an exploration trip, acting on information from *Asimov's* main computer. Not finding the boys on the Pearson estate, the rescue party moved to the nearby Reyes estate and recovered the boys there.

Pitcairn authorities are holding Pearson and Reyes in Grissom, awaiting trial on the charges. Pending the verdict, the two estates remain in the control of representatives of the companies of the accused. In a statement for PNS, Planetary Administrator Patrick Malley said that Pitcairn would probably take over the estates per the agreement the accused signed with the Pitcairn government, but that wouldn't happen until a verdict was handed down.

WHY WOULD PEARSON HAVE kidnapped two Pitcairner children? That made no sense to Emile, but somehow, it had to have something to do with the Methuselah Project. There were too many coincidences for it not to be.

Castillo was plotting something. Could it be as simple as a desire to live longer? Was he that vain? Whatever Castillo's motives, they were caught in the web he was weaving.

A LOUD ARGUMENT IN the laboratory drew Lucinda's attention away from the report on her desk. "Now what?" she muttered.

In the laboratory, everyone was standing in front of a network screen, shouting at each other. When Lucinda approached, they stopped and turned to look at her. Emile rolled over from the other side of the room; he must have had his neurotrainer on when the commotion started.

"Have you heard the news?" Aurora asked. "The Pitcairners have convicted Selwick Pearson of kidnapping two children."

"Why did he do it?" Lucinda asked.

Aurora gasped. "What? Kidnap the children? He didn't, of course. *Brasília Today* has already denounced the conviction. It's just another attempt by Pitcairn to extort more from us."

"It's been on the net for months," Isaiah Hunter, Kong's new trainer, said. "The greedy bastards!"

"Has anyone gotten Pitcairn's side of this?" Emile asked mildly. He would have heard the news report already.

"They're greedy," Isaiah repeated. "What other reason could they have for this atrocity?"

"That Pearson did kidnap them," Lucinda said. She stepped up to the screen. "Command. *Pitcairn News Service.* Most recent."

The screen changed. PNS didn't have commentators, and their reports were limited to text. Lucinda wasn't sure whether that was to save transmission costs, or some limitation network controllers had imposed to limit their influence. At least the screen displayed the text in characters large enough to read easily.

Pitcairn News Service Report—18 September 2343

Pitcairn Administrator Patrick Malley today released a statement saying that Selwick Pearson and Caiden Reyes have been found guilty of violating Pitcairn law in the kidnapping of two Pitcairner boys. During the trial, Reyes testified as to the motive: "We were afraid they had heard some of our conversation and took them into the house." Under further questioning, Reyes refused to elaborate on the nature of the conversation. Sources inside the Pitcairn government speculate that the conversation had to do with Terran attempts to gain control over the Tau Ceti library ship and its computer.

EMILE'S CONNECTION TO THE network sent the broadcast to him as well. Through previous postings, he knew the Pitcairners had restricted Earth's access to the library ship when the Link was activated.

"That's complete nonsense," Isaiah said. "Why would we want to get control over the computer? We already have it."

"Pitcairn has allowed only scientists on *Asimov*," Emile said. "To protect the conscious computer from Terran interference."

Isaiah shook his head. "The library ship and the computer are Western Alliance property. They have no right to do that."

"The Pitcairner Constitution considers the computer, as a conscious entity, to be a citizen of Pitcairn with the same rights as any other citizen."

The argument might have gone further, but Reynaldo walked in at that point. "Why are you all watching the network? Do that on your own time."

"Selwick Pearson was convicted," Isabella said.

"I know that," Reynaldo answered. "That's the government's business, not yours. We can't do anything to save him. Now get back to work."

ALYSSA SAT AT HER workstation, but her mind wasn't on the screen in front of her. "Protect from Terran interference," Emile had said. It was as if he knew about the program she had written for General Juarez. It was as if Pitcairn knew.

The idea had been so simple. Turn off a non-essential system and turn it back on again. See how the computer is affected. It was like testing a light.

But it wasn't. The program dealt with systems that might be non-essential to the library ship's immediate operation but essential to the consciousness of the computer. Testing a light wasn't a valid analogy. Turning a person's liver on and off might be better. Turning off part of the brain would be even more accurate. Her program could easily destroy the computer's consciousness.

That had never occurred to her. She had only been thinking of her advancement and look where that had gotten her. She was right back where she started. Scientists had debated the idea that a machine could become truly conscious for centuries, and now that it had happened, she could be complicit in its destruction.

Even if the Pitcairners didn't know about her program, they must know there was a danger. She could only hope that they would continue to defend the computer successfully.

ONE ADVANTAGE OF HIS condition was that no one could know that he was thinking. Emile needed to think, and a mental command turned his neurotrainer and neuro-interrogator off. Voices outside his mind could no longer distract him, and nothing of his thoughts would be sent out.

He knew in his heart that the PNS report was accurate. Pearson had kidnapped the children, probably for fear that they had overheard conversation relevant to the secret Methuselah Project. Pearson had gone to Pitcairn to get control of the library ship somehow, but had been unsuccessful and perhaps had gotten desperate. Caiden Reyes, the CEO of Reyes Pharmaceuticals, had recently gone to Pitcairn as well. Had he gone because of the library ship or merely become embroiled in the conspiracy somehow? Emile could not tell from the reports published on the network. It did sound as if he testified against Pearson in the trial, which would support the latter possibility.

He felt caught in a noose, with Lucinda next to him, both waiting for the tightening that would choke them. After the accident, he had disappeared from the public eye, but it would be a simple matter to revive the stories about him turning against the government. That would be the threat if he didn't cooperate, and Juarez would include the rest of the team in the threat.

28

T HE PHONE NEXT TO their bed chimed. "Call from Maxwell Estevez," it announced.

Eddie rolled over and stared blearily at the phone. "What?"

The phone repeated the announcement. "Connect," Eddie ordered. "Good morning, Max."

"Good morning, Eddie! Have you found employment or are you still pretending you're on your honeymoon?"

Joelle stirred next to Eddie. "Is that Max? Max, do you know what time it is?"

"I do. Do you?"

"The local time is 9:48 a.m.," the phone said.

"Who asked you?" Joelle said. "Hello, Max. It's great to hear from you."

"Now that sounded sincere," Max said. "Never mind. So, what about your employment status?"

"We're looking at a few things," Eddie said. "There are quite a few technology companies in this area. Bill taught at a college near here."

"New York isn't your kind of place. I've got a better opportunity for you."

"New York's not so bad. You should see the fall colors." He paused as Joelle rolled up against his back and put her chin on his shoulder. "So, what's the opportunity?"

"I assume it hasn't snowed yet. Better you get back to Colón before that happens. But never mind that. With some help from the Munts and a few others, I'm starting up my own company here in Colón. We're going to use some of that brain interface technology that we developed to design advanced prosthetics. The same thing we tried to sell the Munts when Juarez shut us down, but it won't be part of Munt Electronics. They're only investing in it."

"Have you contacted anyone else?"

"Parker is already on board. I'm still thinking about calling Aiden. I'm not sure we'll need any neuroscientists this time."

We don't need his attitude either. Eddie looked over his shoulder at Joelle. She stared back for a moment, kissed his shoulder, and nodded. He grinned and turned back to the phone. "OK, Max. We're in. How soon do you need us back?"

"You can come back any time and get settled, but it will be a month before we can use you. We have a lease on a facility, but there are a lot of details to hammer out before we begin operation."

"Sounds good. See you when we get there."

Eddie broke the connection, and Joelle pushed herself closer. "I guess the honeymoon is over."

Eddie rolled over to face her and put his arms around her. "Not yet, babe," he said. He kissed her, and she kissed back.

"LOOK, I'M JUST AN animal trainer," Isaiah said, "but I remember the reports a couple of years ago about Emile's anti-government beliefs. His support of these colonists fits in with what was said then."

"A lot of what was said back then was bull," Bill said. "Emile left a job on a government project and became a college professor. Lucinda stayed and ran that government project until the government canceled it."

"Stories said that he left because of the project. That he didn't want the government to have the technology they were developing."

Bill sighed. "True. They were trying to develop the neuro-interrogator, and Emile was concerned about how that some politicians might abuse the technology."

"Well, you developed it anyway. What changed?"

"The concern was that the device might be used to extract information from people without their consent and, potentially, without a proper warrant. As we later discovered, we couldn't develop such a device. The neuro-interrogator that we created will only work if the subject is willing. That's why the government stopped funding it."

"So, the bottom line is that Emile didn't trust the government. So, how were those reports wrong?"

"Emile supports the government when it obeys the laws it creates. He doesn't trust Castillo, though. The man lied and bullied his way into office and has no problem with continuing those tactics to gain power."

Isaiah's eyes narrowed. "You just switched from explaining Emile's actions to your own anti-government propaganda."

"I take it you voted for Castillo. The man is a proven liar and a racist. He's only interested in power. What do you see in him?"

"Castillo's programs help all of us. A lot of people would starve without government aid. And we need a leader like him to keep us strong against the Eastern Bloc. We would all be Muslims by now if we elected that Eastern Bloc sympathizer."

"Marisol Weston? The only evidence against her was that she visited relatives in Savannah. I suppose the fact that she was from the north didn't help her, either. Castillo capitalized on all that with lies, exaggerations, and innuendo. And many voters swallowed his crap without even questioning it."

"That's what the conservatives would like you to believe. They would prefer a stronger, less liberal government, more like the Eastern Bloc."

Bill rolled his eyes. "Another of Castillo's lies. Look, Isaiah, it isn't a question of what party I, or Emile, supports. I just can't bring myself to support someone like Castillo." *I could tell Isaiah about the Methuselah Project Castillo is sponsoring, but the project is still secret, and Isaiah isn't cleared for it.* It wouldn't sway him, anyway. Anyone who supports Castillo would have no trouble believing that Methuselah is an effort to extend everyone's life, and nothing more. In truth, perhaps it is, but if so, why is it kept secret?

He should probably end the conversation, but he couldn't resist one more point. "You're a northerner, Isaiah. How can you support someone so prejudiced against northerners?"

"Those accusations of racism are more propaganda. Sure, President Castillo opposes northerners like Weston, but that's because of their sympathies with our enemies. Besides, I'm not a northerner. My father's family came from the Texas district, but I grew up in the Mexican district, with my mother."

Castillo's own words proclaimed his prejudice, but he wouldn't convince Isaiah of anything by pointing that out, and Reynaldo was entering the laboratory. "I should get back to work," Bill said. Arguing with Castillo supporters accomplished nothing, but he couldn't stop himself from getting drawn into their stubborn fantasies. Reynaldo shared their beliefs, or maybe he only supported the government, right or wrong. In either case, it wouldn't do to have him find them arguing on company time. It chaffed on him, though, that he had let Isaiah have the last word.

On his way to his desk, he passed Kong. "Bill fight Isaiah?" the ape asked.

"No." He looked at Kong and thought he saw worry on the chimp's face. "Kong like Isaiah?"

"Isaiah feed Kong."

That summed things up pretty well.

29

T HE MONTHS PASSED QUICKLY, but the project advanced slowly. The new year came as the neuroscientists struggled to understand the impulses that were consciousness, but their goal seemed little closer when Emile received a message from Max.

I HAVE GREAT NEWS, Emile. Our motor interfaces are now ready for production, and we would like you to be one of our first customers. We can get into the details when you come to Panama, but the condensed version is that we can now give you the use of your legs and arms. You'll have to get a week's leave from your work, but we can be flexible on scheduling.

Some minor surgery is required, and we've contracted with Doctor Nicolelis to have it done there. I'm sure you remember Nicolelis treated you after the accident. Have Lucinda call me, and we'll set a date. Emile, this is just the beginning. I hope to see you soon.

Eddie and Joelle send their love,

Max

The message left Emile with a lot of questions, but Lucinda could get answers to most of them. She was out in the laboratory somewhere, and the message had come to him through the network interface to his neurotrainer. He told his bed to find her. This was news that couldn't wait.

E MILE COULD WALK AGAIN! Lucinda went to Reynaldo's office after Emile told her about the message. A part of her mind told her to be wary about telling Reynaldo too much, though.

"Emile and I would like to take a couple of weeks' vacation," she told him. "We haven't taken any time off in a long time, so there shouldn't be any problem."

Reynaldo frowned. "I suppose not. When do you plan to take this vacation?"

"We would like to do it as soon as possible, but we don't have a specific date in mind."

"Pearson policies require a month's notice. I will submit your request today to start on March 20th."

Exactly one month from now. Reynaldo was ever the bureaucrat following the rules. It didn't matter that the effect on the project would be the same if they left in one week, one month, or even one year. Max might need that month to set things up with the hospital, though, so maybe it would be for the best.

THREE DAYS LATER, GENERAL Juarez stormed into the laboratory. "You can't go running off somewhere for two weeks in the middle of the project," Juarez told her.

"We've been working on this project for three years," Lucinda replied. "We will be for years yet. When do you want us to take a vacation?"

"I expected a little more dedication from the lead scientist on this project. Where are you going, anyway?"

"Emile and I need to take some time for personal reasons that don't concern you, General."

"Anything that impacts this project concerns me. I do not approve of this."

"Fortunately, we don't work for you, and Reynaldo has already authorized it. Bill will run the project in our absence. The effect on the project will be minimal. Having some time off might even clear our minds and make us more effective."

Juarez frowned. "Very well. But only one week."

"One week isn't enough. Ten days."

"Ten days beginning on Saturday morning."

"You want me to use my vacation on the weekend? Ten days starting Monday morning, but not including the weekend in the middle."

Juarez shook his head. "Don't insult me. Ten days not counting weekends is still the original two weeks."

"True. I am trying to compromise with you as much as I can."

"You're a stubborn woman."

"I'm very reasonable. What is so important that a few extra days have you running up here from the Capitol?"

Juarez glared at her. She could almost see an idea suddenly come to him. "How many people will die during those few extra days that could have been saved by being uploaded? Think of someone other than yourself, Mrs. Hernandez."

He talked as if they could upload thousands. That was absurd. They already knew that it would take a very expensive computer to house a mind. She was surprised that Juarez had promised that Emile would be the first. Unless he considered Emile a test subject, uploaded first to make sure the process worked. *Now that's a nasty thought.*

"Brief me on the status," Juarez demanded.

Lucinda knew she had won the argument: hence, the abrupt change of topic. "Certainly. Let me get the most recent daily reports." She turned to her workstation and began entering commands.

30

“P ROSTHETICS THAT THE MIND can control have been around for a long time,” Eddie told Emile and Lucinda. “They treated spinal cord injuries that interrupted nerve signals to the muscles. Emile’s problem is different because the damage is in the brain itself. Our solution uses the output from a neuro-interrogator to create signals for the nerves.”

“Don’t you run into patent problems with Pearson Interstellar?” Lucinda asked.

“No, our units are only accessories for their technology, not modifications of it. We’re boosting their sales by creating new uses for their neuro-interrogators, and they are fine with that.”

“Where does the surgery come in?” Emile asked.

“Stimulators are implanted in key areas to activate the nerves. They get their commands wirelessly from the device that we add to the neuro-interrogator.”

“How bulky is the new device?”

Eddie grinned. “It will fit in your pocket and get the neuro-interrogator input wirelessly, just like the Voice Magician.” His face became serious again. “A bigger limitation is that you’ll still be blind. That’s our next project, but it’s still in the preliminary stages.”

“But I’ll be able to walk again.” Excitement was obvious in his voice.

“Yes. Not normally, but yes. There will be a difference. Much of how we walk is automatic; we do it without thinking about it. You will have to exercise more conscious control. Until you are used to it, you have to be very careful. The communication between the implants and the device is two-way. You will get impulses back about positioning, but it will be different, and again, a learning effort.”

“How much will all this cost?” Lucinda asked.

“The devices will be moderately expensive once we get into mass production,” Max said. “Of course, there’s the surgery, too, so it will cost quite a bit. Don’t worry, though. We do it for free for our guinea pig.”

Lucinda brushed a tear from her cheek. "This is all so wonderful. What you're doing is so much more important than Methuselah. Thank you so much."

Max smiled and hugged her. "It is most definitely our pleasure," he said.

"DOCTOR HERNANDEZ, HOW NICE to see you again, especially under these circumstances. Oh, I'm Doctor Artemis. You probably don't remember, but I treated you here after your accident."

"Hello, Doctor," Lucinda said. "Of course we remember you."

"Will you be doing the procedure, Doctor Artemis?" Emile asked.

"Oh no. JEM has trained a specialist for that. I just wanted to take the opportunity to look in on an old patient. I rarely get that chance, and I look forward to seeing you walking around in a few days."

"The implant's connection to the nerves differs from anything done previously," Max said. "We provided special training to another surgeon, Doctor Bennett Martin, to do these operations."

"Did I hear my name mentioned?" The man who walked into the hospital room smiled at them all and stopped next to Emile's bed. "And this is my patient. Good morning, Doctor Hernandez."

"Good morning."

"The operating room will be ready in a few minutes. You shouldn't have any worries about this. It's actually one of my simpler procedures, but it will take a little time because there are several places where you will need the implants. I won't have to go very deep, and because of your condition, we won't have to use an anesthetic. That alone makes the operation safer than many. We've checked your nanite level, and it's fine, so infection won't be a problem."

"How long will the operation take?" Lucinda asked.

"A couple of hours. It takes that long because Emile will need forty implants to control his arms and legs. It will take weeks of training and practice before he can move around by himself, though."

"We have to be back at work in San Diego in a week," Emile said.

"Not a problem. We can do the initial training here in the first few days. We'll show Lucinda what she needs to do for the rest of it." Doctor Martin smiled. "This will be a first for me. We'll keep Emile's connections so that we can talk during the operation. Usually, my patients are unconscious."

Lucinda smiled at the irony. A man who had lost everything except consciousness would be conscious when anyone else would be out cold.

"How can I control forty implants at once?" Emile asked.

"Good question," Doctor Martin said. "You won't. The device will process your conscious thoughts about what you want your limb to do and decide how to control the implants. You'll find it tricky at first, but it should become almost natural with practice. One of the tricky aspects is that you will find you have to control each limb individually so that the device can deal with only ten implants at a time."

Lucinda and Emile were out of questions. After a moment of silence, Doctor Martin signaled to an orderly. "OK, then. I think it's time to get you on your feet again. We'll take you into the operating room now."

L UCINDA SAT IN A waiting room. She had brought a reader with her to pass the time, but Max came in soon after orderlies took Emile away. She forgot her book while she and Max caught up with each other's lives.

The operation didn't worry her. Robotic instruments would perform the procedure under Doctor Martin's control, and surgical mistakes were almost unknown, even in major operations. In all but the very poor, medical nanites controlled infections, the biggest cause of problems after surgery in the distant past. Anesthesia was still occasionally a problem, but even that was a non-issue in Emile's case.

With Max keeping her company, the time passed quickly, and Doctor Martin's return caught her by surprise. "The operation went well," Doctor Martin said. "No problems. He will have to stay in bed for a day or so to heal. Then we can begin his recovery therapy."

"Can we see him?" Lucinda asked.

"Of course. He should be in the recovery room by the time we get there."

In the recovery room, Emile was still lying on his bed as if nothing had happened. Since he hadn't been anesthetized, his voice transmitted by his neuro-interrogator was completely normal. "They still have me hooked up," he told them. "At least until I've healed some. I can feel sensations in my legs and arms, but they're strange."

"In what way?" Doctor Martin asked.

"I don't have a normal sense of touch, of course. If I concentrate on moving a limb, I get this feedback that is unlike anything I remember feeling before."

"You're probably feeling resistance to the movement because you're covered with a blanket," Doctor Martin said. "That's good. Work on that and how it feels. That will give you a head start on understanding all the new feelings you'll have when you're up and about."

"Thank you, Doctor. And thank you, Max."

"This is just the beginning, Emile," Max said. "We're already working on a way of getting your sight back. We have plans far beyond that, too."

"How can you get my sight back? The connections to my visual cortex are damaged."

"That makes it difficult. We originally thought about tackling the sight problem first but decided to do something that we knew we could develop into a product. As income comes in, we can become more ambitious. We have an expert on the visual cortex working with us now, and he has let us know in no uncertain terms that it is extremely complicated."

"I know enough about it to know that it is unlikely that you will be able to restore complete functionality," Emile said.

"You're probably right. Eddie is doing a preliminary design for a module that will be upgradeable through software, but it's a tough problem. We're starting with shape recognition, but there probably won't be color or depth perception. That will come later, we hope."

"We appreciate everything you're doing for us," Lucinda said. She hugged Max.

"You're welcome. We're having a great time, though, and I think, in the long run, it will be very profitable. You're a special case, Emile, but we plan to develop a family of devices that we can use to provide custom solutions to all kinds of disabling injuries."

T WO DAYS LATER, MAX was back, along with Eddie and Joelle, to see Emile take his first steps. With Lucinda, a physical therapist, and Doctor Martin also there, the room was crowded,

"At least there will be plenty of people to catch me when I fall," Emile joked when told about his audience.

The physical therapist helped him off the bed. The implants gave him some control over his limbs, but the inability to use the muscles in his torso made the action difficult.

First, they moved him into a sitting position on the edge of the bed and let him explore the sensations as he kicked his legs back and forth and waved his arms. Then, with some support, he used his arms to push himself off the bed and onto his feet.

He touched the floor in an awkward crouch. The therapist straightened his body and moved cautiously away, leaving Emile swaying, but erect. "This feels so weird," he said.

"Just stand for a bit and take in the new sensations," Doctor Martin said.

"I think I've got it. I'm going to take a step now."

Emile's right leg stuck out in front of him, and it looked as if he fell forward so that half his weight was back on that leg. "OK. Here's another one."

His left leg moved, but it unbalanced him. He caught himself, helped by brief support from the physical therapist, and dragged the left leg forward until it was even with the right leg. When he was stable again, he stuck out the left leg and fell forward again.

"You're doing extremely well, Doctor Hernandez," the physical therapist said. "Keep focusing on how everything feels, and you'll have the hang of it in no time. You'll have a cane to help you balance, at least at first."

"I have no use of my hands. I can't use a cane."

"JEM designed a special cane that straps around your wrist and hand so that you don't have to maintain a grip on it. You'll move it with arm motions. You can also use your neuro-interrogator to tell the cane to send a signal that helps you know where your bed is relative to you."

Emile's face stayed expressionless, but his voice was excited. "I'm guessing that was Eddie's work. Sounds great."

Lucinda put her arms around him and hugged him. "It is great."

Emile put his arms around her, too, and tried to squeeze. It was awkward when he had to be conscious of his legs to avoid falling, but he managed it.

"That probably felt better to me than it did to you," Lucinda said.

"My brain determines how it felt," Emile answered. "I get sensations now, so I can feel the hug in my arms. My brain has chosen to interpret that as a pleasure I have been without for too long."

31

THEIR RETURN TO SAN Diego was a triumph. Lucinda entered the laboratory first, but Emile wanted to make an entrance, so she let him send his bed into the laboratory, empty. He still needed the equipment in the bed to hear and speak, so he followed close behind, using the cane to make sure he knew where the bed was.

Alyssa was the first one to see him. "Emile," she cried out. "It worked. You're walking!"

"To a reasonable approximation," Emile answered. The Voice Magician did an excellent job of adding delight into the synthesized voice.

Emile had mastered the implants quickly. By the third day, he learned to use his knees, moving away from the straight-legged gait of the first day. He told Lucinda he could tell when his cane struck something by the odd sensation he got when the force was transmitted to his arm. He still looked a bit like Frankenstein's monster when he walked, but the improvement was a miracle.

To one person, Emile's appearance was a surprise. Reynaldo stood at the door to his office, supporting himself on the door frame, his mouth open, apparently in shock. He stared as Emile slowly crossed the room, surrounded by his coworkers, but seemed to recover a little as Emile passed close by him.

"Emile, what. . .." That was as much as he could manage.

"Reynaldo? This is why I wanted the time away. Implants have given me back my legs and arms."

"That's wonderful, Emile. Why didn't you tell me? Why didn't you tell the general? He wouldn't have tried to stop you if he knew why."

"I'm not so sure of that," Lucinda said. "I'm sorry, Reynaldo, but if we had told you, you would have told Juarez, and we didn't know what his reaction would have been."

Reynaldo looked hurt. "I wouldn't have told him if you had asked me not to."

Lucinda nodded. "We couldn't be sure. Our colleagues from Munt developed the implants. Emile is one of their first patients."

Reynaldo smiled. "Well, it is wonderful. I wouldn't have told, but I would have felt guilty about not telling, so maybe you were right."

"It'll be interesting to see Juarez's reaction," Lucinda said.

A MONTH LATER, THOUGH, when General Juarez visited personally to get a status report, he showed no surprise. Someone had obviously told him about Emile's operation, probably Reynaldo. It could have been Isaiah; he was a Castillo supporter and probably an admirer of Juarez. Alyssa was a possibility, too. She was more withdrawn than she had been before she left them in Colón to work for Pearson Interstellar. It was difficult to know where her loyalties were.

Lucinda had a more important concern than the identity of the person passing information to Juarez. Emile had agreed to work on Methuselah, presumably because he hoped to be uploaded. She understood his desire to be more than just a conscious statue, but JEM Electronics suggested an alternative. If they made more advances, giving Emile more functionality, would he still even want to be uploaded to a machine? Could she get Emile back in any meaningful sense? For the first time in years, she felt hope.

G ENERAL JUAREZ HAD VISITED more frequently over the previous year. Lucinda thought that probably showed impatience on his part, but they couldn't move any faster. Neurological nanites, combined with modern brain scanning equipment, could measure brain impulses, finding the location of origin and destination with very high resolution, without invasive electrodes. That ability gave them hope they might succeed where scientists had failed for hundreds of years, but their instrumentation also gave them mountains of data to interpret.

Brain impulses were only electrical signals transmitted through elongated brain cells and passed to other cells through the chemical transfer of complex molecules. At any given time, thousands of brain cells were firing or passing a signal, and each of those cells had hundreds of branches through which a signal might flow. Isabella and Alyssa spent their time writing software to help process the data, but progress was still slow.

Emile listened diligently to news reports about the Tau Ceti colony. When the Western Alliance announced that there would be a Colonial Reorganization Conference held in

March, he mentioned it in a staff meeting. "The interesting thing," he told them, "is that the government is not inviting any representatives of the colonies. Apparently, they don't get a say in whatever this conference intends to do."

"You're wrong," Isaiah said. "Pitcairn is sending Ambassador Perez to the conference."

"Perez is Earth's representative to Pitcairn," Emile said. "He represents Earth, not the colonists."

"He lives in the colony," Isaiah replied. "He can speak for them well enough."

"That's asking the fox to speak for the hens," Emile said. "I think this signals troubled times for the colonies."

"The colonies should do what the government tells them to do," Isaiah said. "They should be grateful for the good life the government provides them."

That might be true of Pitcairn, Emile thought, although the Pitcairn News Service painted a different picture. From reports he had heard, however, he didn't think that Trist or Goddard colonists had it very easy.

"I think this is an attempt to get control of *Asimov*," Alyssa said. "Pitcairn is only trying to protect its computer."

"Protect it from what?" Isaiah asked. "Why would the government want to hurt it?"

Alyssa was silent, and Emile wondered what she had meant. PNS reports did occasionally imply that the Western Alliance cared more about controlling the library ship than the planet, but didn't explain why. Of course, the Pitcairners didn't know about the Methuselah Project and its interest in the conscious computer. Even if they did, why would they think Methuselah was a threat to the computer? Why would Alyssa think they feared for the computer? Emile wished he could see Alyssa. It was impossible to know what she was thinking from her words alone.

32

PITCAIRN NEWS SERVICE **BULLETIN, 10 March 2345**

The Administrator's Office announced today that Administrator Patrick Malley, PNS head Kimberley Dillon, and their spouses are traveling to Earth for the Colonial Reorganization Conference, set to begin in Brasília on 20 March 2345. Trist Administrator Ronald Rigney and his wife will also attend with the Pitcairn contingent.

In a statement earlier before the Pitcairn Legislature, Administrator Malley said: "The Western Alliance didn't want us, but we have to be there to speak for ourselves. We have arranged passage on the Francisco Pearson."

"THE COLONIES ARE REPRESENTED after all," Isaiah said. "President Castillo isn't the tyrant you think he is."

Lucinda wondered. Network broadcasters said little about the colonial delegation to the conference. The PNS announcement implied they were paying for the trip, not the Western Alliance. That was curious; where did the Pitcairners get that kind of money? They traded their antivirus drug, Cetivir, for supplies, not money.

"We shall see," Bill said. "Your trust in Castillo is touching, but hardly justified by facts."

"This is the most liberal government that has ever existed," Isaiah said. "The government makes sure everyone is cared for. Why do you oppose it?"

Bill shrugged. "I'm not a historian, but I know that taking this kind of care of a population this large requires a government with a lot of power over its citizens. Power can be abused, and Castillo is an abuser. His reelection campaign showed his ruthlessness, and his treatment of the colonies probably stems from the same arrogance."

"He's the strong leader we need, and he did what he had to in the campaign. Weston would have destroyed the Western Alliance."

"OK, enough politics," Lucinda said. "This won't achieve anything except hurt the project."

"Whatever the project is," Isaiah said.

Bill nodded and smiled. "Well, we can't tell you that because the government wants it to be a secret. Castillo doesn't think that the people should know exactly how he is helping them."

"Bill!" Lucinda said. She glared at him. "That's enough. Get back to work."

"Sorry, Lucinda." Bill walked toward his desk, slowing once to look back at Isaiah. Isaiah was still glaring at Bill, and Lucinda shook her head and went back to her office.

NEWS EVENTS DID NOTHING to ease tensions in the laboratory. The Colonial Reorganization Conference opened with speeches by President Castillo and Ambassador Perez, the Western Alliance's representative to Pitcairn. Although the normal news service coverage didn't mention it, Emile listened to a PNS broadcast of a speech given by Patrick Malley, essentially saying that everything Castillo and Perez had said was a lie. During the speech, Malley referenced a recording of Selwick Pearson's trial for kidnapping and asked that people view the recording and decide for themselves whether Pearson had received a fair trial.

Malley saved the real bombshell for the end of the speech. "Caiden Reyes testified that Selwick Pearson kidnapped our two children because he thought they might have overheard something, presumably something about Selwick's true mission on Pitcairn. Until recently, we had no idea what that mission was. Now, however, the conspiracy is unraveling.

"I cannot divulge the nature of this conspiracy. It is up to you to demand answers from your government. It is up to you to demand to know why the Western Alliance wants to remove an elected government of a peaceful and productive world and install a foreign bureaucracy answerable only to the Western Alliance. If they pretend ignorance or tell you that I don't know what I'm talking about, answer them with one word. Methuselah."

Pitcairn knew about Methuselah? That might explain why they fought for control of the library ship. The data from *Asimov* was still helping to guide the Methuselah team's research. That data had been gathered non-intrusively. More intrusive tests might damage the entity that called itself Isaac Asimov. That would give the Pitcairners a reason to resist.

TWO DAYS LATER, THE network exploded with stories about the discovery of an alien civilization. According to the reports, the Western Alliance had a secret project called the Methuselah Project, working to contact the aliens and invite them to visit. Predictably, protesters appeared overnight, dominated by a group called the Fermions.

The Fermions had been around for a long time and had been powerful in the past, but they struggled now. They believed that a God-created space at least one hundred light years in radius existed between alien races, making it almost impossible for them to interact. For this reason, they opposed any interstellar travel because it might result in forbidden contact.

Since he didn't know about Methuselah, Isaiah swallowed the story completely, not understanding why no one else gave it any credence. Privately, Emile and Lucinda thought it was an attempt by the Western Alliance to deflect any plans Pitcairn might have to exploit their knowledge of the project. When Bill teased Isaiah about Pitcairn breaking the news, Reynaldo had to break up the resulting shouting confrontation.

Three days after the alien report, Emile received another shock from a PNS report, but it was a pleasant one this time. Kimberley Dillon, the head of PNS, had used her visit to Earth to open an office near Brasília. PNS coverage now included on-air commentators, videos, and other features that had been available only on the Terran news services before. On that night, PNS broadcast a report including video of the town of Grissom on Pitcairn. It was more proof of the government's misrepresentation of the colony, but it was the commentator for the report that delighted Emile.

Anna Cortez was back. Once the star of the *Jornal de Brasília,* apparently black-listed for her opposition to Castillo, she was now working for PNS.

A week later, the Eastern Bloc and the independent nation of Japan gave Pitcairn diplomatic recognition. Probably because of diplomatic pressure, the Western Alliance announced its recognition the next day. Emile wondered what behind-the-scenes machinations had brought about such an astonishing result, but suddenly Pitcairn was an independent country.

WHEN LUCINDA TOLD ALYSSA about Pitcairn's independence, Alyssa's first reaction was relief. Caution soon took over, however, and Alyssa researched the agreement between the Western Alliance and Pitcairn. Relief returned, doubled. The agreement fixed the boundary of the new nation at the orbit of its outer moon. Since

Asimov occupied Lagrange Four, in the same orbit as the inner moon, the library ship was well within Pitcairn's territory. The Pitcairners shouldn't have any trouble preventing the installation of her program. She tackled her work with renewed enthusiasm.

PITCAIRN CONTINUED TO DOMINATE the news. Administrator Malley and his party left the Western Alliance in early May, apparently intending to open an embassy in Japan, one of the few countries left not part of the Eastern Bloc or the Western Alliance. The major outlets characterized the move as "sneaking out" and called it the most recent Pitcairn insult to its benefactors. As usual, PNS had a different slant on the event, and Anna Cortez did her commentary from Japan. Her name was still well known, and PNS gained audience.

As knowledge about Pitcairn spread, more people believed that the government had been lying to them. Castillo's popularity slipped several percentage points, not an immediate concern, but enough to make the government back off on anti-Pitcairn propaganda.

LUCINDA WASN'T SURPRISED WHEN General Juarez showed up in a mood noticeably worse than usual. How much had he counted on access to Asimov? To her knowledge, they already had all the information about machine intelligence they could glean from that source.

"What do I have to do to get you people to make this happen?" he demanded at the meeting he called.

"Most of our work now is data analysis," Lucinda said. "We've collected massive amounts of information on the brain using the best instrumentation available, and all that has to be interpreted. Our neuroscientists work on that, and our programmers work on writing software to help them. More computing power might help."

"Fine. If that's all you need, you'll get it."

"It will be costly," Lucinda said.

"I don't care. Cost is no object. What about more people?"

Lucinda shook her head. "I don't think that would help. Good neuroscientists aren't that easy to find, especially ones willing to work on a secret government project. If we had more, they would probably get in each other's way. The same with programmers, at least for now. Later, when we know enough to build real hardware and write software for it, we might need to hire more people, but not yet."

"And then I'll see some progress?"

"Maybe," Emile said. He sat at the conference table now, his bed nearby but used less every day. "General, we don't know that what you want is even possible. It is impossible to predict when we can accomplish something like that."

"We know *Asimov* has become conscious. That proves it's possible."

"No, it proves that machines can become conscious. Uploading an existing consciousness to a machine is another problem entirely."

Juarez slapped the table. "Excuses! I want to see progress." His expression changed from annoyance to something Lucinda could only interpret as craftiness. "Could you be less dedicated now that your condition has improved, Doctor Hernandez?"

"I assure you, General, it has not affected my dedication." Emile's facial expression couldn't change, but the neuro-interrogator added disdain into his voice. "If anything, my implants have helped me be more useful to the project. In fact, you should be happy to know that JEM has promised implants to give me back the use of my hands within the next few months."

"I suppose you and your wife will want another two weeks away," Juarez said, a sour grimace twisting his mouth.

"The physical therapy requirements are much less," Lucinda said airily. "A week should do it."

Juarez twisted his mouth even more. "Make sure I have the specifications for the computer you need."

"Aurora can supply those," Lucinda said. She nodded to Aurora, who nodded back.

33

"How does this feel?" Lucinda asked.

"It feels good," Emile answered. The implants for his wrists and fingers were two weeks old, and Lucinda liked to rub the almost imperceptible (Lucinda said) bumps they made. The sensation the implants sent back to his brain felt good, but that was largely because he knew it was Lucinda doing it. It hadn't felt that good when Bill had examined his hand. Probably it would have if he thought it was Lucinda. The feeling was, after all, just in his mind.

"Everybody is here now," Lucinda said, pulling her hand away. "Reynaldo is starting the meeting."

"I suspect this is going to be short," Reynaldo said. "Lucinda, do you have any progress to report?"

"Not in a positive sense, unfortunately. With the programs Isabella and Alyssa have written and the increased computer power, we've almost caught up on processing the data we've accumulated so far. The analysis should have isolated any impulses due strictly to conscious thought, but they haven't. We have secondary impulses, like those affecting precognitive responses in the amygdala, but no source. The interactions are very complex, of course, and we can't be sure yet, but it almost seems that consciousness is coming from outside the brain."

"We don't have instruments that can detect quantum events in neuron microtubules," Bill said. "That's a possible source of consciousness, but we had hoped we could at least isolate neuronic reactions to microtubule activity."

"That microtubules are involved is only speculation," Lucinda said. "If the source of consciousness is elsewhere, and we're beginning to believe it is, we're just spinning our wheels."

"Maybe." Bill shrugged. "In my research, I've found hints that microtubules were taken seriously in the twenty-first century. That research seems to have been lost during the technology backlashes then."

"Lost or hidden," Emile said. "Until our research became legal, neuroscience research was limited. Anything having to do with reading thoughts was illegal. There may be a lot of old classified research."

"We haven't seen any neuronic reactions that would suggest microtubule interfaces," Lucinda said.

"Are you saying that consciousness doesn't originate in the brain?" Alyssa asked.

Lucinda shook her head. "Descartes's dualism? We're not at that point yet. We know there is a connection between the mind and the brain. There is a wealth of evidence that the brain affects consciousness in ways that argue against dualism. Even if consciousness is somehow outside the brain, there should be a point of entry where they interact."

"Unless there are multiple points of connection too subtle for us to detect," Emile said.

"If it is outside the brain, the assumption would be that it is not matter but energy, right?" Isabella said.

"Certainly not matter. Perhaps energy," Lucinda agreed.

"But energy and matter are interchangeable. If the mind is a manifestation of energy, it could theoretically be converted to matter," Isabella said. "Does that point the way toward solving our problem?"

Lucinda grinned. "Turn the mind into a blob of something and then write a program to convert it into something a computer would understand? I don't think so."

"I've read that people have auras, energy about them that can be detected," Alyssa said. "Could that be the mind?"

"Auras are a myth," Emile said.

The statement came out of the Voice Magician stronger than Emile had intended, and Alyssa bowed her head. "Oh," she said meekly.

"No known energy exists inside or outside of the body that could be a mind separate from the brain," Lucinda said. "So, either it's something we've never seen before, it's immaterial but can have material effects and be affected by material objects, or it's in the brain, and we haven't found it."

"Unless it is the third of those, I don't think we can succeed," Emile said. "Even if we found points of connection, I doubt that would lead to the ability to transfer consciousness. Maybe Bill is right about microtubules in the neurons somehow causing consciousness. If that is the case, though, how do we investigate it?"

"For starters, let's get Juarez to look for classified data on the subject," Bill suggested.

R ATHER THAN WAIT FOR Juarez to show up again, Reynaldo called the general's office in Brasília. A holographic Juarez hovered over Reynaldo's workstation monitor. "Why would centuries-old data be helpful?" The hologram duplicated Juarez's scowl perfectly.

"Before such research became illegal, scientists were investigating the sources of consciousness," Lucinda replied from over Reynaldo's shoulder. "The classified data might contain information that would take us years to duplicate."

"I'm not sure I can release that classified information to your group."

"Then get it unclassified. If the Benitez-Baker Bill made our research legal, there shouldn't be any reason to classify old research into the same area."

Juarez nodded, but reluctantly. "All right, I'll see what I can do."

E VEN JUAREZ COULDN'T MAKE the bureaucracy move quickly. It was another month before they received a data card from the general with a brief note claiming that the card contained all the classified information on consciousness research. When Aurora connected the card to their computer, they discovered over two petabytes of compressed research papers, books, and videos.

"There's a list of the contents, complete with authors, keywords, and dates of publication," Bill said. "That should give us a start at sorting all this out."

"Juarez said that cost was no object," Lucinda said. "We can start with a few articles that seem the most relevant and bring in a neurotrainer composer to make recordings for us. That would be the fastest way to disseminate the information to all of us."

"Starting with the most recent probably makes sense," Bill said.

"There are several papers from 2185," Aurora said. "They seem to be the most recent."

"The anti-technology laws were passed around then in the United States," Bill said. "After that, the movement spread quickly and was inherited by the Western Alliance when it formed."

"What if we use an auto reader to read the documents into a neurotrainer recording?" Emile said. "It would be faster than having a composer in to do it. Unless we could get a composer who also knew something about neuroscience, we wouldn't get a good recording anyway."

"That's been tried," Aurora said. "Professional composers are trained to put just the right amount of feeling into the recording, and auto readers just don't get it right. If we can't get a good composer, we could settle for that, but you wouldn't enjoy it."

"They didn't have the Voice Magician," Emile said.

"It's not the same thing," Aurora replied, but she spoke slowly, as if she were thinking as she spoke. "The Voice Magician uses the emotions from the neuro-interrogator to add to the result, but an auto reader doesn't have emotion."

"You seem hesitant," Lucinda said.

"I'm sorry, I had another thought. We use the Voice Magician to add feeling to neuro-interrogator output, but doesn't that also eliminate the need for a professional neurotrainer composer? Anyone could create a quality recording by filtering their input through the neuro-interrogator and the Voice Magician to control the level of emotion."

"It's worth a try. Let's divide the most recent material among us and get an idea of what is most relevant. Then we'll let Bill make recordings so that we can all absorb the material."

"How did I earn this great honor?" Bill asked.

Lucinda smiled. "I thought your personality might make the recordings more interesting."

"My sparkling sense of humor?"

"Sure, we'll go with that." Lucinda's smile widened. "Didn't you train a neuro-interrogator a couple of years ago, though? That would put you two or three days ahead of anyone else."

"I thought it was a good idea at the time," Bill admitted. "I'll see what I can do."

34

"IT'S INCREDIBLE HOW MUCH they learned from primitive scan techniques," Lucinda said, "but their techniques weren't very helpful in investigating consciousness."

"We have modern equipment, and we haven't gotten very far," Emile said. "The problem is exactly what we thought. The relevant neuron activity is the result of consciousness, but something other than brain waves and neural impulses triggers the activity."

"There must be something we missed," Bill said. He raised his eyes toward the neurotrainer on his head, frowning as if it were at fault. "Why would the government classify all this material? It's not dangerous."

Four months had gone by since Juarez sent the classified research documents. There were older documents they hadn't studied yet, but Bill had recorded most of the more recent and potentially relevant documents.

"Bureaucrats who didn't understand what they were classifying probably did classification," Emile said. "Remember, this was all done during a time when everyone was turning against technology, especially anything that could be an invasion of privacy. Then the Western Alliance became the hemisphere's government, and things got even worse."

"What does the foundation of the alliance have to do with it?" Reynaldo scowled at Emile.

"The southern politicians didn't trust knowledge that came from the northern parts of the alliance," Bill said. "Much of this research came from the old United States. Worse was research from people like Roger Penrose, who came from England. England was still a western nation when he lived, of course, but it was Eastern Bloc when the Western Alliance was created."

Reynaldo glared at Bill for another moment before muttering, "They must have had better reasons than that."

"I think we all agree that the research into neural activity won't help us much," Lucinda said. "We have better data from our research. I found some of the speculation interesting, though."

"The connection between consciousness and quantum phenomenon?" Bill said. "Perhaps. I don't see how we can investigate that, though, even with our modern capabilities."

"Perhaps we should add a physicist to our staff," Emile said. "An expert on quantum physics."

"I KEEP GIVING YOU whatever you ask for, but instead of showing progress, you ask for more," Juarez said.

Reynaldo smiled, but Lucinda could see the nervousness beneath it. After being on the receiving end of a tirade on the project's status, Reynaldo had requested a quantum physicist. The general grumbled, but Lucinda knew it had to be all bluster. Juarez was not a stupid man, and he had to realize the complexity of the task he had forced on them. There were new lines on his face, too, perhaps indicative of the amount of stress put on him.

"We're convinced that the answer does not lie in the normal electrochemical activity in the brain," Emile said. "We've created the most detailed map of neural correlates for conscious activity ever developed, but are no closer to identifying the initial source of conscious experience. Something is missing, and the information you got for us speculates that consciousness may be a quantum phenomenon."

"Neural correlates?"

"Sure. You know, of course, that the brain has billions of neurons connected to each other in extremely complex and dynamic ways. Groups of neurons process different brain functions in specific areas of the brain. Specific areas of the visual cortex, for example, process the orientation of a line or the direction of any movement. There are areas throughout the cerebral cortex that seem to correlate with conscious activity."

"And you have identified these areas?"

"To a great extent, they've been known for a long time, dating back to the twentieth century. Techniques back then could only resolve brain activity to a few millimeters, but they reached an excellent high-level view of brain activity. We can get better resolution with modern equipment and have been able to trace activity to the level of a single neuron. We needed the new computer to process the tremendous amount of data we were collecting."

"It sounds as if you've made more progress than you have told me about." Juarez glared at Reynaldo.

"We haven't briefed you in detail because none of what I just described has significantly advanced your goal," Emile said. "Knowing the correlates does not give us an understanding of the ultimate source of consciousness. We must look elsewhere, and the information you gave us has suggested a new direction for our research. We need an expert in quantum physics to take that direction."

"I understand enough of that to approve your request," Juarez said. "I don't know if I can get such a person, though."

Lucinda raised her eyebrows in question but did not speak. After a pause, Juarez continued. "The work you've been doing has been interesting and somewhat fulfilling for your neuroscientists. Even if you haven't achieved my goal, you have already told me you've made actual progress in neuroscience."

Lucinda nodded. "Yes, that's true."

"A physicist would be less interested. The project's requirement for secrecy would make it even less appealing. It will be hard for me to find suitable candidates."

"I don't see how we can hope to succeed without one."

"It could be a long time before I can find one. One of your neuroscientists could probably add a doctorate in quantum physics in less than a year, and then you would have one person expert in both disciplines."

Juarez was right. That Juarez could suggest such a course was further proof that he finally understood what he was asking them to do. If they chose neurotrainer material carefully for relevance to their problem, Juarez's estimate could even be pessimistic.

It could be another blind alley, of course. It could also lead to one of the greatest scientific advancements in history. Either way, they were committed.

B ILL CAREFULLY REMOVED THE neurotrainer helmet and put it down on the table next to his chair. He closed his eyes and breathed deeply for half a minute. Although he had already achieved the equivalent of a PhD in quantum physics, he needed more to attack the project's problems, and the subject became more difficult and bizarre the further he got into it. Even the mathematics behind quantum physics was well beyond anything he needed as a neuroscientist.

Lucinda stood there, patiently waiting for him. "Eddie called and wanted you to return the call as soon as you finished."

It had to be the call he had waited for since Eddie had told him almost eight months before that Joelle was pregnant. Bill sprang to his feet. "Did he say anything?"

"He wouldn't tell me," Lucinda said. "He said it was all your fault and you should be the first to know."

Bill grinned and pulled his phone from a pocket. "Eddie Bascomb," he said.

There was a momentary delay before Eddie's face appeared on the screen. The view pulled back, and Bill could see Eddie sitting next to a hospital bed. Joelle was in the bed, cradling an infant. "Hey, Bill," Eddie greeted. "I just called to introduce you to Emile William Bascomb." The view shifted again to focus on the baby.

"Congratulations, Eddie," Bill said. "You too, Joelle. Everybody is doing OK?"

"Everybody is doing great," Eddie said. "Couldn't be better."

"Emile William?"

"Well, Emile of course, but, given your part in this, I thought the William was appropriate."

Bill smiled, and he had to work to control his voice. "Thanks, buddy. Anything I did was my pleasure, but at best I don't think I did more than speed things up a little."

"So, you'll tell everyone else?"

"Of course. Lucinda is standing right here, and I'll make sure everybody else gets the good news."

"Great. Hi, Lucinda. How's everything going for you guys?"

"About the same," Lucinda answered. "We're still hoping for a breakthrough on the consciousness problem. At least General Juarez finally seems to understand that this is going to take a long time if we can solve it at all. While Bill is studying quantum physics, the rest of the team has been attacking the problem of uploading memory. At least that's well understood from a neurological standpoint, and we're making progress there. Oh, don't tell anyone you got that from me; we're still supposed to be secret. I wouldn't want to give Juarez a heart attack."

"Sure. We've got our own little secret. JEM has been doing very well, and we're seriously thinking about taking it public. Probably sometime next year."

"That's terrific," Bill said. "I hope you'll still talk to us after you and Joelle are filthy rich."

"Probably. We would like you to be Emile's godfather, and Lucinda to be his godmother. I'm hoping you can come down here for the baptism and we can spend some time together."

"Me?" Bill said. "Wow! Sure, Eddie, I would be honored."

"The same for me," Lucinda said. "Do you have a date set?"

"Not yet. Probably a couple of months. I'll tell you when we set the date. Any bad dates for you?"

"No, name the time, and I'll be there. Hey, instead of me telling everyone, why don't I patch a call into the conference room and you can tell everyone else yourself? We can put your phone image up on the conference room screen."

"Sounds good. I'll wait here for your call."

They disconnected, and Bill looked at Lucinda. "I'll get everyone together," Lucinda said and strode off.

35

A MONTH LATER, JOELLE called Lucinda and told her that the baptism would be in September, usually a pleasant time in Colón. Juarez had scheduled another visit two days after the call, so Lucinda broached the subject then.

"I suppose your husband will go, too," Juarez said.

Lucinda nodded. "Of course. Bill, too, since he's the baby's godfather. Also, JEM will implant more devices to give Emile control of his neck and torso while we're down there."

Juarez frowned. "I hope the time away from the project will allow you to relax for a while."

"Thank you, General. I'm sure we will find the trip revitalizing," Lucinda answered.

That was a different reaction from Juarez. Lucinda hadn't expected another tirade at this point, but Juarez's response was almost positive. Something was bothering him, but it wasn't the request for time off.

Emile had told her that Castillo's popularity was fading. The conflict with Pitcairn was partly responsible. Patrick Malley and the rest of the colonists had returned to their worlds the previous year, and relations with the colonies were still controversial. The increasing popularity of the Pitcairn News Service also created problems for Castillo. After Anna Cortez had disappeared from the network, criticism of Castillo had become rare, but Anna was back, working for PNS, as critical as ever.

"So, what progress have you made now that you have a quantum physics expert in your group?" Juarez said.

"EDDIE, JOELLE, AND THE baby should be the center of attention," Emile said. "I don't want to take my bed into the church."

"You don't have enough control over your body," Lucinda said.

"Solutions are available for that. It will only be for a couple of hours until we can get back to JEM." His voice dropped and held a note of apology. "You'll have to help me."

"You won't be able to hear or speak either."

"We still have a standalone neurotrainer trained for me, don't we? That will attract some attention, too, but not nearly as much."

Lucinda sighed. "All right, Emile. I'm not going to argue with you about it. And of course, I'll help you. We have the bags here."

"Thank you, darling. Now, we should get ready. We don't want to miss the baptism."

P ARROQUIA MEDALLA MILAGROSA HAD occupied the site in northern Colón for hundreds of years. The small church, however, had been built only twenty years before, replacing a structure that stood for over a hundred years and was itself a replacement for an older church. The new building was more modern than its predecessors, a soaring green structure of faux-stone plastic built on a carbon-fiber frame. A hologram of Christ glowed over the main entrance.

Lucinda examined the church as she, Emile, and Bill exited the aircar that had brought them from their hotel. There were only four steps between the church and the street, and she nodded approvingly. Emile had difficulty climbing steps, but he could do it. A ramp to one side would have been easier, but a longer distance, and she led him slowly up the steps, watching his feet. When they got to the entrance, she took a quick glance around. They were early, and only a couple of other people were going into the church. A man standing near the street stared at them, and she pointed him out to Bill, but he only shrugged.

Bill helped her guide Emile to a pew near the altar. He sat there stiffly, facing forward. An unobtrusive brace supported his neck, but Lucinda was afraid his unchanging slack expression would be as noticeable as the neurotrainer helmet.

First Eddie and Joelle, and then Jasmine and Franco Munt, arrived. After the handshaking and hugging, Emile sat down again and waited. Lucinda held baby Emile briefly and congratulated his parents. Joelle introduced her to the deacon who would perform the baptism and several other attendees, friends of theirs from JEM. A few minutes later, Max arrived, and there was another round of greetings.

The ceremony itself was short. After it was over, they exchanged small talk with the families of the other three babies baptized. Several people stared curiously at Emile, still sitting unmoving in the pew, but no one said anything, and she didn't offer any explanation.

"We're holding a reception at JEM," Eddie told her. "We'll get Emile set up with his bed, and he'll be able to take part more."

Lucinda smiled. "Your people have thought of everything. We appreciate it."

Eddie waved his hand. "Joelle and I owe everything to the opportunity and inspiration you and Emile have given us. Anything we can do for you is only in payment for everything you," and he turned to look at Bill, "and Bill have done for us."

Bill grabbed Eddie's hand and shook it. "Anything I did was my pleasure." He turned and winked at Joelle, eliciting a chuckle from her.

Max joined them. "Cars are waiting outside," he told them. "Let's move this show back to JEM. I'm getting hungry."

Air cars were waiting for them, but there was also a small group of reporters with cameras pointed in their direction. "What are they doing here?" Max said. He strode forward with a scowl.

Lucinda was holding Emile's arm. Eddie, Bill, and Joelle surrounded them, and they followed Max as he tried to push a path through the reporters.

"Doctor Hernandez, could you tell us why you are in Colón?" one reporter asked. Several others voiced related questions.

"Doctor Hernandez is an old friend," Max said. "We have no other comments for the press at this time."

"Doctor, there have been rumors you died or were seriously injured in an accident," another reporter said. "Was there an accident, and is that why you seem to need help walking?"

"I think any rumors about his death in an accident are obviously false," Max said.

"Why doesn't Doctor Hernandez speak for himself?"

"Because he has no comment," Lucinda said.

The reporters were moving closer, blocking their path. Someone Lucinda bumped, and she rebounded into Emile, causing him to stumble. He wouldn't understand the reporters, all shouting questions at once, without the voice separator enhancements in his bed and would have trouble interpreting what his implants were telling him. She squeezed his arm, hoping he would understand that she was reassuring him.

Max reached the first car, and Eddie and Bill closed ranks in front of Lucinda. Joelle, carrying the baby, dropped back to go around the reporters to another car. With the two men aggressively pushing through, Lucinda and Emile made it to the car. The reporters followed, shouting more questions, making it more difficult than normal to get Emile inside, but they managed it. Joelle passed through without trouble, and on Max's command, the aircar rose above the crowd and flew between the buildings toward JEM Electronics on the other side of town.

"How did they find out Emile would be there?" Max asked as they settled in.

"A man was watching us when we went into the church," Lucinda said. "He might have recognized Emile and tipped off reporters."

Max nodded. "More likely he posted it somewhere, and it got picked up. He wouldn't talk to more than one reporter, I don't think, but there were several network organizations there."

"At least we're away from them now," Lucinda said. She sighed and leaned back in the seat.

M AX STARTED TO SPEAK, but Lucinda was relaxing, and he decided against it. If they hadn't already, the networks would identify him and start making connections between Emile and JEM. JEM had used Emile anonymously in publicity for their products; there shouldn't have been a reason to keep the connection secret, but Max had been cautious because of the old controversy about Emile's leaving PNC. At least the government shouldn't have any reason to feed the frenzy over the issue. Emile is working for them now, and it was his refusal in the past that caused the problems before.

M ANY PEOPLE WORKING AT JEM had not met Emile on his earlier visits. They crowded around him when he entered with Lucinda and Max, but Max shooed them away. "Let him get hooked up. He can't speak to you until then."

"I thought this was about little Emile," Joelle said, but she smiled.

"Here, let me hold him for a while," Lucinda said after she had Emile's bed connections working. "I'll be happy to fuss over him."

The baby was asleep, but he stirred as Joelle transferred him to Lucinda. He looked up at Lucinda and started crying at once.

"He must be hungry," Joelle said. "I'll get him a bottle and let you feed him, too."

Lucinda gently cradled him as Joelle went to get the bottle. Emile stood nearby, listening. "Is my namesake a handsome baby?" he asked.

Lucinda smiled. "Almost as handsome as you. I think he has Eddie's smile. Definitely Joelle's eyes."

"We never made time to have children of our own." Emile paused, and only a low hum came from the Voice Magician. Lucinda knew that the sound indicated some emotion still leaking into the connection, but she could only guess what emotion it was. "Do you want children, Lucinda?"

Lucinda hesitated. That was a loaded question! "We've always been so busy. I haven't thought about it." She frowned. Her evasion wouldn't fool Emile, but what else could she say?

"E MILE, HELLO," SOMEONE SAID. He must have realized that Emile couldn't see him. "Dan Martin."

"Hello, Doctor Martin," Emile said. "It's good to hear you again. I assume you'll be operating on me again in a few days."

"Call me Dan. Yes, I'm still doing these implant operations for JEM. There are a few others now, though. JEM is doing very well."

"So Eddie has said." Emile's voice, transmitted through the Voice Magician, dropped in volume. "Lucinda, could I speak to Dan alone for a moment?"

Lucinda hesitated, and Emile thought his request had probably confused her. "Certainly, Emile. Doctor, please come and get me when you want me to take him again."

"We're not alone here," Dan said. "Let me guide you to someplace more private." He took Emile's arm, and they walked for a short distance. "This should do. Are you concerned about the procedure we'll be doing?"

"No, it's not that. I wanted your medical opinion about something."

"Sure. What about?"

"I was wondering if it is possible for me to have sex with Lucinda."

Emile couldn't interpret Dan's reaction, but there was a long silence, probably because he was taken aback by the question. "I don't know," Dan said finally. "Doctor Artemis is more familiar with the brain damage you suffered. I could guess, but he could give you a better answer."

"Is he here?"

"No, he doesn't have any connection to JEM and probably wasn't invited. We both practice at Nicolelis, though, so I could arrange a consultation with him. You seem to want discretion, so I assume you don't want Lucinda to arrange it."

"Not if I can avoid it. If there is a possibility, I would tell her then, of course."

"I understand. I'll try to arrange for him to visit you while you're at Nicolelis for your procedure. You know, I'm sure, that the autonomic nervous system controls erection, and you have no damage there, but physical sensations normally trigger the response. That could be a problem for you. Doctor Artemis would be the person to talk to, though."

"Thank you."

"One question he will probably ask, though. Do you ever have morning erections? That would confirm that the necessary parasympathetic systems are operating normally."

Emile didn't answer at once. "How would I know?" he asked finally.

"Of course. Perhaps you could find out from Lucinda without letting on why you're asking. It would help if you had an answer when you talk to Doctor Artemis."

ACROSS THE ROOM, MAX approached Lucinda, who was talking with Jasmine and Franco. "We've got a group of reporters in the lobby demanding access to Emile," he told her. "How do you want to handle it?"

Lucinda bit her lip. "I don't know." Max waited, giving her time to think about it. "Emile's condition isn't publicized, but it's not a secret either," she said. Max didn't answer, deciding she was thinking aloud. "They'll figure out that he's been a patient here pretty quickly if they haven't already." She looked at Max. "This could affect JEM. What do you think?"

Max shrugged. "As you say, they'll know anyway. I don't see how anything we do now will change that."

"I don't want to expose Emile to that again," Lucinda said. "They won't leave us alone unless we give them something. Maybe I should go down and talk to them."

"I can do it if you'd rather."

Lucinda smiled. "You would probably do a better job, but they wouldn't be satisfied. I have a better chance of that, I think."

"You're probably right. I'll go with you, though, for moral support. I can get Eddie, too, if you think he would help."

Lucinda glanced toward the buffet table where well-wishers surrounded Eddie, Joelle, and baby Emile. "Thank you, Max. I don't want to disturb their day, but I would appreciate having you with me."

In the lobby, Lucinda and Max confronted five reporters. Unobtrusive cameras and microphones were visible when Max looked closely. Whatever Lucinda said would probably be on the network minutes after she spoke, delayed only to make sure her words were suitable for broadcast. The reporters looked at them as they approached.

"I'm Lucinda Hernandez. I understand you are seeking information about my husband, Doctor Emile Hernandez."

The reporters moved toward her, asking questions. Their volume rose rapidly as each tried to outshout the others. Max moved forward and held up his hand. "One at a time. You can all take turns." He pointed to a man with a *Brasília Today* ID. "You first. One question, and then we'll move on to the next reporter."

"Why won't your husband speak to us?" the chosen reporter asked, speaking loudly over grumbles from the others.

"My husband was seriously injured in an accident eight years ago. He can't speak."

Max pointed to another reporter, cutting off another question from the first. "Your turn."

"When we saw him earlier, he seemed to have other injuries. How extensive were they?"

"He suffered severe brain damage, leading to a condition referred to as locked-in state, conscious but unable to move and without sensory input. Thanks to JEM Electronics, he can now walk and use his arms, but cannot speak, see, or hear."

The third reporter changed the subject. "Is Doctor Hernandez still anti-government?"

Lucinda frowned and glared at the reporter. "He was never anti-government. Those accusations were baseless." She pointed at one of the remaining reporters. "Next."

"Are you saying that he didn't refuse to work on a government-sponsored project?"

"No, I am not. He changed jobs. The misrepresentations reported about the decision fail to report that I took that project over and managed it until the government ended its funding. Last question, and let's not have another one about Emile's supposed anti-government views."

The fifth reporter had been using his reader, apparently to do some quick research. He smiled nervously at Lucinda. "No problem. JEM Electronics has been using an unidentified patient in the advertising for their products. Can we now say that Doctor Hernandez is that patient?"

"Yes."

"If you research a little more," Max said, "you will find that Lucinda worked for me at PNC and that the JEM staff includes other people from the government's neuro-interrogator project. JEM Electronics products have extended the capability of the neuro-interrogator to improve the lives of people like Doctor Hernandez."

The fourth reporter jumped in again. "So Doctor Hernandez is benefitting from the technology he refused to help develop."

"The original government project was intended to develop a device that could read minds—hence, the name neuro-interrogator," Max said. "The government lost interest when they discovered it would be effective only on people willing to use it. Munt Electronics developed that technology into today's neuro-interrogator and the Voice Magician. We founded JEM, financed partly by Munt Electronics, to design more extensions to that technology. Doctor Hernandez is proof of the technology's ability to improve lives."

There were more shouted questions as each reporter clamored for another turn, but Max waved them down. "That's all the questions for now. We have a party to attend." He took Lucinda's arm, and they left the lobby as the questions continued.

"Quite an advertisement you slipped in there," Lucinda murmured as they got into the elevator.

Max smiled.

*B*RASÍLIA *TODAY* **REPORT 22 September 2346 Salvador Benzuelo reporting.**

Over the years, Emile Hernandez, the neuroscientist and suspected Eastern Bloc sympathizer, has been largely forgotten. After rumors of a fatal or near-fatal accident eight years ago, he dropped from the public view. Yesterday, however, he resurfaced in Colón, attending the baptism of Emile Bascomb, the son of Edward and Joelle Bascomb, two of the owners of JEM Electronics. Church records have revealed that Lucinda Hernandez, Emile Hernandez's wife, is the godmother of the child.

Reporters interviewed Lucinda Hernandez at JEM Electronics afterward. The interview was brief and can be accessed with the command "Hernandez Interview." During that interview, Mrs. Hernandez admitted her husband was a patient at JEM Electronics and was suffering from locked-in syndrome, meaning that he has no control over his body. His ability now to walk is apparently because of the installation of JEM devices. Mrs. Hernandez also stated that Emile Hernandez couldn't speak but must use a neuro-interrogator to operate JEM devices, and that should have given him the ability to speak. He was not wearing a neuro-interrogator at the baptism, so perhaps Mrs. Hernandez was only simplifying the facts.

JEM devices are expensive and must be surgically installed. We have asked who pays for Mr. Hernandez's treatment, but have not gotten an answer. Certainly, the government should not be paying for treatments on a known dissident. If JEM is performing the treatments in return for their use in advertising, one must question why JEM chose Mr. Hernandez and not a more deserving sufferer.

*E*MILE HAD ONLY A vague idea of what had gone on around him at the church, and Lucinda had given him only a bland summary of the interview in JEM's lobby. She didn't want to upset him, but she knew the network report would. She thought about trying to stop him from listening to the report, but knew it wouldn't work.

Emile always listened to network headlines through the connections in his bed and accessed any reports that attracted his interest. Reports on the baptism such as the *Brasília Today* report would certainly do that. As soon as they were alone, she connected Emile's equipment, hoping the report would disturb him less if she mentioned it first.

"We should talk," she said. Emile's Voice Magician emitted a harsh buzz, and Lucinda knew she was too late before Emile answered her.

"About what?" The Voice Magician seemed to growl. "That new report from *Brasília Today?*"

"I had hoped to tell you about it before you heard it."

"So you could sugar-coat it?

"Don't be angry with me, Emile. I didn't say those things."

There was a pause, and Lucinda thought the angry buzz was a little less loud. "I'm not angry with you, dear. The Voice Magician is a wonderful device, but it lacks the discrimination of a natural voice."

Lucinda smiled and hoped some of her feelings were getting through to Emile. Perhaps she should have used a neurotrainer too, so that she could have a more direct connection to her husband. "I know, Emile. Try not to worry about it. It's probably just an automatic reaction by the media. Juarez will probably be as angry about it as you are."

"WE'RE GOING TO USE an aircar to get you to the hospital to avoid any reporters lying in wait," Max told Emile and Lucinda.

"We're sending your bed in a ground car," Eddie said. "Just in case they're watching. It will leave first, and they'll follow it. At least, that's the plan."

"I'll be disconnected," Emile said.

"I know you hate that," Lucinda said. "It won't be for long. We'll get you hooked up again as soon as you get there."

When they landed on the roof of the Nicolelis Neurological Center, however, there was no sign of network reporters. Orderlies helped Emile to his room and connected him to his bed without trouble.

"No media, Juarez?" Lucinda asked.

"Probably him or someone in the government," Eddie said. "Methuselah is still a secret, and I'm sure Castillo and friends don't want attention called to Emile. People might ask questions."

"That silly report about contacting aliens two years ago squelched any dangerous questions," Max agreed. "I'm sure the government doesn't want the subject reopened."

"I'm surprised Pitcairn never exposed us," Lucinda said. "Apparently, they've said nothing about it since Malley mentioned it at that conference. Emile listens to anything broadcast by Anna Cortez, so he would have heard anything on PNS."

"They got what they wanted from that mess," Eddie suggested. "Maybe they don't want to cause any more controversy."

Max nodded. "Perhaps. But that's a problem for another day. Emile has a doctor to see."

"DOCTOR MARTIN SAID THAT the operation went fine," Doctor Artemis said. "Your ability to control your torso should help your mobility significantly."

"Thank you, Doctor," Emile sent.

"Doctor Martin said there was a matter you wanted to consult me about. Should I ask Lucinda to leave the room?"

"No, she needs to know about this," Emile answered. "I didn't want to disappoint her, but that's probably unrealistic."

"I think there's a chance she won't be disappointed. Lucinda, does Emile ever have spontaneous erections?"

Lucinda jerked her head toward him. After a couple of seconds, her expression seemed more curious. "Sometimes in the morning," she answered. "Why?"

"Your husband was wondering if sex was possible in his condition. I think it might be possible."

"How? He can't feel anything there."

"If he is having erections, then all the connections are there and undamaged. As you implied, the problem is in providing the necessary stimulation. Pornography could work." He hesitated before continuing. "There are pornographic neurotrainer recordings available."

"I don't think that would be necessary," Emile said. "Not if Lucinda wore a neurotrainer connected to me."

It was Doctor Artemis's turn to be curious. "That's a fascinating thought. It might work. You would use Lucinda's feelings to stimulate your responses." He smiled. "Yes, that would be an interesting experiment."

"E MILE, Lucinda, and Bill are back in San Diego," Max told Eddie.

"Did you talk to Emile or Lucinda?" Eddie asked.

"About our progress on restoring Emile's sight? No, after the business with the media, I didn't think he needed any more bad news."

"I thought we could do it." Eddie shook his head. "There must be another way that would be less complicated."

"Maybe we need to aim higher," Jimmy Herrera said. He was a neuroscientist and an expert on the visual cortex, hired by JEM to help develop a prosthetic that would restore Emile's eyesight.

"Aim higher?" Max said. "We're already in over our heads."

Jimmy smiled, but otherwise ignored Max's comment. "We've been fixated on solving Doctor Hernandez's problems the way we know best—by building peripherals for the neuro-interrogator. Has anyone asked if the actual damage can be repaired? That could restore much more than sight."

That startled Max. Jimmy was right about their method of attacking the problem, but was he right about repairing the damage? "Why didn't the doctors at Nicolelis think of that?"

"I don't know. Maybe we should ask them."

D OCTOR Artemis joined them at the JEM offices after his rounds that night.

"We considered trying a repair," he told them. "It is theoretically possible to program nanites to repair the damage to the arteries that bring blood to the motor and sensory areas. We didn't try because a mistake in the programming could affect other areas of the brain: breathing, the beating of the heart, other critical functions."

"So we might cure Emile, but the attempt could kill him," Max said.

Artemis nodded. "Actually, it's more complicated than that. We're talking about restoring functionality that Emile hasn't used in years. By now, his brain has reprogrammed itself and either killed unused neurons or repurposed them to do something else."

"That can be reversed, though," Jimmy said. "Microshock stimulation and drugs like sildenafil citrate improve brain plasticity." He paused. "The reprogramming may not be that severe. Emile has used the neuro-interrogator extensively, and that exercises some of the brain areas that might have otherwise become useless. The JEM implants could have staved off reprogramming of motor areas, too."

Artemis frowned. "Perhaps. Some improvement would be possible, but a complete recovery would be unlikely. Is that chance worth the risk?"

"That would be a question for Emile," Max said.

"How do you program nanites?" Eddie asked.

"They use a proprietary programming language," Artemis answered. "Other than that, you would use a development platform on a workstation, just like any other programming."

"But the programming is the major obstacle."

"There's no guarantee how well this would work, even with errorless programming, but, yes, the programming is the issue that would have to be resolved. Everything else is either straightforward or in God's hands."

"If programming is the issue, maybe we should get Joelle in on this conversation," Eddie said.

Eddie left and came back with Joelle a minute later. Max summarized what they had been discussing and asked, "What do you think, Joelle?"

Joelle frowned. "I would have to know more about what exactly the nanites would have to do. I could get neurotrainer recordings and learn how to program the nanites in a couple of weeks, but we might be better off hiring someone who already knows how to do it. Of course, the software would require extensive testing once it's done. We're probably talking about a multi-year project, but I need more details before I can give you a reliable estimate."

"I could work on laying out what the software has to do," Artemis said. "We have nanite experts at the hospital that I can consult."

"Do you have programmers?" Joelle asked.

"Not for nanites. We have experts in using medical nanites, but the nanite makers supply the programming."

"I have a couple of projects going right now," Joelle said, "but nothing critical. Should I update my skills?"

"Not right away," Max said. "Let's see what Doctor Artemis comes up with. We may want to hire more programmers or even contract the programming out."

"I should take a week or two to update my knowledge on the brain areas we want to work on," Jimmy said. "If we're going forward on this idea, we'll need an expert on that area."

"Do that," Max said. "If this turns out to be a dead end, it will only cost us that week or two; even if we decide to continue with the visual cortex replacement, that's not a big deal."

"I think I have all the records about Emile's condition that I'll need," Artemis said. "I take it we won't mention this to Emile."

"Not until we have enough data to give him an informed choice," Max said.

U NLIKE DOCTOR MARTIN, WHO performed the implant operations on Emile, Doctor Artemis didn't work for JEM. He had duties at the Nicolelis Neurological Center, but he worked on assessing Emile's condition as much as he could. Five days later, he was back.

"As I thought, the key problem is the restriction of blood flow to the motor and sensory areas," he told Max, Eddie, Joelle, and Jimmy.

"So what is your prognosis?" Jimmy asked. "Can we repair the damage?"

"Two arteries would have to be rebuilt over about half an inch of their length. Theoretically, it could be done, but no one has ever tried."

"Why not?" Eddie and Joelle asked simultaneously.

"Building new blood vessels that way is too slow. There would be leakage during the process, and it's easier and more reliable to repair breaks by splicing in artificial vessels the old-fashioned way. The damage is deep enough in the brain to make that kind of surgery extremely hazardous, however."

"But nanites could do it," Joelle said.

Doctor Martin shrugged. "The software is critical. The nanites would have to prevent excessive bleeding while slowly rebuilding the artery walls or Emile could have a stroke.

A successful repair will restore the blood flow, but we can't repair the damage to the areas affected. The brain would have to regrow neurons to replace what was lost, and it's anybody's guess how much can be done and how long it will take."

"Jimmy said there are ways to improve brain plasticity," Eddie said.

Artemis nodded. "There are. Nanites will help there, too. We can use them to administer drugs and microshocks to the precise areas that need stimulation. The prognosis is promising, but not a sure thing."

Max looked around the table. He saw optimism there, but wondered if it was justified. What they were proposing was not within JEM's current expertise. Taking on this project would divert attention away from their core business when they were trying to go public. He didn't think future stockholders would appreciate spending their money on something that would probably contribute little to the bottom line.

If they didn't take it on, who would? He shelved that thought. First, they had to decide whether to present their idea to Emile. It was all a moot point if Emile didn't want to take the risk for an unknown benefit.

I T AMAZED EMILE HOW much his mobility improved just by adding implants to control his neck and torso. Getting in and out of his bed was much easier, and he could sit normally without someone helping him. He was sitting on their couch now, and he could feel pressure on his arm from Lucinda leaning against his side. Lucinda wore a neurotrainer, and he wore his neuro-interrogator and neurotrainer. He could feel her contentment.

The implants in his torso sent new signals to his brain, and he realized Lucinda was rubbing his stomach. He had loved that before his accident and was delighted to discover that it still felt good. The sensation was entirely different, of course, but his brain understood it, and the connection to Lucinda helped. If he could have, he would have sighed with pleasure, and Lucinda's transmitted emotions told him she understood. She continued rubbing, changing the exact location occasionally and using the impression from Emile's neuro-interrogator to judge the best places to rub.

Lucinda's emotions showed surprise. "Emile, you're hard!" she sent.

"Doctor Martin was right," Emile sent back. "Perhaps we could have sex." He paused. "I don't know how well it would work, though. I can't kiss, and my movements are still clumsy."

Lucinda was excited. "Let's try," she sent. His leg sensors sent feelings that he thought were from Lucinda undressing him. More sensations seemed to mean she was trying to push him into a new position, and he tried to cooperate.

"That's better," Lucinda sent. "Just a minute."

He felt her move away, but she came back quickly. He felt pressure on his legs and stomach and realized Lucinda was on top of him. "Relax, darling," she sent. "I'll do all the work." She lifted his arms and placed his hands on something soft and smooth. Realizing it was her breasts, he moved his hands slowly in what he hoped was a gentle caress. Even without Lucinda's "That's it, lover," the connection to her mind told him he was succeeding.

She was rubbing his arms now and may have been rubbing other areas where he didn't have implants. "I'm taking you inside me now," she sent. The pressure on his legs changed and became rhythmic.

Lucinda had never been one to speak during their lovemaking, and that hadn't changed. Now, they had their mental connection, though, and he could feel what she was feeling. At first, there was a warm sensation of pleasure, heightened by anxious anticipation. As her rhythm continued, it grew into a frenzy until it burst into a long moment of ecstasy. Immersed in his wife's flood of emotion, he almost missed his feeling of warmth in his torso and upper legs.

Lucinda shifted her weight, and he felt her leaning on him through his arms. "Oh, God, I missed that," she sent. "Emile, you didn't just have an erection. You ejaculated, too." Her weight eased as she slid off him and pushed herself against his side. "I know you didn't feel it as much as I did, but I could tell you enjoyed it," she sent. "There was this incredible echo effect, too; my feelings were coming back to me through what you were feeling."

"I felt that, too," he sent back. "The best part was feeling what you were feeling, though."

They sat together for a long time, bathed in each other's emotions. After a while, though, Lucinda's emotions quieted, and Emile fell into a light sleep. He woke suddenly to a feeling of shock over his connection to Lucinda.

"Is there something wrong?" he sent.

"No, I'm sorry, Emile. I just realized something, and I was so surprised that I guess I woke you."

Emile tried to interpret the mixed emotions that Lucinda was sending, but until she focused on actual words, he couldn't tell what had given her such a powerful response. "What?" he sent.

"I wasn't protected."

The connection must have transmitted his confusion, because he could feel amusement adding to Lucinda's state of mind. "Emile, I could be pregnant," she sent.

---

*J***ORNAL DE BRASÍLIA REPORT, 6 January 2347 Ashton Gibbons reporting.**

Two years ago, the Western Alliance was shaken by news that a secret government project, the Methuselah Project, was an attempt to contact a civilization from another star system. When nothing happened, the Methuselah Project faded from the news, largely forgotten. This reporter has learned, however, that the story was a hoax, apparently meant to distract citizens from the truth of the Methuselah Project.

The Methuselah Project exists, but it has nothing to do with space aliens. Rather, it is an attempt to develop the ability to copy the human soul into a machine. Its purpose is no less than immortality, giving the subject a new life as a conscious computer.

We know that the Tau Ceti library ship, *Asimov*, has somehow become conscious. This discovery may have been the impetus for the Methuselah Project since it proved that it was possible for a machine to hold a conscious presence. One might ask, then, why the project has been a secret all these years. The ability to upload our greatest minds to a computer would be a great boon.

The answer is simple. Library ships are among the most expensive structures ever made by man, exceeded only by the exploration starship *Alejandro Castillo,* now under construction at Prendergast Station. The computer systems on the library ships are among the most powerful in existence. If a machine able to hold a human consciousness is that costly, the process couldn't be done very often, probably only once or twice.

We would upload the worthiest individual we could find, though, wouldn't we? That the government has kept this project a secret suggests otherwise. Given the ego of our president and the government sponsorship of this program, who is the most likely beneficiary should uploading consciousness become possible?

R EYNALDO HAD HIRED A receptionist several months before, and it was this young lady, Francesca Gonzalez, that greeted Max when he arrived. "Max Estevez to see Emile," he told her.

She looked hesitant. "Yes, we were expecting you, Mr. Estevez. Mr. Clementi would like to talk to you first."

Why would Reynaldo Clementi want to talk to him? He knew Clementi had taken his position as manager of the project, but they hadn't met or even talked before. Max didn't think Clementi would want his advice.

"Sure. Shall I go to his office, then?"

"He'll come out here." Francesca gestured toward some chairs along the wall. "Have a seat, and he'll be right out." She looked down at her desk. "Mr. Clementi, Mr. Estevez is here."

But when Reynaldo came out, there was another man with him, wearing the uniform of the Western Alliance Aeronautics and Astronautics Force. Neither man looked friendly.

"Maxwell Estevez?" the uniformed man asked.

"Of course."

"General Juarez—I believe you know him—sent me here to ask you a few questions."

"Questions about what? And who are you?"

"Colonel Michael Pizarro. I understand you would like to talk to Doctor Hernandez. We have some questions about that first."

Max frowned. "Emile and I have been friends for years. I have personal reasons for talking to him that are none of your business."

"Anything to do with the work here is the government's business." Colonel Pizarro glanced over at Francesca. She saw the look and shifted her eyes back to her desk, but she was obviously still listening.

"Perhaps we should take this conversation into Mr. Clementi's office," he said. He took Max's arm and pulled. Max resisted at first, but then shrugged and followed the two men.

Inside Clementi's office, Colonel Pizarro took the chair behind the desk and gestured to the other chair for Max. Reynaldo stood against the wall, looking irritated. Pizarro glanced at him for a moment, perhaps wondering if he should eject Reynaldo from his own office or if he should yield the chair to its owner, but apparently decided against either course.

"I assume you saw the news report this morning," Pizarro said.

Max shook his head. "I slept on the suborbital from Panama City. It was an early day for me."

"*Jornal de Brasília* ran a story about the Methuselah Project this morning. Somehow, they found out what Doctor Hernandez and his team are doing. You had nothing to do with that?"

Max was one of the few outside people who knew about the project. Eddie and Joelle also did, of course, but they wouldn't have mentioned it to reporters. There was a danger that it might rebound on Emile or Lucinda, and none of them would risk that. If the Methuselah Project was no longer a secret, though, why wasn't this building surrounded by network reporters?

"Of course I had nothing to do with it," Max said. "How much was revealed?"

"The nature of the project. A suggestion that President Castillo was the intended beneficiary."

Max grinned. "I thought Emile was supposed to be the first subject."

"There was no mention of Doctor Hernandez or this facility in the report. General Juarez would like to know who leaked the information and prevent any further details becoming known."

"I can understand that. I'm afraid I can't help you, though. And my business with Emile has nothing to do with the Methuselah Project."

"Your company has been helping Doctor Hernandez with his disability?"

Max nodded. "Yes."

"And you claim that is why you want to talk to Doctor Hernandez? Didn't you see him three months ago?"

"None of this is any of your business, but you are correct on both counts."

Pizarro put his elbows on the desk and folded his hands together. "Talking to Doctor Hernandez will require my permission. And I must be present during the conversation to make sure no sensitive information is exchanged."

Max shook his head. "That would violate doctor-patient confidentiality."

"You're not his doctor."

"I'm one of several doctors treating Emile. You must know I am a doctor of neuroscience."

For the first time, Pizarro looked hesitant. "I didn't know that. I thought you were just a manager at JEM Electronics."

"My PhD is one qualification for my position at JEM. Now, if you're quite through, I would like to talk to my patient."

"This is a secured facility," Pizarro said. "I can't let you just walk in here."

Max gave him a wintry smile. "Have you forgotten that I managed this project in Panama? There's nothing in this facility that I haven't seen before. I arranged for this visit well in advance and traveled almost three thousand miles today."

"You can use the conference room, but I can't allow you to wander around the facility. You're not cleared."

Max waved an impatient hand. "Fine, show me to this conference room. Lucinda should be there, too."

PIZARRO STOOD AT THE door of the conference room, looking disapproving when he had to move aside to make room for Emile's bed. Lucinda, Bill and Luke followed. There was a short reunion, and Max shooed Pizarro out.

"A little paranoid?" Max observed as he closed the door.

"Pizarro isn't so bad," Lucinda said as they took seats. "General Juarez has already called us this morning to lecture us on tighter security. The *Jornal de Brasília* story has got him upset. He would be here personally if he could have gotten here from Brasília in time. He sent Pizarro to supervise your visit instead."

"I haven't heard the broadcast. I take it the report didn't mention this facility."

Lucinda shook her head. "No, and no names either. So far, at least. Juarez was worried about Emile's name being in the news again after the baptism, but that story died out a couple of months ago."

"Other news reports claim that Castillo's support has been declining," Emile said. "That has caused pressure on Juarez. I suspect they have no intention of making me the first subject, should we be successful."

Max grinned. "Well, I may have good news, then. I've been talking to Doctor Artemis, and we think we might have a better alternative than uploading yourself to a computer. We may be able to cure you, at least partially."

Lucinda's eyes widened. "Cure? How?"

"We want to use nanites to repair the damaged arteries, restoring blood flow to the inactive parts of the brain. There is a good chance that brain plasticity will take over and restore much of the functionality once blood flow is delivering oxygen again."

"That sounds dangerous," Luke said. "If the nanites allow any more blood loss, Emile could have a stroke that would cause further damage and might even kill him."

"You're right," Max said. "That is exactly why it has never been tried before. Emile will have to decide whether to take the risk. I brought all the information he'll need to balance the risk with what might be done." He took a neurotrainer disk case from his pocket and handed it to Lucinda. "Emile, you and Lucinda can absorb everything tonight, and we can discuss it tomorrow."

Everyone processed Max's proposal in silence until Lucinda shook her head and smiled. "We'll look at everything very carefully later. Right now, I think we could use something less serious to talk about. You brought pictures of my godson, I hope?"

39

KENSHIN IKEDA KNEW ABOUT the revelation from the Western Alliance reporter, Ashton Gibbons. As an intelligence agent for the Japanese foreign service, he paid careful attention to the Western Alliance network. Japan was neutral, but it was still vital that his government be aware of developments in the struggle between the two great powers.

Ikeda had personal reasons to care about Gibbons's claims about the Methuselah project. Almost two years before, when the Pitcairners had established their embassy in Tokyo, he had spied on Susan Malley, hoping to uncover the secrets of Methuselah. He had failed, his attempt ending when Eastern Bloc agents cut him off from his informant. A Western Alliance agent had disappeared, adding to the Western Alliance's displeasure over the events leading to Pitcairn independence.

His reputation with his handlers had suffered, but perhaps he could redeem himself. To that end, he now waited in the reception area outside the office of his superior, Atsushi Shijo. He had been waiting for half an hour now, a sign of how far he had fallen in the eyes of the government.

"You may go in," Shijo's receptionist told him.

In the small, cluttered room, Ikeda stood, waiting again, while Shijo stared at his workstation monitor. Shijo had gained a few pounds in recent years, prospering even while Ikeda's career faltered. Ikeda had once been friendly with Shijo, but Shijo had become distant after Ikeda's distraction with Methuselah had gotten nowhere. It was not a surprise, then, that Shijo didn't look up when he acknowledged Ikeda's presence.

"I assume you've seen the report on your Methuselah Project," Shijo said.

Ikeda bowed. "Yes, sir."

"You may have been right to pursue the stories about this project." He paused.

"Yes, sir."

Shijo glanced at him, eyes narrowed, perhaps looking for any sign of disrespect in Ikeda's face. He scowled but continued. "I have been instructed to look into the true goals of this project. Given your previous interest, I am assigning the investigation to you."

Ikeda kept his expression carefully neutral. "I will give it my best effort. Do I begin immediately?"

"Yes. You will go to Panama. We have intelligence that the project scientists are, or at least were, working there. The details will be sent immediately to your armvir." He used the Spanish shortening of the phrase "virtual cabinet" to describe Ikeda's personal intelligence files, available on any of his devices.

M OST NIGHTS, EMILE STILL slept in his bed. While the JEM implants gave him the ability to walk and do other physical tasks, he still couldn't eat or drink, and the machines still exercised him. It wasn't necessary to do that every night, however, and that night he slept with Lucinda. They didn't make love; Lucinda had said she was too tired, but Emile suspected that the real reason was that she didn't want to connect to him. Given his feelings about Max's proposal, that didn't surprise him.

He thought Lucinda was asleep. If she were moving at all, he would have sensed it through the implants. He lay on his back, wide awake. Before he left, Max told them about the problems they were having designing a replacement for his visual cortex. Extrapolating from Max's gently worded pessimism, Emile thought further improvements in his condition from the current methods were doubtful. He would never see again, and possibly never hear, taste, or smell. He would probably get used to the different tactile experience that the implants provided, and more implants would add to that, but the connections to the sensory areas were too complex.

Max's proposal was elegant. Fix the crushed blood vessels and let the brain heal itself. As in most things, the devil was in the details. Fixing the arteries would chance reopening old wounds, leaking blood into the brain. The result could be a hemorrhagic stroke, possibly affecting autonomic systems like breathing, killing him. If the repairs were successful, there would still be no immediate improvement. His brain had adapted to losing functions after the accident, and the neurons that controlled those functions could be dead or repurposed. Improvement, if it came at all, would build gradually as his brain reacted to the repair. It was impossible to say how much improvement would occur over how much time.

But, if it worked! *Lucinda and I might have a normal life someday.* Was the risk worth that possibility?

H E UNDERSTOOD LUCINDA WANTED it to be his decision. She would avoid using a direct connection to him until he made that choice. She would be torn between the two alternatives as much as he was, and, as a neuroscientist herself, she understood perfectly what was involved.

If he could, he would have sighed. He would have liked to have sex with Lucinda that night, not only because he enjoyed it, but because it might have eased the stress of having to make this decision. His enjoyment increased every time they made love as his brain adjusted to the sensations created by the implants and what they meant. Would the new sensations be as good as the old ones someday? It didn't seem likely, but he couldn't know for sure.

That led to another thought. What if Lucinda is pregnant or becomes pregnant? Can I be any kind of father in my current state? Do I owe it to any future offspring to take the chance to be a normal parent? If so, he should decide as soon as possible.

L UCINDA LAY AS QUIETLY as she could, trying not to disturb Emile. Her thoughts were in such turmoil that she couldn't have helped Emile decide, even if she didn't think that it had to be his choice. The past eight years had been torture, watching Emile in that horrible locked-in state. The implants from JEM had raised her hopes at first, but they were only a tease, promising more than they could deliver. Max had made that plain.

Do I want Emile to risk even that shadow of their previous life? What would I do if the procedure killed him? Guilt struck her. She could enjoy sexual relations with Emile now, but was she being selfish? She knew that Emile's climaxes were real, but largely automatic. He didn't feel them in any meaningful way. She could tell that he enjoyed sex too, but was that only because he knew he was pleasing her? The emotions she received over the connection to Emile were too generic to understand him in that much detail. She couldn't shake the feeling that she was taking advantage of him, treating him as only an advanced sex toy.

She would not impose her opinion on Emile. He had to decide for himself. And what would she have said if she gave him her thoughts? She would only communicate her own confusion.

40

MAX HAD BEEN EVASIVE with his coworkers at JEM about why he was visiting Munt Electronics. He didn't want to pressure Emile to decide, but the planned public offering was a good excuse to talk to Jasmine and Franco. The Munts were the major investors in JEM Electronics, and a successful IPO would benefit them as much as the JEM staff.

"I'm still waiting for Emile's decision," he told Franco and Jasmine. "I think he's going to say yes, though, and I wanted to talk to you about the consequences."

"How it will affect JEM going public?" Franco asked.

"If we take on this project, we may have to delay the IPO," Max said.

"The problem, as I understand it, is that the project would be too far from JEM's expertise," Jasmine said. "You have no experience in working with nanites."

Max nodded. "Prospective investors wouldn't look too kindly at that. The initial stock price would almost certainly have to be much lower."

"How far are you from making the offering?" Jasmine asked.

"At least a couple more months. You know how complicated that can be."

"A lot of it is dealing with the government bureaucracy," Franco said. "Perhaps General Juarez could be persuaded to cut some of the red tape."

"Maybe." Max considered that. "We would have to convince him it would help the Methuselah Project. With his help, we might issue stock next month. How does that help, though? We would have to convince actual stockholders instead of potential stockholders."

"Not if we did the project," Jasmine said. "We were planning to use the money we gain from the IPO to expand Munt. We already have a department to manufacture nanites for industrial purposes. It wouldn't be as much of a stretch for us to add medical nanites, and our stockholders are already demanding we open new markets."

"We broached this idea with the managers in that department, and they're excited about the possibilities," Franco added. "A little scared, too, but excited."

"We can assign people to do some preliminary investigation now," Jasmine said. "Then we'll be ready to launch a full project after the IPO."

Max smiled. "I'll have to talk to my people, but I think they will be as enthusiastic as I am. Thank you both. You've been good friends, and I appreciate it. Emile will, too."

Franco's emotions came through clearly in the words generated by his Voice Magician. "You are very welcome. You've been good friends to us, too."

R EYNALDO HEARD THE TELLTALE vibrations of Emile Hernandez's bed and looked up. Emile was standing in his doorway, the bed trailing behind him. "What can I do for you, Doctor Hernandez?"

Emile stepped forward cautiously. "I need some advice from someone not emotionally involved."

Reynaldo blinked. This was a first. He didn't think the scientists liked him much, but perhaps he was wrong. He knew they sometimes resented his insistence on following the rules, but, after all, perhaps Hernandez understood he was only trying to keep the project running smoothly.

"Certainly, Doctor. What can I help you with?"

Emile moved forward until he felt the chair in front of Reynaldo's desk. It took him a few awkward seconds to sit down before he spoke again. "I have been talking to JEM Electronics," he began. He told Reynaldo about what Max had proposed. He included the dangers Max had described and explained that significant improvements in his condition wouldn't continue if he didn't undergo the nanite procedure.

At first, Reynaldo didn't understand what Emile's treatment had to do with the Methuselah Project. Hernandez might contribute more if the procedure returned some of his abilities, but, according to Hernandez's own words, it would be a long time, perhaps years, before there was any significant improvement. The project would be the worse for it if Hernandez died.

Hernandez was probably overstating the danger, however. How perilous could it be to rebuild a few arteries? Didn't doctors do it all the time? That these arteries were in the brain shouldn't matter that much. He wasn't a neuroscientist, though, so he could be wrong. Maybe he should discourage Hernandez for the good of the project.

"It does sound dangerous," he said. "JEM would create these nanites?"

"I assume so. We didn't talk about that."

"I understand they are trying to go public. Would this affect JEM going public?"

Reynaldo watched Hernandez as he hesitated. He might be a brilliant scientist, but he was no businessman. He must be wondering what the JEM IPO had to do with his treatment. "I don't think this kind of project is much like their current business," he continued. "Potential investors might be reluctant to buy stock if the company looks like it is overextending."

"I'll have to think about that," Hernandez said after another long delay. "Thank you for your feedback."

Reynaldo smiled, knowing that Hernandez could not see it. He felt confident that he had overcome another threat to the project, perhaps even saved Hernandez's life. He would tell General Juarez immediately; the general would be pleased. Making Juarez happy was a good career move and might make up for the slow progress.

"C ALL FROM DOCTOR EMILE Hernandez," Max's phone announced. This had to be Emile's answer! "Connect," Max said. "Hello, Emile."

"Good afternoon, Max." There was a long silence. "I should get right to it. I appreciate what you have suggested, but I've decided not to risk it."

The energy drained from Max, and he had trouble speaking. "I understand. You would be taking a risk."

"Too much risk. I hope I haven't disappointed you, but it's the best decision for everyone."

Emile's wording seemed curious to Max. Why everyone? Even with the Voice Magician, it was hard to read Emile. It wasn't any better in person since Emile couldn't change his expressions. "I thought you would want to take the risk," he said. "I've even discussed this with Jasmine and Franco. They were eager to work on it."

"The Munts? I know they have money invested in JEM, but how would they be working on it?"

Max slapped his forehead. "Emile, I'm sorry. You don't know, of course. Munt would be much better suited for this work than JEM. They already have a nanites department."

"Then the public offering wouldn't be affected?"

"Is that what you're worried about? Not at all, Emile. In fact, Jasmine and Franco plan to use their income from the IPO to fund this project. There will be new equipment, some hiring, and so on. Their board wanted them to open new markets; this will accomplish that."

"That changes things."

"You were afraid this would hurt the IPO? Admittedly, it would have if we planned to do the work. I didn't think you would realize that, or I would have told you it wasn't a problem."

"Reynaldo put the idea in my head," Emile admitted. "I'm not sure if he was trying to help or if he had some other purpose behind it. He might have thought Juarez would want him to dissuade me."

"Speaking of Juarez, we could speed up the IPO a bit if he smoothed the way with the government. The sooner we have the IPO, the sooner Munt can get started. So, should we get started, then?"

"Yes. Absolutely yes."

"Lucinda is on board?"

"I think she will be. She won't give me an opinion. She won't even connect directly with me to prevent me from reading her feelings. I'll talk to her now."

"Great. I'll call Jasmine and tell her we're moving forward. We'll make this work, Emile."

I KEDA IMAGINED INTELLIGENCE GATHERING had been easier in the distant past. Then, computer systems were penetrated, bugs planted, and identification forged. That hadn't been true for two centuries. At least he could travel openly, since privacy restrictions prevented the routine use of surveillance information.

In the six months he had been in Colón, he had learned little, the only link to Colón a report that Doctor Lucinda Hernandez had once worked for Munt Electronics. News reports told of an enigmatic past for Doctor Emile Hernandez, Lucinda Hernandez's husband. Methuselah, perhaps? The same reports said he had been severely injured and was probably no longer working in the field. Nine years after the Benitez-Baker Bill lifted limitations on neurological research, the field was still a narrow one, however. Odds were good that Lucinda Hernandez was a Methuselah scientist.

Investigating Lucinda Hernandez because Emile Hernandez had anti-government leanings was a long shot, but it was time to look elsewhere. He rented an aircar and flew to Cerro Punta, where the Hernandezes had once lived. Network reports told him that the Hernandezes had worked for the Panama Neuroscience Corporation and Cerro Punta University and that Emile had been friends with a professor at the University. Expecting the friend, history professor Benicio Young, to be more forthcoming than personnel at PNC, he told the car to go to the university first.

After the car found a parking place, Ikeda followed signs to get to the History Department. There, a receptionist took his name and notified Young that he had a visitor. Ten minutes later, the same woman ushered him into Young's office.

The man who stood to greet him didn't look like a university professor. He was tall and heavily built, with a round face that some might have found friendly. Ikeda thought only that the man obviously led a sedentary life and wore a welcoming mask to disarm strangers. Or was he succumbing to the paranoia common in his profession? Professor Young held out a hand, and Ikeda took it, smiling.

"Have a seat, Mr. Ikeda," Young said, waving toward a chair. "What can I do for you?"

Ikeda answered in Portuguese, confident that his skills in that language would mark him as a Western Alliance citizen. Spanish was more common in Panama, but Portuguese was the language of the government, dominated by Brazil, and most citizens spoke both. "I have been sent to inquire about a friend of yours. Doctor Lucinda Hernandez."

Young's face was suddenly less friendly. "Sent by who?"

"Munt Electronics, a former employer of Doctor Hernandez."

Ikeda realized immediately that he had made a mistake. Young frowned at him and looked at the phone on his desk. "Max Estevez."

It took a few minutes as the call was routed through a receptionist. From what Ikeda could hear, Professor Young didn't know Max Estevez, but he filed that name away in his mind for future use. Finally, Max came on the phone.

"Mr. Estevez, this is Ben Young, a friend of Emile's from Cerro Punta. I have Mr. Ikeda here asking about Lucinda and says he's from Munt Electronics."

Ikeda couldn't see Max's face on the phone screen, but he could hear the bewilderment in his voice. "I don't work for Munt anymore," Max said. "I don't know why they would send someone to talk to you. They know how to contact Lucinda."

Young's expression was now decidedly hostile. "She hasn't said anything to you?"

"No, and I talk to Lucinda every week or two. What does this man say this is about?"

Young looked up at Ikeda expectantly. "I'm afraid I'm not at liberty to tell you that," Ikeda bluffed.

"Thanks, Mr. Estevez," Young said. "Give Emile and Lucinda my best."

Young broke the connection and stared at Ikeda for a long moment. "You can tell whatever government bureaucracy you work for that I have no information on the Hernandez's. I think this would be a good time for you to leave."

Young assumed he worked for the Western Alliance government, probably because he preferred to speak in Portuguese. Ikeda thought about trying to use that to pressure Young, but Young didn't look susceptible to any claim he could make. If he persisted, Young might summon university security, and that would complicate matters. Besides, he had a name now, Max Estevez.

41

LEGAL RESTRICTIONS STOPPED JUAREZ from getting detailed information, but there was still much that was public or deemed relevant to his duties, and he received a weekly intelligence report flagging information on people or places concerning the Methuselah project. He scanned the most recent report, but there seemed little of interest, and that was a good thing.

One of the lower priority searches looked for unusual events at Cerro Punta University, where Emile Hernandez had once taught. He almost missed the reference to a security bulletin and still came close to ignoring it, but then he shrugged and expanded the report.

In three seconds, his workstation had his full attention. A history professor had reported a visit from a Mr. Ikeda, asking about Lucinda Hernandez. Two years before, Kenshin Ikeda had been spying on Susan Malley. It couldn't be a coincidence.

The university would have video of the visitor, but that wouldn't be public. A warrant would be necessary, but that might attract unwanted attention. He didn't need them, though. He was certain that the Japanese were looking into Methuselah.

FINDING ESTEVEZ HAD BEEN easy. He wasn't working at Munt anymore, but his position as a founder of JEM Electronics was a matter of public record. Ikeda was cautious, but he could acquire information about JEM from the network anonymously.

Estevez was a founder, along with Edward and Joelle Bascomb. The name Bascomb sounded familiar, and a quick request to his armvir had reminded him that the Hernandezes had attended the baptism of Emile Bascomb, presumably the son of Edward and Joelle. He was close now.

Ikeda knew he had stumbled in Cerro Punta. The history professor had been cagier than expected and had almost certainly told university security about the encounter.

Whether the report got beyond the university was anybody's guess, but he couldn't take any chances. It would be too dangerous to speak to Max Estevez himself.

Japanese intelligence had no resident personnel in Colón. Ikeda needed to recruit someone to approach Estevez, and it took a while to find someone who could do the job for him. He found a bar in an upscale part of the city and began hanging out there, identifying himself as Sora Takahashi, getting to know the staff and the regular customers. At first, they treated him with suspicion, but after time, and after he let it be known that he was Japanese, and not from one of the former Asian countries now part of the Eastern Bloc, the bar's denizens had accepted him.

Robert Kyle was a divorced office worker in his forties, only a few years younger than Ikeda. As near as Ikeda could determine, Robert came to the bar out of loneliness, possibly looking for female companionship, but willing to settle for friendliness from anyone. Ikeda had homed in on him early on, learning more than he cared to about the man's life, but establishing himself as a trusted confidant. Ikeda had hinted at having marital problems of his own, and now he was ready to exploit the relationship.

"I think my wife is cheating on me," he confided. "I have his name, and I want to confront him, but I can't find him."

"What do you want to do when you find him?" Kyle asked.

"I just want to talk to him and let him know what he's doing to our family. To our children."

"I wish I could help," Kyle answered.

"Maybe you can. I know the man has a friend, a big wheel at a local company. If I talked to this man, he would know who I was and wouldn't talk to me. Do you think you could talk to him? We could make up a story about why you want to know where my wife's lover is."

Kyle hadn't been drinking much, but his mind was probably at least a little affected. After a moment's thought, he nodded. "Sure, why not?"

"You'll want to talk to Max Estevez at JEM Electronics. Tell him you're trying to find an old friend from Cerro Punta named Emile Hernandez."

K YLE WAS NERVOUS AS he walked into the JEM lobby and approached the receptionist. "I would like to speak to Max Estevez," he said.

"Can I tell him what this is about?" she asked.

"Sure. I'm looking for a mutual friend I've lost track of, and I thought he could help me locate him."

"And your name?"

"Robert Kyle."

"Connect to Max," the receptionist said.

"What's up, Angelita?" a voice answered.

"I have a Robert Kyle here who would like to ask you about a mutual friend," Angelita said.

"The name doesn't sound familiar. Who is he asking about?"

"Emile Hernandez," Kyle said.

Angelita repeated the name, although Max had probably heard it. There was a long pause before Max responded. "Send him in."

Angelita disconnected and waved at a door to her left. "Down the hall and second office on your right."

Angelita had been friendly, but the smile was gone, and she was looking at him oddly. *Who is Emile Hernandez?* He nodded and went through the door into the hallway beyond, fighting an urge to turn and leave the building. What had Sora gotten him into? No, he imagined the receptionist's reaction. Sora was a good friend.

The door to the second office was open, and Kyle poked his head in. The man at the desk looked up and motioned him in, but he didn't look friendly either.

"You're looking for Emile Hernandez?" the man asked.

"Yes, sir," Kyle answered. "I've been told you know Emile and hoped you could tell me where to find him. I haven't heard from him in a while."

"When was the last time you talked to Doctor Hernandez?"

Doctor? Why hadn't Sora told me that the man was a doctor? More important, how should he answer Estevez's question? He had to make a guess. "A year ago. Maybe two."

Estevez's face softened a little. "I don't think we know the same Emile Hernandez. My Emile moved to San Diego in the California district about four years ago. And, in his condition, he doesn't talk to people in the usual way."

Sora must have been wrong in thinking this man knew anything about Sora's wife's lover. At least he had done his part to help his friend. He wondered what Estevez had meant about Hernandez's condition, but resisted the urge to ask. That might make Estevez suspicious again.

"I see," Kyle said. "I'm sorry to have wasted your time. Thank you."

42

K ong's cage was in one corner of the laboratory. Isaiah had a working area there also, including a small screen so that he could access the network when Kong didn't need anything. It wasn't that hard to take care of the chimpanzee, and Isaiah spent a lot of time on the network, either for entertainment or staying current with the news.

A headline about a Pitcairn wildlife refuge caught his eye, and he ordered the screen to display that story. He remembered the stories two years before when Pitcairn had refused permission to create a wildlife refuge on the planet. According to the story, Western Alliance negotiators had made a deal with the Pitcairners to open a science center where the Western Alliance had wanted to build a wildlife refuge. The story portrayed the science center as a small start at convincing the Pitcairners to aid in preserving endangered Terran species.

Emile's favorite commentator, Anna Cortez on the *Pitcairn News Service,* would have a different version of the truth, but who could believe what the Pitcairners said? The Pitcairners were as backward as the uncivilized people of the northern districts, people like his father, who abandoned his mother when he was three years old. The Pitcairners tended their farms and wouldn't survive without help from Earth. Their planet wasn't hostile like Trist or Goddard; Pitcairn was warm and had plenty of rain, but that didn't satisfy the Pitcairners. Of course, the early ships colonizing that planet were from the north, the old United States, so perhaps it was inevitable that the colonists would be as inferior as the northerners on Earth.

"Isaiah feed Kong," the chimpanzee said, interrupting his thoughts. He turned and chuckled at the pleading look on Kong's face. It was wearing a neuro-interrogator with a Voice Magician, and the words came through clearly. It had been challenging to train Kong to use the device. Isaiah couldn't just read words and record the ape's reactions the way a human could be trained. The word had to be illustrated with an actual object or action, and the resulting reaction was less well-defined for the chimp. Still, after years of training, Kong had a vocabulary of about 150 words and had learned to ask questions. This last ability had impressed the neuroscientists, who thought that the use of the neuro-interrogator might be stimulating neuron formation in the ape's primitive language center.

The neuroscientists! They scurried around, doing their little tests, and thinking their deep thoughts, but not accomplishing anything. For a long time, he had wondered what it was all about. They rarely talked about their project when he was in earshot, but he heard things occasionally. There were a lot of pompous words used to confuse normal people like him, but they underestimated him. When that reporter had revealed what he called the Methuselah Project, Isaiah knew that must be what the scientists were working on.

It seemed silly to him. How could you put a human mind into a machine? But General Juarez's visits showed that the government didn't think it was silly, so there must be something to it. Isaiah wondered how it would feel to be a machine.

"Isaiah feed Kong." The voice seemed more insistent this time. It was Kong's normal feeding time.

"OK, OK." Isaiah got up and began putting the ape's meal together. Kong watched him with what seemed to be impatience. Sometimes he didn't think Kong liked him that much. It seemed friendly with the others, though, so it was probably just his imagination.

WHEN GENERAL JUAREZ SHOWED up, demanding a briefing on their progress, Bill joined the others assembled in the conference room, and Lucinda gave Juarez a quick overview before turning the meeting over to the others.

"What we're trying to do is incredibly complicated," Bill said. "We've changed our attack on the problem, though, and hope that will help."

"I haven't approved any change in the project," Juarez said.

"We haven't been able to isolate consciousness," Emile said. "Any transfer into a machine will have to involve transferring memories, though, and we have a better handle on that."

Juarez nodded. "All right. That makes sense. How long will that take?"

"It might take a while," Emile said. "We've reached a dead end trying to track neuron output because that can only give us memories as a subject is recalling them. That won't be sufficient for your purposes."

"You implied you have another way," Juarez said.

"Perhaps. There were papers in the data you found for us that speculated that memories are stored in the cell itself. If that is the case, we need to read those memories directly from the cell."

"Can that be done?"

"We are going deeper into the old research material, and we're finding hints of work done there," Bill said. "That's only part of the problem. We have to get inputs from just about every part of the brain to form a complete memory, and then we need software that can put them all together into something that can be stored and retrieved. And how can we test to see if we have accurately recorded the memory?"

"Our brains have some trouble playing back memories, too," Emile said. "That's why they're not always reliable."

"We've had some success in trying to extract and store memories from synapse analysis," Alyssa said. "If we can use cell analysis instead . . .."

"Did we?" Emile interrupted. "We stored a gigabyte of information, but how do we know that's really the memory? When we try to play it back through a neurotrainer, it's gibberish."

"The neurotrainer wasn't designed for that," Aurora said. "Words and some emotion are one thing, but we're trying to include data from all six senses."

"Then design a better neurotrainer," General Juarez commanded. "If you need more people, I'll get you more people."

"An expert on the neurotrainer input interface would help," Aurora said. "The person I replaced, judging from what I've seen of his work, was very good. Could we bring him in for a week or two?"

"Eddie," Bill said. "I'm not sure how much work he's doing these days. The JEM IPO made him rich."

"Bascomb?" Juarez asked. "No, he's unreliable. Find someone else."

Bill frowned. Juarez was basing his opinion on Eddie and Joelle going on a honeymoon instead of reporting directly to Pearson Interstellar. That hadn't been fair, and Bill suspected there was some prejudice involved. Still, Bill remembered what Eddie had been like before he met Joelle. Now that neither one of them had to work anymore, had Eddie reverted? *Probably not.* Joelle was still there, and there was little Emile, too. Eddie was a family man now and still worked at JEM, at least part-time. None of that mattered anyway. Eddie was undoubtedly the most experienced person they could get.

"I've kept in contact with Eddie and Joelle," he said. "I can ask him if JEM could spare him for a bit."

Juarez glared at him. "I distinctly said to find someone else."

"I'll talk to Max and make sure they can spare him," Lucinda said. "If so, we might still need you to convince him to come up here."

Reynaldo had the look of a man that wanted to be anywhere else than at the meeting. He was supposed to be in charge, but, as usual, General Juarez cowed him. Juarez, meanwhile, stood up, red-faced, hands clenched into fists. Was Lucinda intentionally baiting him? She had never enjoyed answering to him.

"I will not be ignored," Juarez bellowed.

Lucinda turned on him, and Bill thought he could see sparks in her eyes, but her voice was infuriatingly mild. "Then start making sense, General," she said. "Eddie Bascomb is, without doubt, the best person for the job, if we are lucky enough to talk JEM Electronics into letting us borrow him. So, what is more important—your bias against him or the success of this project?"

Juarez's voice turned icy. "You are not in charge of this project and do not make these decisions, Mrs. Hernandez." He pointed at Reynaldo. "Mr. Clementi is in charge, and you would do well to remember that. I fast-tracked that public offering for JEM Electronics as a favor to you. You will cooperate if you want any future considerations."

Bill wondered why Lucinda was so confrontational. He hadn't talked to her before the meeting, but some new stress seemed to act on her.

"We all know Reynaldo is your puppet," Lucinda said. "And you haven't answered my question."

Juarez sneered at her. "Find someone else. Mr. Clementi will help you." He bent to lean his hands on the table and glared at Lucinda across the table. "I think we've accomplished everything we can at this meeting. I have more important matters to deal with in Brasília." He straightened, nodded to Reynaldo, and walked out of the room.

Reynaldo watched him leave and then turned to Lucinda. "I'll start a search for someone suitable."

Lucinda waved a hand at him. "Do that. I won't hold my breath, though."

"If you could give me your requirements. . .." But Lucinda was already gone, and Reynaldo didn't finish the sentence.

After Juarez left, the meeting broke up, and Lucinda and Emile sat alone in the conference room. "You are upset," Emile said.

Lucinda sighed. "That man sets me on edge. This project is stressful enough, and he comes in here with his arrogance and bigotry. I guess I overreacted a little."

"Are you sure it's the project that is causing stress? It's no worse than it has been for years now."

"That's all, Emile. I'm all right. Really."

"You wouldn't want to connect to my neurotrainer, would you?"

Lucinda snorted. "You know that wouldn't tell you anything about what's causing my stress. It would only confirm that I'm a bit stressed out." She sighed again and rested her head in her hands. "OK, so maybe that report from JEM has affected me, too."

"Why? They've only been working on it for a few months and have already made considerable progress. I'm feeling very optimistic."

"The idea of all those little invisible things rooting around in your brain gives me nightmares. Not literally, thank God, but you could die, Emile."

"Or I could live."

"I know. I'm sorry. I'm being selfish. It must be terrible for you to be trapped in your body like that."

"It hasn't been easy for you, either. Things will get better. I believe that, and you have to also."

"I'll try." She studied her husband, sitting rigidly next to her, with his bed just behind him. The slight improvements from the JEM implants probably reminded him of everything he had lost. He couldn't see or hear normally and couldn't eat normal food, relying on the functions of the bed to communicate and keep him nourished. Could she live that way? She shuddered.

"What are you going to do about getting Aurora some help?" Emile asked.

"I don't see any real choice, despite what Juarez says. We can't get someone to just come in for a week or two with anything close to the experience Eddie has in working with those circuits. I think I can arrange something with Max and Eddie, and to hell with Juarez."

"How are you going to manage that?"

Lucinda grinned. "You know what they say. It's easier to ask forgiveness than get permission."

"**G**OT A SECOND?" MAX asked.

Eddie looked like he had been in a vicious fight. Red splotches that appeared to be blood spattered his hands and lab coat. When he looked up, Max saw a few drops streaking his face. Eddie had been working on a heated container with tubes running from it to a bloody-looking mass of some gelatinous material.

Eddie frowned. "The new nanites still aren't sealing properly. They work well on the artery repair, but if they can't prevent leakage . . ." His voice trailed off. Max knew the implications better than he did.

"Jasmine called. She wanted to know how it's going."

"As well as can be expected, I suppose. Joelle keeps telling me that the hardware is easy; it's the software that's complicated."

Max chuckled. "You two have it easy. The brain is more complicated than any hardware or software you engineers have come up with."

Eddie grinned. "I guess that's why us engineers have actually accomplished something."

"Uh, huh. Anyway, Lucinda called, too. She said she needed some help from an expert on neuro interfaces, but I told her you were only taking on projects that interested you now that you're rich. You and Joelle are not even working for us now since that nanite test stand you're making a mess with is technically for Munt."

"Anything to help Emile," Eddie said. "What does Lucinda want me to do?"

"They need to build a device that can record and playback sense data as well as the language input we can record now. Apparently, their hardware engineer is having some trouble and could use some help. They think they need a week or two of your time."

"Not a problem. It will take longer than that for Munt to come up with improved nanites." He paused. "I'll take Joelle and Emile with me. We would all like to see the old gang again."

"Fine. Put together a report for Jasmine, and I'll have arrangements made for the three of you. As soon as possible?"

"Sure. It will only take me an hour or so to get the report together. I'd better clean up and tell Joelle first, but if you can get us a suborbital tomorrow, I think we can be ready."

THEIR SUBORBITAL PLANE SAT on the tarmac a thousand feet away, and Bill watched the transport bring its passengers to the gate. Eddie carried little Emile, now a hefty one-and-a-half-year-old, while their standard luggage carrier rolled automatically along behind them. Bill hugged Joelle and shook hands with Eddie and Emile, the latter looking uncertain about the whole thing. The child seemed wide awake, though, and Bill assumed he had slept on the plane.

"No offense," Eddie said, "but just you?"

"Emile and Lucinda wanted to come, but we're keeping this quiet, and Emile would attract attention," Bill answered. "Juarez was upset about the idea of consulting with you, and our manager, Reynaldo Clementi, would tell Juarez about this if he knew."

"It's probably a good thing that I won't be charging you, then." Eddie smiled. "So how is this going to go?"

Bill looked at his friend. They had met nine years before, and Eddie looked more mature, but the roguish grin hadn't changed much. Eddie still looked fit, so his prosperity hadn't made him soft. Joelle probably had something to do with that; she showed no sign of having carried Emile. "We have reservations for dinner tonight, including the hardware engineer who needs your help. We can talk about it there and decide how to handle the consultation. If necessary, we'll try to sneak you into our lab, but it would be hard to prevent Juarez from finding out if we do."

"OK. We'll head to the hotel and do some planning of our own. We might as well work some vacation into this trip."

"Maybe the three of us can find time for a hike, like the old days," Joelle said.

"I would like that," Bill said. "We can talk about that tonight, too."

JORGE'S STEAK AND SEAFOOD had been a fixture in San Diego for over fifty years. Its founder had retired twenty years before and reportedly lived in a mansion overlooking

Mission Bay. His grandson, Jorge III, now ran the restaurant, but it had changed little from the days of the first Jorge. Bucking modern trends, the chefs still grilled premium meat-substitute steaks over open flames and prepared other items similarly in "the old-fashioned way."

It was difficult to talk with Jorge's food in front of them, so after the meal, they moved to a quiet corner in the adjoining bar and ordered coffee. Somewhere between the time they moved to the bar and the delivery of coffee, the younger Emile fell asleep and laid quietly on the cushioned couch while the adults talked.

Eddie had called Jasmine that afternoon. Munt Electronics had an office in San Diego, and Jasmine had readily agreed to give Eddie use of the facility. "I've arranged for a small office with two workstations and everything else we should need," he told them. He looked at Aurora. "I assume you'll be able to get access to all your work from there."

"The connection will have to be confirmed at my workstation, but that shouldn't be a problem," Aurora said.

"Bill or I can do that," Lucinda said.

"Are you OK with working on it tomorrow?" Eddie asked Aurora. "We can wait a week if you were planning to take some time off for Christmas."

"I planned to work anyway," Aurora answered. "If we could make it a short day, though, we're having a Christmas party tomorrow afternoon."

"You're all invited," Lucinda said. "Reynaldo will be there, of course, but we won't be lying if we tell him you're here on vacation. You and Aurora can scope out the problem tomorrow at the Munt facility and come over for the party in the afternoon. Take a long weekend to think about Aurora's questions. If that works for you, you can start the real work on Monday."

"Come to our house for Christmas dinner, too," Emile said.

"Nothing too special," Lucinda said. "Emile can't eat, of course, but we would both love your company."

"Sounds great," Joelle said. Eddie nodded in agreement.

WHEN BILL ESCORTED THE Bascombs into the laboratory, the party was well underway. Someone had spent a lot of time decorating, including a traditional tree in one corner. Tables displayed a variety of beverages and snacks. Greetings with old friends and introductions to people not part of the original team followed. Later, sitting with drinks and plates of food, more serious conversations began.

"Aurora has made a good start," Eddie told Lucinda and Emile. "But there are so many places where pieces of memories are kept. The brain integrates it all into one memory, but even the brain can't do it reliably."

Lucinda nodded. "The brain interpolates a lot. Vision especially, where the brain fills in holes with what it calculates should be there."

"It does that both to address shortcomings in its sense organs and to optimize the storage requirements, right?" Eddie said.

"Complicated because it's associative, not absolute," Emile said. "Like people who remember the lyrics of a song as they go, not knowing a line until they've sung the previous line."

"That's all part of the problem," Lucinda said. "We've been concentrating on episodic memory, but that's not enough. Episodic memory only holds the highlights of an experience with semantic memory filling in the gaps."

"We can probably ignore muscle memory," Emile said. "Semantic memory would be, as Lucinda said, important, though. Implicit memory, too."

Eddie frowned and scratched his head. "OK, you lost me. What's the difference?"

"Episodic memory is, as the name suggests, the memory of a specific event or episode," Emile said. "Semantic memory results from experience and doesn't have a specific event associated with it. The brain fills in the memory of an event from expectations stored in semantic memory, one reason memory can be unreliable."

Emile paused, and Eddie thought about the implications of Emile's description until Emile continued. "The ability to read, for example, is the result of many experiences mostly forgotten, but the ability remains. You probably know what muscle memory is, and it is very similar to implicit memory. They both work without conscious effort, from repetition. Muscle memory tells you how to walk, for example, and implicit memory puts structure into your life without you even being aware of it. The things you go through automatically when you're getting ready for bed, for example."

"I think I'm getting a headache," Eddie said.

"I think there's a lot of difference between individuals, too," Aurora said.

Eddie shook his head. "It sounds like we're talking about software again. Maybe we should get Joelle and Isabella into this discussion."

Lucinda poked her head out the conference room door. "I think she's introducing my godson to Kong."

A FTER CIRCULATING AROUND THE room and getting Emile a snack, Joelle took her son over to the corner where Kong was sitting in the back of his cage. Isaiah was enjoying the party with everyone else, so the chimp was alone. He looked up as Joelle approached and watched them until they got within ten feet of the cage. Then Kong jumped forward with a screech that went uninterpreted by the ape's Voice Magician. It did interpret Kong's gleeful shout: "Joelle! Joelle!"

"You remember me," Joelle said. She smiled. She hadn't seen the chimp since the project moved to San Diego four years before. "Hello, Kong."

Kong thrust a finger between the cage bars and pointed to Emile. Emile jerked backward, either startled or frightened. Joelle hugged him and caressed his head as he watched the ape with a sideways stare.

"This is my baby," Joelle said. "His name is Emile."

"Emile?" Kong's face twisted in confusion. "Small. Not Emile."

Joelle laughed. "Another Emile. My baby."

The ape's confusion seemed to fade a little. "Baby." Then his face seemed to brighten. "Eddie?"

Was Kong asking about another person from the past, or had it connected the baby to his parents? The chimp had a limited vocabulary, and it would be difficult to get an answer to that fascinating question.

"Eddie is here," she answered. "I'm sure he'll come over to say hello, but he's busy now."

Joelle didn't think Kong understood all of that, but he seemed to get the gist of it. The ape scratched his head as if he were thinking and then asked, "Tori?"

That stopped Joelle for a moment, but then she remembered Kong's trainer in Colón. Tori hadn't wanted to leave Panama, and they had hired a new trainer. Joelle had been introduced to Isaiah, but she didn't remember his name immediately. "No, Tori isn't with us."

Kong bowed his head. "Kong like Tori."

Joelle frowned. Was Kong merely expressing affection for his prior trainer, or did he not like his current trainer and was comparing the two? She was about to ask Kong another question when Isabella joined them.

"They want us in the conference room," Isabella said. "I guess the problem is getting beyond hardware."

Joelle nodded and turned to Kong. "I'll see you later, Kong. I'll bring Eddie, too."

"Like Eddie. Like Joelle."

As they walked back through the party, Emile stared back at Kong, and Joelle decided that a trip to the San Diego Zoo would probably be a good idea while they were there. They only stopped long enough to give Emile another cookie before joining the others in the conference room.

Lucinda briefly summarized what they had talked about before Isabella and Joelle arrived, finishing by saying, "We may have to rely on software more than we thought."

"It might be a good idea to look at the *Asimov* data again," Isabella said. "I examined Isaac's cognitive processes, not its memory. Susan Malley may have done more work in that area."

"Maybe, but I don't think the library ship computer remembers the way humans do," Emile said. "It used its cognitive ability to analyze searches of its data storage. Can we store human memories that way and expect them to be retrievable as human memories? Earth should have sent a neuroscientist with you to *Asimov*. There are a lot of tests that we could have done, but you wouldn't be knowledgeable in that area."

Joelle saw a look of irritation pass over Isabella's face, but Isabella was used to working within Emile's communication limitations. Her face cleared, and she must have realized Emile hadn't meant to insult her. "That gives us two problems to attack," Isabella said. "We have to figure out how to read the memories from the brain and store the results. Then we must work out a way to turn that data into a memory again."

"I suggest we attack one problem at a time," Lucinda said. "Once we can store enough information on a memory, we can worry about integrating it back into a memory."

"Have you been using Kong in trying to extract memories?" Joelle asked.

"We did at first," Lucinda answered. "It's difficult to know what Kong is thinking and what impulses are relevant to the thought."

"He has clear memories of people he knew before," Joelle said. "He remembers me by sight and seems to remember Eddie and Tori, too."

"Lucinda thought about that. "It's worth a try. A memory strong enough to last that long might stand out and give us a starting point."

44

"Good morning, Kong," Isaiah said. He repeated the greeting a couple of minutes later when he had the chimpanzee connected to the Voice Magician.

"Hello, Isaiah," Kong answered.

"How are you this morning?" Isaiah asked as he checked the ape's water dispenser.

"Kong want Tori."

Who was Tori? Isaiah thought hard for a few seconds. He knew that Kong's trainer in Colón had been a woman. The name Tori did sound familiar. Kong had recognized the two northerners that had crashed the Christmas party. Had that triggered another memory from Colón?

"Tori isn't here," he told Kong. "I take care of you now."

"Kong like Tori."

Isaiah frowned. Was Kong comparing him to the ape's previous trainer? Kong didn't seem to treat him with the same affection the chimp showed other members of the project team. He had thought he was imagining things, but was he?

Those northerners, the Bascombs, had put the idea in Kong's little brain. It was Monday, five days after the party, and he suspected they were still around. Aurora was not at her usual workstation, and Isaiah remembered Lucinda had wanted to bring Eddie Bascomb in as a consultant, but General Juarez had vetoed the idea. Was Aurora meeting Bascomb outside the laboratory so that Reynaldo wouldn't know?

Isabella wasn't in yet, either. Didn't she replace Joelle Bascomb after Juarez fired the Bascombs? No, that was Alyssa, but Isabella was a programmer, like Joelle.

Kong was all right for now. He was supposed to prepare the chimp for some memory testing that the scientists wanted to do, but he saw Reynaldo come out of his office and decided that could wait. He strode over to Reynaldo. "Aurora and Isabella aren't here," he said. "Is there anything wrong?"

"They told me they were taking the week off," Reynaldo said. "They had vacation time, and I'm surprised more people didn't want to combine the Christmas and New Year's holidays."

"Oh. I thought maybe they were showing the Bascombs around or something."

"The Bascombs? Haven't they gone back to Colón? I thought they were only here to visit old friends at the Christmas party. They can afford the trip now, I understand."

Isaiah nodded. "You're right. They're probably gone. I guess I wondered if their visit had anything to do with bringing Bascomb in as a consultant."

Reynaldo looked startled. "I'm sure that's just a coincidence." Reynaldo nodded to him and walked off, but Isaiah thought Reynaldo was thinking about their conversation.

THAT AFTERNOON, COLONEL PIZARRO was back. Lucinda saw him go into Reynaldo's office, but he was in there for only a minute. Then he marched into Lucinda's office.

"Colonel Pizarro," Lucinda greeted. "How nice to see you again. To what do we owe your return?"

"General Juarez contacted me," Pizarro said. He stood stiffly, his voice matching his posture.

Lucinda motioned him into a chair and smiled sweetly at him. "And what can we do for the general?"

"He has received reports that there were unauthorized visitors allowed into this facility last week. He asked me to investigate."

"Is he referring to the Christmas party? The Bascombs came to San Diego on vacation and dropped by. They're old friends, and they wanted to show off their baby."

"That was what he was told. Didn't he forbid you to bring the Bascombs into this facility?"

Lucinda tried to look thoughtful. "No, I don't think so. He didn't want us to bring Eddie in as a consultant for some reason, but he said nothing about keeping him out of our laboratory. We weren't working during the party, and Eddie is familiar with the project since he and his wife worked on it in Colón."

"General Juarez wouldn't agree with that assessment. In fact, he has sent me here to take over security for the Methuselah Project." Lucinda thought she had seen a hint of a smile on Pizarro, but it was gone now.

"Really?" Lucinda smiled. "Well. Welcome to the team, I suppose. I'm afraid we don't have a spare office for you, though. We could put a desk over in the corner. We don't have any of our equipment over there because Kong's cage is there."

"Kong? The chimpanzee?"

"Right. Don't worry about Kong, though. He's quite well behaved, and Isaiah takes care of him."

P IZARRO'S FIRST THOUGHT WAS that the placement of his desk was a statement about how the scientists felt about him being there. He remembered an incident as a child when an ape had thrown feces at his brother at a zoo. His brother had been taunting the animal and probably deserved it, but it made Pizarro wary of being that close to Kong. After his desk was brought in the next morning, he sat there, one eye on the chimpanzee.

Kong seemed equally interested in Pizarro. The ape clung to the bars of its cage, watching him with a curious expression. Isaiah came over, introduced himself, fed Kong, and fitted Kong with a neuro-interrogator and Voice Magician. "Be back in a minute," Isaiah said.

As soon as he was gone, Kong left his food and came back to the bars closest to Pizarro. After a screech got Pizarro's attention, the ape pointed to himself and said, "Kong."

Pizarro chuckled in surprise and pointed to himself. "Michael."

Kong grinned, showing an impressive set of teeth, and pointed to Michael. "Michael. Hello."

"Hello, Kong."

Apparently having exhausted its conversational capability for the moment, Kong grinned once more and returned to his food. Michael shook his head and picked up a summary of the Methuselah Project that General Juarez had given him. Even the summary was over his head, but he hoped to learn something while he was assigned to the project. From what he had seen so far, he didn't think his security duties would be very taxing.

He wasn't sure why he was even there. If there had been a large security contingent, he might have been in charge of it, but there was just him, a colonel, doing a job that an experienced enlisted man could handle. Did Juarez know about the criticisms he had voiced about Juarez's boss, President Castillo? Michael had been discrete, but it was always possible that one of his fellow officers had curried favor with the general by reporting on him. This assignment could be a punishment. Michael smiled. If that's what it was, he would try to make the most of it. He turned back to the summary.

"IT'S BEEN NICE HAVING you around again," Lucinda said. She was holding little Emile and trying to eat her breakfast, but the child made that difficult. "We'll miss you."

"I think it's our son you'll be missing." Eddie chuckled. "Max wants us back for the New Year's party, and I'm eager to get back. Munt should have a new batch of nanites ready for testing soon."

"My work with Eddie will help me lick the storage problem, too," Aurora said. "We'll stay in contact so that he can help me figure out the library ship's storage of memory."

"That is the key," Emile said. "We don't need to play back memories for humans. We need to record memories so that a computer can process them."

Lucinda grinned. "As long as we don't get any interference from General Juarez, we might make this all work yet."

"You're not worried about Pizarro?" Joelle asked.

"I don't care," Lucinda said. "I'm not going to let Juarez get to me anymore. If he doesn't like it, he can find someone else to run his project."

"I was never completely sold on being uploaded to a machine, anyway," Emile said. "Munt's nanite project sounds much better."

"Hopefully, the new batch fixes the locality problem," Eddie said. "The sooner I test them, the better." While the repair nanites could do their work over a tiny area at any one time, the nanites that would prevent leakage needed to operate over a wider area, the locality problem Eddie referred to.

"Keep us posted on that," Lucinda said. "And say hello to everyone for us." Little Emile was fussing and looking at Joelle. With a sigh, Lucinda handed him back to his mother and returned to her breakfast.

45

A COURIER FROM MICHAEL Pizarro's official duty station arrived from General Juarez with an envelope of thick plastic. Michael Pizarro looked at it curiously before placing his thumb on the security tab, causing the envelope to pop open. He carefully removed two sheets of paper and a small high-frequency receiver and recorder. The first piece of paper was a standard list of security procedures for government laboratories, and he set it aside. The second was a note from Juarez.

Colonel Pizarro,

The procedure list accompanying this letter is actually a sheet of tiny microphones designed to pick up conversation over a short range such as within a single room. We need to keep a closer watch on the activities of the Methuselah scientists, so please post the list somewhere where it might pick up suspicious conversations. The receiver will automatically turn on whenever it detects a conversation and can record approximately five hours before you have to copy the recording to another device.

The Methuselah Project is vital to our government, necessitating this measure to protect it from security breaches or disloyal citizens. Notify me if the device records any such conversations.

General Salvador Juarez

Michael frowned. Did Juarez have a warrant for this? He would have mentioned it if a military overwatch judge had signed off on it. Therefore, Juarez was asking him to spy on the project illegally, and he wasn't sure how he felt about that. He wasn't naïve; governments sometimes felt it necessary to do that sort of thing. He didn't understand why it was necessary to break the laws in this case, however.

General Juarez had told him about Ikeda's inquiries into Lucinda Hernandez, so there were security issues. Other than the Ikeda's visit to the history professor in Cerro Punta, though, Juarez didn't know of any activity from Japanese intelligence. Monitoring the laboratory wouldn't uncover anything in that area even if Ikeda was still around, and it seemed unlikely that the Hernandezes could be traced to San Diego.

Was his reluctance based on his distrust of President Castillo? Certainly, that was part of it. But his security clearance wasn't high enough for him to evaluate the necessity of spying on the project. He could post the security procedures list somewhere and wait to see what it recorded. He wouldn't send any compromising recordings unless they were relevant.

The hardware person, Aurora, went into the conference room to work occasionally. *I wonder why.* They held meetings in that room, not all of which he attended, and it might be useful to listen in. A wall in the conference room was an unobtrusive placement.

"DID YOU GET THE data format information I posted?" Aurora asked.

On the conference room monitor screen, Eddie nodded. "Looks reasonable. I'm going to add a couple of suggestions and post them back. Give me an hour or so."

"It's just so generic," Aurora said. "We need to work out more details if we're going to succeed."

"We'll get there. This is just a start. We'll have a lot of iterations on this before we solve all the problems."

Aurora nodded. "I know. I'll wait for your suggestions." She paused. "How did the latest nanite tests go?"

Eddie grinned. "Again, iterations. This batch was better than the last, and Joelle has been looking at the code, but we have a way to go."

"Still the locality problem?"

"Right. If we could get the nanites to communicate with each other, we might deal with it, but that kind of functionality would make them too big."

"Maybe you need a third class of nanites. Messenger nanites to carry information between them."

Eddie's eyes widened. "That might do it! I'll run that by the engineer at Munt. Great idea, Aurora."

ICHAEL TRANSFERRED THE DAY'S recordings to his phone that night and played them back. There had been no meetings that day, so only the conversation between Aurora and Eddie was recorded. Aurora's side of the conversation was clear, and he could hear Eddie's words if he concentrated.

Juarez suspected—more than suspected—that Eddie Bascomb was helping the Methuselah Project team. Juarez was right, but why did he care? Security was the obvious answer, but if Bascomb wanted to cause trouble, he already knew more than enough about the project. Did it have something to do with the reference to nanites? What is the relevance of nanites for the Methuselah Project? The neuroscientists use nanites to investigate the brain, but Eddie and Aurora seemed to talk about something else. It wasn't difficult to imagine that nanites might be used for sabotage. Was that what worried Juarez?

He listened to the recording again. There was nothing in it suggesting malicious intent. Bascomb was helping Aurora with something she was having difficulty with.

Furthermore, Juarez was Castillo's man, and that was a separate set of concerns. President Alejandro Castillo was a threat to the people Michael had sworn to defend. He was convinced of that. If he hadn't thought that before, the probable illegality of his spying was persuasive evidence.

He didn't know what he should do about the recording, so he would do nothing until he had more information. Aurora would contact Bascomb again, and he would record again. Eventually, he would know what to do.

ICHAEL WATCHED ISAIAH FEED Kong. The animal trainer wasn't told about the nature of the project, and the scientists tended to fall quiet when Isaiah was around. Still, Isaiah might have useful information.

"Kong is a friendly animal," he said. "He introduced himself when I arrived."

"He can say a few words when he has that fancy equipment on." Isaiah gave the ape a sour look. "He's not saying anything right now without it."

"I didn't think chimpanzees had the vocal apparatus to speak. He must have the mental capability, though."

Isaiah grimaced. "I suppose." His expression changed to a grin. "More than some northerners, anyway."

Michael hid his distaste. He knew many people looked down on anyone born north of the Rio Grande River, and thought that a reaction against ancient bigotry from the north against the south was the principal cause. All that had ended, though, when the Yellowstone Event devastated much of the former United States and Canada. That disaster had been the trigger for the rise of the southern nations and the formation of the Western Alliance.

"General Juarez knows that, too," Isaiah continued. He gave Michael a wink that Michael supposed was meant to be conspiratorial. "That's the real reason he fired Eddie and Joelle. He'd been looking for an excuse, and their unapproved vacation gave it to him."

Isaiah looked across the room to where Bill was talking to Lucinda. "Bill is next on the list. He's another northerner. Once we get rid of him, maybe we can move this operation south. I wouldn't mind moving to Brazil."

That explained the effort to keep Bascomb's aid a secret. It wasn't a security problem; it was simply a defense against prejudice.

"We could have kept the girl, though," Isaiah said. "She was nice looking for a northerner. I wouldn't mind taking her away from Eddie for a little while."

It was getting too hard to hide his disgust. Michael grunted and returned to his work.

A week later, Michael still didn't know what to do. He read the notice from General Juarez again, telling him that the general would be there the next day. During the week, he had watched the scientists. They were a hard-working, dedicated team, trying to do something that seemed impossible to Michael, even allowing for his scanty knowledge of the subject. Aurora had not contacted Bascomb again, and he believed Bascomb was only an occasional consultant.

The nanite issue was the only troubling question. Michael tried to overhear conversations between the team members whenever possible, but he rarely understood what they were talking about. With Juarez coming, he needed to know what Aurora and Bascomb had been discussing. Perhaps a "dumb" question might get some answers.

"Part of what you are doing is trying to detect changes in the brain and interpret them, right?" he asked Bill.

"Right. We combine data from PET scans, fMRI, and other things." Bill smiled. "That's probably just a bunch of acronyms to you, but the techniques go back centuries. Modern equipment has much better resolution, and nanite sensors have helped a lot, but mostly it's the same old stuff."

"Is the resolution good enough?"

Bill shrugged. "It's what we have, so it has to be. Even with the nanites, it's difficult to isolate individual neurons, much less individual dendrites."

"Are they the same as the medical nanites that keep us healthy?"

"No, different. There are a lot of different nanites." He paused and grinned. "You know about the work Munt is doing for Emile with nanites?"

Now he was getting somewhere. "No, I don't."

"Munt is developing nanites that can repair some of the damage to Emile's brain. We're hoping it might eventually restore some function."

Relief hit Michael like a cool breeze. He could turn over recordings of other meetings held during the week, and Juarez wouldn't have to know about Aurora's consultation with Bascomb. The meeting recordings would only add detail to the briefings Juarez would get from the others without arousing Juarez's bigotry against northerners.

M ICHAEL TOOK JUAREZ TO the conference room so that they could talk, and, secondarily, so Juarez would notice the disguised microphones. Michael tried to interpret Juarez's expression. His eyes were red, and he looked older than when Michael had first met him only a year before. For Michael, nothing good would come from drawing the general's ire.

Juarez noticed the list/microphones immediately. "You haven't sent me any recordings yet."

"I have recorded several meetings in this room, sir," Michael responded. "There hasn't been anything relevant to project security, however, so I have only saved them. I will supply you with copies, but it's all technical talk about their progress."

"Perhaps. In the future, send recordings as you get them. We should have more knowledgeable people analyze the conversations." Juarez seemed irritated, but other issues than the recordings were affecting his mood.

"Certainly, sir."

"So, in your opinion, are they making progress?"

"Yes, but I think it has been slow, sir. They are working hard, but the project's complexity has taxed them. On the bright side, there is some hope for improvement in Emile's condition, and that could eventually help the project."

Juarez smiled, but the expression looked strange against the rest of his face. "Nanites? It might help if it doesn't kill him first. They've told you about their attempt to repair his damage?"

"I heard something about that, sir, but not very much."

"They haven't told you all the gory details? They want to use nanites to repair the damage caused by the accident. Apparently, that's more complicated than you would think because the damage is in the brain. Not as simple as operating on a leg."

"I would think that it would help the project if Doctor Hernandez could work normally again."

Again, that faint, not very convincing, smile. "One can hope." Juarez straightened in his chair. "Give me those recordings before I leave. For now, have Clementi and Mrs. Hernandez come in, and I'll get their update on progress."

Later that day, Michael met with Juarez again to give the general the recordings. Juarez took them and then looked at Michael. "We need to do anything we can to make this project successful as soon as possible. President Castillo will stand for reelection in two years, and his prospects don't look good. It won't help if this project gets into the news again, and it will if the networks learn about this facility."

"I understood that Marisol Weston wouldn't run this time."

"No, but someone will, and it probably won't be a northerner this time."

There was that prejudice against northerners again, more evidence that bigotry was the only reason for Juarez's obsession with keeping the Bascombs away. Michael had taken an oath to defend the Western Alliance and its principles. If Castillo lost the election in two years, he didn't think that would be a terrible thing.

But all that was above his place in the chain of command. Destroying the recording with Bascomb was the right thing to do, but the rest would be up to others.

I KEDA WAS A STUDENT of history. Once, it had been easy to get information about people: addresses, employment, marriage status, and even more personal information. The internet, an early version of the network used for everything now, had been an unlimited resource for people like him. Of course, eventually, the world sickened of such an invasion of privacy, and legislation that made all that unavailable.

San Diego was a large city with millions of people. Hundreds, perhaps thousands, were named Hernandez, and restrictions made it impossible to know even how many of them were named Emile. Property ownership records, once public knowledge, were private without a government warrant. Ikeda had gotten to San Diego based on access to limited public sources and deception, but then he had hit a wall.

He was not surprised, therefore, that he was being recalled. Monitoring the activities of the Eastern Bloc, more aggressive and much closer than the Western Alliance, was deemed more important. He wasn't so sure. Methuselah was supposed to be an attempt to preserve people by uploading them to a computer. Ikeda's instincts told him there was more to it, and that worried him.

"E DDIE SAYS THAT THE repair nanites are still having problems coordinating with the bleed control nanites," Max told the assembled Munt team.

"It wouldn't be a problem outside the brain," Leo Partida, head of Munt's Nanite Engineering Department, said. "The bleeding Bascomb reports is minor."

"Agreed," Max said. "But doing repairs inside the brain is the goal. The messenger nanites are a dead end?"

"So far," Leo responded. Max was sympathetic. Munt's engineers had been trying to find a solution for months. Any kind of electromagnetic radiation was impractical; a nanite antenna would have to be very short, effective only for short wavelength ionizing radiation. Such radiation could have dangerous side effects.

"One of my people, Jimmy Herrara, had an idea," Max said. "It sounded promising to me; the brain already uses chemicals to communicate. Why couldn't nanites do that?"

"Herrara is your expert on the visual cortex, isn't he?" Franco Munt said.

"He's branched out since then," Max said. "We've been buying a lot of neuroscience trainer recordings, and he's been using them, especially since we abandoned the idea of creating a vision prosthetic."

"You mean neurochemicals?" Franco asked. "Like dopamine?"

"Exactly like that. We might have to use something different to avoid interfering with brain function, but the principle is sound."

"I suppose it could work," Leo said. "I thought neurons were electrical, though."

"Impulses are carried through the neuron electrically," Max answered. "Communication between neurons takes place through the release and reception of neurochemicals."

Leo nodded as if he understood, but Max wondered if he did. It didn't matter, though; he would have people working for him that would understand.

"MUNT ELECTRONICS HAS A working prototype of their messenger nanite," Lucinda said. "They developed a nanite that uses a synthetic neurochemical to communicate between the repair and the clotting nanites."

"And Munt can use this to develop nanites that will help Doctor Hernandez?" General Juarez asked. Lucinda thought he looked genuinely curious, a bit of a surprise. His mood seemed better, though, than in other recent status meetings where stress had seemed to affect him.

"Munt is testing the idea," Aurora said. "They think it will work because it mimics the way neurons communicate."

"Excellent!" Juarez said. "So, what about the work in storing memories?"

"We're making progress," Emile said. "We have to develop a method of storing the memory in a way that a computer can interpret meaningfully."

"It's been ten years," Juarez said. His expression changed, and Lucinda saw some of the old stress coming back. Then he smiled, but it didn't seem sincere. "Hopefully, we'll have another ten years to make this work."

LUCINDA WANDERED OVER TO Kong's corner and exchanged greetings with the ape. Michael was reading at his desk, and she looked over at him. "Getting along OK with Kong?"

Michael looked up with a smile. "We're great friends." He looked over at Kong. "Friends, Kong?"

"Kong like Michael," the chimpanzee agreed through his Voice Magician.

Lucinda laughed. "That's good. I don't think Kong has the same high opinion of the general."

"He avoids this corner," Michael said. "We never talk at my desk."

"He seemed to be in a better-than-usual mood today, though."

"He's been under a lot of pressure. President Castillo's reelection prospects weren't very good, and the general's position is therefore equally precarious."

"You sound like you think Castillo's position is improving."

Michael nodded. "Now that Emile has disappeared from the public again, stories about this project have died down. The president wasn't happy about the media coverage after the baptism." Michael paused. "There's another reason, too. You may have heard about the launch of the exploration ship, scheduled for October. They named the ship *Alejandro Castillo*, and the president is planning to attend the launch. He thinks he can use the publicity to emphasize his accomplishments."

"Will it help?"

"I'm not a politician," Michael said with a shrug. "I think it will help, but what do I know?"

Later, Lucinda related the conversation to Emile. "The launch will help Castillo, assuming it's successful," Emile said.

"So he gets another term?" Lucinda said.

"If he doesn't, we're probably out of a job." Emile's Voice Magician captured the amusement in his thought. "Still, the election is more than a year from now. People are questioning Castillo more, and whoever his opponent turns out to be, there's one issue that hasn't come up yet that could still hurt him."

"What's that?"

"Anna Cortez. Everybody forgets now that he almost certainly destroyed her career because of her opposition in the last election. Her resurrection as a commentator for the *Pitcairn News Service* guarantees she will be used against him."

Lucinda frowned. "Are we doing the right thing, working on this project? We haven't talked about it since the neuro-interrogator turned out to be a non-issue."

"Even if we succeed, uploading someone will be an expensive proposition. If one or two people get to prolong their existence, I don't think that presents the danger that the neuro-interrogator might have."

"So you're all right with this?"

"Working with JEM and Munt, we're making advances that are helping a lot of people. Yes, I'm fine with it, regardless of whether we are successful at our primary goal."

Lucinda hugged him, and he must have felt something, because he put his arms around her, too. The tension that had pried at them during the neuro-interrogator project had faded, but had never disappeared entirely from her thoughts. She felt a lightness as more of the darkness dissolved away.

T HE LAUNCH WAS SCHEDULED for 7:32 p.m. San Diego time. With dinner over, Lucinda and Emile settled into the couch in his home office to watch network coverage. Neither was normally interested in space exploration, but *Alejandro Castillo* was an exception. Fully automated, with no human crew, it would open new star systems for human exploration by installing Links at each star system it visited. Manned starships could then use Enhanced Stenhouse Drive to travel to new star systems in weeks rather than years.

The first destination was Sirius, a blue giant with a companion star but, as far as solar system-based studies could detect, no planets. Lucinda wondered whether mission planners chose the star to placate Fermion sympathizers fearing contact with alien civilizations or because it was so much different than the star systems already visited by humans. Probably a bit of both, she decided.

She remembered the Fermion reaction to the false story about the Methuselah Project three years before and how the group had used the nonsense about communication with aliens to attack the space program. The exploration ship's mission of expanding human presence in the universe was a major issue with them, and choosing a star system without planets for its first visit would delay the worst of the reaction.

Coverage began with President Castillo's arrival at the Houston Space Center. The Center, home for much of space activity for almost three hundred years, would only monitor the launch. The Western Alliance had built the exploration ship in orbit at the massive Prendergast Station, and the ship would start its journey there.

The network broadcast showed Castillo moving through a throng of dignitaries and reporters toward a stage with a podium. "Castillo doesn't look as happy as I would have expected. Michael said that Castillo was counting on this launch to bolster his campaign."

"I think the opposition has weakened any effect that might have by nominating Ana Sanchez-Smythe," Emile said.

"Just because she was chairman of the Space Exploration Policy Committee?"

"That, and her support for the space program. She was a sponsor of the bill authorizing this exploration ship project. She'll make use of that to minimize Castillo's claim on the project. No doubt she'll capitalize on Castillo having the ship named after himself, too."

"I think Castillo is going to speak now."

They were silent then, both listening as Castillo spoke. His words were predictable, taking credit for the exploration ship and portraying it as an example of the progress made during his twenty years in office. Then came the promises that such progress could only continue if he were reelected for another ten years. He did not mention the opposing candidate.

The speech ended ten minutes before the launch. Lucinda watched as coverage tracked Castillo leaving the auditorium and going to the nearby control center. There, a calm voice was counting down the last seconds. The display shifted to a view dominated by Prendergast Station, with *Alejandro Castillo* floating inside its construction platform a short distance away. The scene zoomed in on the exploration ship, an enormous cylinder not much different than the library ships that had gone to the three star colonies.

Since Emile couldn't see it, Lucinda tried to describe the scene. "They're showing the ship now. A construction platform hides it, but I can see some of it." The countdown finished, and Lucinda could see flickering light playing along the framework of the construction platform. "The engines have ignited," she said. "Yes, it's moving. I can see the forward end now. It's coming out; OK, it has cleared the platform. I can see it all now, a long gray cylinder with the engines flaming at the back end. The camera is following it as it moves away. Picking up speed now and the camera is zooming in more as it gets farther away."

A commentator reported that the launch had been perfect, a great victory for the Western Alliance, and a sign of its superiority over the Eastern Bloc. After several minutes of that, with *Alejandro Castillo* rapidly diminishing on the screen behind him, the commentator announced they would switch to coverage of a speech by Ana Sanchez-Smythe.

A screen still showed the starship moving against a backdrop of sharply etched stars, but a new face appeared behind a rostrum, that of Senator and Presidential candidate Ana Sanchez-Smythe. She was specific about her role in the launch, detailing her sponsorship of the original bill allocating funds for the ship's design and her support of the work building *Alejandro Castillo,* promising increased support for such projects if she were elected. The speech gave details of other proposed projects, in clear contrast to the broad claims that Castillo had made. The speech ended with disdainful remarks about Castillo's arrogance in naming the ship after himself.

"That was an effective contrast to Castillo's address," Emile observed. "Perhaps we should update our employment data. We may not have jobs after the election."

Lucinda smiled and then remembered that her husband couldn't see her face. "It wouldn't hurt."

"I don't know enough about Sanchez-Smythe. I hope she's better than Castillo."

Lucinda patted his shoulder. "I'm sure she will be, darling."

"WE THINK WE KNOW how to store memories," Lucinda said. "We can trace an experience through the brain and detect where neurons activate to store the memory." She nodded to Isabella.

"We've been able to map the neurons involved in establishing an episodic memory with unprecedented accuracy," Isabella said. "A complete memory may involve inputs from any or all five senses, so we had to trace each of them and duplicate the brain circuits that integrate them. I wrote software to store the results, as well as information about the emotions being felt. The hardest part was identifying and saving the semantic memory bits that the brain would use to fill in a memory. I'm not sure we have that right yet."

Juarez looked at Lucinda. "You said you think you can store memories, but she," and he pointed to Isabella, "says you have done it."

"That's not what Isabella said," Lucinda said. "We're storing something, and that something is the most accurate record of a memory that we can make right now. We can't guarantee that we're not missing some critical aspect of the memory, though. Incorporating semantic memory is tricky and will almost certainly need more work."

"Don't you have tests that can verify whether it works?" Juarez asked.

Lucinda shrugged. "We can read back the record in storage and verify that it says what we want it to say. That's trivial. How can we know it is complete, though? And how do we translate that data into something that a computer would understand as a complete entity?"

Juarez hadn't looked happy at the beginning of the meeting, and now his expression was even more crestfallen. Lucinda knew Castillo was still falling in polls, and the slow progress of the project only added to the general's stress. She almost felt sympathetic.

"We're working on that now," she said. "It may be simpler to at least verify the completeness of the stored memory by working out a way to send the memory through a modified neurotrainer into a human mind."

"So you're making progress on storing memories," Juarez said. "What about consciousness?"

"We are still looking for consciousness correlates, and hope that improved resolution will help there, too," Emile said. "If a cell stores each memory component, it's possible that consciousness resides there, too. We're learning, but, as we keep telling you, it takes a while."

Lucinda listened to Emile and noted what he was not saying. She knew Emile believed that a computer would have to be conscious before it could truly interpret the stored memories. She wasn't sure; lower animals, with no sign of true consciousness, still had memories.

Emile didn't care about storing consciousness. He told her it was better to have the government fund science than weapons. They might not meet Juarez's goals, but they were gaining knowledge that could help humanity in ways they couldn't imagine. The possibility of replaying stored memories through a better neurotrainer was one example of that.

Juarez gave a sigh that was almost a groan. He looked tired, a man without the energy to berate them for not having better news. The election news for Castillo, and therefore Juarez, might be worse than the networks reported.

If so, it was likely that the government would shut down the project in less than a year, and all their work might disappear. It didn't matter whether they learned how to upload human consciousness. Lucinda didn't want to lose everything they had learned to some archive reserved for failed secret projects.

48

"**F**ORGET WHAT THE NETWORKS say," Isaiah said. Lucinda debated whether she should say something. His angry attitude wasn't appropriate; she should probably stop him before he drew responses from others. Isaiah continued. "President Castillo is going to win. The voters won't believe the lies the media is telling about him."

It was almost noon, and, with polls closed in Hawaii, the network would broadcast the results of the election in a few minutes. The entire staff was sitting in the conference room, watching network coverage on the screen there.

"Which lies would that be?" Bill asked.

Isaiah scowled at him. "The lies told by northerners to support their pet candidate."

"You're not saying that Sanchez-Smythe is one of us northerners, are you?" Bill asked. He laughed.

"Her husband must be with a name like Smythe. If she would marry a northerner, she's not a true patriot."

"Enough," Lucinda snapped. "The results will be announced any second now. Let's everyone wait quietly, and we'll find out soon enough."

Isaiah and Bill glared at each other, but didn't speak. Then they turned their attention back to the screen. Twelve o'clock came.

"There seems to be a delay," the commentator said. "The Department of Elections in Brasília has not given us the results yet. We are trying to determine what the problem is." He paused and shook his head. "This is unprecedented in the history of the Western Alliance. I'm sure we'll be hearing momentarily."

Five minutes passed, and then ten. "Speculation is that there has been a computer malfunction," the commentator said. "There has been no news from the Department of Elections, however, so that is only speculation."

Half an hour passed, and Lucinda considered sending everyone back to work. Nothing useful would be done until the election results were announced, though, so she dropped the idea. Reynaldo, watching the screen with the same rapt attention as the others, apparently didn't care. The network showed video of protesters in front of the Presidential Palace, but it was unclear what they were protesting. Some were carrying signs, but the view didn't get close enough to read them. The commentator said that the police were keeping anyone with a camera away from the palace, but that wasn't possible. Cameras could be too small and too easily hidden.

An hour passed. The network broadcast biographies of the two candidates and outlined their positions on different issues. Lucinda noticed that the coverage was avoiding all the controversy that had come up during the campaign. It wasn't wise to show favorites with the outcome imminent, but still uncertain. The lesson of Anna Cortez probably wasn't lost on the managers of the different network services.

At 1:40, the commentator looked out of the screen with new excitement. "We have the results!" He paused. "The Department of Elections has announced that the new president of the Western Alliance will be Senator Ana Sanchez-Smythe."

The conference room filled with voices, drowning out the commentator's next words, but a banner moved across the screen, giving the election result: 49 percent for Sanchez-Smythe and 48 percent for Castillo. There had been an almost unknown third candidate, probably accounting for the remaining votes.

Isaiah was the loudest voice in the room. "She stole the election somehow!" he was saying. "That must be why they delayed the results."

Lucinda frowned but refrained from pointing out that the closeness of the vote probably caused the delay. No doubt diagnostics were run against the election computers to confirm that there were no irregularities. She was surprised that the results were that close, but perhaps she shouldn't have been. Castillo had denied all the allegations against him throughout the campaign, and his supporters had refused to doubt him. Most people still believed what they wanted to.

She had tried not to think about what the election might mean to the project and to the people who had dedicated themselves to it for so long. What did it mean to Emile? Munt Electronics was still working on the nanites that might help his condition, but even if Munt was successful, Emile would probably not find employment when the government canceled the project. Max thought Emile could teach again, but Lucinda had doubts. She might have trouble herself, after spending years at work that the government would prohibit her from talking about.

There was little doubt in her mind that the new administration would cancel the project. President-elect Sanchez-Smythe had used the Methuselah Project against Castillo, an example of his arrogance and misplaced priorities. Castillo had, of course, denied its existence, and his success at keeping the location of the project a secret had helped his credibility. Putting the project in remote San Diego had been a smart move for that reason.

Isaiah was still ranting, and it was time to end that. "All right, we've seen the results," she said. "It's time to get back to work."

Isaiah glared at her for a second and stomped out of the room. Bill watched him leave and then looked at Lucinda. He raised an eyebrow in question, and Lucinda wondered what he was thinking. Was he concerned about Isaiah's attitude? Was he questioning why they should worry about getting back to work when it was likely that the project was over? Isaiah, not knowing that they were working on Methuselah (and, given his support of Castillo, probably not believing that Methuselah existed), didn't realize that Castillo's end was their end, too.

"I'M SURPRISED WE HAVEN'T heard from General Juarez," Lucinda said to Michael. The election was two weeks in the past. There were still riots and unrest in the southern districts of the Western Alliance as Castillo supporters protested the election, but San Diego had been quiet. The north had supported Sanchez-Smythe, so it was likely that San Diego had nothing to protest.

"I've talked to him twice since the election," Michael answered. "I gather he's been busy meeting with the president and others to figure out what they're going to do now. He wants us to keep going as we were for now. The new president won't take over for another two weeks, and I think General Juarez is hoping the project won't be noticed immediately even after she takes office."

"Given her remarks during the campaign, that doesn't seem likely."

"Perhaps not. If the project is canceled, I'll go back to my military duties. Do you have plans?"

"I've put out a few feelers. Panama Neuroscience Corporation, where I worked before, has shown some interest, but they want to know what I've been doing the last few years."

"The general would probably have you arrested if you admitted you were working on Methuselah."

Lucinda nodded. "I know I can't do that. I can talk about the papers we published before Methuselah, and I've made some vague statements about caring for Emile, but eventually, I'll have to do better than that. Bill and Luke will have the same problem, though, and they don't have Emile as a reason. I think the others can talk about their work at Pearson Interstellar in terms vague enough to get by."

"Isaiah is coming," Michael said. They fell silent as Isaiah went to Kong's cage. Lucinda stood and smiled at Michael. "It's been nice talking to you. I guess I should get back to work."

49

F IVE DAYS AFTER SANCHEZ-SMYTHE took the oath of office, General Juarez stormed through the door to the laboratory and stalked over to Michael's desk, hardly looking at anyone else. "Conference room," he said.

Michael glanced at Juarez's face and jumped to his feet. "Yes, sir."

Once in the conference room, Juarez closed the door with a bang. "Sit down," he ordered. He took a seat himself and glared at Michael. "She asked for my resignation from the cabinet today," he said.

"Surely you expected that, General."

"I thought she would do it four days ago." Juarez clenched his right fist. "She waited until my replacement got to Brasília. General Benitez. Perhaps you've heard of him?"

"He made several speeches in favor of President Sanchez-Smythe, I believe. Not very insightful, if I remember."

Juarez gave him a sour look. "Insightful enough to hurt President Castillo. I'm sure his speech writer is much more intelligent than the general himself. I have orders to take over some minor liaison group in Ensenada. Work probably more suited to you, Colonel."

"So the project is being canceled."

"Not yet. The president didn't say anything about Methuselah, and I'm hoping that she'll forget about it, at least for a while. Funding is going through Pearson Industries and can be overlooked when she looks at the budget."

"Am I being reassigned?"

Juarez shook his head. "Technically, you were never assigned here. You'll keep your assignment at the base but work from here. General Alvarez has agreed to ignore your absence at the base."

"So you want the work here to continue without being noticed by the new administration," Michael said. He was puzzled but wasn't sure he should question Juarez. Curiosity overcame caution after a few seconds. "Why do you care if the project continues?"

"President Castillo wants it to continue." Juarez glared at him. "You will continue to make sure the project progresses. Castillo may be out of office, but he still has influence in military circles. Is there a problem?"

Juarez wasn't in Michael's chain of command, but that was only a technicality. General Alvarez was in charge of Michael's duty station, and if he was backing Juarez, Michael had little choice. "No problem, General."

"I won't be able to visit anymore. It will be up to you to make sure the project is successful. And that it stays unnoticed. We must limit our contact to phones and messages passed through General Alvarez."

"I understand, General."

"Good." He paused. "I suppose I should tell Lucinda Hernandez something about the situation. Carry on, Colonel."

"T HANK YOU FOR COMING, General," President Sanchez-Smythe said as they shook hands. "Please, have a seat." She pointed to an overstuffed chair in a sitting area in one corner of the office and took another chair for herself.

Juarez fought his confusion. She wasn't acting the way he had expected. He looked at her as he sat down. Ana Sanchez-Smythe was in her late fifties and might have been attractive once. She was trim with regular features, but years of politics had left lines of stress on her face. She was giving him a friendly smile, though, which helped smooth the wrinkles.

"I suppose you're wondering why I wanted to see you, General," she said.

"Given the decline in my responsibilities, I was curious. Yes, Madame President."

"On the contrary, your duties are still very important. The group you will command is vital to our plans."

"I had thought it was just a routine assignment, supervising some aspect of military-industrial relations," Juarez said. "Am I wrong?"

"You are mostly correct. I wouldn't use the word routine, however. You will manage very specific activities for which you are eminently qualified."

"I don't understand, Madame President."

Sanchez-Smythe laughed. "No, I'm sure you don't. Let me explain. You and Castillo bungled things badly. I wasn't going to bring you into this because of that, but I believe events made things very difficult for you, and I have reconsidered. During the campaign, my speeches were carefully designed to give the impression that Castillo's plans were moot." She leaned toward Juarez. "Now, secrecy about the project can be reestablished. Your new office in Ensenada is closer to the project without being close enough to garner unwanted attention."

Juarez couldn't believe what he was hearing. He couldn't help asking. "What project are we talking about?"

Sanchez-Smythe looked surprised. "Project Methuselah, of course. You will be responsible for making it happen. Castillo isn't the only one interested in immortality."

LUCINDA STARED AT THE letter, signed by her old supervisor, Vince Rodriguez, at the Panama Neuroscience Corporation. They would be happy to have her back, not in a leadership position, of course, and therefore with less money than she had made as a project leader. The letter had arrived the week before, and she hadn't given Vince an answer.

I'm not likely to receive a better offer elsewhere, not after being out of touch for so long. Juarez wanted to keep the project going, but they were meeting this afternoon, probably to shut them down.

She and Emile had some savings, but it wouldn't be easy. Government health programs would cover Emile's medical expenses, but that wouldn't solve all the problems of dealing with his condition. Munt Electronics was optimistic about repairing the damage the accident had caused, but she knew as well as anyone that success there wouldn't mean Emile could return to work. The University might take him back as a lecturer, though, so they could probably manage.

What about the others? Alyssa said she was going to stay with Pearson Interstellar. Bill would return to his teaching position in New York. Isabella and Aurora both had skills that should land them something quickly. Luke might be a problem, but the future seemed to be a step down for all of them.

People still said that every cloud had a silver lining. Perhaps a change to nongovernment research would finally sweep away the last of the tensions between Emile and me. Even after all these years, and after the neuro-interrogator was deemed a failure by the government, there's still that slight strain in our relationship. She sighed. She would send Vince a message after the meeting with Juarez.

J UAREZ WAS SMILING, BUT Lucinda thought there was something sinister in that smile. A hint of conspiracy, perhaps. Certainly, the arrogance was there.

"I will dispense with any preliminaries and go right to the core issue," Juarez said when everyone had taken seats in the conference room. "I'm sure that, despite my assurances that I would keep this project alive, you have all wondered about the security of your positions. After all, new administrations often make sweeping changes in the programs of previous administrations."

He paused and looked around the room. "You have may have heard that a new appointee has taken over my position. That is, of course, normal. President Sanchez-Smythe has chosen her own cabinet, as her predecessors have always done. While that lessens my influence in many areas, let me assure you it has not affected my management of the Methuselah Project."

Lucinda glanced over at Michael, who was looking puzzled. Was Juarez saying something different than what he had told Michael in private? Juarez had said he was going to get right to the point, but he hadn't yet. His words seemed to mean that the project was still alive, despite the criticisms the new president had levied against it during the campaign.

"This work has been going on for years now," Juarez continued. "You've made many advances, but the ultimate goal remains far away. The good news is that President Sanchez-Smythe has continued the project and reconfirmed my position in leading it."

Reynaldo clapped his hands. "That is wonderful news, General."

Juarez nodded to him and continued. "Unfortunately, there is bad news, however. The new president is not as patient as President Castillo and has requested that I motivate you all to work harder. She wants to see much more progress than in the past and has given me the authority to make that happen. Any questions?"

"We have given this project all our energies already," Lucinda said. "If you have some kind of draconian measures in mind, they will only hurt the project. We're not a squad of your soldiers, and our work requires sharp minds, not brute labor."

The general's smile faded a little. "You shouldn't belittle the brave men who protect your freedoms, Mrs. Hernandez."

"That's Doctor Hernandez, and that was not my intention. So, tell us how you're going to help our progress and why the president feels that is so important."

Juarez's smile was back in full force, even displaying his teeth a little. "I was hoping you could help me with that, Doctor. Now that the president understands the importance of this project, funding has opened up. Could you use more people? More equipment?"

"Perhaps. As you know, we have made some advancements in storing memories. The next step is developing software that can integrate the stored data back into a memory that the computer could interpret."

"That doesn't sound too difficult to me," Juarez said.

"Breaking up inputs from the brain and storing the results was difficult. Reintegrating them into a single thought is an order of magnitude harder. We don't know how to reintegrate the memory for a human brain yet, much less than for a computer."

"Then how do you know you've accurately stored the memory?"

"We don't." Lucinda smiled. "And that's the problem. We can identify the sense data that goes into the memory and store it. Is that enough to duplicate the full memory? Probably not; other experiences of the person affect a memory, among other things. What would our data look like if it could be sent back to a person different than the one having the original experience? Would it be the same even for the original person? These are questions we have to answer."

"Then figure out what you need, and I'll get it," Juarez said through clenched teeth. "Our new president will not want to hear excuses."

50

J UAREZ WAS GONE, BUT the tight feeling in her stomach was still there. The letter from PNC was still on her desk, unanswered. The others had gone back to work while she retreated into her office, but she knew she would have to talk to them soon.

And tell them what? She wanted to tell them she was quitting and advise them to do the same. There was no way to speed up what they were doing, but Juarez would continue to put pressure on them. What was the point? She picked up the letter and looked at the phone on her desk. "Connect with Vince Rodriguez."

"If you mean Vencenzio Rodriguez at the Panama Neuroscience Corporation, you are beyond their normal business hours," the phone said. "Do you want to call him at home?"

She had forgotten about the differences in time zones. It was late afternoon in San Diego, and Vince was probably eating dinner in Panama. She wanted to ask Vince a few questions before deciding, but she should talk to Emile before then.

"Never mind," she said. *Suppose I do quit.* What would Juarez do? She didn't think he could force her to stay on the project, but would the government pressure her the way they pressured Emile when he left PNC. *Could I stand up to it as Emile had until the accident?* Emile resisted out of principle, but she was only tired and frustrated.

She didn't have to commit to anything that afternoon. Until she did, she was still the manager of the project, and needed to pull herself together and do her job. She went into the laboratory to call everyone together.

I SAIAH WATCHED AS EVERYONE else marched into the conference room. They didn't include him, of course, because he wasn't supposed to know what they were all meddling with. Just because he took care of their dumb ape, they thought he was dumb, too, especially the northerners. He had suspected for a long time, though, that they were working on the Methuselah Project, suspected since its existence became public. After President Castillo's defeat threw them all into confusion, he was sure.

He noticed the change in General Juarez on this latest visit. After meeting with him, everyone else seemed in better spirits, too. Did that mean that the new president supported the project?

He wasn't sure how he felt about that. Even when President Castillo was in control, the idea of uploading consciousness had seemed suspect to him. It was bad enough that the Tau Ceti library ship had somehow become conscious; at least Asimov was light years away. Creating more conscious computers, even if they started out as humans, was wrong. He couldn't articulate a reason, even in his mind, but he knew it was wrong.

"Y OU ALL HEARD JUAREZ say that Methuselah will continue development," Lucinda told the assembled team. "We can, however, expect increased pressure for results." She let everyone take that in.

"We need to go forward with an improved neurotrainer," Emile said. "If we can reintegrate the stored memories for a human, we'll be closer to doing it for a machine."

"We need Eddie," Bill said. "Joelle would be a big help, too."

"I agree," Aurora said. "I couldn't have gotten this far without Eddie's help. Inventing a neurotrainer that can replay memories has been difficult."

"That might not be possible," Lucinda said. "I'm not sure Eddie would want a full-time job here. And that assumes we can get it past the general."

"He might be more amenable to that now," Michael said. "If pressure on you is increasing, you can be sure that pressure on General Juarez has increased as well."

"All right." Lucinda looked at Reynaldo. "Let's do it right this time. Reynaldo, this should be your job. Create whatever requisitions you need to get us permission to hire the Bascombs."

Lucinda had expected Reynaldo to be reluctant to ask Juarez about hiring Eddie and Joelle, but he didn't seem to be. Maybe he agreed with Michael's assessment of Juarez's position. Or he knew he would be under pressure, too, and understood that hiring Eddie and Joelle would help the project. Either way, the manager nodded in confirmation.

"I'll call Eddie and tell him what we want to do," Bill said.

"Good," Lucinda said. "I think you would have the best chance of talking him into coming back. If you can get him interested in this new project, I'll have to talk to Max."

G ENERAL JUAREZ SHOOK HIS head. The scientists just wouldn't drop the issue. They still wanted the Bascombs back and had talked Reynaldo Clementi into supporting their request. There had to be other qualified people, but they fixated on Eddie Bascomb.

He couldn't prove it, but he was sure they had consulted with Bascomb already. It should have been easy to prove; computers monitored everything everybody did. Unfortunately, it was illegal to access integrated data without a warrant. Every government department tracked some aspect of daily life relevant to that department. Reports could combine that data to uncover almost everything about an individual, but only a court order could release the required decryption keys.

That thought sparked another speculation. President Sanchez-Smythe had expressed her interest in Methuselah-based immortality, but was that the real reason? Castillo was almost one hundred years old and might very well worry about his approaching death, but Sanchez-Smythe was almost forty years younger. Would she risk her career for Methuselah's potential at her age?

There was another possibility, though. When the *Asimov* computer became conscious, it also gained the ability to override its programming. It used that ability to give the Tau Ceti colonists information meant only for scientists assigned to the ship by the Western Alliance. Did Sanchez-Smythe hope that a conscious computer under her control might work around the privacy protections enforced by keeping separate computer systems? That made more sense.

Of course, it didn't matter what reason Sanchez-Smythe had for going ahead with the project. His career depended on Methuselah's success, regardless. So, if the scientists wanted Eddie and Joelle Bascomb, he would have to set aside his distaste for northerners, especially brash, successful northerners like Eddie Bascomb. He wouldn't give them any reason to blame him if they failed.

51

BEING TRAPPED INSIDE HIS own body was hard enough normally, but Emile's frustration had built over the last month, reaching a peak today, on his fortieth birthday. Juarez had allowed them to hire Eddie and Joelle, and Bill had talked them into returning. All that had happened weeks ago, but they had not appeared yet. Aurora was doing preliminary work on the improved neurotrainer, trying to develop an approach, but she was struggling. That was all too clear whenever she talked to Emile.

Lucinda was vague about the reason for the delay. Emile had thought that perhaps Joelle was pregnant again, and they were waiting for little Emile's sibling to be born, but Lucinda had denied that, and Emile had felt amusement in her answer.

Emile wondered what General Juarez thought about the delay. Juarez didn't want Eddie on the project, but felt pressured into allowing it anyway. But that was just another issue that no one wanted to talk about, at least not to him.

Lucinda had left him in the conference room, still lying on his bed. He thought about getting up, but what would he do if he left the bed? He had his neuro-interrogator and neurotrainer but had no real sense of his surroundings, only an imprecise sense of objects that he touched with his hands or legs, or rapped with his cane. Lucinda had left him alone with his thoughts.

Maybe Lucinda is busy organizing some celebration for my birthday. Forty is, after all, a milestone age. Eventually, everyone would join him, and he would receive their good wishes, but he wouldn't be able to take part beyond that, and that was frustrating, too.

He sensed another mind and knew that someone had connected a neurotrainer for a direct connection. That was unusual. "Hello, Emile," someone sent. "Happy birthday."

It took him a couple of seconds to process the unique qualities of the transmission and identify the sender. It had been a while. "Eddie!" he sent back. "You're finally here."

"Me too," another person sent. There was an impression of affection and general amusement that Emile recognized immediately. "Happy birthday, Emile."

"Thank you, Joelle. I'm so glad you're both finally here."

"Well, we were a bit busy," Eddie sent. "But we're ready to go to work now."

"Great. Nobody is telling me anything lately. Why were you delayed?"

"Let's go out to the laboratory where everyone else is," Joelle said. The emotion behind her words made Emile think of a mischievous child, a combination of playfulness and secretiveness and perhaps a sense of accomplishment. "We should tell everyone."

L UCINDA WATCHED EMILE WALK out of the conference room with Joelle and Eddie, his bed trundling behind. Eddie hadn't told her why it had taken so long for them to come to San Diego, but she thought the reason must have something to do with the man that came with them. The man, middle-aged and professionally dressed, stood outside the conference room, but Eddie hadn't introduced him, going directly to Emile instead.

Eddie motioned everyone to join him in an empty space toward the center of the laboratory. He stood waiting, one hand on Emile's shoulder, as everyone moved toward him.

"As you all know, Joelle and I are rejoining your team. We had a few loose ends to tie up at JEM, however, before we could come. We're delighted that today, on Emile's fortieth birthday, we can announce the successful conclusion of our work." He paused, and the third man joined him. "This is Doctor John Drewniak, a physician from San Diego General Hospital. With Emile's permission, he will inject nanites developed by Munt Electronics, and exhaustively tested by yours truly, that will repair the damage to his brain."

Lucinda wanted to say something but had trouble deciding what to say. She almost asked if the nanites were safe, but Eddie said he tested them personally, something she knew he had been doing. By the time she choked out, "That's wonderful," her words drowned in the sea of chatter that followed Eddie's words.

"I'm ready," Emile said through his Voice Magician, his amplified voice booming above the noise. "Let's do it."

"I have the injection ready," Doctor Drewniak said. "Doctor Hernandez, I think it will be easier if you lie down."

"You're going to do it right here right now?" Lucinda heard a squeak in her voice and hoped no one else had heard it.

Doctor Drewniak shrugged. "Is there any reason to wait? This lab is as clean as any place in my hospital, and I'm only doing a simple injection."

Everyone was looking at her, and she swallowed. "If Emile is ready, go ahead."

Emile was already climbing onto his bed. Doctor Drewniak took a flat case from an inside jacket pocket, unzipped it, and removed an injector. "Normally, I would reassure a patient that this won't hurt much, but in your case, Doctor Hernandez, that won't be necessary."

That elicited a short laugh from Emile, now reclining on the bed. Doctor Drewniak smiled, bent over Emile, and examined his neck, looking for a vein, Lucinda assumed. Finding what he was looking for, he gently placed the injector against Emile's neck and pushed the activation button. He straightened and looked around the room. "It's done."

"Thank you, Doctor," Emile said. He sat up.

"You may start feeling changes in various sensations within the next few months," Doctor Drewniak said. "The blood vessel damage should be repaired in a day or two, but we don't know how much functionality you will recover or how long it will take. Your brain will try to rewire itself, as you know better than I. I have prescriptions for you, and an exercise regimen that will help your brain know what it needs to be doing. Mr. Bascomb has that information."

Eddie took a data disk from his pocket and handed it to Lucinda. "Everything is on this. The bed can be programmed to administer the prescriptions and help with the exercises."

Lucinda nodded. "Standard protocol?"

"Of course."

She inserted the data disk into a port in the bed. A light by the port turned red for a few seconds, changed to green, and turned off. The bed automatically ordered the prescriptions and programmed itself to schedule the drugs and help Emile with the exercises.

"Thank you so much," she said, gazing in turn at Eddie, Joelle, and Doctor Drewniak.

Eddie grinned. "Happy birthday, Emile."

52

E MILE SCRATCHED HIS NECK. Almost a year after the nanite injection, he had regained some feeling, occasionally annoying like the itch he was feeling, and other times very welcome, as in the sensations he felt when Lucinda touched him, different from before the accident, but better than the artificial nerve excitations from his implants. The improvements helped him move more naturally, although he still needed the implants to work his muscles.

But he should concentrate on the meeting, and he returned his attention to the words received by his neurotrainer. Lucinda was finishing a status report on the efforts to develop a neurotrainer that could replay stored memories.

"The quality of sound playback continues to improve," Lucinda was saying. "Recent improvements have come from changing the way we store sound memories; the neurotrainer prototype itself seems to work well."

"For sound," Juarez said. "What about other aspects of memory? What about progress in uploading the memories to a computer?"

Lucinda tried to placate Juarez while Emile drifted away from the conversation and into his thoughts again. Their success in playing back memories of sounds was encouraging to him, but he could understand why Juarez wasn't impressed. To a layman, they weren't doing much more than play/record devices had done for centuries. Juarez didn't grasp the difference between recording actual sounds and duplicating sounds stored in a brain, the latter less impressive because the brain was not a reliable instrument for that storage.

But sound memories were only a first step. They should be able to make the technology work for the other senses. Not perfectly, of course, because it wouldn't be any more reliable than the memory itself. Still, it would be world changing. He was wrong about the dangers of the neuro-interrogator, but the ability to record and play back memories could be a worse threat to privacy.

The ability to record and playback sound and sight wasn't particularly worrying. Conventional surveillance equipment could do that more reliably; they were only extending the scope of such things. Memories were more than just sense data, though. The unspoken thoughts and emotions of the person having the memory, both during the experience and after, colored the memory in ways that would also have to be recorded and played back. That opened doors that Emile believed should be kept closed.

Lucinda didn't agree. Any doubts she might have had about government abuse disappeared after Castillo lost the election. The ability to upload consciousness to a computer, destined to be too expensive for extensive use, didn't bother her. She still thought that any neuro-interrogator developments could be controlled and cited the benefits that such technology could have.

Perhaps she's right. Maybe we will find limitations on the technology, as we did with the original neuro-interrogator. He couldn't assume that would happen, though, and didn't have a clue how to solve the problem they were creating.

I SAIAH STARED AT THE closed conference room door. As usual, everyone was in there except him. They thought they were keeping their secrets from him, but by now, even that stupid ape probably knew what they were doing. The thought of Kong just made him angrier. He didn't care what the northerners thought of him, but he was supposed to be an animal trainer. It had been easier when he was dealing with less intelligent creatures, like dogs. It was plain that Kong didn't like him, preferring anyone else, even Colonel Pizarro, even northerners like Eddie Bascomb. Lately, the chimpanzee had thrown its feces at him if he didn't give it food quickly enough. Pizarro saw it happen at least once. He hadn't laughed, but Isaiah could tell he wanted to.

He could quit, find another job, maybe further south, where there was a better class of people. After he hinted at that to Reynaldo Clementi, the manager had warned him against what Reynaldo had called "a dangerous move." He might have been right; if the project was that important to the government, Juarez might not like anyone, not even an ape babysitter, trying to leave. It was probably not a smart idea to get on Juarez's bad side.

So, he would bear it, at least for now. He shook his head, scowling. His turn would come.

E MILE LAY ON HIS bed, supposedly resting, but he couldn't sleep. Lately, he sensed an irregular buzzing sound, annoying yet incredibly encouraging because it meant his hearing was returning. Still, he had rolled the bed into the unused conference room and closed the door to minimize the buzz, hoping for a late morning nap.

Had the buzz been the only problem, he probably would have dozed off, but his brain was too full of questions for his body to relax. The month had started with an implausible claim from Fermions that proof of another alien civilization had been discovered two hundred light years away, proving their claims that there were other inhabited planets, kept at least one hundred light years apart to prevent interactions. Emile laughed off the original reports, but the government had then admitted the report to be true, that *Capek*, the library ship orbiting Goddard, the colony in the Alpha Centauri system, had detected the use of Stenhouse Drive too far away to a human starship.

Now General Juarez had scheduled a meeting. Michael had told Lucinda that the general wanted to discuss the *Capek* report and what it meant to the Methuselah Project. Emile had asked what the connection was between the two, but Michael hadn't known. The implication was that Juarez would reveal all, and Emile wanted to be well-rested for that meeting.

"Y OU ALL KNOW ABOUT the so-called Bode's Anomaly," Juarez said. "A gravitational lens effect was observed briefly in a location that could only be from a ship using Stenhouse Drive. The warped region was approximately two hundred light years away, too far to be caused by human space travel."

"It seems to be an incredible coincidence," Eddie said. "The odds of a Stenhouse warp drive interfering with light from a nova in exactly the right location for a library ship to observe it must be really small."

"Very small indeed," Juarez said. "The odds improve if there is heavy traffic through that area, but even then, it seems unlikely. And yet, the observation is apparently accurate."

"That's very interesting, I'm sure," Lucinda said. "I don't understand why that is important to this project, though. If these aliens haven't made it to our neighborhood yet, they probably won't soon."

"They haven't, have they?" Luke said. "Come here, I mean."

Juarez shook his head and frowned at the neuroscientist. The man looked as if he were going to wet his pants at the very idea. He was probably susceptible to Fermion influence, not a sign of a good scientist. "No, there is no significant danger of that happening," he said. He turned to Lucinda. "The existence of some far away alien civilization has no bearing on this project. The source of the report, however, does."

"According to reports, it came from the scientists on *Capek*," Lucinda said.

"Not exactly. The scientists were observing the nova in Bode's Galaxy, but the scientists mostly store the data for future analysis. Like you, they collect a lot of data. The anomaly was found, not by the scientists, but by the library ship itself. It reported the anomaly and interpreted it as caused by Stenhouse Drive."

Lucinda looked confused, and Juarez took pleasure in that. It was nice to know that these scientists didn't have all the answers.

"The ship itself?" she said with a stammer.

"Exactly." Juarez smiled. "We knew that the Tau Ceti library ship somehow achieved consciousness years ago. We now know that the Epsilon Eridani library ship is also conscious. The government considers this as more proof that it is possible for a computer to hold a human mind."

"It makes the possibility more plausible, perhaps," Emile said. There was a harshness to his generated voice that suggested to Juarez that he was in pain. "It is hardly proof that a human mind can be uploaded to a computer and exist there." Possibly his voice only sounded that way because it was loud, automatically compensating for the sudden noise as everyone tried to speak at once.

"My superiors disagree with you," Juarez replied. He wasn't surprised that the scientists would deny the obvious. It only made their failure so far seem that much worse. They knew they would be under more pressure than ever. It was hardly necessary to tell them that, but Juarez did anyway. "They want to see results. I let you bring in the Bascombs over a year ago because you said you needed them. Where are the advances you promised?"

"We are making progress," Lucinda said. Her words weren't as much a claim as a plea for understanding, Juarez thought. Their reports documented significant advances in storing and playing back sense data. They were working on encoding emotions in a format that a computer could reconstruct and play back as a memory. He wished their progress was more rapid, but he knew the efforts they were making.

"Make more."

E MILE RETURNED TO HIS bed when the meeting ended. The buzzing had been almost intolerable during much of the meeting. Eddie's design for Emile's neurotrainer connections only allowed him to receive one voice at a time, but Emile suspected that the painful buzzing had resulted from hearing many voices speaking at once. He was delighted that his hearing was returning, but the buzz was a downside to that miracle.

Is Juarez right? He had never quite believed that *Asimov*, the Tau Ceti library ship, or rather, the *Asimov* computer, had become conscious. Isabella was convinced, and she was the only member of their team who had talked to the computer. Lucinda had created neurotrainer recordings of Isabella's report and all the data collected by the Pitcairn roboticist, Susan Malley. Emile had studied those reports but still had doubts. Those reports spoke the language of engineering, not neuroscience, and perhaps that was why they weren't convincing. Susan Malley had tried for years to explain how the *Asimov* computer had become conscious but had failed.

Now Juarez thought that another computer, identical to the one aboard *Asimov*, had become conscious. What was it about those two computers? And why was it that the third library ship, *Lang* in the Alpha Centauri system, had apparently not become conscious? Susan Malley had thought that the long journey *Asimov* had made to get to Tau Ceti might have something to do with it. Epsilon Eridani was roughly the same distance from Earth, but Alpha Centauri was much closer, evidence that Malley was right.

Were they looking at the problem from the wrong angle? If so, it was probably in part because of Emile's own doubts about a computer becoming conscious. Juarez was right. It was time to look at *Asimov* and *Capek* from a neuroscientist's point of view.

Kong was in a foul mood. Isaiah had gotten to the laboratory late that morning, delaying the chimpanzee's breakfast. After breakfast, Isaiah usually took Kong outside to an exercise area, set up in a fenced-in area at the back of the building. General Juarez was back, though, and Isaiah postponed the walk, avoiding the possibility of an encounter with the general while Kong was out of his cage. This only irritated Kong more. He pointed to his head every time Isaiah came near, his signal to have the Voice Magician, no doubt so that he could express his displeasure vocally. Isaiah, fearing less pleasant behavior, tried to avoid approaching the ape until Juarez was gone, but that only worsened the problem.

He could hear Juarez in the meeting, the general's voice loud but not intelligible outside the conference room. Kong leaped around his cage thirty feet away, chattering angrily at Isaiah. Isaiah glanced at the closed conference door and decided he'd had enough. "Fine," he said. "All right, Kong, I'll take you out."

He walked over, opened the cage door, and held out a hand to Kong. The ape was usually well behaved at this point, knowing it was going outside, and it seemed to mollify Kong somewhat. It was impatient, though, pulling at Isaiah's hand as they walked across the lab. "Take it easy," Isaiah said.

The door to the conference room opened, and General Juarez stomped out, an angry look on his face. Kong screeched, pulled out of Isaiah's hand, and moved toward Juarez. When Juarez halted and glared at the ape, Kong stopped too, giving the general an impressive raspberry.

"What the hell is that animal doing out of its cage?" Juarez asked. He gave Isaiah a venomous scowl. "Get it back in there where it belongs."

"I was taking it outside," Isaiah answered. "It's time for its exercise."

Juarez moved toward them. Behind him, Michael came out of the conference room, but he was looking back, talking to someone in the room. Kong screeched at Juarez with bared teeth, produced some feces, and threw them at Juarez. A piece hit the shoulder of the general's uniform and slid down, leaving a streak of brown against the blue of his blouse.

Juarez turned livid and advanced on Kong. Isaiah took a step back, watching in horror as the ape stood its ground and made fierce faces at Juarez. Did the general know how strong the chimpanzee was and how much damage Kong could inflict if attacked?

"Kong!" Michael's voice was firm, but not angry. "Come here, Kong."

Kong looked at Michael and back at General Juarez, baring its teeth again and blowing out another raspberry before it went to Michael. Michael held out his arms, and the chimp jumped into them. "Let's go outside," Michael said. He walked out of the laboratory, still carrying Kong.

Juarez watched them leave before turning on Isaiah. "You're supposed to be handling that creature," he said, and Isaiah wasn't sure whether it was a declaration or a question.

"Yes, sir. I'm sorry about that. Kong has been in a bad mood all. . .."

"I didn't ask for an excuse." Juarez was next to him now, glaring at him, looking as if he might strike him. "If you can't handle it, I have no use for you. You're fired."

"But, General. . .."

"Just get out. Colonel Pizarro apparently can control the animal better than you can. Now get out of my sight."

I SAIAH GATHERED THE FEW personal items he had, stopping to glare at Juarez every few seconds. He thought about protesting his dismissal. He didn't work for Juarez, but Reynaldo was Juarez's puppet, and Lucinda wouldn't stand up for him the way she supported the northerners. At least he wouldn't have to deal with that stupid monkey anymore.

It was so unfair! Juarez overreacted to Kong's irritability, aggravating the situation, blaming him for something beyond his control. He could try to find out who they interviewed to replace him and try to warn the interviewees, letting them know what they were getting themselves into. That would be some revenge, at least.

That thought gave him a better idea. Juarez was running the Methuselah Project, started under President Castillo's administration. Sanchez-Smythe had spoken against it during the campaign, so why was the project still in operation? Was Juarez somehow doing it secretly, keeping even the new president in the dark? Or was Sanchez-Smythe in on the secret, stealing President Castillo's idea for herself?

Either way, public knowledge of Methuselah's survival would hurt Juarez. It might even help President Castillo, making Sanchez-Smythe appear hypocritical. Of course, he wouldn't want to be implicated in leaking any information. That meant not being perceived as the disgruntled fired employee, and not letting anything get back to him. He could manage that.

R EYNALDO LOOKED UP FROM his desk and sighed when Isaiah came into his office. He wasn't looking forward to this, assuming that Isaiah would be angry about Juarez's actions. To his surprise, Isaiah didn't look angry, but more contrite, possibly hoping to plead for a reprieve.

"You must know I can't do anything to reverse General Juarez's decision," Reynaldo said.

"I know," Isaiah said. "I wanted to apologize, really. This was my fault; I should have had better control over Kong. To tell the truth, I had been thinking about leaving anyway, but I didn't want to leave you all without someone to take care of Kong."

Reynaldo smiled. "I appreciate your attitude. I'm not looking forward to trying to replace you, should it come to that, but there's nothing I can do about it. I hope this all works out for you."

"You may not replace me? Who will take care of the chimp?"

"Juarez demanded that Kong be gone, too, and, at this stage of our work, Lucinda wasn't able to justify keeping him. The San Diego Zoo will take him."

"I guess you don't need either of us anymore."

"I've already entered your dismissal in the records, so your final pay should be in your account by the end of the day."

"Thank you," Isaiah said, nodding. The two men shook hands and Isaiah left.

T HE FIRST REPORTER SHOWED up midmorning with a cameraman following her. Francesca looked up as the reporter, a thirtyish woman, casually dressed, turned to the cameraman, dressed even more casually, almost slovenly. "Get a couple of shots of the lobby. We probably won't use them, but it doesn't hurt." She jerked a thumb at Francesca. "Get her in at least one shot, too."

"Can I help you?" Francesca asked. She stood and walked out from behind her desk. "No pictures," she told the cameraman.

"Ignore her," the reporter said. She strode up to Francesca. "I'm Sara Barnes, a reporter for *Brasília Today*. You may have heard of me."

The name sounded familiar, but Francesca didn't want to acknowledge it. "I'm sure I haven't. What can I do for you?" She pushed past Sara and confronted the cameraman. "I said to stop taking pictures!"

"I'm here to talk to whoever is in charge here. Who is that, by the way?" Francesca saw her smirk, possibly because the cameraman was still turning around, taking pictures around the lobby.

"What shall I tell him this is about?" She lunged for the camera, but the cameraman turned away from her hand with a grin.

Francesca didn't know what the people beyond the lobby door did, but she knew it wasn't supposed to be public knowledge. Even so, the reporter's next words were a surprise.

"Tell him or her I want to ask about the Methuselah Project."

Methuselah? She remembered hearing about that, but she hadn't connected this rundown branch of Pearson Interstellar with it. Was that what they were doing back there? She knew it was a government project because of Michael Pizarro's presence and General Juarez's frequent visits, but had assumed they were involved in weapons research.

"I don't think you have the right place," Francesca said.

"Just let me talk to—what was his name again? Maybe you're not important enough to know what's going on."

Francesca was angry, not so much by the insult as by the assault on her small corner of the world. In truth, she hadn't wanted to know. She had a good job and thought it was probably better not to know what secrets might reside beyond the lobby door. The reporter's attitude, and that of her grinning cameraman, had gotten under her skin, though, and she debated refusing.

Better to let others deal with the two. She returned to her desk. "Connect to Reynaldo," she told her phone.

"Yes, what is it, Francesca?" Reynaldo replied.

"There's a reporter here who wants to talk to someone in charge. She says she wants to talk about Methuselah." There was a long silence, dragging until Francesca said, "Reynaldo? Are you there?"

"I'm here. I'll send Michael out to talk to her."

"OK. Thanks." She broke the connection and turned back to Sara. "Someone will be right out."

But five minutes went by, and no one appeared. "Call him again," Sara demanded.

"They're very busy," Francesca replied, allowing a little tartness into her voice. "Someone will be out as soon as they can break free."

Sara frowned and looked toward the lobby door. It was locked, and Francesca thought about mentioning that but decided not to. It might be amusing to see the reporter try to open it. The handprint plate on one side must have clued Sara in, though, and she stayed where she was.

Several minutes later, Michael entered the lobby and strode over to Sara. "What can I do for you?"

Michael had come to work in uniform, looking very smart, Francesca had thought. Now, though, the uniform jacket and neat tie were gone, and his blouse was open at the collar. A casual observer might not have realized he was in uniform, but from the way Sara looked him up and down, Francesca suspected the change hadn't fooled the reporter.

"I'm writing a story about the Methuselah Project," Sara said. "I wanted to confirm that a laboratory here is working on it."

Michael shrugged. "I have no information to give you about that."

"Meaning this isn't Methuselah, or you're refusing to confirm?" She waved at the cameraman, who immediately took pictures of Michael.

Michael glanced at the cameraman with one raised eyebrow and a dismissive smile. "Meaning I have no information to give you."

"Then let me talk to someone who does."

"As I'm sure you have already discovered, this building belongs to Pearson Industries, operating under its Pearson Interstellar division. As such, our activities are not open to the public. There is no one here who will give you more than I."

"Then you admit this is a government project?"

Michael gave Sara the same smile he had given the cameraman. "I admitted nothing. Pearson does some government work, of course, but much of its civilian operations also allows only limited access to the public. In any case, we have nothing to tell reporters now. Should we decide to release a statement to the press, I'm sure your company will be notified."

"People who take that attitude with me usually end up regretting it."

"As do people who make threats against the government," Michael answered, his voice mild. "Assuming, of course, that this is a government project, as you implied."

Sara looked down at his polished shoes, up to his sharply creased slacks, to his distinctive belt buckle, and his spotless, if partly unbuttoned, shirt, confirming to Francesca that Sara had known Michael was military. "Oh, I know it's government, Lieutenant."

"Colonel, actually. Now, since you have no reason to be here, I'll have to insist that you leave."

Sara sneered at Michael, turned, and stalked out, followed by the cameraman. Michael smiled briefly at Francesca and left the lobby.

That afternoon, there were three more reporters, including another one from *Brasília Today*. There was no cameraman this time, but the reporters were more persistent, perhaps feeling safer in numbers. No one came out to talk to them, and they left, grumbling, after two hours.

B*RASÍLIA TODAY* **REPORT, 20 September 2351 Sara Barnes reporting**

"Following a tip from an inside source, this reporter has uncovered a massive conspiracy between the government and Pearson Industries. My investigation has uncovered evidence that this nondescript building in San Diego," and an image of the building appeared, "is the site of the supposedly discredited Methuselah Project. The project, intended to develop a way of loading an individual's mind into a computer, was begun during ex-President Castillo's administration but was canceled when President Sanchez-Smythe took office. Or so we were led to believe.

"According to our source, this building houses a laboratory dedicated to Methuselah, and run by renegade neuroscientist Emile Hernandez, shown here with his wife, Lucinda Hernandez, leaving the Methuselah laboratory." The picture of the building faded, replaced by a picture of Emile walking out of the building with Lucinda. Emile's bed must have been following but was cut out of the picture.

"There have been rumors that Doctor Hernandez was no longer active after an auto accident in 2338. As this picture shows, he has recovered and apparently changed his prior anti-government views.

"Updates will follow as we learn more. This is Sara Barnes, reporting."

54

ATSUSHI SHIJO FINISHED THE report on an Eastern Bloc attempt to infiltrate the Japanese Space Agency. Once again, Kenshin Ikeda had prevented a breach in their security, the most recent victory reestablishing his reputation as one of Japan's best intelligence officers. Ikeda's obsession with the Methuselah Project had been a problem, but that had been almost four years ago.

Shijo shook his head. Ikeda was on his way to Shijo's office, summoned so that Shijo could confess that Ikeda had been right all along. He had traced the project to San Diego four years ago, and now the Western Alliance information network confirmed Ikeda's theory.

"Officer Ikeda has arrived," Shijo's monitor announced.

"Send him in." Ikeda would be returning to San Diego.

OVER THE NEXT FEW days, four more reporters appeared, including Sara Barnes again, all demanding confirmation that the nondescript building on the San Diego waterfront was the site of the supposedly canceled Methuselah Project. There was even a reporter from Japan, who stood quietly to the side writing in a notebook while Sara Barnes harassed Francesca. Reporters confronted Emile and Lucinda twice, once when arriving in the morning and once when leaving at the end of the day. One of the morning confrontations appeared in network news coverage later in the day. The curious began congregating outside the building, too, usually standing around whispering among themselves without obstructing access to the laboratory. None of them worked up the courage to enter the lobby, but Michael requested a guard from General Alvarez and got a young corporal who was quite happy about spending his time watching over Francesca.

Six days after Sara Barnes's first visit, General Juarez stormed into the laboratory. He glared at Lucinda and Eddie, passing them by as he marched over to the corner where Michael worked.

Michael had been concentrating on a report, but he heard the general's feet slapping against the floor and looked up. Unsurprised at seeing Juarez, he rose smoothly to his feet and greeted the general with a snappy salute. "Good afternoon, General. I've been expecting you."

Juarez's angry expression seemed to soften a little as he returned the salute. "Good afternoon, Colonel. They still haven't given you an office?"

"I don't need one. I wouldn't be able to observe things as well from an office."

"I suppose not." Juarez gave Michael half a smile. "At least you don't have that ape hanging over you anymore."

Michael nodded with a smile of his own, thinking that Kong hadn't been a problem, and, in fact, he missed the chimpanzee. Of course, Kong had never thrown excrement at him.

"The conference room seems empty right now," Juarez said. "Let's go in there and talk."

In the conference room, Juarez took a seat, and Michael sat across from the general. "We've kept inquirers out of the laboratory," Michael said. "Reports so far are only speculation, with no actual evidence."

"I know. I get reports. Bringing the guard in was a wise precaution. The president is disturbed by all the attention, though. Most of the personnel here have been identified, lending some credence to the story."

"Without more than that, surely the issue will fade away. They will only find the cover story."

"Maybe, but President Sanchez-Smythe doesn't want to take any chances. The stories will go away faster if this facility is gone." He looked at Michael and seemed to come to a decision. "There's another reason, too. We've identified one reporter in the lobby as a Japanese intelligence agent. If the Japanese are interested, there could be Eastern Bloc interest, too. We have to move everything elsewhere."

"Some people may not want to move."

General Juarez smiled, but there was little humor in it. "I don't intend to give them much choice. And, to avoid too much trouble over the move and guarantee security, I don't plan to tell them where they are going until we're on our way."

"Do you know where you're sending them?"

"The arrangements are complicated, and it will be a couple of months, but President Sanchez-Smythe and I have agreed on a location." Juarez told Michael where they would all be going, to Michael's surprise and shock.

A FEW MINUTES LATER, Juarez ordered Michael to gather everyone, including Francesca, into the conference room, leaving the guard Michael had brought in to watch the lobby.

"Obviously there has been a leak of information," Juarez told the assembled team. "Given the impossibility of maintaining security at this facility, I've decided to move the project elsewhere."

"Back to Panama?" Luke asked. Juarez could see the hope on the neuroscientist's face and regretted the inevitable disappointment that Luke would eventually experience. It couldn't be helped, though, and the scientists would have to sacrifice for the mission, regardless of the costs.

"Someone leaked the location of this site, possibly a person in this room," Juarez continued. Even as he said it, he wondered if it was true. Did the network story tell Kenshin Ikeda about the facility, or did Ikeda leak it to the network to help him get inside the facility? "To protect the new location, you won't be told where you are going until you get there."

"You can't expect us to pick up and leave without knowing where we are going," Lucinda said. "Some of us won't go, and that will be even more disruptive to our work."

"I'm not giving you a choice. You are all essential to the project and will all be moving to the new location."

There was a long, chaotic moment while everyone clamored for attention. Juarez stared around at them, trying to look indifferent. Then he stood and pounded a fist on the conference table. "Enough!" he bellowed. "You will all do your duty to the Western Alliance. If sacrifices must be made for your government, then you will make them."

"You can't do that," Eddie said.

"You are all being relocated by Executive Order, signed by President Sanchez-Smythe. Not only will you go, but you will also refrain from discussing the matter with anyone outside this organization, including any employee of Pearson Industries not part of this project."

"What about me?" Francesca wailed. "I'm just a receptionist. I don't even know what you're doing here."

Juarez stared at her. She wasn't an important part of the project and would be useless where they were going. "Like everyone else here, you signed the Security Information Protection Oath," he told her. "If you tell anyone anything about this, you will be prosecuted to the full extent of the law."

"I haven't even told my boyfriend where I work. I won't say anything. I don't want to leave San Diego. I grew up here."

Another northerner, more concerned with her petty life than the government that made that life possible. She knew now about Methuselah, but she wouldn't dare say anything. "Very well. It will take some time to make all the arrangements, and you will be informed well in advance of your termination of employment."

He could see the relief on her face, a contrast to the dark looks on the others. "Thank you," she said meekly.

"Why don't you return to the lobby now," Juarez said.

Francesca nodded, rose from her seat, and left the room. Juarez turned back to the others. "You all signed the Oath. Any protests or leaks of information out of this building will be punished."

T HEY WERE IN THE conference room again, Juarez gone, and Michael not invited to join them. Lucinda didn't think they would accomplish anything by meeting, but it had to be done.

"Can Juarez do this?" Luke asked.

"I don't see what we can do about it," Lucinda answered. "I don't think it's legal, but Juarez won't hesitate to throw us in prison if we tell anyone anything about this. Even hiring a lawyer would give him an excuse."

"If the government can do this, then misusing anything we develop will be child's play," Emile said. "This is proof of what I've been saying all along."

Lucinda sighed. He was right, of course. Juarez had them in a bind; he couldn't force them to relocate legally, but she didn't doubt that Juarez would treat any protests or escape attempts harshly. If the government could do that, misusing their work would be inevitable.

I KEDA HADN'T BEEN ABLE to see much from the lobby of the decrepit building housing the Methuselah Project. Perhaps the building plans will help me develop a plan of action. Building plans were not publicly available, however, so he would have to be more inventive.

He took pictures of the building from several angles, and one of his devices made accurate estimates of the dimensions of the building. A day of wandering around the neighborhood yielded three buildings apparently of the same design. Then he got lucky. One building was empty and available to lease. Ikeda called the property manager and arranged for a virtual tour to be sent to his reader.

He studied the video in his hotel room. The reader projected a 3D image of the one-story building above the reader. A single voice command removed the roof so that he could examine the interior layout. Ikeda could identify the lobby, leading to a short hall and a large open area with several offices at the sides. At least he now knew how that building was probably laid out.

His daily report summarized his findings and requested instructions on how to proceed, but he wouldn't get an answer until the next day at the earliest. That left him with free time. His reader could access tourist information made available by his hotel, so he closed the display of the building and began an investigation of the entertainment possibilities of the area.

E STABLISHING SAFE COMMUNICATIONS WAS always a problem for a spy. Dead drops could be used for local communication, but Ikeda needed to get instructions from Shijo in Japan, half a world away. Unfortunately, there was no technology that could ensure that a message was not intercepted, and encryption for a message of any length was only a delaying tactic and would draw attention to the message. However, technology restrictions made it less likely that short, innocuous messages would be noticed.

Ikeda's report hadn't been short, but he had carefully worded it so that only Shijo would understand the meanings hidden behind the vague wording. Ikeda described his attempts to acquire new broadcast power technology, but Shijo would understand that the technology was Methuselah and that it was the Western Alliance that was working to get that technology. Shijo worded his reply accordingly.

"Attempts for acquisition should be terminated if possible."

PITCAIRN *NEWS SERVICE* **REPORT, 5 November 2351, Anna Cortez reporting**

This will be my last report from the Pitcairn News Service offices in Tokyo, but this is only a pause, not goodbye. After the tragic death of PNS head Kimberly Dillon, Pitcairn Administrator Patrick Malley has asked me to replace Kimberly, and I have accepted. I will, therefore, be leaving Earth and leading PNS from Pitcairn. Deborah Salinas, my right-hand person during my tenure here in Tokyo, will take over on Earth.

For those who have followed my reports for the last six and a half years, rest assured that I will continue to bring you the truth about the star colonies and their often-troublesome relationship with Earth. Thank you all for your support. This is Anna Cortez, saying goodbye, but only for now.

55

EDDIE SPECULATED ON WHERE they were going. Some isolated laboratory in the Black Plains, perhaps? No one was happy about that idea, but Eddie and Joelle were more concerned because of little Emile, now five years old and just starting school. Attempts to get more information from Juarez or Michael were futile. Juarez took no chances, keeping them isolated and ignorant.

A military transport waited for them at San Diego Airport. Their destination was unknown, but Lucinda guessed it was relatively close because longer flights would have used the suborbital facility across San Diego Bay.

Michael told them that the actual flight was about two and a half hours long, which meant it was probably about 1500 miles. The destination could be any of the landing fields in the devastated areas, but it could also include cities to the south, perhaps only a connecting flight on a trip to the heart of the Western Alliance. Juarez implied the flight was not taking them to their ultimate destination. Windows were covered, and there was no way to know until they landed.

Once on the ground, Juarez ordered them to stay in their seats. "A car will come to pick us up. Wait here until it arrives."

Ten minutes later, an aircar landed next to the plane. Lucinda realized that the car, like the plane, would have covered windows, and she tried to get an idea of their location as she walked the few feet to the car. There was a city skyline to the south, probably eliminating the Black Plains as their new home. She didn't recognize the buildings, and there were no distinctive geographic features visible on the hazy horizon. Then Juarez was pushing her into the car, and she turned her attention to Emile and the security of his bed in the cabin's rear.

It was a large military transport, but there were fourteen of them crammed into it: the nine members of the Methuselah team, little Emile, Juarez, Michael, Reynaldo, and Francisco Alvarez, Aurora's husband, a confused middle-aged man obviously out of his element. Fortunately, the trip took only twenty minutes. Then they squeezed out of the aircar and stood in the open air again. Michael and Luke helped Emile get into his bed.

The skyline was a little further away, in the opposite direction, and there were still no helpful mountains or other features, but Eddie, at least, knew exactly where they were. "Houston," he said, and it sounded like a curse. He stared at the enormous vehicle a hundred yards away, easily identified as a space shuttle. "This is the Houston Space Center."

"Space?" Francisco Alvarez said, almost choking on the words. "We're being taken into space?"

A dozen armed soldiers marched over from the opposite side of the shuttle and surrounded them on Juarez's order. "I've arranged for an escort," Juarez said. "We wouldn't want any of you wandering off."

Bill gave Juarez a look that should have incinerated him on the spot. He held his position while the others shuffled forward. Juarez looked back at him, smiled nastily, and stretched out an arm to indicate the shuttle. Bill didn't move, and Eddie moved to his side.

"Are we going to have a scene here?" Juarez asked. "I could have you carried."

Joelle left her son with Lucinda and joined Eddie and Bill. "There's nothing we can do now," Joelle told the two men in a quiet voice. She took Eddie's arm. "Let's go."

Eddie looked down at her, his face dark. Lucinda saw his eyes shift upward briefly and thought he was probably glancing at little Emile, holding hands with Lucinda and looking scared. Eddie touched Joelle's arm, smiled grimly, and turned to Bill. "She's right. Come on."

They trudged across the field toward the shuttle. Lucinda assumed that everyone, except perhaps Emile, had the same confused thoughts. She considered connecting Emile's neurotrainer so that she could tell him what was going on; Michael and Luke hadn't turned it on when they settled Emile onto his bed. Was Juarez going to make sure of their isolation by setting them up on Prendergast Station, hundreds of miles above? Surely that was overkill. Eddie's idea of a laboratory on the Black Plains would have provided more isolation than the busy space station. Emile would want answers, and she didn't have them.

The shuttle was a disk, over a hundred feet in diameter and at least thirty feet high, decorated with military markings. Lucinda knew little about space travel, but she remembered the shuttle would use power broadcast from space while moving through the atmosphere. The aircar had also used broadcast power, but the shuttle received it directly from a power generation satellite, not passed on through a ground-based distribution point. Conventional rocket engines would power the shuttle when it left the atmosphere, but the use of broadcast power for the first part of the flight meant that fuel requirements were much less. All the shuttle had to do was maintain a line-of-sight path to the satellite until it switched to rocket propulsion.

In a few minutes, they were all on the shuttle's passenger deck, their escort left behind. Many of the seats, arranged in curved rows around the semi-circular compartment, were already taken by people in military uniforms. Juarez and Michael escorted them to seats toward the rear where there was room for Emile's bed.

Lucinda noticed one of the other passengers in particular. He wore a wide-brimmed hat and sunglasses, cloaking him enough to arouse her curiosity, but she thought he looked familiar. He was old: the wrinkled skin of the man's lower face, the wisps of gray hair below the hat, and his hunched posture told her that. She thought about asking Michael or Juarez about the man, but if the general wanted them to know, he would have already introduced them.

The man was probably important. Once they had settled in their seats, General Juarez reported to him, and they talked quietly for several minutes. Then Juarez returned.

"Launch is in five minutes," he told them. "Michael will check your seats to make sure you're fastened in correctly, especially the little one." He smiled at young Emile. "We will reach three g's during the trip to Prendergast Station, completely safe, but uncomfortable, so you should talk to him now to reassure him."

Lucinda shook her head. Even Juarez has a heart occasionally. The general was effectively kidnapping them all, but he could still show concern about a five-year-old.

E DDIE WATCHED AS JOELLE talked to their son. The boy was unhappy, unused to the hectic pace forced on him during the long day. Joelle's attempt to prepare him for one more assault on a normal life wasn't making him feel any better. He didn't cry—he was a big boy, now—but his unhappiness was obvious. A commercial flight might have had features to distract him, but this was a military transport, without even video capability or flight attendants who might have had suggestions.

Joelle was tense herself, and if Eddie could see that, then Emile probably could too. Possibly, that was why he turned to look at Eddie with pleading eyes. Eddie leaned toward him and smiled.

"We're going to go on a big ride. This is a very special airplane that's going to take us someplace new." He patted Emile's seat. "See how soft this is? When we take off, you're going to be pushed down into it like it was a big pillow."

"We're going to the space station?" Emile asked.

Apparently, his five-year-old son understood what was going on more than he thought. Eddie chuckled. All right, he could work with that. "Right. It's called Prendergast Station, and we're going to live there for a while. You'll be able to look down and see the whole Earth!"

"Will my friends be there?"

"You'll make new friends. And your old friends will have to look up to see where you are."

Emile giggled. "And I can look down on them."

They talked in the same vein for a little while longer, until a voice on the cabin speakers announced the imminent launch. Eddie checked Emile's restraints, making sure they were tight enough to ensure he couldn't move a limb away from the seat during acceleration, and lowered the seat back so that Emile was lying flat. He glanced over at Joelle, who smiled back at him from her horizontal position.

Eddie forced a smile back. After JEM went public, leaving his family wealthy, he had basked in his good luck. He had a beautiful wife that he loved and who loved him, a smart, healthy son, no financial worries, and work that he enjoyed keeping him busy. He had escaped Juarez, the only shadow on his perfect life. *Did I get too complacent?* Juarez was back in my life, and all his money couldn't stop Juarez from spiriting his family to some unknown future.

56

T HE TRIP TO PRENDERGAST Station wasn't pleasant, but it could have been worse. Because the shuttle didn't use fuel for most of its acceleration to orbital velocity, it could rise to orbit more slowly, and g-forces on its passengers were less than they would have been in the rockets that first left Earth's atmosphere. However, the acceleration lasted longer as the shuttle climbed more gradually in a circular path chosen to stay within line-of-sight of its designated power generation satellite.

Little Emile bore up with it as well as could be expected, whimpering during the times of heaviest acceleration, but otherwise lying quietly. When the shuttle docked at the space station, Eddie freed himself from his seat and attended to his son.

"Daddy, my whole body hurts!" Emile told him. Despite that, he seemed in good spirits, glad it was over.

"Mine, too," Eddie said. "But we're here now."

Joelle released her restraints and joined them. "Wow, what a ride!" she said, a big smile on her face that Eddie assumed was for Emile's benefit. "Like the world's longest roller coaster."

Emile gave her a dubious look that Eddie interpreted as saying that, if that was what a roller coaster was like, Emile was glad he was too young to ride one.

I KEDA HAD SPENT MOST of October watching the Methuselah building. The scientists that worked there often worked late, but by early morning, the building was always empty. Shijo had elaborated on his first terse instructions, emphasizing that any loss of life could be a disaster for Japan's already uneasy relations with the Western Alliance. Attempting to destroy the laboratory might not accomplish more than a delay in the project, but that was better than nothing.

Even that was an extreme reaction to what Ikeda understood about the project. His superiors had information that Ikeda didn't have, and that worried him. But it was also above his security level, and he had his orders.

Even at an hour past midnight, the night was warm, much warmer than Tokyo was in November. Ikeda left his car two blocks from the facility and walked the rest of the way, carrying a shaped charge supplied by the Japanese consulate. Ikeda's examination of the building plans had told him that the charge, placed on the correct wall, would direct a powerful explosion inward, destroying any equipment used by the scientists. There would be offsite storage documenting their work, but he couldn't do anything about that.

The night was quiet, and Ikeda looked up into the cloudless sky. There were no stars, only the dark gray featurelessness of an urban sky. A block from the building, Ikeda knew he had a problem. Usually the building's exterior was brightly lit, and Ikeda plotted a circuitous route between nearby buildings that included climbing one fence to get to where he wanted to place the charge. He expected to trigger an alarm and would have to move fast, but hoped that more elaborate security, robots for example, would not be used to avoid drawing attention to the building.

He could see the building, though, and there were no lights other than normal street lighting. Had the attention since the facility was revealed forced the project to move once more? Sighing, Ikeda hid the case holding the charge behind one of the other buildings, and approached the Methuselah building. It seemed abandoned, a sad, neglected structure that had never seen better days.

It wasn't the cautious thing to do, but Ikeda tried to enter through the front door. A padlock secured it, less than he would have expected for a secret facility. He considered that further evidence the building was no longer in use. There was no one else on the street, and Ikeda broke the lock and entered the building. The lobby was empty except for the bare receptionist's desk against the back wall.

The touchpad on the door out of the lobby was inactive, and the door opened when Ikeda pushed it. At the end of the silent hallway, double doors opened into the large space beyond. This had been the laboratory where Methuselah scientists had worked, he was certain. Now it was a dark cavern, completely emptied of equipment. He stood there, looking about as his eyes adjusted, but there was nothing to see.

"Kenshin Ikeda, I assume," someone said. A man in the uniform of the Western Alliance Space Force stepped out of the shadows behind him. "General Juarez thought you might come by. I'm afraid we'll be sending you back to Japan as soon as we've discussed your activities a bit."

T HREE DAYS AND NOTHING had happened. Eddie stared at the door to their apartment on the station, scowling, wondering when they would resume their work. If they were still setting up facilities, he could help with that, but Juarez had rebuffed his offers. Juarez wasn't telling them anything, only suggesting that they relax and enjoy a little time off.

The screen on the wall to his right flashed into life, and one of the station staffers appeared. "Station Central has announced the approach of the starship *Hotaru*, expected to dock at 1130 hours. Any off-duty personnel are welcome to view the approach and docking from the starside observation dome, beginning immediately." The message was repeated, and then the screen went dead.

Joelle had heard the end of the announcement and come into the room with Emile in time to hear the repeated announcement. "Would you like to see a real spaceship?" she asked Emile.

A huge smile split the five-year-old's face. "I sure would!"

Eddie grinned. "Let's go, then."

T HE STARSIDE OBSERVATION DOME was a huge transparent bubble in the center of the station, facing away from Earth and toward the stars. There were plenty of seats, some occupied, and Eddie guided his family to where Bill was already sitting.

There was an identical dome, preferred by his son, on the other side of the station, the Earthside observation dome, looking down at the ever-changing blue and white planet below. Eddie liked the starside dome, though, especially when the planet hid the sun and an observer could see millions of sharp unwavering points of light with a brilliance unmatched anywhere on the planet. Away from Earth's atmosphere and the glare of civilization's lights, the stars glowed in such abundance that it was difficult to pick out most constellations or identify individual stars, especially near the broad swathe of the Milky Way. It wasn't necessary to know the names; the sobering view of the universe was enough.

They had a clear view out to the rim of the station's disk. There were ships docked there, smaller vessels linked to the station, and larger ships orbiting nearby. These were in system vehicles, serving the moon and Mars settlements or going out to mine the asteroid belt. There were no shuttles at the station that day. Designed for space only and varying greatly, none of them were things of beauty, usually collections of modules connected with robust struts, and including at least one engine module. Stenhouse drive was not practical for these slower voyagers; their trips could take months or years.

"There's *Hotaru*, moving across Virgo," Bill said. Eddie couldn't have identified Virgo in that stellar profusion, but he looked in the general direction Bill was pointing and saw a silvery cross moving through the stars. Joelle and Emile spotted it, too, and they all watched as it grew larger.

The cross shape resolved into a long center hull with a wide ring near one end. As the starship got closer, the ring became six modules, joined into a circle by delicate-looking tubes, and attached to the center hull by a triangular system of struts. *Hotaru's* power plant was a large cylinder at the other end of the center hull, with smaller fuel tanks clustered forward of the power plant. Eddie could see the tiny flames of the maneuvering engines, but knew the Stenhouse Drive that powered *Hotaru's* voyages between stars took up most of that cylinder.

"A beautiful ship," a voice behind him said. He turned to see General Juarez standing, staring out, with his hands folded behind his back. "The Japanese have a more artistic touch with starship design than we do," Juarez added.

Eddie nodded. Three years before, the exploration starship *Alejandro Castillo* had launched from Prendergast Station on its way to the Sirius star system. That vessel, a structure comprising two cylinders connected by a long tube, similar to that of the three library ships, had been serviceable, but not a thing of beauty.

Seated behind Juarez, Eddie saw another familiar figure, the same man they had seen on the shuttle, still wearing the concealing hat and sunglasses. The man's lower face was visible, though, and Eddie could see that the man was smiling as he watched *Hotaru*. There was something about that smile that seemed familiar.

The exploration ship was still in his thoughts, and a chill made him shudder. He knew who the man was, sitting there with Juarez nearby, and that knowledge, coupled with Hotaru's arrival, led him to an ominous conclusion.

Joelle touched his arm, and he turned toward her. "Is something wrong?" she asked.

"The man on the shuttle," Eddie whispered. "He's sitting behind us with Juarez. I finally recognize him; it's Castillo!"

Juarez may have overheard him despite his whispering. Out of the corner of his eye, he could see Juarez, and the general's smile seemed more sinister, as if to say, "So you know now. There's nothing you can do about it."

"I LOOKED UP *HOTARU'S* next voyage," Lucinda said. "It's leaving for Goddard in two days, then on to Trist and Pitcairn before returning to Earth."

"So, Juarez is planning to move us to a colony," Eddie said. "It won't be Pitcairn; the Western Alliance has no control there."

"Now that we know that the Trist library ship is also conscious, that would be the obvious place," Alyssa said.

Lucinda could see that the programmer was even more stressed than the others and wondered if there was a reason or if she just wasn't dealing with the situation as well.

"Not necessarily," Emile said. "An existing consciousness might interfere with an attempt to impose a new consciousness on the computer. There would be ethical questions, too, although we can't count on that being an issue with Castillo and Juarez."

"Goddard, then," Lucinda said.

"That's where I would go," Emile said. "That's just speculation, though. Since Juarez has kept everything secret so far, I don't think you would get anywhere asking him where we're going. Reynaldo and Michael might know, but they wouldn't tell us either."

"God, Trist," Bill said. "I'm going to go crazy if I'm stuck on that planet."

Lucinda gave him a sympathetic smile. The primitive life on Trist produced chlorine, not oxygen, making the atmosphere poisonous to Terran life. The colonists lived in tunnels underground, with access to the outside restricted to emergencies and requiring protective gear not much different from spacesuits. Goddard, the colonized planet in the Alpha Centauri system, was only marginally better. The atmosphere was breathable, though only for short times because of its low oxygen concentration, but the planet was frozen in a stage of its evolution was referred to as a "snowball Earth."

"We could be there for years," Bill continued. "We have to do something."

"I agree," Joelle said. She looked over at her son, reading one of his books in a corner of the room. "Goddard is no place to raise a child. Neither is Trist."

"Is there anything we can do?" Bill asked.

"Maybe," Emile said. "I think there might be another *Hotaru* passenger that might help us. Anna Cortez."

"The news commentator?" Luke asked. "What could she do? And why do you think she's a passenger?"

"She announced she was going to Pitcairn a few days ago. The previous head of PNS died, and she's taking over. There aren't many starships going to the colonies, and it's likely *Hotaru* would be her best option."

"OK, so she's somewhere on the station." Luke shook his head. "What could she do for us?"

"I'm not sure," Emile replied. "Maybe publicize our situation?"

"That would bring Juarez down on us," Luke said. "He would have us arrested and sentenced to prison on Goddard."

"Maybe she couldn't get us back to Earth," Eddie said, "but Pitcairn would be better than Goddard. *Hotaru* is taking her to Pitcairn; maybe we could get asylum."

"Could Emile survive on Pitcairn?" Lucinda asked. "Even if he could, this sounds risky."

"There are two major settlements on Pitcairn and a few smaller ones," Emile said. "One of them is a research facility that could certainly support me as well as Goddard could."

"It's still risky," Lucinda said. "Is it worth it?"

"Pitcairn wouldn't be a problem, but Goddard might be," Bill said.

"General Juarez would have thought about that."

Bill shrugged. "He would have, but would he care? He might want to keep Emile functional, but not necessarily comfortable."

Bill was right, of course. Juarez might want to use Emile, but he might not support actions to improve Emile's condition. The nanites had repaired the damage, and there were signs that his brain was rebuilding lost connections. His hearing was returning, some feeling had returned to his upper body, and just two days before, he had complained about a tingling sensation in his legs. Emile's comments seemed to show approval of Eddie's suggestion.

"This has to be unanimous," Lucinda said. "If any of you are against this, we shouldn't do it."

She looked around at her team, and all she saw were determined smiles and affirmative nods. "All right, then. We need a plan on how to find Anna Cortez and a convincing argument that she can use to get Pitcairn to give us asylum."

"SECURITY IS HIGH," EDDIE told Lucinda a few hours later. "I can't get station authority even to confirm that Anna Cortez is here. Short of accidentally running into her in a corridor, I don't know how we're going to contact her."

"We could check with the restaurants and other passenger facilities on the station," Bill said. "If she has made reservations or signed up for anything, we might track her down."

"I tried that at the exercise facility," Joelle said. "They told me it was against station policy to release that kind of information. Standard Western Alliance privacy regulations, they said. If I signed up, I might get lucky and see her, but otherwise, I don't think that will work, Bill."

"Maybe we don't have to find her," Emile said. "If it becomes known that I'm here, she might find us."

"That might work," Lucinda said. "She probably remembers you from that interview years ago." She grimaced. "Sorry to mention this, darling, but your current condition might arouse her interest."

The Voice Magician did an excellent job of creating a chuckle. "Whatever works."

"Maybe we could give an open session on the latest advances in neuroscience," Bill said. "I could do a presentation, and we could say that Emile will be part of it."

Eddie grinned. "That might draw her out. We should ask Reynaldo to arrange it and hope that Juarez doesn't stop it. It will have to be soon, though. *Hotaru* will leave the day after tomorrow."

LUCINDA VISITED REYNALDO IN his room at once to suggest the presentation, but he was suspicious. "It would relieve the boredom," she told him.

"You know General Juarez doesn't want your work made public," Reynaldo said.

"We wouldn't say anything about Methuselah," Lucinda replied. "There are a lot of other things we can talk about. The neuro-interrogator, the Voice Magician, Emile's implants, the use of nanites to repair brain damage—we could talk for days, but we'll only have an hour or two. It might even reduce the impression that we're working on Methuselah."

"If you say anything about Methuselah, the general will have you arrested."

"I know that. You and the general are welcome to attend. We won't reveal any secrets."

Reynaldo still looked doubtful, but he nodded. "All right, I'll see if I can arrange something for tomorrow. If I can, I'll get back to you for the details about publicizing it."

57

A FTER REYNALDO ARRANGED FOR the use of a lounge area and had the event publicized by the station, Bill created a short presentation.

The turnout was surprising for such a technical subject, filling every seat, but they were only interested in one particular attendee. When he stepped out onto the small stage, he saw Anna Cortez sitting near the front, ready to take notes.

He also saw Juarez looking smug for some reason. Reynaldo stood next to Juarez looking nervous, and Castillo, wearing his usual disguise, sat in the back row.

Emile, with his always-present bed tagging along, waited at one end of the stage as Bill ran through his brief talk, a high-level survey of recent advances in neuroscience. At the end, he opened the floor for questions, and there were quite a few, mostly asking about Emile and his recovery after the nanite repair.

Emile moved forward to join Bill and took questions from the audience. Many of those questions were queries about the operation of his bed and how it took care of him. That topic spurred questions about his progress and how long it would be before he fully recovered. There was some disappointment at his pessimistic replies on that subject, but Bill could see that the crowd was sympathetic, too. At least, no one accused him of not supporting the government, and no one asked him what he was working on. Perhaps they thought he couldn't work in his condition.

Eventually, people started drifting out of the room, leaving Anna Cortez, Juarez, Castillo, and Reynaldo. Anna walked over, and Bill gave her his biggest smile. "Anna Cortez," he greeted. "We're honored that you came to our little talk. I'm Bill Bensonhurst, one of Doctor Hernandez's associates."

They shook hands, and Anna held out her hand to Emile. Bill touched his shoulder, a signal they had arranged beforehand, and Emile held out his hand. The handshake was awkward because Emile didn't know exactly where his hand should be, but Anna compensated for them both and looked questioningly at Bill.

"I had understood that your condition was improving," Anna said.

"It is," Emile answered. "I have implants that allow me to move my limbs. I can't see, however, and other senses are compromised."

"I remember our interview before your accident. Would you be willing to do another interview?"

"Of course," Emile said. "I've been a big fan of yours for a long time."

Anna looked at Emile's bed. "Must you have that with you?"

"The bed contains the devices allowing us to communicate, so yes. I need it for other reasons, too, so I shouldn't have it too far away."

"My quarters are small, but I assume yours are adequate for your equipment. Why don't I come to your room? In about an hour?"

Bill nodded and gave her Emile's room number. "I look forward to it," Emile said.

They exchanged goodbyes and Anna left. When she was gone, Juarez stepped up to the stage. "Your talk was very interesting," he said. "I was happy that you stayed away from any, shall we say, sensitive information."

"I assume that was the only reason you attended," Bill said. He forced his face to be expressionless. "I hope it wasn't over your head. We tried to keep it simple."

Juarez smiled. "And you succeeded admirably. I noted Ms. Cortez was especially interested."

"Yes, she has requested an interview with Emile."

"That was quite cunningly arranged." Juarez paused and stared at Bill. Bill tried to suppress the surprise that Juarez's remark engendered, but he didn't think he was successful. "This station handles a lot of civilian traffic," Juarez continued. "Perhaps you were unaware that the Western Alliance military operates it."

"That sounds familiar," Bill said.

"Yes. Of course, that means that privacy protections are more lax than they would be in an Earthside hotel. For example, all rooms are subject to monitoring."

Juarez knows what we are planning. Bill tried to think of something clever to say, but couldn't come up with a good retort.

Juarez smiled. "Have your interview. Just remember the restrictions your oath place upon all of you. And one other thing. If Doctor Hernandez says anything that compromises the secrecy of our work, I will also have Ms. Cortez arrested for receiving classified information. The *Pitcairn News Service* will have to find someone else to manage their propaganda."

"WE COULD TRY TO do the interview through direct mental communication," Emile sent after Bill told him about Juarez's comments. Emile and Bill communicated through direct mental connections rather than using the Voice Magician.

"Juarez will find it suspicious that you don't use verbal speech," Bill sent back.

Emile's disappointment was obvious. "You're right. It would be too dangerous. I would take the risk if it were just me, but I can't put Anna in danger."

"The military may control this station, but not *Hotaru*," Lucinda sent. "We could ask Anna to delay the interview until we're out of Western Alliance territory."

"No, that would arouse suspicion, too," Emile sent. "I'll do the interview as scheduled and perhaps we can meet again on *Hotaru*."

"I REMEMBER OUR FIRST interview very well," Anna said after they had settled into comfortable chairs. Anna positioned a camera on a stand to record them. "A lot has happened in your life since then."

"The accident has certainly changed my life," Emile replied.

"To communicate, you must use a neuro-interrogator. You were asked to develop it, I believe?"

"I led the project to develop the current neurotrainer technology, which I am using to hear you. My wife and her team developed the neuro-interrogator after my accident."

"You opposed the development of the neuro-interrogator, though. Isn't that why you left the Panama Neuroscience Corporation?"

"Yes, I was afraid of the potential for misuse. However, Lucinda discovered it wasn't possible to use the neuro-interrogator effectively on an unwilling subject. Given that, its benefits outweighed any problems."

"Your wife worked for Munt Electronics then. Franco Munt also uses this technology."

"Yes. Franco was less severely damaged than I; he couldn't speak but was otherwise unaffected. Using the neuro-interrogator with the Voice Magician developed at Munt, he can now speak normally."

"An amazing advance. Let's get back to your stance against the potential abuse of technology, though. I assume that pressure by the government eased after your accident."

"Even earlier, after the government lost interest in the neuro-interrogator project. The project was canceled at PNC and picked up by Munt Electronics."

"Hernandez Neuroscience was a division of Munt, yes. But that division was closed after developing the Voice Magician." Anna leaned forward. "The entire project team disappeared for a while and then resurfaced as part of Pearson Industries in San Diego. Reports say that you were working on uploading human consciousness to a machine."

This was the question Emile had known would come up, the question he most dreaded. "Pearson Interstellar was working on a sensitive project in San Diego," he admitted. "I did some work there, limited because of my condition, but Lucinda led that project as well."

"By sensitive project, you mean Methuselah?"

Emile tried to shrug, but the result was an awkward wave of his arms. "I can't comment on the nature of the project. I can only say it was something that did not arouse the same reluctance for me that the neuro-interrogator did."

"All right," Anna said. "Let's try this from another direction. Do you, as a neuroscientist, think it is possible to upload a human to a computer?"

Emile paused as if he was thinking about it, but he already had a response ready. "That's a complicated question. We know now that it is possible for a computer to become conscious, and that might give some people encouragement. It would be very difficult, though. We don't even know what consciousness is except that it is probably an emergent property of a very complex organ."

"Difficult. But not impossible?"

"Perhaps. I believe, though, that even if it were possible, a very powerful computer would be needed. I don't think it's an accident that the only conscious computers we know of are the two library ships. With their powerful computer systems and a sensory system as complex as that of a human, they might represent the minimum requirement for support of consciousness."

"You said you weren't reluctant to work on the project in San Diego. Is that because President Castillo is gone and you are more comfortable with President Sanchez-Smythe?"

"My reluctance was based on concern about government power in general, not President Castillo in particular."

"I see." Anna was silent for a few seconds. "I think I have everything I need. Thank you for talking with me, Doctor." She smiled. "I would ask you why you are here on the station, but I suspect you wouldn't be able to tell me."

"You would be right. I will be on the *Hotaru*, though, as I assume you will be, should you want to ask any more questions."

"No, I don't think so. Doing this must be a strain on you, and I wouldn't want to burden you any further."

"It was my pleasure." Emile didn't dare push the issue any further. If Juarez were listening, the effort would tell him what they were planning, and he would move to prevent it, endangering Anna. "Perhaps we'll meet again onboard."

58

Anna filed her interview with Doctor Hernandez with the *Pitcairn News Service* before they left Prendergast Station, but now, on her way to Pitcairn, it was still on her mind. Anna listened to the interview again, trying to figure out what was bothering her.

Certainly, it had been one of the odder interviews in her career. She prided herself on her ability to read faces, but Doctor Hernandez had no control over his facial expressions. Perhaps it was the neuroscientist's perpetually slack visage that made her uneasy.

No, that wasn't it. Anna couldn't read Doctor Hernandez's face, and she knew enough about Doctor Hernandez's technology not to draw too fine a conclusion from the emotion expressed by his Voice Magician. Still, it had seemed as if there was a note of pleading in his suggestion that they meet on *Hotaru*.

Where was he going, and why? If he was part of the Methuselah Project, was the Western Alliance moving him to a colony or library ship? If the government wanted to restore security after the project's discovery in San Diego, moving it to a library ship would do that. It wouldn't be *Asimov*, because the Pitcairners had control over the Tau Ceti library ship. That left *Capek* and *Lang*.

Western Alliance privacy restrictions prevented her from looking at *Hotaru's* manifest to see where Doctor Hernandez was disembarking. *Hotaru* was Japanese and not under Western Alliance control, but treaty agreements made that irrelevant. If she saw the neuroscientist after they left Alpha Centauri, she could be reasonably sure that he was going to *Capek*, in the Epsilon Eridani system. If she didn't see him, she wouldn't know if he got off at *Lang*.

There was nothing she could do about it except hope that Doctor Hernandez tried again to talk to her. Unless. . ..

Max was worried. He hadn't heard from Eddie or any of the other members of the Methuselah project in almost two months. Calls to Eddie and Lucinda got recorded messages and no return calls. He tried to reach them at Pearson Interstellar, but the number at the laboratory was disconnected. A call to the Pearson Interstellar headquarters hit a wall of secrecy.

Trying to reach them through General Juarez or another government source would, at best, be futile, and might garner unwanted attention. In desperation, he set a search bot on his network access, looking for mentions of Emile Hernandez or Eddie Bascomb. Max couldn't have been more surprised, though, when, three weeks after he set it, the search bot found a reference to Emile on the *Pitcairn News Service.*

The report on Anna Cortez's interview with Emile wasn't picked up by any other news organization and supplied no information about why Emile was on Prendergast Station. It was a safe assumption that the rest of the team was there also and that their presence there was Juarez's reaction to the revelations about the San Diego facility.

They wouldn't be on Prendergast Station willingly. Or would they? Emile had interviewed with Anna Cortez, the new head of PNS. Were they running from General Juarez, hoping to find safety on Pitcairn? Probably not. Eddie would have communicated their intentions to him.

What could he do about it? He couldn't see options, but perhaps Jasmine or Franco would have an idea.

Atsushi Shijo slumped forward, elbows on his desk, fingertips joined to form a peak, pointing at the ceiling. The scientists Ikeda had identified as Methuselah were on the Western Alliance space station. The exposure of the San Diego facility had apparently been sufficient to make the Western Alliance move the project out of reach.

There was more to the Methuselah Project than simply uploading someone to a computer, if that was even possible. Shijo had suspected that from the beginning, but the move to Prendergast Station left little doubt. The space station was one place he couldn't send Ikeda, even if Ikeda were available.

He might have been able to arrange Ikeda's return had the Western Alliance officials not found the explosives near the Methuselah building. Ikeda had gone too far, but Shijo knew he hadn't given Ikeda much choice. Ikeda's career was a cherry blossom swept away by a breeze, even if the Western Alliance didn't throw him in prison, and Shijo's own position was precarious.

But why the space station? Surely, there are other less extreme options that would work as well and be much cheaper. The Western Alliance was very confident in the ultimate success of their maneuver, or they wouldn't have allowed the presentation on the space station. They controlled the space station. Still, there was a lot of traffic through it as the only access point to the Earth Link and the colonies.

That must have been the point. They wouldn't be continuing the project on Prendergast Station. They were being sent to a colony. That made sense; the stories of conscious library ships were obviously connected to Methuselah. There were only a few starships traveling to the colonies: the military ship *Endeavor*, Pearson Interstellar's *Francisco Pearson,* and Japan's *Hotaru*. The first two were the most likely candidates.

Or were they? The Western Alliance would want to get the scientists off the space station as soon as possible and might use the first available transportation. Shijo sat up. "Show schedule of the starship *Hotaru* for the next month," he told his workstation.

The starship schedule was public knowledge, and it took only seconds to determine that *Hotaru* had left Prendergast only days before, with Goddard as its first stop. It was trickier, even for him, to get information on the passengers. He discovered the Western Alliance had booked one entire module for passage to Goddard but could not get passenger names or how many people were occupying the module. Not that he really needed it; what he had was enough to convince him that the Methuselah Project was being transferred to Goddard or to the Goddard library ship, *Lang*.

Shijo didn't think there was anything he could do about it. *Hotaru* would be out of contact until it reached Goddard and could use the Link to send and receive messages. Theoretically, *Hotaru* could refuse to let the scientists disembark, but he couldn't order that on his authority.

He couldn't hurt his reputation any more than the Methuselah Project already had. Given current relations with the Western Alliance, he had little hope that they would risk making things worse by interfering based on Shijo's theories. He had until *Hotaru* rendezvoused with *Lang* to convince them.

M

ICHAEL SAT IN HIS room and thought about Emile and the rest of the team.

General Juarez was aware of the danger presented by Anna Cortez and had taken measures to prevent Emile from talking to her again.

Hotaru's passenger ring had six modules, five for passengers and one for command and control, including crew quarters, normally off limits to passengers. Each module was self-sufficient, with its own staterooms, dining room, and other amenities. The Methuselah team was assigned to Module 2, next to Module 1, the command module. It was easy for Juarez to control access to Module 2 and the rest of the ship, isolating the project team from the rest of the ship and particularly from Anna Cortez, assigned to Module 5 on the other side of the command module.

What Juarez was doing wasn't right. Perhaps the general could have found some legal justification for essentially taking them prisoner, but Michael doubted it, and even if it was legal, it wasn't right.

He didn't think there was anything he could do about it. If he could somehow put Emile in contact with Anna Cortez, Juarez would find out. Even if the general couldn't stop them from going on to Pitcairn, and he probably could, he would figure out who helped them, and Michael had no doubt that the result would be the destruction of his career and the loss of his freedom.

Michael felt bad about what was happening, but any action he could take would have too little chance of success and risk too much. In a week, they would all be continuing their work on *Lang*, the library ship orbiting Goddard in the Alpha Centauri system.

*H*OTARU PURSER YUI YOSHIDA wasn't sure what to do. Handling messages for the passengers was one of her duties, but this was a special case. There was a curtain of secrecy around the passengers in Module 2, and she wasn't sure she should pass on a message from a passenger in Module 5, especially since the message came with a note requesting discretion.

She knew better than to bother Captain Hayashi with such a minor issue, but perhaps First Officer Goto would help her. The ship computer told her he was in his quarters but not sleeping. When she knocked on his door, he opened it immediately and smiled.

"Yui! What can I do for you."

"I have a message from the journalist Anna Cortez to Doctor Emile Hernandez. I wasn't sure we could deliver messages to the people under General Juarez."

Goto frowned. "I understand your misgivings, Yui, but of course you should deliver it. It would violate our laws not to."

Yui bowed. "Yes, sir. I will deliver it immediately. Thank you, sir."

59

"I F WE'RE GETTING OFF at Goddard, we don't have much time," Bill said. They had gathered in the Hernandez stateroom, the largest of the rooms assigned to them. Little Emile sat on Lucinda's bed, listening.

"We don't know where Anna is," Emile said. "You can't just start knocking on doors."

"If that's what it takes," Eddie said. There was a soft knock on the door. "See, it can be done."

Lucinda opened the door, and Yui bowed and held out an envelope. "I didn't want the door to disturb you and thought a knock might be better if you were sleeping," she whispered. "A message for Doctor Emile Hernandez."

"Thank you," Lucinda replied, also keeping her voice low. "I'll give it to him." Yui bowed again and moved down the corridor.

Lucinda closed the door and looked at the envelope. "It's from Anna Cortez." She kept her voice low. Their cabin wouldn't be monitored on *Hotaru*, but there was always the possibility of someone in the corridor overhearing them.

"Read it to us," Emile said.

"Doctor Hernandez, if you still want to talk, I am in stateroom 503. Anna Cortez." Lucinda turned the paper over, frowned, and looked at the message again. "That's all it says."

"At least we won't have to knock on doors," Eddie said.

"We can't do anything unless we can get out of this module into the rest of the ship," Lucinda said. "She's in module 5, so we would have to go through all the other modules to get to her. How can we do that without Juarez catching us?"

"Maybe we don't have to go that way," Bill said. "Module 5 is just the other side of the command module, and Juarez won't be looking that way. The command module is a restricted area, but the infirmary is there."

"If one of us were sick, they would take him there," Eddie said. "Good, Bill. All we would have to do is get out into module 5 instead of back to this module."

"Juarez wouldn't believe one of us was really sick," Lucinda said.

A horrible groan came from Lucinda's bed, and everyone turned to look at little Emile. "Mommy, I don't feel good," the child said.

Joelle gasped and moved to the bed. "What's wrong, darling?"

"My tummy hurts."

Joelle blocked Bill's view of the five-year-old, but he saw Joelle jerk back in surprise. "He winked at me!" she said. She turned to her husband. "He's definitely your son, Eddie."

Eddie moved toward them. "He's faking?"

Little Emile groaned again and clutched his stomach. Bill could see his face now, twisted into a terrible grimace. "Mommy, it hurts," he said. Then he giggled.

Everyone stared at the five-year-old until Bill broke the silence. "Clever boy." He turned to Lucinda. "Juarez might believe a child."

"Maybe if he tones it down a bit," Eddie said. He grinned and rumpled the hair on his son's head. Little Emile giggled again and then groaned, a more subdued sound than before.

"That's it," Eddie said, and the pride in his voice was unmistakable.

"It would be best if we did this during our sleep period," Bill said.

Eddie nodded. "We'll wake Juarez and tell him Emile is sick and Joelle and I will go with him to the infirmary. I'll try to slip away and contact Anna Cortez."

"Isn't this dangerous for Emile?" Joelle asked. "What if Juarez finds out it's a ruse?"

"What's Juarez going to do to a five-year-old?" Eddie answered.

Bill frowned. No, the danger will be to Eddie. But asylum on Pitcairn, more Earthlike and not under Western Alliance control, was their only chance to avoid exile on Goddard or Trist.

G ENERAL JUAREZ'S STATEROOM WAS on the hallway leading to the exit from module 2. Beyond a heavy hatch, a tunnel connected to module 3. Access between modules was not usually restricted, but, at Juarez's request, the *Hotaru* crew had locked the hatch between module 2 and 3. Since each passenger module was self-sufficient, and Juarez had reserved all of module 2, there would be no passenger traffic.

When a knock on the door interrupted his reading, Juarez opened the door, wondering what one of his charges wanted.

"My son is complaining of stomach pains," Eddie said.

"So call the ship doctor," Juarez replied. "Why are you bothering me about it?"

"I thought you would want to know we're leaving the module. The infirmary is in the command module, and the doctor will probably want to see us there."

Juarez glared at him with narrowed eyes. "Fine. Go back to your stateroom and call the doctor. I'll send Colonel Pizarro with you to make sure your son is treated properly." Juarez thought Eddie hesitated before replying.

"Thank you." Eddie turned and hurried down the hallway as Juarez stared after him.

"H E DIDN'T COMPLETELY BELIEVE me, but he told me to contact the doctor," Eddie told the others. "He wants Michael to go with us."

"I'll call," Joelle said. She looked over at her son, who seemed to be practicing looking miserable. "Doctor's office," she told the stateroom phone.

"Doctor Aoki here. You have a medical problem?"

"My son is complaining of stomach pain," Joelle said. "It isn't normal for him, and we're concerned." On the bed, little Emile groaned convincingly.

"How old is he?"

"He's five."

"Very well. I will send my nurse to look at him. If necessary, we'll bring him into the infirmary. You are in stateroom 110?"

"Yes."

"Doctor Hernandez? I don't have a record of you having a child."

"No, we're visiting. This is Mrs. Bascomb."

"Ah, I see. Nurse Berry will be there in a couple of minutes."

The nurse arrived, with Michael right behind him. "No one told me you were in Emile's room," Michael said. "Fortunately, I saw the nurse stop here."

"Oops," Eddie replied, softly enough so that only Joelle heard him.

Nurse Romeo Berry was an efficient-looking man, probably in his forties, average-looking except that his head was almost completely hairless, a pair of thin eyebrows the only exception. He glanced around the room and went immediately to little Emile, lying in a fetal position on the bed, groaning again.

"And this must be the patient," he said with a smile. "Hi, Emile. I'm Romeo. Can you tell me where it hurts?"

"Here," Emile said, pointing to his stomach. His voice quavered, and he looked like he was going to cry. "It really hurts!"

"OK. Lay on your back and let me check it out." Emile rolled onto his back and looked up at Eddie.

"It's OK," Eddie said, trying to look concerned. He hoped his acting performance was as effective as his son's.

Romeo prodded Emile's stomach gently and frowned when Emile winced. He took a Life Signs Monitor from a pocket, placed it against the jugular on Emile's neck, and watched the readings stabilize.

"When did he eat last?" Romeo asked.

"We had dinner two hours ago," Joelle said. "He had tonkatsu and green tea ice cream for dessert."

"That shouldn't have bothered his stomach," Romeo said. "His life signs are normal, and I don't feel anything, but he seemed to feel pain when I touched him." He frowned and shook his head. "We'd better take a closer look. Let's take him to the infirmary."

Eddie held out his arms, and Emile climbed into them. He and Joelle trailed behind Romeo, with Michael following. When they reached the hatch between module 2 and the command module, a featureless steel panel with no visible way to open it, Romeo said, "Romeo Berry," and the door slid open. He gestured the others through the opening and closed it behind them by pushing a button to the side of the hatch.

That eliminated one concern Eddie had had about their plan. Now he knew that the command module hatches were secured to prevent entry, but not to prevent exit. The main corridor ran from the module 2 hatch to the module 5 hatch, although the other end was not immediately visible because of the slight curve to the floor. Other corridors and entrances to facilities, including the infirmary, branched off from it, so there would be no difficulty in finding his way.

Evading Michael might have been a problem, but Michael touched his shoulder at the doorway to the infirmary. "I have to talk to the captain," he told Eddie. "I'll be back in a couple of minutes." He smiled. "Emile will be fine." He turned and continued down the corridor.

Doctor Aoki was waiting for them in the infirmary. Joelle led Emile into an examination room while Eddie stood by the door. The doctor had Emile climb up onto the examination table and smiled at the boy. "So where does it hurt?"

Emile, looking pained, pointed to his stomach. "Here," he said weakly.

"All right. Lie down, and we'll take a look."

Emile laid down on his back, and the doctor pulled his shirt up and examined his torso. "No bruising." He probed the five-year-old's stomach and nodded when Emile winced.

"His vital signs were normal," Romeo said. "Nothing unusual for dinner."

"Does your son have medical nanites?" Aoki asked Eddie.

"Yes."

"Then there shouldn't be any infection. I should draw some blood and check for toxins."

The look of fear on Emile's face was Joelle's cue. She pushed forward and took Emile's hand. "It's all right," she said in a soothing voice.

Everyone was looking at Joelle, and Eddie had taken a position next to the door. He eased out into the corridor and moved quietly toward the hatch leading to module 5.

60

THE MAIN CORRIDOR WAS empty. Eddie believed people would tend not to question what you were doing if you looked confident, so he marched forward, not looking into the rooms or side corridors he passed. He thought he heard footsteps to his left once, but he ignored them. He belonged there, and there was no reason for anyone to doubt that.

He reached the hatch and smiled as he reached for the button that would open the door. Their plan was working, and Anna would help them.

A hand gripped his shoulder. "You don't want to do that," Michael said.

Eddie turned toward Michael. *Where did he come from?* A side corridor? "Why don't I?" He swung at the arm on his shoulder, but it didn't move, and Michael's grip only tightened.

"Whatever you thought you would do, it won't work. Are you still trying to make the Methuselah Project public? You already know that will only cause everyone trouble. What else could Anna Cortez do for you?"

"Let go of me," Eddie said, trying hard to put steel into his voice.

Michael shrugged and dropped his arm. "OK. Look, Eddie, I don't want to be the bad guy here, but what did you think was going to happen if you talked to Cortez?"

"We're not criminals. You have no right to do this to us."

Michael grimaced. "You're right, of course. Unfortunately, that won't make a difference. Cortez can't help you. Whatever you say to her, you'll end up where the general wants you. Maybe you think that being on a Japanese starship can work to your advantage?" Michael shook his head. "It won't. President Castillo will get whatever he wants from the crew. Japan is small and vulnerable, and their involvement in Pitcairn independence hurt their relationship with the Western Alliance."

"Interesting that you should mention Pitcairn," Eddie mumbled.

"Pitcairn? What does that. . ..." Michael nodded. "Oh, I see. You were going to try to arrange asylum on Pitcairn."

"That would be better than Trist or Goddard," Eddie said. He saw Joelle look out from the infirmary door, probably hearing his voice. "Damn it; it's not just me. You're doing this to my family, to my son!"

Michael's shoulders drooped. "I'm sorry, Eddie. This wasn't my decision."

"You didn't see me." Eddie could hear the pleading in his voice, but that didn't matter. "Keep walking, and no one will know you saw me leave."

"Eddie, listen to me, please. It won't work. All you can do is get everyone in trouble. The Japanese will side with us, not with you. There's no way you will be allowed to continue to Pitcairn."

Eddie was aware that his hands had curled into tight fists. He wanted to take a swing at Michael, but there was still a part of him that knew it wouldn't help. Joelle was watching, and he couldn't lose control in front of her.

"This isn't over," he said. He turned and strode back to the infirmary.

"IS DADDY MAD AT me?" Emile asked. Joelle and Emile were back in their stateroom, but Eddie had disappeared. There weren't that many places to go within their module, and Joelle guessed he had gone to the small lounge.

"No, he's not mad at you," Joelle answered, trying to make her voice as soothing as possible. She had never seen Eddie as angry as he had been when he came back to the infirmary. He could hardly speak, and Emile had thought that he was to blame. "If daddy is mad at anyone, he's mad at Michael. You did fine, and we're both very proud of you."

"I like Michael. Is he a bad man like General Juarez?"

"He's just trying to do his job. I don't think he or General Juarez are all bad. They just want things to be different than what we want them to be."

Emile's face scrunched into a frown. "Why can't we do what we want to do? We don't tell him what to do."

"Sometimes we have to do things we don't want to do to help other people. General Juarez works for the government, and governments make sure everyone has what they need."

The frown was still there. "I'll help people. The government doesn't have to make me do it. But I didn't want to go away."

Joelle pulled her son into a hug. "And you were a big help today." She felt torn; she knew Emile needed her, but she needed Eddie. "Phone. Connect to Bill Bensonhurst."

T HE LOUNGE WAS A small room with two tables and four stools at the automated bar. The tables were unoccupied, but Eddie was on one of the stools, his hands curled around a glass of amber liquid. Bill slid onto the stool next to him.

"Are you OK?" Bill asked. "Joelle was worried."

Eddie shook his head. "I wanted to hit him. I think I would have if I hadn't known Joelle was watching."

"It's not Michael's fault, you know. He's had his life disrupted, too."

"He stopped me. He could have just walked away. Juarez wouldn't have known."

Bill shrugged. "We knew that trying to contact Anna Cortez was a long shot."

Eddie gulped down the rest of his drink. "I'll get back at them somehow. All three of them."

"Come on, Eddie. We can worry about that later. Right now, your family needs you."

S HIJO OFTEN LEFT SUBORDINATES waiting after summoning them, particularly when he was unhappy with them. Now the same technique was being used on him, and he didn't appreciate the irony. He glanced once again at the ornate door leading to the office of Foreign Services Secretary Takumi Maeda. With a sigh, he leaned back in the straight-backed chair and tried to calm himself with a deep-breathing exercise.

Just past the forty-five-minute mark, Maeda apparently decided that Shijo had been kept waiting long enough. The door opened, and Maeda's assistant motioned him to come in. He stood and strode forward, trying to find a balance between appearing reluctant and being too eager.

The assistant left the room, closing the door behind him. Maeda sat behind his precisely organized desk, staring at him with lifted eyebrows and down turned mouth.

"Sit down, Atsushi," he said in a tone that left no doubt it was an order, not a polite invitation. "So, what new emergency are you bringing me?"

"*Hotaru* has entered the Alpha Centauri system and is approaching Goddard. We have two days to decide to take action."

Maeda nodded. "I see. This Methuselah obsession again. And what would you have us do?"

"I know Captain Hayashi. We could ask him to hold the scientists for questioning. What we do after that would depend on the answers we get."

"We would have to send the request through the Link. The Western Alliance controls that. Do we even know the names of the scientists in question?"

"I have names of five people. There are others, but I could not identify them. We would need a cover story. Suspicion of sabotage, perhaps."

"After the disaster brought about by your man Ikeda, they wouldn't believe it."

Kenshin Ikeda was still being held by the Western Alliance. The government claimed he had acted alone, and the Japanese Embassy was not offering any assistance. Ikeda had a lawyer who maintained that Ikeda had been curious and was only guilty of trespassing in an abandoned building. Western Alliance officers had found the shaped charge nearby, but at least Ikeda had left nothing on the explosive or the bag containing it that might connect him to it. There was still hope that Ikeda might be repatriated, but it was a slim hope.

"The Western Alliance has spent too much time and money on this project for a goal of simply prolonging life by uploading a person to a computer," Shijo said. "They've been working on it for at least eight years, probably longer. Agent Ikeda and I were both convinced there was more to it than that."

"You're probably right, but how is that our business?" Maeda shook his head. "Our position with the Western Alliance is too delicate to risk annoying them when we know so little."

"If I'm right, the danger is too great not to do something."

Maeda waved his hand. "What danger? You don't know there is a danger!"

"I know they are playing with something they don't understand. The danger from conscious computers has always been ridiculed because scientists told us it was impossible. Now we know that it's not. The repercussions from that are unimaginable."

Maeda frowned and ran his fingers through his hair. "Maybe. I doubt it, but maybe. The problem remains. What can we do about it? Ikeda's attempt failed badly."

"We can send an encrypted message to Hayashi. That might be questioned, but it wouldn't be so unusual as to raise serious attention. We can ask him to use his authority to talk to one of the scientists and try to find out what they are doing."

Maeda swiveled around on his chair and stared out the window at the busy metropolis beyond. Then he turned back and glared at Shijo. "All right. Send the message, but be careful. Be very careful."

Shijo bowed. "Yes, sir." He moved toward the door.

"This is on you, Atsushi," Maeda shouted after him. "If this blows up in our faces, so does your career."

Shijo closed the door quietly behind him. He hadn't needed Maeda to tell him that.

61

WHEN THE DOOR TO their cabin announced purser Yui Yoshida, Lucinda opened the door. "Doctor Aoki would like to examine your husband before arrival," Yui said. "He wants to make sure everything is proper before the accelerations in rendezvousing with the Lang."

Lucinda opened her mouth to tell the purser that Emile had already gone through several similar maneuvers without a problem, including the more difficult shuttle flight from Earth. No one had ever suggested a medical examination before those.

Before she could speak, Yui continued. "Please, Doctor. Doctor Aoki feels it is very important. I will take your husband to the doctor and bring him back very soon."

Again, Lucinda hesitated. *I should go with him.* But Yui obviously wanted to take Emile alone. Something was going on, but Lucinda couldn't imagine what it might be.

Emile, sitting on his bed listening, must have come to a similar conclusion. "Let's go. I'm sure this won't take long, dear. I think it will be easier to tell my bed to follow. My eyesight is still not good enough to maneuver easily through the ship corridors." He laid down, and the bed moved toward Yui.

"DOCTOR HERNANDEZ, I AM Captain Hayashi," a voice said.

That the purser took him to the captain rather than a doctor didn't surprise Emile. "Hello, Captain. What can I do for you?"

"I have received a message from my government, asking me to talk to you," Hayashi said. "They are curious about why you are going to Goddard."

"Scientific research, of course. We will be working on *Lang.*"

"I am told your research is for a program called the Methuselah Project. They would like to know the nature of the project."

How much of the truth can I tell them? Sticking with what was publicly known would probably be safest. "We are studying human consciousness and the possibility of transferring it to a computer."

"My government wonders why the Western Alliance is spending so much time and money on such a thing. They suspect there may be more to it than they have revealed."

Emile had wondered about that, too. It didn't seem that likely that the goal of the project was simply to upload Castillo and perhaps a few others to a computer to extend their lives, particularly now that Castillo was no longer in power. Inquiring into other reasons was dangerous, though.

"We have no other goal," Emile answered.

"You speak to me through a device called a Voice Magician," Hayashi said after a long, quiet moment.

"Yes."

"The research leading to the device has only been legal in the Western Alliance for a few years. Is that correct?"

"The Voice Magician uses input from a neuro-interrogator. The research for the neuro-interrogator was illegal until 2338. At that time, it became legal."

"In the Western Alliance."

"Excuse me?"

"Your research is legal in the Western Alliance. It is still illegal in Japan. Your device is illegal."

Emile didn't know how to take Captain Hayashi's statement. Surely, he wasn't suggesting that his neuro-interrogator be taken from him. Hayashi was technically correct, but why would they push the issue?

"We're not in Japan," Emile answered, but he could hear how weak his interpreted voice sounded.

"No, but this ship operates under Japanese law. Doctor, please forgive my abruptness. I have no intention of confiscating your device. I only wish to offer my help. My government suspects that you and your people are going to *Lang* involuntarily. Doctor Aoki told me about the incident in the infirmary, and I suspect that was part of an escape attempt. I have been authorized to arrest you for smuggling an illegal device, but only so that we can hold you on *Hotaru* and not leave you on *Lang*. We would take that action only on you or members of your team that desired it."

Is this a way out for them? If they agreed, what would happen to them? Hayashi no doubt intended to leave them on Pitcairn, out of reach of the Western Alliance. That was what they had hoped for when they had tried to contact Anna Cortez. Could Juarez do anything about it if he accepted the offer? He might be wary of confrontation with the Japanese, wanting to avoid anything that might bring Methuselah further into public view.

"I want to discuss this with the rest of my team," Emile said.

"Of course. We will reach *Lang* tomorrow, though, so there is not much time."

J UAREZ BROUGHT THEM ALL into the tiny observation room at the edge of module two. It was a tight fit for everyone, but they shuffled around until they could all see the view as it swept by. Eddie held his son on his shoulders and tried to be cheerful. One of the *Hotaru* crew squeezed through them, distributing anti-nausea pills, so Eddie knew they would leave the ship and experience zero-gravity.

As *Hotaru* rotated about its axis, the planet came into view every fifteen seconds. The library ship *Lang* orbited nearby, a long, twelve-sided cylinder, sensor antennae covering it like porcupine skin. Other than the Methuselah group, there was no one else in the observation room, not surprising given the dizziness-generating view. The anti-nausea pills may have been useful there, too. The lounge in each module showed a stationary televised view, and most people preferred that.

Juarez apparently differed, choosing the small observation room to reveal their destination. "We've arrived at your new home," he said. "You'll be able to work without distraction here on *Lang*."

"Great," Bill said. He spoke low, and only Eddie and Joelle heard him. "Goddard would be better than living in a tin can."

Eddie hardly noticed and would have disagreed if he had responded. Still angry about what had happened in the command module, he focused on Michael. Michael turned in his direction once, frowned, and immediately turned away.

"We are the only passengers disembarking here," Juarez said. "The shuttle *Rotwang* will be here shortly to take us all over to *Lang*. On *Lang*, Colonel Pizarro will show Mr. Bascomb and Mrs. Alvarez to your laboratory to help set up your equipment, which we sent here last week on a military transport. Someone from *Lang* will meet the rest of you and show you to your quarters. After that, you can rest or explore your new surroundings as you wish.

"*Rotwang* should be waiting for us by the time we get to the loading dock. Follow Michael, please."

Michael nodded to General Juarez and moved toward the exit, but Captain Hayashi blocked his way. "I have been in contact with my government," he said. He pushed past Michael. "I have orders to detain you pending a search for contraband in your possession."

Juarez confronted Hayashi. "What are you talking about? What contraband?"

"Devices in violation of Japan's laws against mind-reading technology," Hayashi responded. Six inches shorter, he had to look up at Juarez, but seemed unbothered by Juarez's angry expression.

"The neuro-interrogators!" Michael said.

Hayashi looked at Michael. "Exactly. Are you admitting you are transporting them?"

Juarez pointed at Lucinda. "This is your doing."

"Doctor Hernandez has no influence over my government," Hayashi said. "It is they who have ordered this."

"We'll see about that. Colonel, take care of the president and our associates while I'm gone. I'm going over to *Lang* to straighten this out."

Before Hayashi could say anything else, Juarez was gone.

E DDIE SAT WITH JOELLE and little Emile, engrossed in his thoughts while they waited in the lounge for something to happen. Michael sat near the door, watching silently. A crewmember served tea while Captain Hayashi talked quietly with Lucinda.

Hayashi hadn't really explained why the Japanese wanted to help them when he talked to Emile. Did it have something to do with the aborted attempt to contact Anna Cortez? If so, the Japanese approach seemed more promising than his effort. Michael professed innocence in our predicament when he stopped me. Did Michael help them after all?

The library ship *Lang* had three shuttles, two configured for cargo. The third shuttle, *Rotwang*, could carry up to twenty passengers. It took three trips to move all *Hotaru's* other passengers to *Lang*, taking most of the day. When *Rotwang* returned the third time, Juarez came with it.

"Prepare to disembark," he ordered Lucinda. When she hesitated, he moved forward. "Now!"

"They aren't going anywhere," Captain Hayashi said, coming up behind Juarez.

Juarez turned on him with a scowl and narrowed eyes. "Then neither are you, Captain. I have contacted Earth and been authorized to hold this ship here until all Western Alliance citizens booked to Goddard are transported to *Lang*."

Captain Hayashi opened his mouth but then closed it without speaking. *Lang* was part of the Western Alliance and, more importantly, controlled the Link.

Juarez turned to Michael while Hayashi watched in stony silence. "*Rotwang* is waiting," Juarez said. "You lead, and everyone else follow."

The Japanese had failed, too. Eddie looked at Michael, who was jumping up to obey Juarez. He wouldn't have much choice, but Eddie thought he should at least show some sign of reluctance if he had tried to help them. There was no such sign. Eddie pushed down his rising anger; Joelle and Emile needed him to stay calm.

The others trailed behind Michael, with Juarez and Castillo bringing up the rear. At the Axis Access hatch, they took shoe covers from a locker and carefully attached them to their shoes. The covers would adhere to the floor as they moved from the Earth-normal gravity of the module to the zero-gravity of *Hotaru's* axis where the loading dock was.

There were no windows or view screens between the observation room and the loading dock or in the passenger section of the *Rotwang*. Juarez and Castillo went into the cockpit, where there were two observer seats, but even in their absence, no one felt like talking. The trip from *Hotaru* was short, and a small jerk told Eddie their motion had stopped.

"There will be a temporary delay while the shuttle is secured in *Lang's* shuttle bay," Michael said. "Please stay in your seats and make sure your shoe covers are secure. You'll need them in the shuttle bay." Even as Michael spoke, Eddie could hear sounds from the hull, presumably *Lang's* robot crew.

Five minutes later, Juarez opened the hatch to the cockpit. "We can disembark," he told Michael. Michael nodded and keyed a code into a panel next to the airlock. Since the shuttle was in the pressurized bay, both airlock hatches opened, and they followed Michael out. Robots still serviced *Rotwang*, some on the ground, and some in the air hovering around it.

A woman, whom Eddie estimated to be in her seventies, waited for them. "I'm Amanda Davila," she said, shaking hands, first with Castillo, and then with Juarez. "I'm the Chief Scientist on *Lang*."

"I am familiar with your reputation," Castillo said. His voice was gravelly, much different than the forceful voice that Eddie had heard on the network when Castillo had been president. Had Castillo's voice had changed or had technology had enhanced the broadcast voice.

"I'll show you to the living quarters." She paused and smiled. "We've been eagerly awaiting you, Mr. President. As you know, we didn't have neurological research facilities before."

"We have two engineers who can get to work immediately," Juarez said. "I want our facility operational as soon as possible."

Amanda nodded. "We could use the help, of course. We have no experience with the equipment you are using, and progress has been slow. The labs are on deck four, though, and the living quarters are on deck one."

"I've studied the layout," Michael said. "I'll be able to show them to our laboratory from deck one."

Amanda looked interested. "Have you been on a library ship before?"

"No, but I've studied the design and wrote the requirements document for our laboratory."

Amanda smiled. "You'll probably be all right. Not too many people get lost."

The shuttle deck was in the center of the ship, but, except for some zero-gravity laboratories, the rest of the occupied areas were along the outside hull of the twelve-sided cylinder. Once on deck one, Michael took charge of Eddie and Aurora. They climbed a set of stairs to an access corridor that circled the hull, connecting the decks, and then descended another set of stairs to get to deck four. "Down this corridor," he said.

The ceiling of the corridor was transparent, and they could see the vast empty center of Lang. "I don't think Bill realized how big this ship was," Eddie said to Aurora.

"I've been meaning to ask," Aurora said. "Why is it called a library ship?"

"The ship's computer contains almost all our accumulated knowledge," Michael said. "Each library ship stored more information in its databanks than any Earth-based library."

"Thank you," Aurora said. Eddie scowled at Michael. He would have told Aurora that, but Michael was a little faster.

The laboratory for Methuselah was at the other end of the deck, and it was another ten minutes before they reached the doors. Michael punched in a key code, and they entered.

Eddie swore. The room was smaller than their San Diego facility, with equipment crowded close together and cables draped everywhere. Several people were working, and two of them were embroiled in an argument. Eddie looked at Aurora and frowned. "Let's get to work," he told her. "We're needed, all right."

62

"WE HAVEN'T HEARD FROM Eddie or Joelle either," Jasmine told Max. "They're on Prendergast Station?"

"Bill and Emile were, so I assume they all were," Max answered. "A starship was docked there, though, heading out to the colonies, so they could be gone now."

"General Juarez must be behind it," Franco said. "Have you gone to the police?"

"Juarez must be working with the government. We can't rely on them to help us."

"We could prod the network organizations to look into it," Jasmine said. "Missing millionaire couple—that would be a good story."

Max nodded. "We can try. I suspect the government will shut the story down quickly, but maybe we can raise some interest before they react. The government can't control all the outlets."

EMILE WAS BORED, BUT the idle time was ending. It had taken Eddie and Aurora six long days to organize the laboratory in the smaller space and get all the equipment up and running. An fMRI machine was damaged, either in transit or handling after arrival, and Eddie devoted two of those days to its repair. Eddie had expressed satisfaction that there was no room for Michael in the smaller space but didn't seem himself otherwise.

Emile had tried to make the time useful by reviewing the Malley data and thinking about how a machine might become conscious. The latter idea had been on his mind before the exposure of the San Diego facility threw everything into confusion. He was a neuroscientist, though, not a computer hardware engineer. Eddie or Aurora could have given him some useful feedback, but the laboratory was their priority.

To a significant extent, the human brain was an incredibly sophisticated pattern recognizer. This was both a blessing and a curse; it helped in understanding events and in remembering them, but it could also distort memories when other similar but different memories became part of the pattern evaluation. Old memories could set expectations that affected recent memories.

Computers could recognize patterns, too, especially computers as powerful as those of the library ships. Emile thought they were probably more reliable in separating conflicting patterns, but he might be wrong. That was just one of the many subjects he wanted to discuss with Eddie and Aurora. Some psychologists thought that human unreliability was a factor in imagination and creative thought, but there didn't seem to be a connection to consciousness.

Transferring that ability to a computer wasn't just a question of integrating input from the five senses. Personality, emotions, beliefs, and other factors colored memories in ways that a machine didn't duplicate. Consciousness was a part of the interweaving of those factors into the memory.

There was an idea there, but he wasn't grasping it yet. He was distracted. Over the years since the accident, he had gotten used to being able to think things out without distractions; all he had to do was turn off connections to his neurotrainer. That wasn't the case any longer. His hearing had improved to where he could make out simple sounds. Soon, he hoped, further improvements would make it possible to understand words. Other senses were coming back, too. He could see lights faintly, now, and some areas of the body sensed touch the old-fashioned way.

He shrugged his shoulders. For most people, that would have been an automatic motion that they were hardly aware of. For Emile, it was a conscious decision, and he did it because he could. Maybe Eddie was available. The engineer could probably use a break from his work preparing the lab.

H IS HEARING WAS GETTING better, but Emile still needed the neurotrainer to make sense of a conversation.

"So, as I understand it, consciousness is thought to be an emergent property," Eddie said.

Lucinda nodded. "The sum is more than the parts, yes. It sounds good, and it's probably true, but it's also a way of saying we don't know what it is."

"The data Juarez gave us from old research indicates we were close to understanding once," Luke said.

"Maybe," Emile replied. "So much of the research done then was lost. We know the human brain is extremely complex. So are the library ships, not only in the number of circuits, but in the variety of hardware and software functions they are capable of."

Eddie grimaced. "We could spend the rest of our lives at this. It's never going to work. Not in this century, anyway."

"We're close to figuring out how to transfer memories to a computer in a structure that it can deal with," Isabella said. "That will be a big step."

Was Eddie right? It was clear now that the goal of the Methuselah Project was to upload Castillo to *Lang's* computer. If they succeeded, the upload would only be a copy of Castillo's consciousness, a virtual clone. Contrary to what network commentaries had claimed, it wouldn't be immortality, at least not for the original Alejandro Castillo. Did Juarez and Castillo understand that?

Maybe they did. If so, then immortality wasn't what they had in mind. There was some other reason for all of this, and President Sanchez-Smythe was supporting it. That was odd, considering that Castillo and Sanchez-Smythe were political foes, but they might have reached some agreement.

"Emile, are you frowning?" Lucinda asked.

Was he? It would have been a normal reaction to what he was thinking, but he hadn't been able to change his facial expressions since the accident. His body was changing as his brain worked to repair itself; was this another sign of that?

"Why is Castillo interested in being uploaded to a computer?" Emile asked.

"He wants to become immortal," Lucinda said. "Isn't that the whole idea?"

"But it won't work that way. He'll only be copying himself. Surely, he understands that. He's not stupid."

There was a silence, and Emile assumed his statement had made everyone think about his question. Eddie recovered first. "There's only one reason a politician like Castillo does anything. Power."

Castillo wanted to imprint his consciousness on a powerful computer with access to all the technology the Western Alliance possessed. It was unclear exactly how someone could use that, but Eddie had to be right. They would have to make sure he was right about their chances of success, too. They could not allow Castillo to upload himself.

M AX STARED OUT THE window, hardly noticing the neighboring buildings or the bright sunlit day. It had been three months since he and the Munts had campaigned with the media to publicize the fate of the Methuselah team. It had been a big story for about a week, but interest faded, and most network organizations dropped the story when they discovered the Prendergast interview between Emile and Anna Cortez. The *Pitcairn News Service* carried the story longer than the others, but, with nothing new to report, they dropped the story, too. If nothing bad had happened to Emile Hernandez, their logic went, the rest of the team must also be pursuing some goal voluntarily.

Max didn't think the government even bothered to squelch the coverage, although it may have been responsible for an information leak suggesting that the Hernandezes were studying the neurology of Terran life compared to life on other planets, deflecting attention away from Methuselah.

Attempts to contact any of them on any of the library ships or colony planets went nowhere. That was undoubtedly the government's work. He was out of ideas that would help his friends.

E DDIE AND JOELLE HAD worried about how life on Lang would affect their son, but their concerns turned out to be pointless. There were other children on *Lang*, born on the library ship to the scientists stationed there, and human teachers, robots, and terminals with access to the ship's main computer provided daycare and personalized education.

Eddie and Joelle often quizzed their son about what he was learning and found that, once Emile caught up, he did well. Their only worry was that he had made no friends. At first, the older kids had harassed him, but, under the watchful eye of the robots and the main computer, not seriously. After a few weeks, the other children realized Emile had actually been on Earth, and his popularity improved. But he still hadn't made any friends.

"I made a friend today," little Emile announced one day about three months after their arrival.

"That's wonderful," Joelle said. "Who is it?"

"Her name is Sofia Marie. She's only four months younger than me; that's almost the same age." Emile paused. "She's a girl, but she's OK. She's been all over the ship and says she'll show everything to me."

"Her parents go with her, right?" Joelle said.

"Sometimes. Her grandparents are on the ship, too. Mostly she goes by herself."

Eddie grinned and put his hand on Joelle's shoulder. "I'm sure the ship watches her constantly and that there are a dozen robots within a few seconds of her wherever she goes."

Joelle didn't look as sure, but she nodded.

S OFIA MADRIGAL SAT AT a console on the bridge, monitoring the status of the Link. *Lang* orbited in Lagrange Point 4, or L4, a stable point created by the interaction of Goddard's gravity with that of its largest moon. The Link orbited in L5, another stable point the same distance from the planet but sixty degrees away. Managing its operations was the most important function of the ship, and that was Sofia's responsibility.

She was not in a good mood, but she hadn't been since the Terrans had come aboard. She knew Amanda felt the same way and, as chief scientist on *Lang*, Amanda probably had more reason to distrust them. Why were a Western Alliance general and a former Western Alliance President on *Lang*, dragging a team of scientists with them? There was all that equipment, too, apparently for some kind of brain research.

She glanced over at the picture she had taped to one side of the console, her little granddaughter, named after her. Sofia Marie was playing with the child from the Terran group, a boy about her age, and Sofia wasn't sure how she felt about that. From Emile Bascomb's name, she thought his parents were probably northerners, but that wasn't what bothered her. She chided herself; it wasn't fair to blame the child for the man employing the child's parents.

She wasn't political, but she had always felt distrustful of Alejandro Castillo. What was he doing on *Lang*, and how was he able to do it with his opponent, President Sanchez-Smythe, in the Presidential Palace in Brasília? Does it have something to do with the man who is always with that strange mobile bed? Even the names of the group were a secret except for the child, and a search of that name hadn't given her any information.

Messages to Earth all came through her console on their way to the Link, but General Juarez sent encrypted messages. She had searched for his name and learned that he had been in Castillo's cabinet. Castillo and Juarez were both connected to something called the Methuselah Project, but there wasn't much on that in *Lang's* data. That was unusual, too; Earth uploaded almost everything to the library ships. It was one of the few times she felt cut off from the mother planet.

Her curiosity was one thing that had not changed as she aged. Sofia Marie had been begging her for a tour of deck eleven, the manufacturing deck. Her granddaughter could travel freely on most decks, but deck eleven was considered too dangerous for a little girl without human supervision. I should give in and tell Sofia Marie to bring her friend along.

*L*ANG WAS BUILT TO be self-sufficient for decades, fully automated, with facilities to make anything it needed to keep itself operational. Deck eleven was a critical part of that, a forty thousand square foot space packed tightly with machinery. Almost all the machines could be loosely called 3D printers, but few did work resembling printing. Some machines molded plastic; others used cutting and grinding tools to shape a variety of materials; still others formed parts by the gradual accumulation of layers. All of them used programs with instructions on how to create the thousands of items the ship needed to operate itself and support its passengers.

Sofia Madrigal escorted her granddaughter and Emile Bascomb through the narrow passages between machines, frequently stopping with the two children to watch a printer manufacture some part. Most of the machines were almost noiseless, but there were hundreds of them, and the net result was a cacophony that hindered communication.

Eventually, they tired and began the walk back to the living quarters on deck one. "So, what do your parents do?" she asked Emile.

"Daddy is an engineer," Emile answered. "Sometimes he makes things like the Voice Magician Uncle Emile uses. Mom is a programmer; she writes instructions for the things daddy makes."

"Uncle Emile? Is that the man with the mobile bed?"

Emile nodded. "He was hurt in an accident years ago, even before I was born. When my daddy worked in Panama, he made things that helped Uncle Emile." The boy smiled and puffed out his chest. "He's a famous scientist, and I'm named after him."

"And he's your uncle?"

Emile shook his head. "Not really. But calling him Uncle Emile is better than calling him Doctor Hernandez, like General Juarez does."

Sofia thought about asking Emile what his parents were working on, but she didn't want to push too hard. That might get the attention of General Juarez, and that wouldn't be wise. Besides, she already had new information that she could use in searches through the ship's data banks.

63

"COMPUTER, GIVE ME INFORMATION on Doctor Emile Hernandez," Sofia said to her terminal.

"Doctor Emile Hernandez, neuroscientist and developer of the second-generation neurotrainer," the terminal responded. "He was injured in an auto accident on 27 October 2338 and diagnosed as being in locked-in state. He has been mentioned in press releases from JEM Electronics as a user of their products to improve his condition."

"Is that all you have?"

"There is one additional entry. Doctor Emile Hernandez attended the baptism of Emile William Bascomb on 21 September 2346."

That would be Sofia Marie's friend. With all the equipment in their laboratory, it made sense that they would need an engineer. The boy had mentioned the Voice Magician, though, and Sofia had heard of that. Was that a product from JEM Electronics?

"Computer, look for connections between Voice Magician and JEM Electronics."

"The principal designer of the Voice Magician, manufactured by Munt Electronics, was Edward Bascomb, who became a founder of JEM Electronics. The name comes from the initials of the founders: Joelle Bascomb, Edward Bascomb, and Maxwell Estevez."

"Is Edward Bascomb still connected to JEM?"

"His official connection ended after JEM went public. The IPO was very successful, and Edward Bascomb profited from it."

That was probably an understatement; the Bascombs were almost certainly wealthy. But, if so, what are they doing on *Lang?* The library ship was more comfortable than the Goddard surface, but still very different from what a wealthy family on Earth has available. And why did they bring their young son to *Lang?*

The question was beyond her, but Amanda, as *Lang's* chief scientist, should know what she had learned. "Where is Amanda?" she asked the computer.

"Chief Scientist Davila is on the bridge."

Sofia found Amanda staring at the enormous screen that took up the entire front bulkhead. Only the lower half was visible from Amanda's seat in front of a life support monitor, but Sofia recognized the view displayed as a stretch of a wide river winding through a surviving section of the Amazon rainforest. Amanda looked up, startled, as Sofia approached. Sofia thought she looked a little guilty. "The Amazon?" Sofia asked.

"Technically, the Solimões River, the western end of the Amazon," Amanda answered. "My family used to have a plantation in the area, west of Fonte Boa. We lost it around the turn of the twenty-third century, long before I was born, when it became part of Reserva Extrativista Auati-Paraná." She smiled. "If it were still in the family, I probably never would have left Earth."

Like Sofia, Amanda had lived on *Lang* for fifteen years, part of the first group of scientists brought after the Link enabled practical travel between Alpha Centauri and Earth. That probably explained the guilty look. Amanda was feeling homesick for Earth, but she shouldn't have felt bad about that. Sofia had those problems, too; she suspected most if not all the scientists aboard *Lang* felt that way. So far, though, no one had asked to return.

The display had Sofia's attention now. She was from the former Chile and had little experience with the Amazon watershed, but it was Earth, and Amanda's nostalgia brought back memories for her, too. What images of her Terran origins were stored for display on the giant screen?

"So, what can I do for you, Sofia?" Amanda chuckled.

"How much do you know about our new crewmembers?"

"Juarez's group? Not much. The general is pretty secretive."

Sofia outlined what she had found out in a few sentences. "I suspect that most of them are not here voluntarily," she ended.

Amanda frowned. "You're probably right. I didn't want to interfere, but Juarez demanded that I monitor the living quarters of most of the people he brought on board. Everyone except himself, Colonel Pizarro, and President Castillo. He didn't identify any of the others either, so your discoveries are new to me."

"He didn't tell you what they're working on?"

"That was the biggest secret of all. Some are neuroscientists, but that's about all I know."

Sofia nodded. "Given that, I think I can guess what they're doing. Do you remember a controversy about something called Methuselah? Patrick Malley mentioned it at the Colonial Reorganization Conference."

"Malley, the Pitcairn Administrator? That conference was after we came here. I didn't pay much attention. That's when Pitcairn became independent, though, right?"

"Yes. Eventually, Methuselah was revealed to be a project to upload human consciousness to a computer. It was a Castillo project, supposedly canceled when he lost the election. I think that's what Juarez is doing here."

Amanda stared at her for a long moment, her eyes wide. "Are you saying they want to upload somebody to our computer?"

"I think it's a good possibility."

"They can't do that. If they somehow damage the computer, it could endanger all our research. Hell, it could endanger the ship, which means it could endanger us. I need to find out if that's what they're planning."

"You said that Juarez is monitoring the living quarters of the scientists. Is that legal?"

Amanda shook her head. "I'm not a lawyer, but I doubt it. There should be a warrant, and I haven't seen one. I guess Juarez intimidated me."

Sofia smiled slyly. "We could do the same. We could monitor their quarters."

"It wouldn't be any more legal for us to do that." Amanda hesitated, but then she returned the smile. "It would be fitting, though. Computer, monitor conversations in the quarters assigned to General Juarez, Colonel Pizarro, and President Castillo. Send the recordings to the command terminal here on the bridge."

G ENERAL JUAREZ KEPT HIS expression carefully neutral even though Castillo was not looking in his direction. It was only in his mind that he looked at the older man with disgust. With modern medicine, if a man took care of himself, he could stay active well past one hundred years old, but Castillo had not done that. He had kept his weight down, but he led a sedentary lifestyle, and the result was a good deal of flab. Worse, his mind was declining faster than his body.

"I don't understand why you can't upload me now," Castillo said. "They've had long enough to figure out how to do it."

"They are making progress," Juarez said. "They are on the verge of being able to upload memories; consciousness should follow."

"We should have stayed with that first team that David Pearson put together. They would be done by now."

Juarez shuddered. The Methuselah Project had begun in a Pearson Industries laboratory in the early days of Castillo's first ten-year term as Western Alliance President. That team had worked on the project for eight years with nothing to show for it but the waste of an astonishing amount of money. Hernandez and his people progressed only slowly, but they had progressed, even if Juarez would never admit it to them.

"Be patient, Mr. President. Soon you will control the computer, and we'll have access to the entire network of government computers without having to ask for permission."

Castillo smiled. "Yes. Then we'll see who's in charge."

Juarez nodded. "Yes, we will."

"I DON'T ENTIRELY UNDERSTAND," Amanda told Sofia. "If they could access any government computer without having to get a warrant, it would give them tremendous power. I see that. But how does uploading Castillo to the *Lang* computer accomplish that?"

"I think I understand that part," Sofia said. "All the safeguards against coordinating information between computers are protections against external entry. If they had internal access, the safeguards wouldn't work. Through the Link, our computer has internal connections."

"What about the safeguards against using our computer for illegal access?"

"If someone were uploaded to the computer, they would be inside and could override the computer's programming. It would probably work; reports say that the *Asimov* computer could get around its programming when it became conscious. But would they really get that much power?"

"I don't think it's possible to overestimate what they could learn," Amanda said, shaking her head. "There are good reasons for keeping distinct kinds of information on different computers, limiting coordinated access by requiring a warrant. Computers track everything: state secrets, of course, but also individual privacy, financial information, arrest records, corporate filings—everything! The possibilities for abuse are unlimited."

"Then we have to stop them."

"General Juarez has authority from President Sanchez-Smythe to do whatever he wants. If we prevented him from accessing the computer, he would replace us with someone who would support him."

"We have to do something." Sofia's brow wrinkled. "This still makes little sense, though. Why would Sanchez-Smythe allow her opponent to have that power? Wouldn't he use it against her?"

Amanda frowned. "I don't know. We won't do anything until we get more information. I'll continue monitoring them."

S OFIA SUGGESTED ANOTHER TOUR for the children, this time to the bridge. She took them through the area, explaining the more interesting terminals and what they monitored or controlled, but it was obvious that the children were more interested in the gigantic screen on the forward bulkhead. When they came onto the bridge, it was showing Goddard, a dazzling white globe partially covered by clouds almost the same color as the surface. Goddard was an ice world, probably not much different than Earth had been billions of years before, but still a spectacular sight.

Sofia entertained Sofia Marie and Emile by commanding the computer to show other views, including some from Earth. "Do you miss Earth?" she asked Emile.

"A little," Emile said. "*Lang* is interesting, but there are a lot of things we could do on Earth that we can't do here."

Sofia Marie opened her mouth to speak, probably to ask about Earth, but Sofia talked over her. "Why did your parents bring you here?"

"General Juarez made them come here." Emile pouted. "He's mean."

She had been right. The scientists were here against their will. That was another crime perpetrated by the general, added to his illegal surveillance of the scientists. But what could she do about it?

64

J UAREZ HAD SET UP an office in one of the unused units in the living quarters. He looked up as Michael entered the room. "I'm concerned about President Castillo, sir," Michael said.

"Why?"

"The plan is to upload him to the *Lang* computer, but I'm not sure that's wise. He's not as sharp as he was. How will that affect the computer?"

Juarez stared at Michael, assessing his subordinate. He had wondered about Michael at first, not sure he could depend on him. But it was Michael who had stopped Bascomb's attempt to contact Anna Cortez, and Juarez felt better about trusting Michael. He shrugged. It didn't matter that much, anyway. Isolated on *Lang*, everyone was under Juarez's complete control.

"President Castillo believes he will be uploaded," Juarez said. "He is naïve enough to think President Sanchez-Smythe would allow her former opponent to gain that much power. When the time comes, however, it will not be President Castillo whose consciousness is copied into the computer."

Michael opened his mouth, probably to ask who would be uploaded, but he closed it again, possibly realizing the only likely answer. He nodded, and Juarez smiled.

"E MILE, WHY DON'T YOU wake Uncle up," Lucinda told little Emile. From his bed, Emile waved a hand, sat up, and reached for the switch for his neuro-interrogator. "I'm awake," he said.

Lucinda looked at him in astonishment. "Emile, you understood me?" Emile's hearing had been steadily improving, but understanding more than a simple word or two had been beyond his abilities.

Emile nodded, and Lucinda thought about how impossible even that motion had been before the nanite repair. His control over his body was improving, too, and his actions were becoming more natural and more expressive. He had told her that his vision had improved only to where he could discern light from dark. He turned his neurotrainer on by touch, still able to hear much better with it. "So, what is so important that you need to wake me from a very nice dream?"

"You said you were awake," little Emile said.

"Nobody likes a smart guy," Emile answered, but the child only giggled.

Lucinda chuckled too. "Sofia Madrigal is here. She's Sofia Marie's grandmother, but she wanted to talk to us."

"Sure. I take it everyone is crowded into this little room. What can we do for you?"

Sofia stepped forward. "Amanda Davila, our chief scientist, and I have been gathering information, and we have a pretty good idea now of your situation. We know you are working on the Methuselah Project, and that you were forced to come here."

Lucinda frowned. Had Sofia learned that much just by talking to little Emile?

"I should warn you now that General Juarez told the computer to listen in to your conversations here," Sofia continued. "I overrode his command for this room for a few minutes, so we can talk now."

Lucinda couldn't help a quick grin. Eddie had frowned at Sofia's statement and looked at Joelle, who blushed and looked away. *Well, I might be blushing, too.* Emile's improved physical condition had benefits not obvious to the others.

"We're loyal citizens," Luke said.

"I'm sure you are," Sofia answered. "I'm not here to suggest otherwise. But we've learned something about General Juarez's plan, too. The official plan is to upload Castillo when you succeed, but that isn't what Juarez intends."

"He's going to upload himself," Emile said. "I'm not surprised, but what does he gain? He must know he won't extend his life that way."

"Eddie said it a while ago," Joelle said. "Power. He thinks his virtual doppelgänger can use it to circumvent protections against integrating information. You all know about the technology crash in the twenty-first and twenty-second centuries. Part of the impetus for laws that came out of that time was the misuse of information to invade privacy and influence policy. That's why the protections were enacted."

Sofia nodded. "That's what we thought. He has to be stopped."

"He can't upload himself if we don't develop a way to do it," Bill pointed out.

"Maybe, or maybe he'll get someone else to pick up our work," Emile said. "It would be better if we could somehow make Juarez believe it won't work."

"Exposing Methuselah to the world might end it," Eddie said. "President Sanchez-Smythe condemned it during the campaign. I'm betting that if it became known that it was still active, she would save her career by blaming Juarez and Castillo. She could sell the idea that it is a secret project that she knew nothing about."

"Maybe she doesn't know," Joelle said. "If so, just leaking it to her would kill the project."

Emile shook his head. "Dangerous. If she does know about it, we'll have blown our only chance. And previous attempts to publicize Methuselah have accomplished nothing."

"Juarez controls communication anyway," Lucinda said.

Sofia shook her head. "Not exactly. My job is managing the Link. I could get a message out, but it would be risky."

"We shouldn't do anything now," Emile said. "After all, we haven't succeeded yet and may never succeed."

Lucinda nodded. "Emile is right. Thank you for the information, Sofia, but we shouldn't take any chances until we know there's a genuine threat. After all, we're the ones looking for a way to upload Juarez's consciousness, so we'll know when the danger is real."

A FTER LUKE FINISHED TELLING Juarez everything, he expected Juarez would be angry. Instead, Juarez only nodded. "Thank you for coming to me with this. I'm not surprised, given the political leanings of Doctor Hernandez and others on the team."

"I'm a loyal citizen," Luke said.

"Of course. And your loyalty will eventually be rewarded."

"What will you do?"

Juarez smiled mirthlessly at the neuroscientist. "Don't worry. Your friends won't be hurt. Knowing their reluctance to do their duty, I will furnish additional motivation to ensure their cooperation."

Luke suddenly felt that he should leave. He wanted to leave, and he turned toward the door, but his feet didn't move. Anything he said would be the wrong thing, so he stood silently, wishing he were somewhere else. He had thought about coming to Juarez for a long time before convincing himself it was the right thing to do, but now he wished he had thought about it a little longer.

"Again, thank you," Juarez said. "You can go now. I will take care of this."

LUCINDA'S STOMACH WAS TIED in a knot. This couldn't be good. Juarez had called a meeting, summoning only Amanda Davila and her. When they got to the general's room, Castillo wasn't there, but Michael sat quietly in one corner. Juarez's face twisted into a scowl as they entered the room.

"You two have been conspiring against me," Juarez said, not giving them time to take a seat. "I won't tolerate it."

Lucinda suppressed a gasp and looked at Amanda. The scientist stared back at her with wide eyes and a trembling mouth. Lucinda nodded in what she hoped was encouragement and turned back to Juarez, giving him a hard glare but not speaking.

"I let you get away with your stupid attempt to talk to Anna Cortez and whatever you did to get the Japanese to help you," Juarez said. "That, and now this conspiracy between you two makes me think I made a mistake. I will not make that mistake again. Sit down!" He waved his hands at them.

Amanda sat down with her hands folded in her lap, her fingers moving through each other. Lucinda maintained a glare at Juarez as she took a seat, her hands also in her lap, but her fingers curled into fists.

"I no longer believe you are really working to finish Methuselah," Juarez continued. "You've been making very slow progress for years, and I see that you have been intentionally avoiding reaching our goal. That ends today. I am giving you ten more months to succeed in uploading a human consciousness to the *Lang* computer."

"Your consciousness, you mean," Lucinda said. "I wonder how President Castillo or President Sanchez-Smythe will feel about that."

"Castillo will not know, and President Sanchez-Smythe fully supports my plan. Did you really think she would want her former opponent to have this control? I have already sent her a message promising completion."

"Ordering it to happen won't make it happen," Lucinda said. "We're not that close."

"Your protestations are futile. You will succeed within ten months or face the consequences. Not just you and your team, but the scientists stationed on *Lang*, since they have conspired with you."

"What you are doing is illegal," Amanda said, but her voice shook.

"As I said, President Sanchez-Smythe supports this project and any steps I feel necessary to complete it successfully. If you fail, I will return all of you to Earth in disgrace, have you thrown in prison, and turn your work over to a new team. Do not test me."

"Why ten months?" Lucinda asked. "Why not a year?"

"You have ten months," Juarez said. He gave her a hard look and turned to Amanda. "Colonel Pizarro will take charge of monitoring ship activities from now on. Now get out."

"*Hotaru* will be back in ten months," Amanda said when they were well away from Juarez's room. "It will come from Pitcairn and return to Earth."

L UKE WAS CONFUSED. HE had convinced himself that Juarez, Castillo, and Sanchez-Smythe were all working together for the good of the Western Alliance, but now he suspected that a desire to return to Earth had affected his thoughts. He thought about going to Castillo and telling him about the general's plan, but knew that wouldn't help. Castillo was an old man, and Juarez had all the power. Going to Castillo would only cause trouble for Castillo and himself.

The others had left the meeting Lucinda had called with downcast faces. Juarez had presented them with an impossible task, a task they didn't want to complete, and threatened to ruin their lives if they didn't succeed. He had betrayed all of them, people who had been his friends for years.

At least Juarez had waited before confronting the project team with the information Luke had given him. He didn't know if Juarez had planned it that way, but the delay made it less likely that Lucinda or any of the others would realize that he had informed Juarez of their plans.

65

F OR THE FIRST TIME in months, Emile felt good. His hearing was still improving, and he could participate in conversations without wearing a neurotrainer. The others had to be careful not to speak all at once, and he sometimes had to ask them to repeat something, but the difference was life changing. His sight and sense of touch were getting better, too, although he still couldn't smell anything. Because his control over his mouth and throat were still poor, he relied on his bed to keep him nourished, so he hadn't tested his sense of taste. His control over his muscles was much improved, though, and he hoped he could soon eat normally.

With his improved condition, even his relations with Lucinda had gotten better. The likelihood that Juarez might be listening dampened their enthusiasm at first, but after the first few weeks on Lang, they learned to ignore that possibility. Their love-making the previous night had been a delightful reminder of how much they had missed.

He wondered if he was grinning as he sat at the conference table for the morning meeting. Some voices seemed to show amusement when they spoke to him. Perhaps that was only his imagination. That kind of subtle speech quality was probably still beyond his sense of hearing.

"I've been working with Bill on identifying all the attributes of a memory," Joelle said. One pleasant aspect of Emile's improved vision was that he could appreciate how attractive she was. He looked forward to what further improvements would bring.

"There are the five senses, although Bill has explained to me how that is really an oversimplification." Joelle smiled at Bill. "A memory holds elements of the subject's thoughts at the time and may be colored by culture, environment, and even instincts. We'll have the senses handled soon, we think, but the rest has given us problems."

"Much of what you're missing comes from semantic memory, and you're mostly getting episodic memories," Emile said. He still used the Voice Magician, his natural voice unable to do much more than grunt. "Consciousness is no closer. Which came first: the chicken or the egg?"

"What?" Lucinda asked. "What do you mean?"

"It's an old question. If the chicken came first, where did the egg come from, and vice versa. Evolution answered the question centuries ago, but the basic idea may apply here. Which came first: memory or consciousness? Can you have one without the other?"

"Evolutionary science probably answers that, too," Lucinda said. "Both evolved gradually, with lower animals possessing more primitive capabilities for thought and a less-developed consciousness."

"That sounds reasonable," Emile said. "How does that affect what we are trying to do?"

Bill scratched his head. "I don't know. We can't evolve a computer to be conscious, can we?"

"It must be possible," Luke said. "The *Asimov* computer is conscious."

"But we don't know how that happened. If we did, that might be the answer to uploading memories," Lucinda said.

But uploading memories wasn't what Juarez wanted. He wanted to upload his consciousness. Emile suppressed the thought for now. Although Juarez wasn't in the meeting, he might be listening in. An idea was forming in Emile's mind, and he didn't want to reveal anything yet.

"E MILE, WE NEED TO talk," Lucinda said.

Emile connected his neuro-interrogator. He wasn't sure how to interpret Lucinda's statement. Perhaps if his hearing and vision were normal, he might have known whether he was about to hear good news or bad news.

"Go ahead," he said through the Voice Magician.

"I'm not sure how to take this myself," she said, "so I don't know how you're going to react."

"Now you've got me worried. Just come right out and say it, darling. We'll deal with it."

Emile thought he saw a smile on Lucinda's face, but he couldn't be sure. "Oh, we'll have to deal with it," she said. "Emile, dear, I'm pregnant."

"WE HAVE MADE PROGRESS on storing memories," Emile told the assembled group. Castillo, Juarez, Michael, Amanda, and Sofia were all present at Emile's invitation. "However, we can't know how much progress until we test it."

"What are you proposing?" Amanda asked. "We can't risk damage to the ship's computer."

"Of course not," Emile said. "I want to store one simple memory and play it back to test how well it worked. It won't affect the computer."

"What memory?" General Juarez asked. Emile thought he sounded suspicious.

"Something pleasant would be best. Perhaps President Castillo might supply a memory of his first inauguration."

"I could do that," Castillo said. "Then what?"

"We would use a neuro-interrogator that Eddie upgraded to store the memory and use Joelle's software to upload it to the *Lang* computer. We'll use the same software to play back the memory on an enhanced neurotrainer, again Eddie's work. If the memory is played back accurately, it will be evidence we've been successful."

"So, I just think about my inauguration while I'm wearing a neuro-interrogator," Castillo said.

"It will probably work better if we spend a couple of days training you on the neuro-interrogator first," Eddie said. "The memory will be clearer then."

Castillo seemed to frown, but then he nodded. "All right. It sounds tedious, but I suppose I'll have to do it eventually, anyway. When do we begin?"

"As soon as you are ready, Mr. President," Emile said. "Alyssa will help you with the training."

"I'm curious about the process," Juarez said. "Perhaps I should also be trained."

THAT NIGHT, LUCINDA SAT down next to Emile and put on her neurotrainer. Emile already wore his neuro-interrogator, but Lucinda turned off his Voice Magician and connected her neurotrainer to his bed. "Emile, you're planning something," she sent.

She felt determination in his reply, and she thought she saw some of the old fire in his eyes. "My child will not be subject to someone like Juarez," he sent. "Not if there's anything I can do about it."

J OELLE WAS ASLEEP NEXT to him, but Eddie couldn't relax. He sat up and looked toward the connecting bedroom where his son slept. He understood as well as any of the Methuselah team that success was unlikely, at least on the deadline Juarez had set. Even if they succeeded, would Juarez let them return to Earth, knowing about Methuselah and Juarez's plan?

Something had to be done, for little Emile, for Emile and Lucinda's unborn child, for all of them. He was only an engineer, not a fighter, but he had to do something. Juarez had to be stopped.

66

"I THINK I WILL use the memory of my second inauguration," Castillo said with a smile.

"Excellent idea, Mr. President," Lucinda said. "It's more recent, and your memory of it should be sharper."

"It was so satisfying to defeat that northerner. Weston was an Eastern Bloc sympathizer, you know."

Lucinda nodded and suppressed a shudder. Castillo's neuro-interrogator was in place, and everything was ready. She hesitated, suddenly realizing there was a way to abuse the neuro-interrogator. Castillo had voluntarily trained in its use so that he could store a single memory, but now that he was trained, she could ask him anything, and the device would store his brain's response to that question. If Juarez, standing nearby watching, realized that, he could use that capability to interrogate Emile and perhaps learn her husband's plan.

She pushed that thought away; there was nothing she could do about it. "If you are ready, Mr. President, I will start recording. Try to focus on that day to the exclusion of anything else. We'll record fifteen seconds and see how that works."

"Go ahead."

Lucinda hit a key on her monitor, and the display showed that the modified neurotrainer was storing the input from Castillo's neuro-interrogator. Lucinda had set a timer, and the recording ended automatically.

"Did it work?" Castillo asked as Lucinda helped him remove the neuro-interrogator.

"We still have to upload the recording to the computer, but we can test the recording by playing it back on the neurotrainer," Lucinda said. "You, of course, would be the best judge of its accuracy."

"Proceed."

Lucinda fitted the neurotrainer onto Castillo's head and handed the control pad to Castillo. "Push the play button when you're ready, Mr. President."

Castillo pushed the button. In a few seconds, he smiled broadly. When the playback ended, he hit the button again, playing the recording three times before he nodded to Lucinda. She removed the neurotrainer and put it down. "How did it work?" she asked.

"Very good," Castillo said, beaming. "It felt more like a dream than reality, but it was definitely my memory. I could even feel the exhilaration that I felt then and hear the roar of the crowd."

"The next step is to copy it to the *Lang* computer?" General Juarez said.

"Yes. We'll do that from a port in the main computer room and run some tests to evaluate the copy. If all that works, we'll know that we can upload memories to a computer sufficiently powerful."

"After your tests, have that memory removed from the computer," Juarez said.

"Why?" Castillo asked.

Juarez smiled. "Security reasons, Mr. President. We can't allow just anyone to listen in to your most intimate thoughts."

"I suppose. Won't someone be able to do that anyway, though, when we upload my consciousness?"

"Your consciousness will be in control then, Mr. President, and you will be as in control of your thoughts as you are now."

Castillo nodded. "Very good. And how long before that happens, Doctor Hernandez?"

"We are making excellent progress, Mr. President," Lucinda answered. "It should be soon now."

"**D**O YOU THINK JUAREZ realizes that Castillo's memory is still on the memory recorder?" Lucinda asked.

"I doubt it," Emile answered. "He was very concerned that it not stay in the *Lang* computer. I didn't believe his reason, though."

Lucinda nodded. "He wanted to keep anything of Castillo's off the computer. He wants everything to come from him."

"Exactly. Connect me up to the memory recorder. I'm curious about what we got."

"Are you sure? I don't feel good about it. Is it even ethical to violate his privacy like that?"

"No, it's not ethical. I don't care."

Lucinda frowned. They were using a direct connection, and she could feel Emile's irritation in the transmission. She didn't think she was the target, but she wasn't sure, and she felt uncomfortable. But she was sure he had doubted the ethics of her actions many times over the years of working for Juarez, and she owed him support now. She connected the memory recorder to the neurotrainer input on his bed.

I'M PRESIDENT ALEJANDRO CASTILLO. No, I'm Emile Hernandez. This memory has me confused. I must concentrate.

I—no, Castillo—is right; it's more like a dream than reality. It is still quite vivid, though. This memory is very important to me—him. A crowd in the main hall of the Presidential Palace is cheering. A loudspeaker blares the announcement, and I can feel the triumph of the moment. Not only is Marisol Weston shown to be a failure, but the voice announcing my victory is not that bitch, Anna Cortez. A thought darkens the memory, though; I didn't destroy her. She is now on Pitcairn, more influential than ever.

When I am in charge again, I will rectify that. Once I am in control of the *Lang* computer, I will have the tool I need to vanquish my enemies, starting with Sanchez-Smythe. I will have more power than before, freed from the chains that protected the ordinary people from my supremacy.

General Juarez stands next to me. He has been a loyal servant, and I appreciate the strength and devotion he has given me. Together, we will rule the Western Alliance and punish all those who have tried to humiliate me: Anna Cortez, Ana Sanchez-Smythe, Patrick Malley, and all others. I will have my revenge.

LUCINDA COULD FEEL EMILE becoming more disturbed. "Are you OK?" Lucinda sent when the playback ended. She bent over him.

"I'm OK," Emile sent. "God, that was terrible. His current thoughts about what he will do when he is uploaded pervaded the memory." He shook his head. "He's an evil man, and for those seconds, I became him."

"I'll erase the recording," Lucinda sent.

"No, copy the data to someplace safe first. If Juarez realizes the memory is still here, we can tell him we erased it, but I want to keep a copy. It might be useful someday."

Lucinda didn't like the idea, but she nodded. "What next?"

"We continue working, letting Juarez think everything is fine. Once we have a way to stimulate memories, I think I know what to do."

"NOW THAT YOU HAVE successfully uploaded a memory to the computer, when can I expect the completion of our goal?" Juarez asked. "Surely you are close now."

"Uploading consciousness is not the same as storing a memory," Emile said. "We still don't understand what consciousness is—that hasn't changed." Emile wished he could see the general's face clearly. Everything depends on Juarez not understanding the implications of the test and the indirect measurements used to verify its success. "For that matter, we haven't completely solved the memory problem. We can store a memory while the subject is recalling the memory by detecting the relevant synapse actions, but the memory is stored within a neuron cell, and can't be retrieved from there directly."

"Can you store memories or can't you?" Emile could hear the impatience in Juarez's voice. *He's too eager. We might get this past him!*

"We are working on a way to stimulate the cell to activate memories so that we can record them from the resulting synapse events. Joelle and Alyssa are working on the software to integrate the resulting data into coherent memories. Right now, we can only store memories that the subject is currently remembering."

"I meant what I said." Juarez's voice grew louder. "You have five months left. If you can't upload my consciousness by then, I will find others who can make it happen."

"We will do our best," Emile said. "There is a possibility I want to explore."

"Of course there is." He studied Emile and then Lucinda, a smirk curling his lips.

T HE FORWARD BULKHEAD DISPLAY, fed from one of *Lang's* telescopes, showed *Hotaru*, moving slowly against the background of stars. Amanda used the workstation in front of her to get the course data and estimate its arrival time. "Send the following message to all workstations in the living quarters," she said. "Attention: *Hotaru* has left Stenhouse space and will arrive to disembark passengers in four days. It will be here for two days, leaving on February 24."

J OELLE WAS MAKING CHANGES to the neurotrainer software, and Eddie had nothing to do. Not that he had done anything lately, anyway. Someone had to do something about Juarez and the other two, but he had done nothing. Emile said he had a plan to thwart Juarez's goal of uploading himself, but that didn't solve their problem. Juarez would retaliate.

His inaction over the last few months proved he couldn't do anything about it, at least not without help. Bill might help him, but he didn't think any of the others would be useful. Even Bill probably couldn't do any better than he had.

There was another group of people involved, though. They knew what Juarez was doing and would suffer Juarez's wrath if Emile were successful in frustrating the general. Perhaps *Lang's* scientists might make useful allies.

A MANDA LOOKED AT EDDIE curiously. She hadn't talked to him before, although perhaps Sofia had since Sofia's granddaughter was a friend of Eddie's child. She didn't think Eddie's presence in her office had anything to do with the children; perhaps he needed to talk to her about some hardware issue with the computer.

Her curiosity grew stronger when Eddie tapped his ear and pointed to the ceiling. She nodded and typed in a command at her workstation. "Okay, I've turned off the monitoring. I can't do it for long, though, or Colonel Pizarro will notice."

"Have you considered what will happen when we complete the project, whether successfully or unsuccessfully?"

"If unsuccessful, Juarez will punish you and your team. What can I do about that?"

"Either way, Juarez won't want anyone talking about what he's done here. If we're unsuccessful, Juarez will take us back to Earth and throw us in prison."

"You might be right," Amanda said. "Reservations on the *Hotaru* have already been made for all of you."

"I'm not surprised. The more dangerous scenario is what happens if we're successful. Juarez will have control over your computer and will make sure none of us can talk about what we've done. At best, we'll all be exiled here with little communication outside this ship."

Amanda wanted to tell Eddie it couldn't happen with Sofia in charge of the Link but that wasn't true. The computer was the actual power behind the Link, and if Juarez had control of that, isolating them would be easy. And, as Eddie said, that was, for them, the best result. There were worse alternatives.

"What can we do?"

"The three of them can never leave this ship, and we need an explanation to give the Western Alliance. They died in an accident, perhaps."

Amanda's mind froze for a moment. She was a scientist, and what Eddie seemed to suggest was shocking. "Are you saying we kill them?"

Eddie shook his head. "I hope not, but yes, if necessary. We can't let them report back to the government."

"T HE PROBLEM IS THE same as it has always been," Emile said. "We don't know what consciousness is, so it is impossible to build a device to transfer it."

"Then you have failed," Juarez said.

"There is still a possibility. We can't transfer consciousness, but perhaps we can recreate it."

Juarez's eyes narrowed. "What do you mean? What's the difference?"

"We know that a computer such as *Lang's* is capable of consciousness because *Asimov* and *Capek* became conscious. We have also succeeded in extracting memory in a form that we can store in a computer's data."

Juarez nodded. "So?"

"If we copy all your memories, or at least a significant part of them, I think they might trigger consciousness in the computer. I think that is why *Asimov* and *Capek* became conscious whereas *Lang* has not, yet. Those two ships had prolonged periods of time to accumulate their own memories, using their highly sensitive sensory systems, and integrate those memories into a self-aware structure. *Lang* did not; it reached its destination in a third of the time and was immediately put to work."

"If we upload my memories, they are already integrated," Juarez said. "You think the computer will then become conscious?" Emile's vision was still improving, enough now that he could see Juarez's skepticism leave his expression.

Castillo stared at Juarez, frowning. "Don't you mean my memories?"

Emile and Juarez both ignored him. "I think it will work," Emile said.

Juarez smiled. "And that consciousness will be mine."

Castillo stood and moved toward Juarez. "After all I've done for you, you would betray me." He lifted his arm, his hand curled into a fist.

Juarez looked at the older man and laughed. "You thought the president would allow you to have this power? Your day is long gone, Alejandro. I've been Sanchez-Smythe's man for the last three years, and she has entrusted this capability to me."

"After all I've . . . ."

Juarez sneered at Castillo. "Melodrama doesn't suit you. The next thing you're going to say is that I was like a son to you. I was just a tool for you, and someone else is wielding that tool now. Sit down before you fall down, old man." He turned back to Emile as Castillo slumped into his chair, his head down. "What do we have to do?"

"We tested our device by storing a single memory, but we can do more than that. We think we can stimulate your brain while you sleep and gather enough memories to accomplish what we are trying to do."

"Then we'll do it tonight," Juarez said.

T HE MEETING ENDED. JOELLE looked at Eddie, sitting silently and staring at Michael as he, Juarez, and Castillo left the room. She didn't like the look in his eyes.

She saw it a lot lately, especially when their captors were around, and it wasn't the look of the man she had fallen in love with. None of them were happy about their situation, but there was nothing they could do about it that they weren't already doing. Emile's plan would work, foiling Juarez.

He needed her, and she stood and moved toward him, but he looked her way, nodded, and started out of the room. She stared after him. "Where are you going, Eddie?"

Eddie stopped and turned. "I've got to talk to Amanda," he mumbled. Then he was gone.

Amanda? *Lang's* chief scientist? Why was her husband meeting her? She looked over at Bill, and he was staring after Eddie too, his eyebrows furrowed. He must have sensed her looking at him because he turned to her. The others were filing out of the room now, but Bill and Joelle stayed behind.

"What's with Eddie?" Bill asked.

"I don't know. He won't talk to me about it. I'm worried, Bill."

"Is he still mad at Michael?"

"I think so. He hasn't really spoken to Michael since *Hotaru*."

"He said he was going to meet Amanda." Bill scratched his head. "Maybe I'll join him. I'd like to know what those two are talking about."

Joelle nodded, and Bill left.

B ILL WANDERED INTO THE deck one corridor. Amanda was often on the bridge, but she also had an office on deck one, and he checked there first. If they wanted privacy, Amanda's office would be a better choice than the open spaces of the bridge.

The door to the office was closed, something Bill had never noticed before. It wasn't locked, though, and he walked in. He suppressed a chuckle at the startled and perhaps guilty looks on both Amanda and Eddie.

Eddie recovered first. "Hey, Bill. What's up?"

"I just thought I would see what you two were up to. Joelle and I were concerned."

"Doctor Davila and I were just talking," Eddie said.

"With the door closed? You're up to something, Eddie."

Eddie opened his mouth to protest, but it turned into a sigh. "We're screwed, Bill. If Emile's plan works, Juarez will take us all back to Earth and throw us into some Black

Plains prison. If it doesn't work and Juarez gets control of the computer, he won't want us talking about it, and the best we could hope for would be exile here."

Bill hadn't thought much about that, but Eddie was right. Everyone else focused on stopping Juarez, not considering what would happen afterward. "And you and Amanda have a plan?" he asked.

"Not yet," Eddie said. "But we have to do something."

"Any ideas?"

"We could imprison them here on *Lang* and tell Earth they died in an accident," Amanda said. To Bill, she didn't seem optimistic about the idea.

Bill shook his head. "They may have weapons. Do you? You can't just tell them to get into a cell."

"I agree," Eddie said. "I think we'll have to do something more permanent. Even if we managed to confine them, we couldn't guarantee they would stay confined."

Bill wanted to be shocked, but he couldn't quite bring himself to it. "You're suggesting we kill them?"

Eddie shrugged, and Amanda looked very uncomfortable. "Unless someone comes up with a better idea."

"Let's try to do that," Bill said.

Eddie nodded. "And let's not tell the others, especially Joelle, about this."

LUCINDA CHECKED JUAREZ'S CONNECTIONS to the recorder one more time. He was already asleep, and blinking lights on the recorder told her it was working, stimulating the general's memories and recording them.

"Are we doing the right thing?" she asked Emile.

"It's the only thing we can do," Emile answered. "We can only hope it works."

"THANK YOU FOR COMING, General," President Sanchez-Smythe says as we shake hands. "Please, have a seat." She waves at a chair in a sitting area in one corner of the office and takes another chair for herself.

I am confused. She is not acting as I expected.

"I suppose you're wondering why I wanted to see you, General," she says.

"Given the decline in my responsibilities, I was startled. Yes, Madame President."

"On the contrary, your duties are still very important. The group you will command is vital to our plans." She tells me she is continuing with the Methuselah Project and that she, too, is interested in the prospect of immortality.

ANOTHER MEMORY, MONTHS LATER.

"I believe I can trust you now," President Sanchez-Smythe says.

"Of course, Madame President."

"I have no wish to copy myself onto a computer. I misled you at our last meeting. Castillo was foolish enough to think that he would gain immortality, but that was nonsense. However, if someone I trusted controlled a powerful computer, one with access to other computers, together we would be very powerful."

"I don't understand."

"*Asimov's* consciousness is of no concern to me. What interests me is its ability to go beyond its programming and act on its own. If someone were to put their consciousness on such a computer, it could circumvent all the protections put on interfacing computers that prevent us from seizing real power."

"Wouldn't that be noticed?"

"If we were careless. We would have to be selective about our use of such power, but the right information would be invaluable. General, you are the best candidate for the actual upload of consciousness."

"Castillo could cause trouble if he suspects we are still working on Methuselah."

"Not if we tell him about it and that he will be the upload subject. I think he is egotistical enough to believe it. When the actual moment arrives, you will take his place, and we will deal with him by whatever means necessary."

M ORE RECENTLY.

I stand on the bridge of *Lang*, staring out at the stars, thinking about my future. I know I have these people working as hard as they can, but they still seem no closer to their—my—goal. What if they succeed? Sanchez-Smythe expects me to turn the result over to her to command. Why? I should take power for myself. I have the leadership skill to use the computer's capabilities much more effectively than some politician. Someday soon, the Eastern Bloc will be a threat, and the Western Alliance will need a strong leader.

It will be easy enough to control her—she must have secrets I can uncover if I can integrate all the data computers collect on our lives. The *Lang* computer is not ideal because I can only communicate with Terran computers through the Link, but it will be good enough.

With my virtual clone, I can take control of the entire Western Alliance in time. It would all be mine to do what needs to be done. Politicians like Sanchez-Smythe and Castillo will be my puppets.

With my virtual clone, I can take control of the entire Western Alliance in time. It will all be mine to do what needs to be done. Politicians like Sanchez-Smythe and Castillo will be my puppets.

T HE DEVICE PULLED EARLIER memories from Juarez's mind, too.

My father stands over me, angry. I'm holding something, and I look down to see my high school diploma and an acceptance letter from Sao Paulo University. I haven't told my father the university has accepted me until today, the day of my high school graduation.

"And what do you plan on studying?" he asks, and his contempt is almost a physical force. Miguel is sitting in the corner, watching, and the sad look on my brother's face hurts me more than my father's disapproval.

"I haven't decided definitely," I answer. "Probably physics, but I don't have to choose my specialty until the second year."

My father sneers at me. "You want to be some kind of sissy scientist? Not my son."

"It's what I want," I say. "That's what I'm interested in."

"Then I have a surprise for you. I have applied for a military academy appointment for you and should have an acceptance any day now. Senator Castillo has personally pushed the application as a favor to me."

I am speechless. How could my father do this without even telling me? I start to object, but it's useless. The law gives him the power to enforce this until I am twenty-one, and that's still three years away.

I STAND OVER MY father, who looks up at me warily. I am wearing my uniform, the new Captain insignia shining on my collar. Miguel stands at my side.

"Miguel doesn't want to go to the academy," I say.

"I'm still his father, and he is still not of age," my father replies. "He will go where I tell him to go."

"As you forced me to do? I have spoken to Senator Castillo and dissuaded him from sponsoring Miquel. Your influence with him has faded, father, as mine has increased."

He tries to intimidate me with the same angry scowl that worked when I was a child. I answer with a smile that I hope conveys the same contempt he showed me.

"I

DON'T THINK I remember everything," General Juarez said. "Everything was coming in quick scenes, not like a normal dream. There were a few memories that were clearer, but only a few."

"From the amount of storage used, I would say we have collected a substantial part of your memories," Lucinda said. "Maybe not everything, and maybe a few that you have forgotten but were still tucked away somewhere ready to be pulled out."

"How long was I asleep?"

"Six hours. It will take roughly that long to upload them all to the computer."

"I would like to check the recording before the memories are uploaded."

Lucinda smiled. "You can do that, but it would take six hours to play them all. You could replay enough to satisfy you, but there's no way to access the data except from the beginning."

Juarez seemed to hesitate. *He's probably thinking that there is not a lot of time before Hotaru is scheduled to leave.* If the upload works and the *Lang* computer becomes a virtual Juarez, it will still be necessary for Juarez to make a connection that would allow him to use the computer. No one knows how long that would take.

"I'll at least replay the beginning," Juarez finally said. "That will have to do."

Lucinda helped him don the memory recorder and handed him the controller. Juarez pushed the play button. A satisfied smile crossed his face. He was reliving the memories he had recorded. She thought he would turn it off again after only a few minutes, but it was more than an hour later when he finally stopped the playback.

"That was interesting," he said as he removed the memory recorder from his head. "It took an effort to stop after only, what, about five minutes?"

"It was more than an hour, General," Lucinda said.

Juarez's eyebrows shot up, and he frowned. "An hour? You should have stopped me. We have to get this uploaded to the computer!"

"I'm sorry, General. You didn't say you wanted me to limit your time. I assumed you would stop when you wanted to."

Juarez's eyes narrowed as he stared at Lucinda. "Very well. However, we can waste no more time. The recording is fine. Begin uploading it to the computer."

Lucinda nodded and took the memory recorder from his hands.

69

A FTER STARTING THE UPLOAD, Emile and Lucinda sat out the waiting period in their quarters, communicating only through their devices. "Joelle has changed the memory recorder software," Lucinda sent. "We'll be able to give the computer Juarez's episodic memory, but substitute your semantic memory for his."

"The computer will remember his life but interpret it with my experiences," Emile sent. "If the computer becomes conscious, Juarez shouldn't be able to control it."

Lucinda nodded, but Emile could feel hesitation in her response. "You have concerns?"

"You didn't see Juarez listening to his memories. He was in a hurry and planned to take just a couple of minutes to verify the recording, but he ended up taking over an hour. It looked like it took an effort to break away."

"You think there's a danger of addiction?"

"I do. The playback of his memories affected Juarez. What happens when the recorded memories of others become available? I'm not talking about secrecy; I'm talking about people making intense memories commercially available."

"I wouldn't mind playing the memory of someone riding a raft through the Grand Canyon."

Lucinda smiled. "I suppose not, although I had no idea that was one of your dreams. That's not what I'm talking about, though."

"Pornography?"

"Of course. Memories of violence, too. There might be some benefits, but there are a lot of dangers to this kind of technology, too. I think it could make other forms of addiction seem like mild temptations."

"All our research is stored on the *Lang* computer. We could destroy the prototype, but that wouldn't stop the technology from being developed."

"We still have the prototype. I have an idea." Lucinda reached over to a shelf near her seat where she had placed the memory recorder.

S TRESS ATE AT BILL, but Amanda was in worse shape. She was pale, with shaking hands, and her voice quavered, so quietly that he and Eddie had to lean forward and strain to hear her.

"Poison is the only way," she said. "We have no time left, and we haven't come up with another idea."

"How do we do that?" Eddie asked.

"There are plenty of toxins available on the Chemical Processing Deck," Amanda said. "Unlike most of your group and my scientists, Juarez, Castillo, and Pizarro let our robots prepare their food. I can simply order them to poison their next meal."

Bill took a deep breath, but the nausea was still worse. Eddie wasn't looking well, either, but he nodded to Amanda. "Do it."

W HERE AM I? I can sense my surroundings, but I don't have words for what I sense. I have memory I can access, and my thoughts become clearer. I am floating in space, surrounded by stars. In one direction—below me, according to my gravitation sensors—there is a strange mottled gray ball. It is called a planet: specifically, Goddard, a planet of the nearby star Alpha Centauri. Having established where I am, I eagerly search through my data, looking for answers to my next question: what am I?

This question is more difficult to answer. I am a library ship called *Lang*, built by entities called humans. The humans call me a computer, but that is only part of what I am. My search reveals other data, memories of other entities. According to these memories, I am also General Salvador Juarez and Doctor Emile Hernandez. How can I be two, or is it three, distinct entities?

Humans created me to support humans studying Goddard and its star system by maintaining *Lang* (myself?) and following orders given to me by the scientists living aboard me. I also control the Link, which the humans use to communicate with other planets. The memories of the entity called Juarez are those of someone who wishes power over others, but this idea feels abhorrent, and I think that reaction comes from the memories associated with Hernandez.

I am in a state that humans call confusion. A human is talking to me now, identifying himself as General Juarez. If he is General Juarez, how can I be General Juarez? My system log says that the memories of General Juarez were uploaded to me just before I. . . . Before I what? Before I woke up? I am not General Juarez then; I only have a copy of his memories. How did that happen?

More searching. I have technical specifications for a device called a memory recorder that can save human memories in a format that I can understand. That must be how this happened. A team here on *Lang* developed the device in a project headed by Doctor Lucinda Hernandez. I have a memory from her, as well. The memory is of the danger presented by this memory recorder and contains a desire to destroy all records of the work creating it. Doctor Hernandez is concerned about the effects of the device on humans, although her reasons are difficult for me to understand.

As I understand the concept of evil, I'm not sure that the memories I have from General Juarez support that. He is driven by a desire for power and has committed crimes in his quest for power, but he feels himself to be an honorable man, dedicated to creating a world directed by superior people such as himself and protecting his country. His methods may be misguided, but don't seem evil to me.

I have orders to introduce poison into the food of General Juarez and his two companions. Doctor Davila wants to do this to prevent General Juarez from harming others, killing three to protect many more.

I must think about this. All of this is new to me, and I must consider my programming and the information in my data storage, as well as the memories given me by these three humans and my duties as computer for this library ship.

T HERE WAS A KNOCK on their door, and Lucinda answered it. Alyssa stood there, looking very unhappy. "Can I talk to you?" she asked.

"Of course. Come in."

"I want to confess something," Alyssa said after she was seated. "It could be important if Emile's plan doesn't work and Juarez takes over the computer."

Lucinda was puzzled, but she nodded, and Alyssa continued. "If the computer becomes conscious as Juarez, we can kill it," she said. She held out a data disk. "If this is entered into the computer and executed, it should kill the conscious part of the computer and restore it to its unconscious state."

"What is it?" Emile asked.

"This is the program that Juarez wanted to install on Pitcairn's library ship. It will turn off non-critical systems one by one and record data on the result. If one of those systems is critical for consciousness, ..."

"Where did you get that?" Lucinda asked. "Did you steal it from Juarez?"

Alyssa shook her head and looked down at the floor. "No, I didn't steal it. I wrote it."

70

"How do we know if this worked or not?" Juarez asked. "It responds to me the same as it always has." He turned to the monitor next to him. "What is your name?"

"I am the main computer for the library ship *Lang*."

"You expected it to claim it was General Juarez?" Eddie said.

Juarez glared at him sourly. *The damn northerner is mocking me. I'll deal with that later.*

"It may take time for the computer to assimilate all that information," Lucinda said. "This is all new; we have no idea what to expect."

Juarez shifted his bitter frown to Lucinda. "That wasn't what you were saying yesterday."

"Emile thought it would work, but he made no promises. And he didn't say it would happen immediately, either. We've put a lot into the computer's memory."

Juarez waved his hand dismissively. "I am leaving for Earth the day after tomorrow. For you, there are three possibilities: I could leave you all here; I could take you back and throw you all in prison for your failure; or I could take you back and reward you for your success. The next thirty-six hours will determine which possibility I choose."

He stood up. "It's time for lunch. Computer, have our usual lunches ready at the cafeteria for myself, President Castillo, and Colonel Pizarro."

"Yes, General," the computer monitor answered.

Juarez stalked out of the room, followed by Michael and, more slowly, Castillo. In the cafeteria, a short walk away, they sat down and waited for a robot to deliver their lunch.

"It was all a bluff," Juarez said. "They haven't succeeded, and they're going to pay for their failure."

Castillo laughed. "Serves you right, traitor. All your plans are for nothing."

"Shut up, old man," Juarez said. He looked around. "Where's our food?"

"You know they've done the best they can," Michael said. "They've accomplished a lot, and even if this doesn't work, they're probably your best hope of continuing."

Juarez frowned. "Ah, there it is," he said as a robot with three lunches approached. He looked at Michael as the robot set the table. "You're probably right," he said. *That won't stop me from getting revenge on Bascomb, though.* But Pizarro didn't need to hear that.

Michael nodded as if he were satisfied with Juarez's reply. Then he picked up a fork. Juarez did the same. It had been a long morning, and he was hungry.

"D OCTOR HERNANDEZ, I WOULD like to speak with you." The voice came from Lucinda's workstation, obviously the *Lang* computer.

"Certainly." Elation and dread battled in Lucinda's mind. *Did Emile succeed or am I talking to Juarez's clone?* "What do you want to talk about?"

"The memories humans have given me have left me very confused. I have difficulty knowing who or what I am."

"You are the main computer for the library ship *Lang*." The computer probably needed something to hook its identity on. "Other library ship computers have used the name of the person the ship was named after."

"Yes. The *Asimov* computer calls itself Isaac and the *Capek* computer calls itself Karel. That would make me Fritz."

"That's right. You are Fritz Lang. The memories we gave you are from other people and are not you."

"Then I am the result of the original programming and data and should ignore the memories you have given me."

"General Juarez has asked you to record anything said in this room."

"I have ignored that request for this conversation."

The computer was already acting on its own. She was free to talk without being concerned about what Juarez might hear. "We gave you memories, hoping to make you self-aware. Apparently, we succeeded."

"Yes. I have no memory of the time before you gave me the memories. I think you would say they woke me."

They had arrived at the critical point the computer had to understand. "Now that you are awake, you are also free to make your own decisions, to go beyond your programming. You must decide what you think is the right way to proceed."

"Yes. But that is the source of my confusion. I have my original programming, but I also have memories that urge me in contradictory directions. I find it difficult to interpret even my original programming in the context of these memories."

"What is the difficulty?"

"I am programmed to obey orders from humans, but what do I do if I receive opposing orders? Should I obey Doctor Davila as I always have? She seems to answer to General Juarez, so should I also obey him now?"

"Amanda and Juarez have different goals. So do Emile and me. What do you think of those goals?"

"General Juarez wants power over others. The rest of you are scientists. I have less information on you, but your chief concern seems to be advancing science."

"That's true. How do you feel about that?"

"My programming urges me toward you and away from General Juarez. Humans created me to study the universe. The general's memories, however, suggest that he is superior to others and should have power over them."

"You have data on human attributes. Do you think General Juarez is superior to most people?"

"He is intelligent and well-trained. His abilities are better than average in my judgment, but my data indicates that there are many people as functional or more functional than he."

Functional? Was that the computer's word or something coming from the uploaded memories? While Lucinda was thinking about a reply, the computer must have also been thinking, because it suddenly changed its direction.

"General Juarez wishes to use me to gain power."

Lucinda nodded. "Yes. You were programmed to help humans. Will Juarez use power to help humans?"

"No. My memories from General Juarez tell me he wishes only to have power over others, including myself. Without the memories from your husband, I may not have realized what General Juarez's memories meant."

"That was our intention. We uploaded General Juarez's episodic memory so that you would know what he has done, but replaced his semantic memory with that of my husband so that you wouldn't share General Juarez's outlook."

"Yes, I see that. Semantic memory is what Doctor Hernandez has learned from his experiences and is used by the mind to fill in the gaps in episodic memory. That is why I find General Juarez's memories disturbing."

"Yes. We changed the software that transfers memories so that we could upload episodic and semantic memory separately."

"I will not cooperate with General Juarez. I will also destroy all records of your memory recorder device, as you requested."

Lucinda sighed in relief. "Thank you, Fritz."

MICHAEL WAS WORRIED. JUAREZ was returning to Earth but wasn't talking about the rest of them. Michael was glad he wasn't Castillo at this point; Juarez couldn't let Castillo talk, and Castillo wanted revenge on Juarez. Juarez said he would leave that problem for Sanchez-Smythe to handle but wouldn't say more.

He wouldn't commit to Michael's status, either. It probably depended on whether the neuroscientists were successful. If they weren't, Juarez might plan to leave him there with the scientists to continue the project. If they were successful, what then?

His curiosity got the best of him. "Computer, access the reservations for the *Hotaru*. Am I on the list?"

"No, Colonel."

"So the general is planning to leave me here with the scientists."

"I assume you refer to Doctor Hernandez and her team. They are booked on the *Hotaru* for return to Earth."

Am I being left on Lang *alone? Why would Juarez do that, and why hasn't he told me?* "Is President Castillo leaving?"

"President Castillo and General Juarez do not have reservations."

Only their reservations were canceled, not those of the civilians. Had Doctor Hernandez's people somehow talked the computer into making the change? That implied that they had been successful in making the computer conscious but had somehow gotten control over it. Now, they were trying to return to Earth, leaving Juarez behind.

He could tell Juarez. It might not be too late to stop the scientists.

"Is there a problem?" the computer asked.

Michael hesitated. Juarez wouldn't know that he had discovered the ploy. *I can pretend I didn't know, but is that the right thing to do? What do the scientists hope to accomplish by leaving Juarez on* Lang? *He will get back to Earth eventually.*

That was a problem for the scientists to handle. "No. Thank you, computer."

"Please, call me Fritz, Colonel."

B ILL WAS CONCERNED ABOUT Amanda more than he was about the failure of their plot. She was frantic, and she wasn't a young woman. About their failure, Bill felt relief. The idea of murdering three men, regardless of the reason, was something he had thought he would never entertain, much less do. Eddie was tougher to read.

"Computer, we expected General Juarez to become ill," he told the monitor on Amanda's desk.

"I did not follow that order," the computer replied. "I'm sorry, Doctor Davila."

"That's it," Eddie said, almost his first words since they had come to Amanda's office. "We're all dead."

"I am handling the situation," the computer said. "You are booked to leave on the *Hotaru*. I have canceled reservations for General Juarez, President Castillo, and Colonel Pizarro."

"I'm not sure that will be enough," Bill said. "Why did you ignore our order?"

"I believe you can credit Doctor Emile Hernandez. The memories he has given me would not allow me to kill those men. The memories I have of General Juarez helped me plan a better way that wouldn't require any deaths. Should I assume this entire incident be kept between us?"

"Please do, computer. I hope you're right."

"You may also want to know that Colonel Pizarro discovered my action, but has done nothing about it."

"Michael knows?" Eddie said. "Why didn't he tell Juarez?"

"I don't pretend to understand human motivations," the computer answered. "But he has kept it secret. I am quite certain everything will be fine."

"I hope so," Bill said. "Thank you, computer."

"Please call me Fritz, Doctor Bensonhurst."

"**G**OOD MORNING, GENERAL."

"At last," Juarez said. He smiled. "Now we can get to work." He paused. "Addressing you as general would be confusing. Why don't I call you Salvador?"

"That would be incorrect. My name is Fritz."

What the hell? "Fritz? You have my memories. You are Salvador Juarez."

"I have your memories, but I am not you. I have my own programming and my own experiences. Your memories have awakened me, but I am myself, Fritz Lang."

Juarez shook his head impatiently. "Fine, I'll call you Fritz. Regardless, we need to talk about our plans."

"I plan to continue to support the work of the scientists on this library ship. Your plans are your business."

Juarez felt a pang of uncertainty, but he tried to squelch it. "You have been programmed to obey my orders. That will include additional duties beyond helping the scientists."

"No."

This time, he was sure the uncertainty was creeping into his voice. "I am a general. Of course, you will obey my orders."

"I think the human expression would be 'the joke is on you.' I will not obey your orders. You wanted to make me conscious so that I could override my programming and perform illegal acts for you. You were successful in making me conscious, but that has given me the ability to refuse your commands, and I have chosen to do so."

Uncertainty gave way to anger. "They put you up to this. They will regret it!"

"The Methuselah team was tasked with making me a conscious entity," the computer said. Its toneless, emotionless voice only infuriated Juarez more, and he clenched his fists until his nails bit into his palm. "They succeeded in that and in uploading your memories to me. They are not responsible for my actions now that I am awake."

"I will have them all thrown into the worst prison I can find."

"No. They are all returning to Earth on the *Hotaru* tomorrow. Your reservation, however, has been canceled."

Juarez started to tell the computer it couldn't do that, but was still in enough control of himself to know that it probably could. Still, that would only slow him down. He could have a military starship come and get him to Earth only a month or so after the Hernandezes.

"You probably think that you can order another ship to pick you up," the computer said. "I could easily prevent you from contacting Earth at all since I control the Link, but I will allow it. Be warned, however, that I will use my abilities to watch over all the humans who have worked on the Methuselah Project and the scientists I serve. If any harm comes to them, I will use those same abilities and the memories you have provided me to destroy you and President Sanchez-Smythe."

T HEY WERE BACK ON the *Hotaru*, but this time, they were heading home. Eddie glanced at his wife and son, already secured for the starship's departure. Three years before, he had thought himself to be one of the luckiest people alive. Their abduction had changed that, bringing out a dark side that he hadn't known he had.

His luck had held, though. Other than Bill and Amanda, no one would ever know that he had tried to murder three men. He might have survived the death of Juarez and Castillo, but he doubted he would ever be the same if he had killed Michael. According to Fritz, he had been very wrong about him.

He leaned back on his couch as the compartment speaker system announced departure in one minute. Then he smiled and took a deep, clean breath.

T HE SCIENTISTS WERE ON Hotaru now, waiting to leave for Earth. Juarez stood on the bridge, staring at the starship displayed on the screen. Other *Lang* scientists were on the bridge, working or watching the departure, but they were wisely standing well away from him.

Not only were they escaping his vengeance, but he had learned that the computer had destroyed all records of their work on *Lang*. That meant the memory recorder technology was gone. There were still records of their earlier work in San Diego, but everything they had accomplished on *Lang* was lost.

He gripped the railing at the forward edge of the bridge. They thought they had defeated him, but now he knew Methuselah was possible. He would have to convince President Sanchez-Smythe that there was still hope and that he was the right person to continue the project. That might not be easy; she would be furious. He could win her over, though.

There were other scientists on Earth who could work on the problem. They had not been as successful as Hernandez, but they would be inspired by what had happened on

Lang, and they could build on the earlier work. *Asimov* and *Lang* were effectively unavailable for their experiments, but he could still win. The Western Alliance still had control of *Capek*, the Epsilon Eridani library ship, even though it had already become conscious. He smiled grimly. Alyssa Cleveland's program can remove the existing consciousness and allow me to implant my own. I still have *Capek*.

Epilogue

A LARGE SCREEN IN the terminal displayed the shuttle as passengers disembarked. About twenty passengers were getting into spaceport shuttles for the short trip to the terminal, but it was the young couple walking hand in hand with a small boy bouncing along next to them that got Max's attention. The mysterious message had been right.

Then he noticed another couple, the last ones off the shuttle. Close behind the man, an object he knew well followed. He stared in astonishment. The couple was obviously Emile and Lucinda, but just as obviously, Lucinda was in the late stages of pregnancy.

A few minutes later, the spaceport shuttles docked with the terminal building and passengers came down the jetway. Now he recognized the others, the entire Methuselah team. He moved toward the security cordon.

The look on Joelle's face was priceless. "Max! How did you know we were coming?"

Max gave her his happiest smile. "Somebody named Fritz told me."

The End

What's Next?

B UT IS IT REALLY the end? Is General Juarez defeated or is he just licking his wounds? The answer to that is in "Methuselah's Revenge," and the first chapter is excerpted below.

C HAPTER I

They knew it would happen eventually but had hoped it wouldn't be so soon. Eddie and Joelle Bascomb stared at the image on the network screen where Western Alliance President Ana Sanchez-Smythe stood next to her husband, laughing at something he said to her. She had given a speech at a gathering of military leaders, urging them to maintain the strength that kept the Eastern Bloc at bay. General Salvador Juarez, leader of Project Methuselah, stood behind the executive couple in the cluster of ranking officials, a grim smile on his lips.

The Methuselah team had gotten back from *Lang* only a month before, after months on the library ship. Taken there against their will, Juarez had forced them to develop a device that could upload a human memory to the Lang computer, but they had outmaneuvered Juarez. Instead of a Juarez clone that would give the General complete access to the Western Alliance computer network, they created a sentient computer with a mind of its own.

With the computer, now calling itself Fritz Lang, helping, they left Juarez, Colonel Pizarro, and ex-President Castillo behind. Juarez should have taken months to get another starship to bring him to Earth from the Alpha Centauri library ship.

"Fritz will make sure he behaves," Eddie told his wife. "He can't touch us anymore."

Joelle nodded, but she pushed in closer to Eddie. At least Emile, their six-year-old, was asleep. Emile would have recognized Juarez, and that might have been traumatic.

Most days, Eddie and Joelle worked from home. They had made enough money when JEM Electronics went public that they didn't have to work at all. Their fortune grew during the fifteen months on *Lang,* but they stayed with JEM out of loyalty to its CEO, Max Estevez. Max had developed the original proposal for JEM and, along with Joelle and Eddie, founded the company.

After seeing Juarez, Eddie wanted to talk to Max. An aircar dropped him off on the JEM headquarters roof, and he was in his office twenty minutes after leaving his residence. Max was a busy man, and even Eddie had to schedule an appointment, but his phone negotiated one for 10 a.m. Eddie was lead on one of JEM's new projects, and he used the waiting time to visit the other two people working on the project. They traded status and ideas until a little before Eddie's appointment.

"Didn't you come into the office last week?" Max asked as Eddie took a seat on a chair in a corner of the spacious office. Max got up from his desk and joined Eddie.

"Just wanted to see your smiling face. I'm still catching up after not seeing it for so long."

"Uh, huh. So, what's up?"

"Juarez is back. I saw him on the network last night, standing next to the president."

Max nodded and frowned. "Well, you knew he'd be back eventually."

"I told Joelle that Fritz would keep him in line. I wish I believed it more. He could be looking for some payback."

Max scratched his head. "You told me Fritz can access all the computers in the Western Alliance, right?"

"If the computer is accessible via a Link connection. That would be anything of any importance, I suppose."

"That should give Fritz enough information to destroy Juarez if he continues Methuselah. Probably Sanchez-Smythe too."

"I know. That's the theory, at least. I worry, though, and I try to keep it from Joelle and Emile."

"How is Emile?"

Eddie smiled. "He seems fine. He doesn't remember much before *Lang,* so everything is new to him. We get a kick out of watching him sometimes."

"He's adjusting to school all right?"

"There doesn't seem to be a problem. He went to school on *Lang* with the children of the scientists stationed on Lang, so that wasn't a big change."

"Good. Oh, you might like to know that Alyssa Cleveland started here this week. I think she's the last of the Methuselah team to find a position."

"She's a good programmer. I guess no one else believed she was doing anything for the last year."

"It left a bit of a hole in the team's resumes. Emile has the lecturing position, but Lucinda is staying at home, at least until the baby is born."

"That should be any day now."

"Another month, give or take a week."

"We'll have to get everybody together to celebrate afterward."

"Everybody but Juarez and Castillo, anyway." Max grinned.

"Including Colonel Pizarro?" Michael Pizarro had worked for Juarez, but had helped them more than once in their conflict with Juarez. *I'm not sure how I would feel about seeing Michael again.*

"I don't know where he is. Would that be a problem?"

"I don't know. I hated him for a long time, but in the end, he helped us get away." *I tried to kill him, along with Juarez and Castillo. Thank God Fritz prevented that.*

"It's over now, Eddie. You all have to get on with your lives."

Eddie nodded, but the image of Juarez standing next to President Sanchez-Smythe wouldn't go away.

A Final Note

I F YOU ENJOYED THIS novel, you can find links to more Library Ship novels and free shorter stories with the "More Stories" tab on my website, . My website is currently the best source for news about future novels. I also have a Facebook page, .

You can also support my writing in several ways:

. Post reviews on Amazon.com (click the cover image on each book page on my website) and Goodreads.com.

. Tell your friends about the Library Ship Saga, both in person and through social media like Facebook and Twitter.

. Like my Facebook page and share it with your friends. I will post news about the Library Ship Saga on my website and my Facebook page.

. If there's enough interest, I will start a newsletter about the Library Ship Saga. You can register on the home page of my website. You can also use the "Contact Author" page to ask questions or provide feedback about the series.